TENDER CAPTOR

"No!" cried Carmen. "You must not!" She struggled to free her hand from his grip. When Puma would not release her hand, she used the other to push at his arm, trying in vain to free herself. "Let me go. You cannot—must not—"

"Must not what?" Puma was grinning down at her. The little Spanish captive was certainly struggling to free herself. He loosened her hand suddenly, and she fell back on the robes.

Puma bent his head toward her, his breath soft on her lips. She looked so delectable, felt so soft.

Carmen watched him, her lustrous eyes locked on his. "No," she whispered again. His touch was gentle, relaxing, and she wanted to let him continue, but she knew she must not.

"Sí," he whispered. "I have been wanting to kiss you ever since I first saw you." His head came down then and gently, ever so softly, he touched his lips to hers. It was a sweet kiss, the sweetest he had ever tasted. And he wanted more.

Other *Leisure Books* by Theresa Scott:

FORBIDDEN PASSION
BRIDE OF DESIRE
SAVAGE REVENGE
SAVAGE BETRAYAL

APACHE CONQUEST

THERESA SCOTT

LEISURE BOOKS　　NEW YORK CITY

For the next generation: Alysson, Gervaise, James, Richard, David, Dove, Alastair and Tianna.

My sincere thanks to Mrs. Wilma T. Phone of Dulce, New Mexico, for graciously answering my questions about the Jicarilla People. *Ihéedn.*

Prologue

Mexico City
December, 1689

"You don't want *him*, Fray Cristobal. He's even worse than the others." An obscene gesture of the comandante's thumb in the direction of the filthy captive accompanied his tone of contempt.

Fray Cristobal did not turn his tired gaze to the captive that Comandante Diego had indicated. Not just yet. *Madre de Dios*, it was hot! He mopped the sweat from his pink brow with a much-used gray rag. Then he stared once again at the long line of seventy silent prisoners. In all manners of shape and size, they awaited his judgment. He sighed.

When he finally turned to look at the prisoner

Diego had spoken of, Fray Cristobal flinched. Proud, piercing blue eyes glared back at him out of a filthy, sparsely bearded face with a hawk-shaped nose. Tangled blue-black hair grazed broad, bronzed shoulders. The dirt and filth sticking to the brown skin did little to hide the proud stance of the man and his muscular size. And, like the rest of the prisoners, this one stank.

The churchman took a step back and covered his nose with the rag. The captive looked untamed and vicious. Even in this line of criminals and misfits he stood out.

Yet the good brother found he was suddenly reluctant to let the comandante have final say over which men he, Fray Cristobal, would choose. Fray Cristobal surprised himself. He wanted to defy the comandante, this smooth, cruel son of Spain. For a moment, Fray Cristobal stared, fascinated, at the long black hairs that sprouted from the comandante's nose. Then, with a sigh, the priest turned to peer at the prisoner once again. Immediately the prisoner shifted, came alive, the coldness in his eyes like that of a bird of prey; he watched the churchman warily.

Fray Cristobal blinked. He saw a glint of something in those icy eyes—an intelligence, an awareness, a desperation. Fray Cristobal tore his gaze away from the captive's as an idea half formed in his mind. "He looks no different than the rest. Mayhap tougher . . ." Fray Cristobal swiped ineffectually at his forehead, the sweat running into his eyes and momentarily blurring the bright sunlight of the pink adobe plaza.

The comandante swung his impatient gaze back to the pale, aesthetic face of Fray Cristobal. As did most soldiers of the civil government of New Spain, he hated this man, this thin brother of the Church. He hated him, not because of the man himself, but for what he was—a representative of the most powerful institution in New Spain, the Church. The comandante knew that the Church could only stand in the way of any gains he and the military could hope to make in settling this vast new land and conquering its peoples.

Then Comandante Diego studied the cold, granite face of the prisoner. "*Sí,*" he said at last and spat casually on the ground. "He is a murderer, a thief and a cutthroat like the rest of this scum."

Fray Cristobal grunted. His fine plan to bring fifty soldiers to the rescue of Santa Fe, the struggling capital city in the north of New Spain, had met with limited success in Mexico City. When the Viceroy of Mexico City had first agreed to Fray Cristobal's plan to take back soldiers and supplies to the weakened Santa Fe, Fray Cristobal had been ecstatic. But when he had found out the caliber of the soldiers he was expected to take, Fray Cristobal's ecstasy had quickly evaporated.

The dregs of Mexico City's prisons had been opened to him—every murderer, every criminal, every drunkard, every whoremaster behind bars in Mexico City was now Fray Cristobal's for the taking. The Viceroy of Mexico could spare none of his own men at this critical time, the Viceroy had explained. Take it or leave it, the Viceroy had sneered further, then opened his arms expansively as though he had offered the good brother the choicest men of his best regiment.

Fray Cristobal wiped at his forehead. *Madre de Dios*, it was hot. He eyed the blue-eyed murderer glaring at him. "I'll take him," Fray Cristobal heard himself announce and sighed.

The comandante shook his head, muttering to himself while he made an official notation beside the soiled, ragged list he carried. "One more murderous cutthroat added to your regiment," he observed sourly. Then he turned suddenly crafty eyes upon the man of the church and for a moment Fray Cristobal forgot his anger at the Viceroy and at the military in the battle he waged for souls. Fray Cristobal frowned, suddenly wary. "What is it?"

"Mayhap you spoke too soon," Comandante Diego said smoothly. He was enjoying the moment, Fray Cristobal could tell, and he felt his stomach tighten.

"This one is a thief, a murderer, like the others, *sí*," said the comandante softly. "He is also an Apache." He waited to see fear strike the spindly brother's pink face. He was not disappointed.

"Apache?" Fray Cristobal had recovered at last, though there was a tremor in his voice. He

12

turned weary eyes upon his opponent. "Why, Comandante Diego, I—I would wager that even this Apache has—has a soul." Brave words; he wondered if he believed them himself.

Diego laughed, the sound striking a jarring note in the quiet, hot afternoon. A few chickens scratching in the dust of the plaza scattered at the sound. "No, good brother, he does not. The *indios* of Mexico, now, mayhap they have souls. . . ." Diego shrugged. "But the Apaches?" He shook his head confidently. "They have none."

Fray Cristobal turned his gaze back to stare at the *indio*. Unreadable blue eyes glared back at him. He thought he caught a glimmer of cruelty. He would wager that somehow this *indio* had understood every word. "He looks almost Spanish," mused Fray Cristobal aloud. "Where did he come from? How long has he been locked up in prison?"

Diego shrugged again. "The north, somewhere. He's been locked up a year, mayhap more. Hard to say." He straightened, watching the good brother sweat in the hot afternoon sun. "He was supposed to hang in two days."

That caught Fray Cristobal's attention quickly.

To his nervous look, Comandante Diego answered grimly, "He killed one of my soldiers. A lieutenant." He swung hard black eyes upon the captive. "If it were up to me, I would hang the son-of-a-bitch, not make a *soldado* out of him."

"My son," murmured Fray Cristobal, nervously crossing himself. "Do not say such things. To have such words upon your soul . . ." He looked at the prisoner with renewed interest. To thwart the military in this one little thing would not be a sin, Fray Cristobal assured himself. And it would give him a tiny victory in the face of so much defeat. It would also make him feel immeasurably better. "Mayhaps this—this Apache will be of use on our *jornada* north. He can speak with the other Apaches, the other *indios* we meet . . . tell them to let us pass."

Diego swung to face the good brother. "The other *indios* we meet," he repeated thoughtfully. Then he smiled again, that amused smile that Fray Cristobal was coming to hate. "The only *indios* we have to fear on our journey north *are* the Apaches, you fool."

Fray Cristobal gasped at the insult. Such lack of respect for a representative of the Holy Church!

"The Apaches will take every opportunity to raid us. The Apaches have done so every time we have ventured north into their accursed country." Diego surveyed the sleepy plaza. "It is one reason I am here, in Mexico City," he added. "No accursed Apaches." His black gaze settled for a long moment on Fray Cristobal, and the man of the church could read the hatred in the other's eyes. "I do not want to escort you to Santa Fe," snarled Diego bluntly. "I wish to stay here. But the Viceroy has proclaimed it otherwise. So I will go. But I do not like it."

14

He waved the dog-eared list he was making to show the Viceroy. Everything must be recorded, official. The Spanish prided themselves on their excellent records. The comandante shook the list in Fray Cristobal's face. "It is only *I* that stands between ignorant fools like you and vicious animals like *him*."

Both turned to stare at the unblinking, silent prisoner.

"But Comandante . . ." Fray Cristobal looked taken aback at the other's open attack. "I had no idea. I will ask the Viceroy . . ."

"Do not bother," sneered Diego. "I won't have you run crying to the Viceroy saying I cannot do my job! No, I will go. And I will do my duty, which is to train and deliver these diseased lice to Santa Fe." He surveyed the barred windows that lined the little plaza. Behind them were the rest of the murderers that he was expected to whip into shape as soldiers. "But more I will not do. Do you understand?"

His angry gaze quelled Fray Cristobal, who looked away only to catch the captive *indio* watching him. A fierce, cruel smile crossed that tanned face, and Fray Cristobal shivered. It would be a six-month journey to Santa Fe. He wondered suddenly how many of them, himself included, would survive it. He shivered again.

Chapter 1

Eyes narrowed, Puma slouched against the barred prison wall along with the other hand-picked criminals. The thin, pink churchman was still choosing his soldiers. Soldiers, pah! Puma spat into the dry dust of the plaza to show his contempt, his face impassive. Little did he care if these Spanish dogs knew of his contempt or not. He was Apache. What did he care about these foreigners?

Without warning came a fleeting memory of Puma's Spanish father, his blue eyes crinkled in a smile. Puma squashed it. He was Apache! And Apaches raided these fools, the Spanish. As they raided the Pueblos, the Tewas, Tiwas, Keresans—anyone who had food or horses or slaves was fair game for the Apache! Puma himself had raided Spanish caravans many times, and Tewan vil-

16

lages, and more until—. Until he had been sold into slavery himself, by his own people—more specifically, by Angry Man, the headman's son.

Puma's large hands tightened into fists as the memories washed over him. A long, thin scar on his right arm glared white, a constant reminder of the evil betrayal.

Angry Man had just tried to kill Puma for the second time. The first time, he had been thrown into a herd of thundering horses racing past. Angry Man had succeeded in making that murderous attempt look like an accident, and no one had contradicted him. The second time Angry Man was not so fortunate. He had jumped Puma as Puma had been grooming his favorite stallion. The horse had snorted a warning mere seconds before the downward stroke of Angry Man's knife sliced into Puma's arm. Nearby warriors had quickly seized Angry Man and Puma and dragged them before the cacique, the headman of their tribe.

"What is this, my son?" the old man had asked. When Angry Man had refused to answer, the headman had turned to Puma. "Why are you here, Puma? What has happened to your arm?"

Puma ignored the dripping blood. His face was set in stone. It was not Puma's place to tell the headman that Angry Man, his only son, had just tried to murder Puma.

The headman waited patiently until one of the warriors spoke. "These two were fighting. Angry Man attacked with a knife."

The headman frowned. "This is most serious. It is wrong for Apache to kill Apache!" Indeed, the murder of another Apache was a most reprehensible crime to the Jicarilla people.

"He is not Apache!" erupted Angry Man. "I say, drive him out of our village! Force him to live with the coyotes and the rabbits. Perhaps the Spanish dogs will take him. After all, he is the son of a hated Spanish dog!"

There were several gasps from the crowd gathered around Puma and Angry Man.

The cacique waited until the crowd grew silent once more. His wrinkled face remained impassive. "It is wrong for an Apache to speak so about another. Puma is Apache born. His mother is a member of our tribe."

"I do not demand that his mother leave," clarified Angry Man shortly. "I demand that *he* leave!"

Time went by. The silence grew. Finally the old man spoke again. "I want you to tell me that you will not fight again with Puma, Fearsome One." He was looking directly at his son as he spoke his son's true Apache name. Few times in their lives were Apaches addressed by their true names. At such times, it was with utmost seriousness.

Fearsome One, nicknamed Angry Man, glared at his father. "I cannot say that to you, Father, and speak the truth."

A look of pain flickered across the headman's face. He was silent again. The crowd began to stir restively. Even so, the old man held his silence. At last he spoke. "It is a sad day for me. It is with a terrible pain in my heart that I say that it is *you* who must leave our people, Fearsome One. You are banished for four years." He turned and shuffled slowly, painfully, through the entrance to his tipi. The flap closed after him.

People continued to mill around in front of the cacique's dwelling, then gradually drifted away, leaving Angry Man and Puma to face each other. "Be warned," snarled Angry Man. "I will kill you, banishment or no." His dark eyes were beads of hate. He jerked around and stalked off to his tipi.

Puma stared after him, then shrugged his broad shoulders and sauntered over to where the horses were corralled. Angry Man had hated him for some time. Puma had first noticed Angry Man's hate when they were boys, after Puma's father had left the village, left his mother, left him. Angry Man's hate had seemed to grow with the increasing presence of the Spanish in the land.

Puma went quietly back to grooming Raids the Enemy. This time when the pinto stallion snorted, Puma swung sharply, alert and ready. But it was not Angry Man.

Puma relaxed. "You go with him?"

Takes Two Horses stood silently before him, watching the horses. At least he answered, "I go."

Puma continued to brush Raids the Enemy's hide. It was not his business what Takes Two Horses did. "Once we were friends. But now, no more."

"No more," agreed Takes Two Horses.

"It was not I who changed." Puma gave smooth strokes to the horse's white and brown hide. Raids the Enemy rolled his eyes. They were blue, one of the reasons Puma had chosen him. He and his pinto stallion were the only ones in the village with blue eyes.

Takes Two Horses said enigmatically, "There are too many Spanish on the land. Apache land."

Puma said nothing. What was there to say? He could not remember a time when there were no Spanish, though the old ones spoke of such a time. For the Apache, the Spanish provided rich pickings on raids. That was all. "Renegades," observed Puma, "live on the run. No place do they call home. No place is safe. Any one of The People who sees them tries to kill them."

Takes Two Horses laughed. "I would rather die like a warrior than live like an old woman."

Puma swallowed the angry retort that rose to his lips. Instead he said mildly, "A man is not a warrior who makes war on women and children."

"I do not make war on women and children."

"But you will." The young man stirred uneasily and Puma added, "Angry Man will be driven to it. He will seek slaves to trade with the Utes, the Comanches, the Spanish, just to live. And to get weapons. He is ruthless. It is the kind of man he is. It is the kind of man you will become if you go with him."

His listener moved away from him.

20

Puma closed his eyes and his hand went still on the stallion's back. A breeze cooled his eyelids. When he opened his eyes, he said, "It has been a long time since we were boys. And friends."

"You are not my friend. Angry Man is my friend!" Takes Two Horses turned away and walked several steps toward the village.

Puma's next words halted him. "I will watch over your mother and sister," said Puma. "I will see that they have meat to eat—and protection."

Takes Two Horses swung around to face Puma with a grudging look. Wary, he said nothing, only started for the village once more.

"Go, and may our paths cross only in peace," called Puma.

"Only in peace," echoed Takes Two Horses sullenly, now trotting. Then he was gone.

The next time Puma saw Takes Two Horses was out on the desert when Takes Two Horses and Angry Man and the renegades with them traded a sullen and bound Puma, still atop his pinto stallion, to their lifelong enemies, the Comanche, as a slave.

A snarl from the Spanish commander brought Puma's attention back to the present. The churchman was finished choosing his criminals. The *soldados* guarding them shifted nervously.

"Back, you filthy scum!" ordered Comandante Diego, waving his sword at the rejects. "Back to your cells!" He kicked a prisoner in the butt

21

who was moving too slowly for his liking. The man stumbled and fell, then got to his feet, his face contorted in anger. Diego raised his sword threateningly, and the man sullenly joined the long line of captives slowly winding their way back into the dark adobe prison. Puma watched from the knot of chosen ones. How he had loathed his tiny, dark prison cell. How he loathed the brutal treatment meted out to the prisoners.

Puma glanced rapidly around the plaza. It was deserted except for a chestnut mare tied to a rail at one end. Puma had no intention of being turned into a *soldado* for the greater glory of Spain. Now was a perfect time to escape. Whilst one of the soldiers was preoccupied with hitting another captive, Puma darted around the corner of the building. Like a sleek shadow, he slid along the wall for some distance, then raced swiftly to the horse. He had almost reached the mare when a cry rang out.

With a bellow, Comandante Diego gave chase, sword out. He yelped for help. Three *soldados* joined him. Puma clung to the mare's back and yanked on the bridle to turn the beast's head. The commander grabbed the reins, the three soldiers grabbed Puma, and in seconds he was sprawled in the dirt, two of the soldiers on top of him.

"It's the son-of-a-bitch that killed Lieutenant Martinez!" cried Diego. He raised his sword to decapitate Puma when Fray Cristobal rushed to intervene.

22

"No, no!" cried the churchman, rushing up. "In the name of God, no!"

The cry checked Diego's fury momentarily. Fray Cristobal threw himself between the sprawled *indio*, the *soldados*, and the livid comandante.

Panting, still furious, Diego stepped back. One of the *soldados* shoved Puma to his feet. "Put him with the others. I want that son-of-a-bitch out of my sight!" snarled Diego at two of the soldiers. He whirled upon Fray Cristobal, his frustration and fury seeking an outlet. "You!" he sputtered. "You can have him and you are welcome to him! Just keep him out of my sight!" Diego stalked away, ramming his sword into its scabbard.

Fray Cristobal, shaken, stood to one side, wiping at his forehead and the dust on his long brown garment as if trying to forget the whole sudden episode.

Puma, hauled by a *soldado* on each arm, looked filthy, beaten and yet strangely exultant at his close escape as he was dragged back to the huddle of chosen ones. Elation shot through him. He could still run, still fight. He was not dead yet!

And his next escape attempt would be in Apache territory. He would not fail; he knew it.

Chapter 2

El Paso del Norte
March, 1690

"His Excellency is prepared to meet with you now."

Carmen swept past the unctuous little man bowing her into the well-appointed office of the Alcalde of El Paso del Norte. He had kept her waiting for a day and a half in the hot little parlor, assuring her every few hours that his Excellency would see her momentarily. Hummph!

Carmen flounced past the toady official, glancing neither to left nor right. She stopped in the middle of the room and stared at the man writing at the broad desk. The scratch of his quill pen was the only sound in the room. She waited, hands on hips, for him to look up and acknowledge her.

When he did not, she looked around, nervousness betraying her for the first time.

She ignored her black lace-swathed dueña, Doña Matilda Delgado who had marched silently into the room behind her. *This* room was not hot and baking, Carmen noted with impatience. This room had wide-open windows that let in a lovely breeze that fluttered the expensive hand-woven curtains, no doubt imported from Spain at great expense. The lovely paintings on the walls, the hand-carved furniture, the beautiful rug on the hard brick floor—no doubt also imported from Spain—testified to the owner's expensive but excellent taste.

The scratching of the quill was becoming irritating. When the alcalde still did not look up, but kept writing his report or dispatch or list of household purchases, or whatever he was writing, she could stand it no longer. He might be the Alcalde of El Paso del Norte and the surrounding province, but *she* was Carmen Yolanda Diaz y Silvera, a woman of Spanish nobility and lately a citizen of the great city of Seville, Spain. She could trace her lineage back several generations, including and past her ancestress imprisoned in the seraglio of a Moorish sultan before the Spanish troops had retaken the city in 1248! How dare this insignificant alcalde keep her waiting! She had already waited six months.

"I must speak with you," she began and was pleased that her voice came out cool and confident.

The pen faltered, then took up the scratching once more.

How dare he! she fumed. "Your Excellency—"

"One moment." His voice was also cool, but also clipped and impersonal.

Carmen sighed. She thought she heard a smothered cough behind her, but when she swung around to chastise Doña Matilda, that woman was silent, her pointed nose busily engaged in studying a painting entitled "A Spanish Lady of the King's Court."

Finally, the incessant scratching stopped, and the alcalde laid down his quill pen. He got to his feet, and Carmen was surprised to see that he was not very much taller standing than he had been sitting in his leather chair. She took a step forward.

The alcalde studied the woman in the turquoise taffeta dress, then hastily said, "No, no, let me." He came around his desk to greet her. "Had I known I was keeping such a beautiful woman waiting, I would have dropped everything immediately!" he said gallantly.

Carmen smiled tightly, not at all fooled by his hollow compliment. Through gritted teeth, she said, "You met me six months ago, your Excellency. Then three months after that. I have been waiting ever since."

He took a step back then and stared. The blond hair, those magnificent turquoise eyes— *sí*, he had seen her before. "Six months?" When his brow wrinkled, the top of his partially balding head wrinkled too. "I am sorry it has been so long. . . ." He spread his hands. "Perhaps you could refresh my memory. You wanted . . . ?" he paused delicately.

Patience, she warned herself. Sister Francisca would counsel patience at a time like this. Taking a deep breath, Carmen said steadily, "I must get to Santa Fe, and I am seeking an escort. I have been told it is too dangerous to travel alone." Her flashing eyes made him wonder why she had not charged out into the desert alone, such was the passion he detected in her. "I am to marry my *novio*, Juan Enrique Delgado, who lives in Santa Fe. Surely you remember?" She wanted to shriek at the man, to wring her hands in agony. "I had an appointment with you when I first arrived."

"Of course, it is coming back to me." The alcalde touched his forehead. "So many things, you understand. I am a very busy man. I hope you understand."

She did not. How could he forget something that was so important to her? She cleared her throat. "Six months, Your Excellency, I have been waiting. . . ." Anger choked the words in her throat. She could not insult the man, but oh, how she longed to scream at him. Or throw something.

The alcalde turned from her and stepped to a window. *Madre de Dios*, the breeze felt good. He got so tired of so many people pleading with him for favors. He wished she had realized that, had she but paid him—oh, not a great sum, just enough to jog his memory—then she would not have had to wait so long. These nobles from Spain just did not understand how business was done in the New World.

He sighed, wishing the woman and her problem gone from him. He glanced out the window and down at the plaza. Chickens scratching, children playing quietly. His glance slid back, then paused as he caught sight of the dusty figure of the recently arrived Fray Cristobal down in the plaza. The alcalde remembered their interview two days previously. The priest was a do-gooder—an unworldly one at that, in the alcalde's opinion. Attending the churchman was Comandante Diego and some of his *soldados*. A good man, that Diego, thought the alcalde.

Suddenly the alcalde stiffened, calculated quickly, then turned to face the blond woman, an expansive grin upon his face. "I have news," he said. "Very good news."

Carmen was startled at the sudden transformation in the alcalde. Previously he had seemed vague, unaware of her and her request. Now he was positively beaming. She glanced toward the window, amazed at what a fresh breeze could do to revive a man.

"There is a detachment of fifty *soldados*, fifty well-trained soldiers newly arrived from Mexico City. They guard a caravan bound for Santa Fe. They leave within the next few days. You would do well to seek a place for yourself with them."

Carmen was stunned. She did not know what to say. For six months, she had been stranded in

28

this colonial town of adobe and dust, waiting, waiting, and now he was telling her she could leave?

A beaming smile spread over her face, and for a moment, the alcalde stared. The lady really was lovely. Then he cleared his throat and bowed politely. "You and your dueña are welcome to travel with this escort. I will give you this note to deliver to Fray Cristobal. Fray Cristobal," he repeated carefully so that she should have no doubt as to whom to contact—or whom to blame if it came to that.

Again the scratching of his quill pen filled the room, but this time the sound trilled in Carmen's ears.

The alcalde finished writing, folded the note in half, then in half again, and handed it to her with a prim smile.

Carmen took the note and pressed it to the richly embroidered bosom of her turquoise dress. The alcalde's eyes followed it. He tore his eyes back to meet her wide ones.

"Oh, thank you, Your Excellency, thank you!"

He smiled and waved a hand benignly. He had made no money on this transaction, true, but he had gotten rid of another pleader. He waved his hand again. "No need to thank me, Señorita . . ." He faltered.

"Doña Carmen Yolanda Diaz y Silvera," she pronounced with dignity, her eyes flashing.

"Doña Carmen Yolanda Diaz y Silvera," the Alcalde repeated dutifully and bowed.

Carmen understood that she was dismissed. Happily waving the missive at Doña Matilda, she left the room in a swish of turquoise skirts and ruffles.

The room lacked something—excitement, mayhap—now that she was gone, thought the alcalde. Then he shrugged and picked up the next paper from the pile on his desk. Soon the scratching of his quill pen filled the room once more.

Chapter 3

Doña Matilda was asleep. Carmen was certain of it as she stared down at the softly snoring woman on the bed. Let her sleep, Carmen told herself as she glanced away. The woman was worn out from packing.

Carmen's turquoise eyes barely took in the four wooden walls of the hotel room that had been her home for the past six months. Tomorrow. Tomorrow she would leave this room and continue her voyage to Santa Fe. Carmen's heart beat rapidly at the thought. It was one reason she had not been able to fall asleep as easily as her dueña.

And tomorrow she would be one day closer to Juan Enrique Delgado. "Juan," she whispered the name softly. "Juan Enrique Delgado." She sighed. When would she ever see him? And when she saw him, would he like her? Would she like him?

Pensive, Carmen stopped folding the clothes she was placing in the elaborately carved wooden trunk. Juan Enrique Delgado was the whole reason behind her voyage to New Spain. A rude little voice in her mind wondered if he was worth the trouble she had gone to. She shrugged and wandered aimlessly around the room, touching this candle, that crudely carved box, little things in the room that had been her home for six long months.

She wandered over to the window. The cotton curtains hung listlessly in the hot evening air. A purple dusk crept across the town of El Paso del Norte. The smell of mesquite smoke in the air told Carmen that the locals were preparing their evening meal. She sighed once more. It was so hot.

From the cantina far down the narrow street came the sounds of laughter and music. Carmen had heard such sounds on many of the nights she had been in El Paso. She peered in the direction of the noise but could see nothing. Several loud whoops escalated into high cries. The locals having their fun, she thought and suddenly felt left out. What would it be like to walk along a street freely, to go wherever she wanted to, without a chaperone? To go to the cantina? Oh, not to go in, of course, but just to peek in. One peek. One peek without her dueña. Doña Matilda, kind soul that she was, was always so prim and proper.

Then Carmen shrugged, impatient with herself that she had even let herself wonder what it would be like to wander out into the night, into the intensity and excitement of the cantina.

Elbows resting on the rough wooden sill, she turned back to gazing at the tiny lights of the town, which held back the encroaching darkness. She stood there for a while, staring out into the twilight.

On the street below, five men staggered by. One of them tripped and fell. He was helped boisterously to his feet by his laughing companions. Arms about each other's shoulders, they sauntered on down the street, waving wide hats at the newly rising moon.

Carmen turned away, a small smile playing about her full lips. There was the reason she did not venture out without Doña Matilda, she thought. The men. Here in the frontier town the men were—well, wild. *Sí*. She had seen it with her own eyes. They were boisterous, loud and dangerous. She had even seen women accosted in the street below. Of course, *she* had never been accosted, thanks to her dueña. And also thanks to her own good sense that she had never ventured from the hotel room at night.

The men had passed by now, their laughter and shouts fading and blending with the music and laughter of the cantina patrons. A door opened. Closed. The night went quiet again.

Carmen leaned on the window sill and sighed. She looked at the golden crescent of moon low in the sky. Was Juan Enrique Delgado looking at the moon tonight? Of course he was. Somewhere in Santa Fe, he had risen from his dinner, walked to his door, and was even now staring out at the beautiful moon, thinking of her.

Carmen giggled to herself at her fanciful speculation. Of course she did not know if Juan was really looking at the moon and thinking of her, but it was pleasant to think that mayhap he was. She turned, a small smile on her lips.

A movement at the end of the street, across from the cantina, caught her eye.

Soldados, she thought, watching two men tie their horses to the hitching post. Probably from Fray Cristobal's caravan. She had approached the good brother directly after her interview with the alcalde. She had liked Fray Cristobal immediately, and even more so when he had readily welcomed her to his caravan.

Carmen glanced at the soldiers once more. The street would not be so dangerous with the likes of these men to guard it. They were no doubt well-trained and protective of the good brother. She had seen several of them standing around examining the horses that traveled with the caravan. They were big men, well-armed with spears and swords and arquebuses. She had seen them from a distance, of course. And when she was with Doña Matilda.

Carmen stole a quick glance at her dueña, a sly thought crossing her mind for the first time. What if—? No. She must not even consider it. Pushing the hasty idea from her mind, she sought to calm herself by watching the *soldados*. Just watching them, she felt the town of El Paso del Norte to be safer than it had been in months. *If it is so safe,* the little voice in her mind speculated, *why not venture out?*

Never. What would Sister Francisca say? Or Doña Matilda? Carmen resolutely pushed the thought from her mind and stared at the moon. Juan—she must think of Juan Enrique Delgado, the reason for her travel. *But Juan is so far away,* came the little voice, plaintive now. *And adventure is so close.*

Carmen considered. Then, without further thought, she got to her feet, grabbed a dark cloak and tiptoed from the room.

"Woman," muttered Miguel Baca. "I want a woman." The tall dark *soldado* with him merely lifted a brow at his scrawny companion. Miguel Baca was unusual for a soldier. The Spanish military did not customarily take someone so frail-looking. Miguel Baca's skinny body was a legacy of his starved boyhood spent among the rest of the thieving, orphaned riff-raff of Mexico City. A scrappy fellow, the day he had been accepted, at age fifteen, as a *soldado* for the King of Spain was the second happiest day of Miguel Baca's life. His first happiest day was the day Hortensia Amiga, a popular Mexico City prostitute, had taken him to her bed. Free.

"Let's go to the cantina. I'll find a willing one there." His companion merely shrugged his broad shoulders and sauntered along with him.

The cantina door opened; music blasted forth, and harsh yellow light illuminated the hard faces of the two *soldados*. Baca had the black eyes of a Spaniard, but his companion's eyes were an icy blue. He too had darkly tanned skin, and his shoulder-length hair shone blue-black in the harsh yellow light of the cantina.

Baca sauntered up to where three soldiers sat playing cards at a table. His companion followed, face stony. "Baca," greeted the others. Wary nods were directed at his companion. The two sat down.

Obviously Baca's friends had been in the cantina for some time. Their drinks were low and their conversation stupid. Baca's stony-faced companion looked around in a bored fashion while the others continued to drink. In one corner of the adobe room, two men were singing and playing maracas and the guitar. A woman danced, her lovely face an entrancing combination of her Indian mother and Spanish father. Her movements were quick, bright, well-practiced; her dark eyes were flat and contemptuous. Baca's hungry eyes fastened on every move of her flashing legs and breasts.

"Forget it," slurred one of Baca's companions. "Josefita does not even look at *soldados*."

"My money is as good as the next man's," frowned Baca.

"You're a *soldado*. Josefita hates us."

"That's not what I heard. I heard Josefita loves us."

"That was last week—before a damn *soldado* broke her heart and stole her money. Now she won't even look at us." Tears formed in the eyes of the speaker at Josefita's cruelty.

"Son of a bitch," sighed Baca, relaxing back in the chair. "I suppose next week she will love us again. After I have left town."

The others nodded glumly and continued to watch Josefita's lovely long legs as she pranced and stamped to the quick beat.

"Where are all the women in this town? I have not seen even one." Baca's voice had a distinct whine.

"Locked up," explained another man.

"By their husbands, their lovers, their dueñas, their mothers. . . ."

Baca took another swig of his drink. He set the cup down with a bang and got to his feet. He swayed a little as he swung to look at the man who had entered the cantina with him. "Are you coming?"

The silent *soldado* heaved himself to his feet and headed for the door. Baca followed several unsteady steps behind. The three soldiers watched as the door closed behind them.

"Goddamn Apache," murmured one.

The others nodded. "Tough son of a bitch though. Wouldn't want to have to fight him."

The others nodded again. One took a long swig of his drink. "Baca's the only one who can stomach him."

A loud, guttural burp interrupted this comment. "Nah, it's the Apache who tolerates Baca. Baca's a skinny little runt—sly, too. Always out for a piece of silver. Can't trust him."

"How come the Apache's with him?"

"Mutual admiration. No one will talk to the 'Pache, and no one likes Baca."

"The 'Pache saved Baca's life. Lead bull of the herd tried to gore Baca. That's why Baca is civil to the Apache. And Baca's never tried any of his thief's games on him, you can be sure. Why his throat would be slit so fast—"

"Señores," purred a lovely voice.

"Josefita!" chorused the men. One of them moved the chair that Baca's companion had recently vacated. He opened his arms to the woman. "Come to me, *querida*! You love us again, *sí*?"

"*Sí*," muttered Josefita, her face a smiling mask as her thoughts worked furiously. Conchita, her youngest daughter, was sick, even now fighting a high fever. The two older ones were probably frantic with worry. There was not much food left in the *casa*, either. Curse that thieving *soldado* she'd let move in with her. She had been so certain that he would stay. . . . She widened her smile at the three staring men. Her eyes glittered. "How much silver you got?"

"*Mucho, mucho*!" they chortled, reaching into pockets and throwing coins on the table.

Josefita sat down.

Puma was the first to see the cloaked woman. Baca, lurching along the street, had yet to spot the dark figure, her face hidden by the heavy hood, but Puma knew it was a woman. He was half tempted to point her out to Baca, then squashed the impulse. Let Baca find his own woman.

But Baca, with an unerring sense, looked up and spotted the woman walking past the church. She paused, lifting her nose as if to smell the clean desert air. She glanced in their direction, but to Puma's surprise, she did not move away or run. Either the woman was looking for this night's customers or she was a fool.

With a grunt, Baca changed course and headed for the woman. Puma followed, wondering what the Spaniard was up to now. Ever since Puma had saved Baca's life, Baca had acted as though he must protect the Apache, much to Puma's amusement. Baca had run interference between Puma and the other Spaniards. When the bully, Rodrigo Gomez, had wanted to pummel Puma for some slight, it was Baca who stepped in and smoothed the moment over. Gomez had been all too willing to accept the smaller thief's peacemaking attempts, especially after he caught sight of the gleaming blade of the razor-sharp knife in Puma's palm. Baca had moved his bedroll closer to the Apache's at night. In the six months they had been on the trail from Mexico City, Puma had grown used to the smaller man's company and now tolerated it, though he had been a loner after he was imprisoned by the Spanish.

Baca bowed low in front of the woman, muttering something that Puma could not make out—the words were too slurred. The woman drew back in surprise, and her hood slipped off, exposing a cascade of thick hair that picked up the light. She reached for the hood hastily, but she was too late. Baca and Puma had seen the golden curls before she quickly covered her head again.

Baca's breath hissed. He reached for the woman and grasped her arm. Frightened, she tried to pull away, but the small man's grip was too strong for her. "No, no," she cried. With huge eyes, she turned to Puma. "Please help, señor," she pleaded, tugging frantically against Baca's pull. Why, oh why, had she ever ventured forth alone? wondered Carmen frantically.

Puma stared at her. He had never seen eyes the color of turquoise stone before. They were like jewels!

"Come with me," cried Baca, yanking on the woman's arm. Her fear and appearance seemed to have driven the smaller man past some point of sanity. He started to drag her along the street, crooning to her all the while. Puma watched the woman struggle, wondering suddenly if she was indeed the loose woman of the streets that he and Baca had taken her for.

The woman was digging her heels into the dust of the road and hitting at Baca with her free hand. The blows did little to sway him from his intent.

When she saw that she was getting nowhere, Carmen tried kicking at the man to dislodge his grip. Her booted foot struck shinbone and the man yelped, but he hung on. Oh, if only she had stayed in the hotel room!

Despite her best efforts, the man was dragging her along in a direction she did not want to go.

She glanced wildly at his companion who had chosen not to aid his friend so far. This man, bigger than her attacker, was watching her calmly out of narrowed eyes. "Please, señor," she tried again. "Do not let him hurt me. *Por Dios!*" She lurched in his direction, though she truly despaired of his help. She would be ruined in mere moments.

Carmen's eyes widened as they met those of the watching man. He was large and powerful, but he was something more. His eyes were fastened on hers, seeming to devour her. His lips were a thin slash in his face.

This time when the woman looked at him, Puma's blood froze in his veins. He stared back into magnetic, turquoise, jewel-like eyes that were framed with thick, dark lashes. Puma's world stopped. Something in the woman's pleading eyes reached out to him. It was as though her very soul touched him. Pounding blood roared in Puma's ears, and his breath quickened. It had been a long time since he had had a woman. Two years or more. He had not wanted any of the hated Spanish, and the Pueblo Indian women who waited on the Spanish were too afraid of him when they found out he was Apache. He had been waiting until he could return to Apacheria. But this woman! He had never seen a woman like her. Beautiful and fiery and desperate.

In a moment his decision was made. "Baca, let her go."

Baca swung around to him. "Are you crazy? She is magnificent! I want her!" He swayed a little.

"Let her go," repeated Puma in a voice that bore no reckoning with. But Baca was too far gone with drink and lust to recognize the danger. He clutched the woman's arm tighter and swung her between the two of them. "Stay out of this, 'Pache," he warned, his teeth bared in a grimace. "I found her first. Go get your own woman."

Puma did not wait to bandy words with the man. With a deft swing, he tapped the side of Baca's head and watched as Baca's eyes rolled into his head and he slowly sank to the dirt. Puma caught Baca's head and laid him carefully on the ground. He turned to the woman. She was watching him with wide, frightened eyes.

"Oh, no," she moaned. Was this man about to pluck her from where she stood and carry her off now that her tormentor lay on the ground? Oh, where was Doña Matilda? She took a step back.

Puma saw the fear in her eyes and was surprised at it. Before he had seen anger, pleading, but not abject terror. "Cowering, *querida*?" he drawled, his Spanish only slightly accented. He had put his time in prison to good use.

He reached out and clasped her wrist with a grip that was firm and unyielding.

Carmen's eyes widened. She straightened. "Never!"

Puma glanced at his prone companion. "Then I suggest you return home," he purred.

Carmen glanced around the deserted street. Noise and music and laughter were still coming from the cantina. She had not had a chance to peek in there before these two had come along. She wanted to run headlong for the hotel, but a thought halted her. It would not do. It would not be dignified to make so hasty an exit, not in keeping with a member of the Seville nobility. Not at all. With head held high, she met his gaze as an equal, though she had to look up to do so. *"Muchas gracias, señor,"* she said with as much dignity as she could muster. She was glad her voice did not tremble, though her body did. She was very aware of his grip on her wrist, and she thought her skin felt warm there. Her face certainly did. "I will thank you to let me go."

He bowed and promptly released her wrist. "Of course. You are free to go," he said, taking away the last tiny fear she had that now he would be her attacker.

She turned quickly away. "I must—must go." She took several steps, halted, and swung back to face him, a safe distance between them now. He was staring at her.

"What—" She swallowed. "What is your name?"

He stared at her, expressionless.

Her lips trembled. "So that I may know whom to thank," she explained, the words forced. What she really wanted to do was turn and run and never stop until she reached the safety of her hotel room.

She met his eyes bravely, and Puma marveled again at the feeling that had touched him when she had pleaded so desperately with him. "Puma," he said at last.

"That's all?" she asked, taken aback. "Just 'Puma'?"

He nodded. She was Spanish, obviously. He distrusted the Spanish. He had reason to. He wondered briefly where she was from; he had detected a slight difference in her pronunciation. What did it matter? He would not see her again. Fray Cristobal's caravan was pulling out in the morning, heading north to Santa Fe, and Puma was going with it. The Apache part of him mused that if she were in Apacheria, his territory, he would steal her and take her with him. But he was not in Apache territory. He was in Spanish territory, enemy territory. No, he would let her go.

None of his regrets showed on his face.

Carmen took several slow steps toward him. When she reached him at last, she touched his hand.

He flinched. It was not the Apache way for a strange woman to touch a man. Carmen felt the swift reaction and, mistaking it for fear, felt a little strengthened. "Do not fear," she said softly, kindly. "I but wish to thank you for—for saving my life. Thank you, Puma."

He gaped at her, his visage revealing his astonishment. "Fear?"

But she had turned away, lifted her skirts, and was running for the hotel at the far end of the street. He watched her go, shaking his head. Then he chuckled. "Fear," he muttered to himself, incredulous.

Baca, behind him, still lying on the ground, began to stir. He moaned and Puma walked over to give him a hand up. The smaller man swayed on his feet for a few moments, holding his head. "I had the most wonderful dream. . . ." he muttered.

"You must tell me about it." His companion laughed good-naturedly as they headed back to where the caravan was camped.

Heart pounding, Carmen reached the hotel. Just before entering the door, she paused and stared down the street to where the tall, strong *soldado* had been. He was gone. Inexplicably, she suddenly felt lonely. Thoughtfully, she pushed open the hotel door and stepped across the threshold.

Chapter 4

It was him! He was on the caravan! Carmen's heart pounded erratically as she gripped the slats of the ox-cart and peeked out. When she'd first spied him on the caravan, she'd thought her dreams had miraculously invaded her waking hours. For she'd dreamed of him, tossed and turned restlessly, finally falling asleep at dawn with thoughts of him. Of course she had not told Doña Matilda. And now here he was—traveling on the same caravan as she. Her eyes brightened with excitement. He looked so tall, so strong, so . . .

Her breath quickened. She leaned forward and stared intently at him as the big sorrel stallion galloped past toward the front of the caravan. Her hands gripped the slats tighter as she pressed forward to follow him with her eyes.

Dios, he looked magnificent! He wore the

armor of the Spanish Empire as one born to it. Carmen craned her neck, straining to see him, but he had disappeared into the dust cloud. She sank back, disappointment flooding over her.

Then Carmen noticed Doña Matilda staring at her, those piercing eyes narrowed thoughtfully. Suddenly conscious of her eagerness, Carmen glanced away.

Mayhap it was unseemly to be staring after him, she mused. She must not forget that she was Carmen Yolanda Diaz y Silvera, a noblewoman of Seville, Spain. Nor must she forget that she was traveling to marry Juan Enrique Delgado of Santa Fe. She must not let her heart, nor her head, be turned by a handsome *soldado* of the Empire who quite took her breath away. . . .

Carmen gazed dully out the side of the ox-cart as it lurched over the rough ruts of the dirt road. Red dust stuck to her face and her hands. Her hair was coated with the dust, her clothes had dust in every seam. Though she was thankful that her dress was long, the heavily embroidered front panel only topped her breasts and she could feel the infernal dust clinging to her neck, breasts, and every pore of her skin.

She and her dueña had made a roof of blankets across the high wooden sides of the cart to protect them from the merciless rays of the sun. Just ahead of Carmen's cart rode Comandante Diego, followed by six *soldados*, riding two abreast.

They led the way along El Camino Real, the King's Highway.

Behind Carmen's cart trailed ten more carts. They were loaded down with supplies that Fray Cristobal was delivering to Santa Fe and included one hundred new arquebuses, a type of musket. There were also saddles, swords, daggers, and bushels of corn meal and grain to feed the colonists in Santa Fe.

Straggling behind the ox-carts were the hundreds of cattle and scores of goats that would supply food for the remaining three-month journey and for the inhabitants of Santa Fe. Twelve men rode on either side of the cattle, urging them along the dusty road. Behind the cattle trotted a huge herd of a thousand horses. Thirty *soldados* guarded the horses. Fray Cristobal's remaining recruits were scattered along the line of the caravan.

Occasionally Carmen would see Fray Cristobal ride past on his large gray mule, Gabriel. Fray Cristobal rode sometimes to the rear of the ox carts, sometimes just behind Comandante Diego, depending on whether Gabriel felt like walking that day or not.

Carmen's turquoise eyes searched across the endless vista of reddish brown desert and huge, brown, cracked boulders. She was searching through the ever-present dust cloud that hovered over the caravan, looking for some sign of life besides the cactus.

Every morning for the past week, she had stared out at what seemed to be the same scene. First the interminable wait in El Paso del Norte—and now this! Why, the plodding caravan could be going in gigantic circles and she would never know the difference. If only they would reach Santa Fe. . . . And Juan. . . . She resolutely pushed the memory of ice-blue eyes from her mind.

The cart lurched again, and Carmen grabbed at a wooden side railing. She muttered softly under her breath, careful not to let Doña Matilda, crouched across from her, hear the naughty words. And how the nuns in the convent would have been shocked to hear their star pupil repeating such words, thought Carmen. She supposed she did it to relieve the boredom, for it was awfully boring to look out at leagues and leagues of desert day after day.

Carmen glanced across at her dueña. Matilda Josefa Delgado had been Carmen's loyal and constant companion since the day they had left Carmen's home in Seville over a year before.

When Carmen's father died, everything had changed. Even now, the memory of her father's death brought tears to Carmen's huge turquoise eyes, and she turned for a moment to gaze out the slits in the cart wall, hoping the scorching heat would soon dry the welling pools of her tears.

Carmen shook silently, but she still pretended that she was enraptured with the view, when in reality all she could see was her deceased father's face as though through a white mist. It seemed that his face was getting more and more difficult to recall. What if she should forget him entirely? Her breath came short and quick and she pressed a pale, slim hand to her mouth to stifle a moan. The desert blurred in front of her eyes, and she choked back sobs. How much it hurt to be left alone in the world.

After some time had passed, the terrible ache of unshed tears finally lessened. She straightened a little, striving to regain her composure. She brushed carefully at her eyes and coughed, as though the dust had become too much. Carmen leaned back, eyes closed, striving desperately for some peace of mind. She was unconscious of the picture she presented.

Long, naturally curling blond hair rippled over her shoulders and down her back. Earlier, she had taken off her mantilla to free her hair, and the black lace of mourning lay draped over a blanket beside her. Her favorite turquoise taffeta dress, the one she had worn at the successful interview with the Alcalde so many days before, was now wrinkled and dust-coated. It was the first colorful garment she had put on since emerging from the mourning period for her father, and she had worn it despite a disapproving sniff from Doña Matilda, who had been reluctant to see the year's required mourning pass. Now Carmen regretted her rash action because the dress had wrinkle upon wrinkle from being slept in, crouched in, and walked in for several days. Great dark stains had spread under her arms, thanks to the infernal heat of this desert country.

Still, Carmen looked reasonably presentable, her high wide forehead giving her a noble appearance commensurate with her birth. Her black-fringed turquoise eyes, now closed, were set in a truly angelic face, or so Sister Francisca, her favorite nun at the Seville convent, had always told her. Then Sister would get flustered and sternly warn Carmen about the terrible sin of vanity. Privately, Carmen had wondered how terrible a sin it was when her appearance brought such a gentle tone to the usually reproving voice of Sister Francisca.

Carmen's eyes opened as she mused upon Sister Francisca. Mayhap soon Carmen would stop the cart and walk, just as she had done for the past several days. She found the exercise helped her body and her thoughts. The ox-cart would become too sweltering, too dust-filled, and too hot, so she and Doña Matilda would walk beside it. The plodding pace of the oxen was easy to keep. The carts did not really need any guidance because the beasts just plodded along in the wake of the cart before them. After some time, the clouds of red dust and the hot sun would ally to give Carmen a choked, aching feeling, and she would be back in the cart once more. 'Twas the exchange of one misery for another, Doña Matilda said. At such times, Carmen reminded herself of the stifling boredom of the convent and thus encouraged herself that she was having an adventure far beyond her wildest dreams.

But oh, how she would love to be able to gallop over these vast desert hills on a swift horse, like her beloved Andalusian mare, Margarita. Thoughts of her horse, with her gray glistening hide, her strong muscles bunched as they galloped across her father's fields, filled Carmen with bittersweet memories of home.

But Margarita was gone, gone like the rest of Carmen's old life. After her father's death, his younger brother had taken over as the head of the family. Tío Felipe had insisted that the beloved horse be sold. Of what use was a horse on the ship and then on the overland route to Santa Fe? he had scoffed, deaf to Carmen's desperate pleas. Margarita would probably die from such an arduous journey, her uncle had informed Carmen coldly. At last, reluctantly, Carmen had agreed to part with the mare because she had seen that it was the only way to save the horse. Later, she learned that her uncle had been unwilling to pay the costly tax for the special license required to ship the mare to the New World.

Carmen sighed. How she wished that Margarita were here now, to gallop over these hills, to outrun the oppressive heat and dust. . . .

The ox-cart lurched again and Carmen's rambling thoughts jerked back to the present.

How lonely the desert was, she mused. Why, anything could happen to the unwary traveler. That was why she had been forced to wait for six months in El Paso del Norte for an escort. Now, seeing the desolate countryside, how few the missions were and how far apart, she was glad she had waited. And there were *indios* to watch out for—Comanches, Utes and the most dreaded of all, Apaches. The presence of the Spanish *soldados* on the caravan gave Carmen a sense of security. Not a single Apache would dare attack these fine soldiers!

On two of the nights they had been fortunate and stopped at a mission. The missions were clusters of adobe huts surrounding a larger adobe church. The padres and their Indian servants had been very welcoming and had been hungry for news from the travelers. The women and children—dark-eyed, black-haired and unsmiling—had stared at Carmen and at her clothes until, uncomfortable with their silence and their stares, Carmen had sought out her ox-cart once more.

The sparseness of the colonists' material lives was not a surprise to Carmen. She had seen poverty before. Though most of her life had been spent living in relative comfort at the Catholic convent in Seville which her father had chosen for her, there had been those excursions—escorted, of course—that she and Sister Francisca had taken from the convent. The narrow streets of Seville were crammed with refuse and animal entrails and all manner of filthy garbage. The contents of slop jars nightly doused the city streets after the ten o'clock deadline allowed by law. She and Sister Francisca had walked to the Arenal, the public promenade and market that followed along Seville's Guadalquivir River. The good sister always held tightly to their money, for fear of cutpurses. On these occasions, Carmen had seen all manner of beggars. Though Seville was a city of gardens, monasteries, and even palaces, there were also the poor, the hungry, and the ragged—and they all seemed to flock to the Arenal. *Sí*, Carmen had seen poverty.

Her father's home had been furnished on a modest scale. Carmen had known that the orchards and vineyards had provided some of the wealth that he did have. Her father, though a member of the Spanish upper-class, had for years been losing money on ill-fated trading ventures in the New World. First, one of his ships sank, then another was destroyed by pirates. While the Diaz family's name was still honorable, it was true that the conspicuous wealth of prior generations was absent for this present generation. Don Carlos's marriage, for love, to Carmen's mother, the daughter of an impoverished *hidalgo*, had not helped the family fortunes either.

Traveling in the New World, Carmen again saw hungry children, and it greatly saddened her. She began to ask herself why God had seen fit to parcel out the good things on such an unequal scale. Or was it man that had allowed the inequality?

And while her life in Seville had been fairly comfortable materially, it had been much the poorer in relationships. Back in Seville, on special feast days and holy days, she had been allowed to visit her father for a few hours, only to return to the convent at night. Her father had preferred it that way. For a long time, Carmen never really knew what she had done to deserve such a cold upbringing. Many times she had yearned for her father's approval, for some warmth, some display of affection on his part, but alas, he was always cool and distant. She supposed she should not have been surprised when his younger brother, Felipe, turned out to be of similar ilk.

One day, after Carmen had reached adulthood, her father's sister, Tía Edelmira, had discovered Carmen crying. It was on one of Carmen's rare, brief visits to the family manor. Tía Edelmira's black eyes had narrowed thoughtfully, then she had taken her sobbing niece aside. She explained that it was not that Carmen had disappointed her father, it was that her father was that way with everyone. He could not tolerate intimacy and had never been able to, not since the death of Carmen's mother at Carmen's birth eighteen years before.

Through tear-filled eyes, Carmen had asked if her father blamed her for her mother's death, and Tía Edelmira had reluctantly acknowledged that such might be the case. Then she had risen from the settee and set about briskly straightening the already neat room, giving it all of her attention.

Carmen had understood then that her aunt had said as much as she was able to about the painful subject. As Carmen wiped away her tears, she knew in her heart that her father had unjustly judged and condemned her. With leaden feet, she had left the room, the rustle of her aunt's cleaning whispering behind her.

Strange that she should be thinking about all this now. What she should be thinking about was her *novio*, Juan Enrique Delgado, a man she had never met, nor heard of, until that fateful day when Tío Felipe had called her into what was now his study and informed her of her betrothal.

Juan Enrique Delgado, her uncle informed her, was the third son of an illustrious Spanish grandee from one of the oldest families in Seville. As a third son, he of course was not his father's heir, but he apparently was an ambitious man. He had traveled to New Spain, far away in the New World, to seek his fortune.

Carmen's uncle was impressed by the man's lineage and the information that had filtered back to the noble families of Seville from New Spain. He had been impressed, too, Carmen knew, by the well-written letters of Juan Enrique himself that told of his thriving quicksilver mine and salt mines.

Juan had also financially established himself by the sale of a shipload of African slaves to Mexico, a fact that caused Carmen a certain uneasiness. She glossed over it, however, as Tío Felípe went on to enumerate the fine qualities of her prospective husband—his lands, his mines, his house . . . Deciding it was time to settle down and take a wife, Juan Enrique Delgado had petitioned for, and won, Carmen's fair hand. Even now, on her white hand there gleamed a small ruby surrounded by emeralds, a gift from the unknown Delgado.

As she had listened to her uncle, Carmen had begun to understand that this marriage was his desperate attempt to right the Diaz family fortunes. It sounded as though Juan Enrique Delgado was also an up-and-coming merchant, and the Diaz family's waning fortunes could swiftly be reversed by Carmen's brilliant marriage to such a man.

Her lips tightened when she realized that she was to have no say in the marriage agreement whatsoever. She could only hope that Juan Enrique Delgado was an honorable, decent man, important qualities to her.

When she pressed him for details, Tío Felipe had admitted that her *novio* was several years older than Carmen, but that was to be desired, her uncle had added sharply. An older, more stable man would settle a flighty convent girl who was constantly getting herself into escapades.

Carmen had let that comment pass, but she had wondered what kind of escapades her uncle thought were possible in a convent, where one was surrounded by stern, sharp-eyed nuns. The only nun Carmen had ever been able to sway, who had a soft side was Sister Francisca, and Carmen was certain that the good sister had never reported their occasional visits to Seville's outdoor market. Surely such sorties could not be called "escapades." Carmen shrugged and concluded that her uncle was making things up.

Not to be deterred from her goal of finding out about her *novio*, she had then asked her uncle where in the New World Delgado lived.

"Santa Fe," she was told curtly. Her uncle then lifted a thickly bound book off his desk. The pages were yellowed and crinkled. The author was Tomás de Torquemada, a leader of the Inquisition two hundred years before.

"This should tell you all you need to know," her uncle had pronounced. Bewildered, Carmen read the title: *How To Be A Perfect Wife*. Her uncle waved a hand dismissively; her interview was at an end, and Carmen left the room, dazedly clutching the thick volume to her breast.

And now here she was, traveling in this terrible heat, across perilous terrain, to marry a man she did not know. She could only hope that he was kind. Indeed, if the truth be told, Carmen hoped he was more than kind. In her mind, she had turned to her *novio* as someone who had rescued her from the boring existence of the convent. He was the man who had come into her life to replace the loss of her father, and though Juan Enrique Delgado was unknown to her, Carmen had begun to feel a special concern for and attachment to him.

She hesitated to call it love, yet it was a very strong concern that had seen her through the long, long sea voyage, and then the overland trip from the Gulf of Mexico to Mexico City and then to El Paso del Norte. That same dogged determination to reach Juan Enrique Delgado had made the six-month wait in El Paso del Norte so difficult, and that same determination now kept her pursuing the dusty trail to Santa Fe.

Idly, for something to do, Carmen said, "Doña Matilda, please read to me from the Torquemada book."

Obligingly, the older woman picked up the thick, precious, swaddled volume, one of the two valuable books they'd brought with them from Spain. The second book, especially beloved by Doña Matilda, was a thin volume of poetry by one of Spain's great poets, Lope de Vega. She set the thin book aside and settled the heavy volume on her knees.

Doña Matilda cleared her throat and began to read. " 'Rule Number 237: The perfect wife keeps her husband's home tidy at all times.' "

Carmen nodded thoughtfully. "Go on," she encouraged.

" 'Rule Number 238:' " read Doña Matilda, " 'the perfect wife is always ready to listen to her husband's wise words.' "

Carmen frowned. She hoped that Juan Enrique Delgado would have wise words. Of course he would, she chided herself. He was handsome, charming, wise—all the things she hoped for in a husband. And once again, gratitude swept over her that her cold uncle had thought to include this marvelous book for her journey. *How To Be A Perfect Wife* had proved to be a most valuable guide on what a wife should be, Carmen thought in satisfaction. "Go on," she repeated.

Her dueña's voice droned soothingly on and on. " 'Rule number 265: The perfect wife never raises her voice to her husband. Rule number 266: The perfect wife defers to her husband in all things.' "

Carmen let Doña Matilda read on. Truth to tell, Carmen had memorized the entire book. Every single one of Torquemada's four hundred and seventy-three strictures was engraved on her mind over the course of her long sea and land voyage.

" 'Rule Number 274: The perfect wife allows the servants to serve her the choicest morsels. Rule Number 275:—' "

"That will be all," sighed Carmen.

Doña Matilda re-wrapped the book in its cloth covering once more.

Carmen fidgeted, wanting something else to do. Finally, she slipped off Juan Delgado's ring and groped around the floor of the ox-cart until her fingers settled on what she was seeking. Her dueña looked questioningly at her mistress for a moment, but forbore to comment. Instead she gazed, seemingly entranced, out at the broad, red expanse of desert, giving her charge a small measure of privacy.

Carmen straightened and pulled a dark brown leather bag into her lap. She took one last look at the ring, then opened the leather drawstring and popped the ring into the sack's interior. A dull clank sounded as the ring fell atop more jewels. Carmen smiled secretly.

She held up the sack, swinging it pensively. Her sole wealth, her dowry, all she had in the world, was in this sack. Her uncle had decided that jewelry was the safest form of dowry for traveling the vast distance between Seville and Santa Fe, so he had liquidated all that Carmen's father had left her and bought jewels and gold coins.

Carmen had spent most of the gold her uncle had given her to buy food and lodging on her journey for herself and Doña Matilda. Carmen had purchased the ox-cart and the oxen from a family who had traveled up from Mexico City with the caravan and then decided to settle in El Paso del Norte. Food and lodging for this trip, the last leg of Carmen's journey to Santa Fe, had taken her last coins.

Inside the brown sack were magnificent rubies, some far finer than the one in the ring Delgado had bought for her, though Carmen was reluctant to admit this. She thought mayhap Delgado had needed to put his money into the quicksilver mine or the salt mine, and so had found himself short of funds when he went to purchase a ring for his bride-to-be. Besides, she had so many jewels now. Why be so particular over his ring?

Also in the sack were topazes, sapphires, gleaming diamonds, and rare jewels of all colors in a vast array of settings. Some were mounted as rings, others were pendants, necklaces, bracelets, brooches, whatever the human mind had ever devised to decorate a woman.

Sometimes, when her dueña was taking a nap, Carmen would take out the sack and play with the jewels—they were like so many pretty toys. She would run them through her fingers like waterfalls, stringing the necklaces around her neck, one atop the other. Tiring of her play, she always wrapped them back up carefully, placed them back in the sack, and wedged it between the blankets on the floor of the ox-cart.

"My lady," came the voice of Doña Matilda, "it would be best if you left the ring on your finger. Your *novio* will not be pleased if he notices it absent."

Carmen smiled. "Of course," she agreed. "I had forgotten." Mentally, she chastised herself. How could she have put Juan's precious ring in with her own jewelry? What had she been thinking of? It was a gift from him, a cherished keepsake, meaning far more than its mere monetary value. She must henceforth remember to keep it always on her finger.

She studied her companion. The spinster maiden aunt of a distant cousin of the Delgado family, Matilda Josefa, while noble, had never received a decent marriage offer in her younger days, and so she had been obliged to support herself by chaperoning various female members of the Delgado family as they came of age. Each young Delgado had gone on to marriage, leaving behind a Matilda Josefa who grew a little older and a little grayer before she took up the next Delgado. Carmen sometimes wondered how many young Delgados she had run through, but thought it impolite to ask.

"Did you ever meet Juan Enrique?" asked Carmen now. She had asked about him before on the long journey, but each time had found it difficult to get Doña Matilda to part with any important information. The older woman, usually so blunt, had always seemed rather reticent to discuss her relative.

While the older woman took her time in answering, Carmen searched for the slim packet of letters she carried with her. There, wrapped with a purple ribbon, next to the crushed, yellowed letter from Tía Edelmira that had fortunately caught up with Carmen in El Paso del Norte, was the single missive from Juan Enrique Delgado.

Carmen opened it up once more to read the fine, curling script. She sighed happily. The flowery language set her heart to beating as fast now as when she had first looked upon the words. She finished reading the text she had memorized and closed her eyes, savoring the noble sentiments expressed in the letter. Was there ever a finer, more cultivated man than Juan Enrique Delgado? Sternly, she quashed an image of a square-jawed, rugged face with ice blue eyes. No, of course not. Not anywhere in the vast lands of New Spain.

And Carmen had written to Juan. She had undertaken to inform her betrothed, in her own dainty handwriting, of the departure and arrival dates and everything she thought he might like to know about his intended bride's travel plans. She had no way of knowing if her letters had reached him, but she hoped that they had.

"Juan Enrique," said her dueña, with a slight cough, "was always a good boy." A blatant lie, Matilda Josefa thought uncomfortably. But then she could hardly tell his *novia* the truth. Juan Enrique had been the terror of the manor where he had been brought up. Matilda Josefa mused that she could easily tell the young woman numerous stories about her precious *novio*. There was the time he had set fire to the barn cat's tail and the frightened beast had run madly through the stalls, almost setting the whole barn on fire. A quick-thinking groom had doused the poor animal with water, but the unfortunate animal had died from the terrifying experience.

Then there was the time Juan Enrique had rolled a neighboring simpleton boy along the road in a barrel and was about to roll him off a bridge when he was halted in this amusing diversion by his older, more responsible brother.

And how well the family had hushed up the little incident with his half-sister and the illegitimate child.

Matilda Josefa guessed that most of the money that Juan Enrique claimed came from his quicksilver and salt mines actually came from the family coffers. The old grandee was still sending funds to his rapscallion son to keep him out of Spain forever. An excellent bargain, thought Matilda Josefa privately.

Ah, *sí*. She could tell this young woman a tale or two about the man she was going to marry. Her eyes narrowed consideringly. She sighed. But she would not. Better to say nothing. During the many months of travel, Matilda Josefa had come to care for *La Carmencita*, the nickname she had given the young woman. Though headstrong at times, La Carmencita had always made certain that her dueña was well-treated and fed. Matilda Josefa appreciated this very much and was inclined to shrug off her charge's impulsiveness as mere youthful high spirits. She did not like to think how marriage to Juan Enrique would change this spirited child. There was always the hope, of course, that he had changed, become more mature, more caring. Matilda Josefa sighed doubtfully and glanced out through the slats of the cart.

The truth of the matter was that there was no longer any place for her in the family home in Seville. The unfortunate half-sister, whom Matilda Josefa had also doted upon, had been removed to a small cottage in the country, far from the family's estates, and Matilda Josefa had no wish to share her lifelong exile. She had been forced to look for another position.

No, were La Carmencita to know the kind of man she was going to marry, she would turn the ox-cart around. Matilda Josefa had seen enough of La Carmencita to understand that the young woman seated across from her was intelligent and kind. She could be headstrong and impulsive when she wished. Those traits, coupled with the independence her dowry gave her, would probably lead La Carmencita to renege on her stupid uncle's contract once she met Delgado. And Matilda Josefa knew that when that moment came, she would not desert her charge, but stay with her even if they must leave Santa Fe in disgrace. Far better the disgrace than seeing such a lovely one torn down by the likes of Juan Enrique.

Matilda Josefa coughed as a nondescript sorrel trotted by, kicking up more dust.

Carmen froze. Her eyes darted to the man sitting so straight in the big saddle. "There he is again," she muttered.

Her companion peeked through the slats. "Who?"

Carmen flushed. She had not meant to speak aloud. "Mmmmhm," she murmured, hoping to put Doña Matilda off.

But the older woman's curiosity was piqued. Her bright black eyes followed the trotting stallion. The man riding the animal had broad shoulders, narrow hips, and long legs. Black hair showed under his Spanish helmet. "Who?" She asked again. "That *soldado*?"

Her pointed nose was actually sticking out over a slat.

Carmen sighed. She did not want to lie, but she also did not want to tell Doña Matilda that the man who had just ridden past had rescued her that last night in El Paso del Norte. Duenna would be horrified to know that her young charge had been wandering around the town alone.

For Carmen, however, the man's presence on the caravan was a constant irritant, a reminder of her impulsive behavior.

It was also something like a secret between the two of them. One morning, as she was packing away the bedding, Carmen had felt the hairs on the back of her neck stir. She had looked up to find him watching her. He was sitting atop the sorrel, and his impassive face gave away nothing. Bristling, Carmen had frowned imperiously at him, in her best noblewoman-of-Seville manner, daring him to say anything. He had continued to stare at her until she had grown flustered and dropped a blanket. His stony countenance had revealed nothing, yet when he nudged the horse away, she was left feeling unaccountably let down, as though she was prepared to do battle and her opponent had declined the challenge. She had to admit that the ice blue of his eyes and the look in them had shaken her. Since then, she had found herself watching for him at odd moments of the day, but she could not tell whether it was attraction or guilt or curiosity or anger that drew her.

Doña Matilda drew her nose back into the cart and examined her young charge's face intently.

Why, La Carmencita was blushing, and her eyes suddenly looked bright and vital.

Her sharp eyes thoughtfully followed the *soldado* on the sorrel.

Chapter 5

Puma rode along in the wake of the caravan, the thin cloth covering his nose and mouth keeping out the clouds of red dust. Soon they would be in Apacheria. Then he would leave these Spanish invaders to their fate.

It had been a long, strange journey for him since he had last seen Apache territory, he mused. Now he felt himself to be older, wiser, harder than he had been when he had lived with his Jicarilla Apache people.

Being sold into slavery had done that to him. If he had had a knife, he would have hacked off his braids in his grief at being separated from his people. When the Comanches, always his people's feared enemy, had ridden south and sold him to the Spanish, Puma had not known whether to be relieved or infuriated. The Spanish had chained

69

him like an animal and dragged him to Mexico City and thrown him into prison. What they had intended to do with him, Puma never did find out. But once he had killed the Spanish *soldado*— Lieutenant Martinez—it mattered little. The Spanish were set to hang him.

Lieutenant Martinez had made the fatal mistake of trying to beat Puma. A cruel man, Martinez was fond of beating the prisoners, and he had often forced the families of the prisoners to give him expensive presents in payment for visiting with their men. If a prisoner's wife or daughter was of particular beauty, Lieutenant Martinez would demand that she sleep with him. He was greatly hated by the captives.

Some of the prisoners, after Martinez's death, had smuggled Puma extra corn cakes, or the swill that passed for soup, or left him little presents of fresh fruit in gratitude.

So Puma had waited in that dark prison cell, far off in a foreign land, waited for death and tried to pray to God. But it had been difficult. He had not wanted to accept death at the hands of the Spanish and he had not been able to pray. He had not been able to chant the Death Song. The words had choked in his throat. And at night when he dreamed, he dreamed of his home, of his mother and cousins and friends, and it was as if he was with them once again. When he awoke, he would feel renewed, refreshed—and even more desperate to escape.

70

But Puma had not been able to escape. When freedom finally came to him, it was in the unexpected guise of thin, pink Fray Cristobal. After Puma had finally left the dark little hole of a prison, he had been given a Spanish uniform and a horse to ride and a measure of freedom, Spanish-style. It was as if Puma was suddenly reborn. The reprieve from death, the chance to return to his homeland—it was too much for him to take in at once. The other *soldados* on the caravan had ceased to jump at the fierce yells and yips of freedom that had passed his lips those first few days.

Over the duration of the six-month journey from Mexico City to El Paso del Norte, Puma had had time to study the men around him and especially Fray Cristobal. He wondered about the man and his motives. Puma decided, to his surprise, that the man meant well. Several times Fray Cristobal had handed out extra grain to the dark-eyed inhabitants of the missions, though Comandante Diego had chided him for his generosity to the peons. Once Fray Cristobal had even won a confrontation with the wily military leader over delaying the caravan for two days while he prayed over a deathly sick Indian child. When the child miraculously recovered, even Comandante Diego treated the good brother with more respect—for two whole days.

Comandante Diego was a man Puma kept away from. Early on in the journey, Diego had ridden up to Puma and snarled tersely that he would be watching for any excuse to kill him. Lieutenant Martinez had been a personal friend of Diego's. Further, Diego warned Puma that the weak Fray Cristobal, indeed the entire membership of the Holy Mother Church, could do nothing to save him—the next time. The flat black eyes of the comandante had met the icy blue of the Apache. The two understood each other well. Puma found that while he did not like Comandante Diego, the man did a fair job of leading the caravan through hostile territory. He was brave—or arrogant—to the point of foolhardiness, and Puma's Apache soul could grudgingly respect that. So, while Puma did not fear the comandante, he did nothing to provoke him either and kept well out of his way. Puma had a far more important goal than besting Diego—he would survive until he could leave the caravan and rejoin his Apache people once more.

Puma glanced around. The sun would be setting soon. Diego would halt the caravan, and camp would be set up for the night. The cattle would settle down and so too would the horses and, of course, the people. Puma's eyes wandered to the first ox-cart. Inside, he knew, was the turquoise-eyed woman and her companion. Every night the two set their blankets at some distance from the others. Puma had learned something of Spanish customs during his forced stay with them, and he knew that the old woman was supposed to guard the young one from the advances of men. There was a similar custom among his own Apache people.

But he could not help reminding himself that were he to steal the turquoise-eyed woman, one old woman would prove a pitiable deterrent. Strange how the thought of stealing the lovely one had come to him more often, the closer he got to Apacheria.

Their meeting in El Paso del Norte had, contrary to Puma's expectations, not been their last. He had first noticed her the next morning when her ox-cart had joined the caravan. Sitting astride his horse, he was certain that his face had given away none of his shock at the first sight of her, though his heart had beaten faster until he had taken several deep breaths and reminded himself that she was Spanish.

Ever since they had left El Paso del Norte, Puma had been uncomfortably aware of the lovely woman. Now he watched the jerking, bumping course of the ox-cart and wondered about her. Too bad she was Spanish.

Even when he was a small lad, Puma had sensed that he was different from his fellow Apaches. None of them had blue eyes. None of them had been deserted by their father. His mother spoke little of the man who had sired Puma, and Puma did not ask.

He had vague memories of his father. He remembered his father as a big man, holding him, laughing with him. He remembered his father, arms filled with wildflowers, riding toward Puma and his mother. Puma's father was laughing, and his light brown hair was stirred by the wind. There were other memories, too—

confusing ones. Of his father, sitting, staring at the fire, not answering any of his mother's questions. Of his mother, crying in the night. And finally, Puma remembered his father riding away. He remembered the hot tears brimming as he watched his father's broad back disappear over a hill. Puma never saw his father again.

So Puma had been content to bury the Spanish side of his heritage until Angry Man had begun bringing it up, taunting Puma and goading the People about it. Puma had not wanted to face his Spanish heritage, and he had succeeded in ignoring it, mayhap even running from it, until Angry Man had sold him into slavery. And once the Comanches sold him to the Spaniards, he had had to stop running. Being a captive of his own father's people had forced him to look at a part of himself that he didn't want to face. He had mixed feelings now about himself and about the Spanish.

When Puma had first been taken into captivity, he had hated the Spanish, every one of them he had seen. Beatings, poor food, slavery itself—little in Puma's prior experience had prepared him for the brutality that the Spanish meted out. He had not known people could treat one another so cruelly.

And what prison did to his Apache soul . . . he shuddered even now to think on it. To be locked up, confined—he who had once had the right to wander wherever he wanted, to fly as free as the eagle and the hawk, to run as far and as fast as the wolf, to climb as high as the sheep—

to him the confinement was pure torture. To have God's great sky reduced to the tiny view he could see from a barred window . . . Puma shook his head, grim-faced, recalling. At first he had blamed Angry Man, then the Comanches, then the Spanish. And he had hated them all.

After some time in prison, he began to notice that not all the Spanish were cruel. Some of them treated him kindly—one or two of the *soldados*, several of the prisoners. Puma had been reserved and uncommunicative with his fellow captives, and they had accepted his silence, mayhap respected it, and allowed the wounded part of him to heal. Slowly, tentatively, he had begun to talk with them; talk was about the only thing one could do in the prison where each man was kept apart from the others. Occasionally, prisoners were thrown in together if there were more than the jail could accommodate, but usually a man was left alone in a tiny cell. Puma found that he had a facility for the Spanish language. As he learned more of the words, it was almost as if he'd already known the language. More memories of his father returned, and he guessed that his father had taught him Spanish during Puma's early years—before he had deserted Puma and his mother.

And though Puma continued to regard the Spanish as unwanted invaders in his land, he had begun to determine differences between them. The Churchmen, he saw, were different from the *soldados*. The Churchmen wanted to build missions and churches and make the Indians do the labor. They spoke of souls, of saving the Indians. Puma knew this because the prison was visited regularly by a man referred to by the Spanish prisoners as Padre—"Father"— and all his talk was of the Indians as children. Puma did not see the Indians as children. He saw them as adults, trying desperately to cope with the chaos brought by the invaders.

The *soldados*, the warriors, were constantly bullying the Indian people, wanting new land. Sometimes, when a Spanish *soldado* was thrown into prison to sober up after a fight, he would speak of the Cities of Gold for which the military were searching. There were supposed to be seven of them. At such times Puma would merely shake his head; there were no cities of gold that he knew of, and the Indians he spoke to thought the Spanish were merely crazy when it came to golden cities.

Yes, he had seen a strange variety of people, Spanish and Indian, come and go through the prison while he was there. He had learned the Spanish language and some of their customs— but for what? His new freedom gave him cause to wonder why he had been shown such things, why he had experienced such devastating captivity. Did God have some plan for him?

And while Puma's anger and rage had abated somewhat, he knew he would never accept these foreigners as belonging to his land. For if that were true, what about himself? He, who had the blood of the Spaniards running through his own veins? He was having great difficulty accepting that his Apache blood mingled with that of the invaders. He wished he could just forget the whole thing, but he had come too far, learned too much, to go back now. When he did reach his people, everything would be changed—for him.

Puma frowned as the caravan slowed and moved off the trail to camp for the night. He watched the first ox-cart roll to a halt under a pinyon tree. In this spot there was green grass for the cattle and horses, and the dust was not so thick. A small creek ran nearby. Puma grunted. Diego had been fortunate in his choice of camping place this night.

The two women were climbing out of the ox-cart now, the younger first, reaching back to help the older one out. The turquoise-eyed woman glanced about and stretched. Puma's eyes fastened on her breasts. He stared at the elaborately embroidered front of the turquoise dress she wore, wishing he could see more of her. She took several deep breaths of the clear air. Puma gripped the high wooden pommel of his saddle, hard. He should be helping with the horses, the cattle, something, anything but watching the rise and fall off that turquoise-clad chest.

The woman began to move off, presenting her delectable backside to him. He wondered if she knew he was there, watching her. She bent over to gather sticks of wood for a fire, and with a last sigh, Puma turned away. What was the matter with him? How could he find a woman of the invaders attractive? For that was what he was beginning to think—that the turquoise-eyed woman was very attractive indeed.

Chapter 6

Puma watched in amusement as Miguel Baca hurried up to the two Spanish women struggling with the heavy trunk. "Here, allow me," Baca said politely, nearly tripping and falling over the trunk in his haste. The blond woman stared at him and took a step backward. Puma wanted to tell her that Baca did not remember anything of the evening he had accosted her. Puma's tap on the head had apparently wiped the memory from Baca's mind. But Baca's fawning smile seemed to reassure the woman that she had nothing to fear from him. It was either that or the way the black-swathed dueña planted herself firmly between Baca and her young charge. She thrust a sharp nose in Baca's grinning face and stated, "Leave. We do not need your help!"

Baca gave a yelp when the dueña followed up with a stomp on his foot, and he quickly made his retreat. Puma grinned to himself as he unsaddled his horse. The dueña certainly took her role seriously.

Puma reached for the bridle, but his movements were too swift. The sorrel mount he was unsaddling rolled his eyes and suddenly swung around to bite Puma on the arm. Puma flinched. He had learned to take precautions with the big beast, but his attention had been distracted by the women. It was not the first bite he had received from the horse. The irritable young stallion was very unlike Puma's pinto stallion, Raids the Enemy.

Still, the horse was proving to have stamina, and Puma was glad of that. When he left the caravan, he might have to travel several days to find his nomadic people, and a strong horse would make the search easier. He muttered softly to the beast in an attempt to calm him, then wrestled with the heavy Spanish saddle. He finally got it off the horse's broad back and let it sink to the ground.

Later, Puma joined Miguel Baca at a small campfire the skinny *soldado* had made. On the caravan there were eight cooks—six of them men, two heavy-set, middle-aged women. The cooks rode in the ox-carts during the day and prepared food for the fifty soldiers every evening.

Puma and Baca walked over to help themselves to the contents of one huge pot. One of the cooks, Lopez, joked with the men as they helped themselves to corn cakes. Puma saw that there was even fresh meat for the evening meal.

While Lopez and Baca talked, Puma spotted a moving turquoise dress out of the corner of his eye. It was the blond woman. She and her dueña slowly walked up to the big pot to take some food. Silence fell among the three men as the women approached.

Puma watched as Lopez, wearing a look of utter concentration, carefully spooned a huge helping of beans onto the blond woman's plate. The blunt, strong fingers of the cook next deposited a warm corn cake precisely next to the beans. With a flourish, Lopez then scooped up a large chunk of meat and placed it delicately on the other side of the beans. With a huge grin, he bowed as though presenting the lovely woman with the finest meal ever made.

She smiled, nodded, then stepped to the side as she waited for her dueña to be served. With a quick *plop!* the beans were on the dueña's plate; a loud *thunk!* and a corn cake rested next to the beans; finally, a mushy *splat!* and a chunk of meat slid across the heavy plate. The old woman harrumphed, glared at the cook, and marched away, her charge hurrying behind her.

Lopez watched them go, his eyes following the young woman. Baca, too, watched her, a hopeless, yearning look on his face. Puma merely shook his head.

"What is her name?" asked Baca without taking his eyes off the retreating women. Lopez, too, kept his eyes on them as he answered in a voice filled with reverence, "Her name is Doña Carmen."

"Doña Carmen," repeated Baca, drawing the name out lovingly in the same awed tone of voice. Both men continued to stare at the woman, who moved towards their own campfire.

Lopez sighed. "I think," he said thoughtfully, "that she has the nicest *tetas* I have ever seen on a woman." He paused then nodded. "*Sí*, the very nicest."

Miguel Baca nodded too, a look of wonder and bliss upon his face as he continued to stare after the woman.

Puma could stand it no longer. He walked back to the small campfire where his bedroll waited for him, leaving the two Spaniards to their dreams. Finishing his meal in the gathering darkness, Puma checked on the sorrel once more before wrapping himself in a blanket for the night.

He was awakened suddenly out of a wild dream of turquoise jewel eyes and howling coyotes. Puma sat up, disoriented. His Apache skills were leaving him, he thought, as he crouched and reached for a spear that Comandante Diego had seen fit to make standard issue to every *soldado*.

The coyote had given several yips. But Puma sensed that it was not a coyote. It was Comanches. They were giving each other their hidden locations so they did not accidently shoot each other.

Puma was on his feet, wide awake now, glancing around. Some of the cattle moved restlessly. He heard a horse nicker. His eyes strained in the darkness. There, over by the pinyon tree where the two women had bedded down. A movement.

Stealthily, glad the fire had burned itself out so that his movements could not be seen, Puma stepped soundlessly through the darkness. He reached the pinyon tree. Nothing. His Apache skills did need honing, he thought again. The Comanche must have heard him coming.

He glanced over to where the two women slept on, unaware. Now the coyote yips were distant, back in the next arroyo. The Comanches were withdrawing. They must have scouted out the size of the caravan and the number of men and decided not to chance an attack. He shook his head. If they had been Apache, they would have attacked.

Puma stood for a long while, listening, eyes searching, poised in the dark like an avenging angel over the two sleeping women. Then with one last longing look at the blond woman, Puma returned to his dead, blackened campfire and rolled himself in the thin blanket once more. It was some time before he was able to go back to sleep.

The next morning, Puma bent to check the ground under the pinyon tree. He counted the tracks of at least seven moccasin-footed Indians. So they were on foot and there were only a few of them. He grunted. Comandante Diego must learn of this. They would have to guard the horses closely. The Indians were probably after the horses—portable wealth. Suddenly Puma caught himself. What did it matter to him if a few Spanish horses were stolen by Comanche Indians? With a grim smile to himself, he straightened. It did matter. He had a score to settle with the Comanches, too. No Comanche would capture a horse while Puma was on this caravan. Of that he was certain!

He swung around, his grim smile still in place, and nearly walked into the blond woman.

"What—what are you doing?" She stood there looking at him, curiosity and something else—fear?—in her eyes.

Puma sighed. He had not even heard her. His Apache skills did indeed need further honing.

Chapter 7

"What are you doing?" the blond woman asked again. Her ever-present dueña marched up behind her. With a warning, "Doña Carmen . . .", she placed herself directly between the girl and Puma.

He met black, deep-set eyes that dared him to touch the young woman. He waited with interest to see if the old lady would stomp on his foot as she had on Baca's, but she did not.

Puma took a step back and said politely, "I am checking the trail."

"Trail?" asked Carmen in bewilderment. "What trail?"

"The trail left by the Comanches. *Indios*."

Carmen's hand went to her throat. "*Indios*? I—I do not understand. . . ."

Puma saw her shock and wondered what she would say if she knew that the man standing in front of her was also an *indio*. He gazed into her eyes. "Last night there were several *indios*. Here. Under this tree."

Carmen gripped her dueña's shoulder with tight fingers, and Puma saw the other woman wince. "Easy," he cautioned. "You were in no danger."

"No danger?" cried Carmen in disbelief. "But if they were so close . . ."

"They left."

Three curious *soldados* strolled up to them. Comandante Diego pushed his way through them. "Here! What is going on? Is this man bothering you?" He bowed to Carmen and her dueña and swung a steely-eyed gaze on Puma. "You had better not be bothering these fine ladies—"

Carmen flushed. "No, no, Comandante. Everything is fine. It is just that—"

"What? Tell me. If he has been rude—"

"This man is not rude," spoke up Doña Matilda. "You are. What my young charge is trying to tell you is that this man has important information."

Comandante Diego's black eyes met the dueña's black eyes. Neither wavered. The comandante was the first to look away. He frowned at Puma. "What are they talking about, *soldado*? What important information?" His eyes narrowed as they rested on Puma. "You! You are the troublemaker. . . ." He swung back to the women. "This man will not bother you again." He bowed to the women once more.

Puma regarded Diego thoughtfully. The man was trying to impress the women. Then Puma shrugged. It was nothing to him what the Spanish did with their women.

"Comandante," the dueña spoke sharply. "I believe he has *very* important information—"

Diego focused a frown on Puma. "Well? Speak up!"

"Tracks," Puma answered. "Comanches. In the night."

He walked over to the pinyon tree. Diego strutted after him. Puma knelt and pointed to the soft imprints in the ground.

Comandante Diego bent down to look. He straightened slowly. "How do you know they were Comanche?"

Puma shrugged. He did not feel like explaining that the type of moccasin and the coyote cries were signs of Comanche or that, had the tracks been left by Apache, they would all know because the caravan would have been attacked by now, so he said nothing.

"How many?"

"Seven."

Commander Diego bristled. He eyed Puma. "They wanted the women." It was not a question.

Puma paused. "No," he said at last. "They wanted the horses."

"Hmmmph." Comandante Diego frowned. "Then we had better guard the horses. Can't have them being stolen before we get to Santa Fe."

Puma nodded.

Diego took a step closer and thrust his bearded face at Puma. "And keep away from those women."

Puma kept his face impassive. Resentment welled in him. "I am like the Comanches. I, too, prefer horses," he sneered.

Diego flushed. "Look, you son-of-a-bitch," he snarled. "Keep away from those women or I'll—I'll hang you from the nearest tree."

Puma surveyed the horizon pointedly. There was nothing but low scrub and the occasional skinny tree. Nothing that would support a man's weight for a hanging. The comandante followed his gaze and flushed as though he had read Puma's thoughts.

"We will be in my territory soon," observed Puma. His face was stony, though he kept his voice neutral. "Soon you will need me more than I need you." His icy-blue eyes met Diego's squarely.

The Comandante's face was so red that he looked sunburned. "You think so, Apache?" he sneered.

Puma flinched. The word had sounded like an epithet.

"Oh, *sí*, I know all about you," gloated Diego.

Puma kept his face impassive. He would not let this man goad him into saying anything more. He had said too much already.

"We'll see how smart you are when you are no longer a *soldado*."

Puma looked at him quickly.

Comandante Diego smiled, showing teeth but no humor. "As of now," he said, "you are a scout. No longer a *soldado*. You have just been demoted!"

Puma felt like laughing aloud. Did the Commander think Puma cared for Spanish trappings of honor? Being a scout would be far better. He could ride ahead of the caravan, look for water, watch for hostile Indians, possibly even meet some of his own people. He would be in a far better position to escape as a scout than he was now, riding herd on cattle and horses. He began to remove his heavy metal vest.

Diego snatched it out of his hand. "And get some other clothes. I do not want to see you further disgrace the proud uniform of a Spanish *soldado*." He spat in contempt. "Strip, *indio*!"

Several of the *soldados* standing around took up the whisper. "*Indio. Indio.*"

Carmen and Doña Matilda watched from a distance. Carmen felt bewildered. "Why is—?" She gasped. "Who are they calling '*indio*'?"

"Him." Matilda Josefa's face was equally grim. "It appears that the man you were talking to is an *indio*."

Carmen flushed scarlet. Her hand sought her throat. "You mean he—" The *soldado*! The man who had rescued her in El Paso del Norte, the very man that she had watched for every day, hoping to catch sight of him riding by—an Indian! That meant dangerous! "He cannot be."

"He is." Doña Matilda turned her back on the men. "Come, Doña Carmen. We must see about repacking our ox-cart. Let us leave the men to their business. I am sure that Comandante Diego knows what he is doing."

Carmen stumbled after her. She managed one swift peek over her shoulder at the demoted *soldado* and caught a glimpse of broad, naked chest. She gave a little squeak when she saw him reach for the waist of his pants and start to undo them.

"Doña Carmen," reproved Doña Matilda sharply. "Come along."

Carmen's eyes were huge as she hurried after the departing back of her dueña. "Wait for me!"

Chapter 8

Another long day in the ox-cart. Carmen was becoming very, very weary with this part of her adventure. Things moved too slowly—by her guess, at the rate of three leagues per day. The dust, the cows, the horses, the soldiers, the desert, the cactus, the sky—she had seen it all for what seemed like years. In reality, it had been four weeks.

She sighed and glanced across at Doña Matilda, slumped against the side and snoring softly, her head nodding from time to time at the jerking of the ox-cart.

Carmen supposed that her own impatience lay in the fact that they were getting closer to Santa Fe. Soon she would actually meet Juan Enrique Delgado. Soon she would know what he was like, how he looked.

She had been traveling for almost a year across the known world to meet this man. A little rebellious voice wondered if he were worth it. Of course he was. She squashed the little voice. Juan would love her. He would be a handsome, tall, dark-haired man who would love her madly.

She smiled a tiny smile. His eyes would be— what color would his eyes be? She must remember to ask Doña Matilda his eye color. Would they be icy blue? She squashed that thought. No, he would not have eyes the like those of the dangerous man on the caravan—the man that Comandante Diego had ordered to scout. The caravan now had two *indio* scouts.

Carmen sighed. She did not see him ride by so often on his sorrel. Sometimes, in the evenings, she caught a glimpse of him when he rode into camp to report to Comandante Diego, but it was not as often as she would have liked. It was not that she thought the scout handsome, oh no. It was that he was so— so different, so interesting, so dangerous. . . . Carmen shivered despite the heat in the oxcart. On impulse, she threw off the blanket that protected her from the dust, grasped the top of the cart rail, and pulled herself up, swaying.

She glanced across the broad vista of desert the caravan was passing through. To her right ran the almost dry creek bed of the Rio Grande which *El Camino Real* had crossed numerous times on the trip north. Why the river was so misnamed had bothered her until she found out that at times it grew from the present little trickle and flooded until it was very broad across. She learned from Fray Cristobal that the caravan had had to wait three months to ford the flooded Rio Grande before they had finally reached El Paso del Norte.

The thin Churchman often mentioned that delay in his rescue plans for Santa Fe and always with regret in his voice. Carmen could understand his impatience. She noted, however, that he did not make up the lost time by traveling on Sundays. Fray Cristobal was most insistent that the caravan rest on Sundays. Comandante Diego went along with this demand, whether out of practicality, to refresh the men and beasts, or for religious reasons, Carmen could not determine.

To her left, far off in the distance, were the mountains, their crests covered in snow. Carmen always enjoyed looking at them. The setting sun cast beautiful yellow and pink and lavender streams of color in the sky beyond the mountains. Her eyes lingered on the sight.

When Carmen swung back to face the front, a small burst of dust caused her to clap her hands in delight. It was the dust trail of a roadrunner. Carmen laughed as the bird darted full-speed along in the wagon ruts made by the ox-cart ahead of her. The bird's head was lowered, its tail raised as its enormous strides carried it over the ruts. She watched the roadrunner for some time before the bird veered off to race across the desert after something only it could see.

Carmen stood, relaxed, swaying with the cart. She glanced to the front of the caravan. Would the *indio* scout be returning soon? This was the time of evening when she had observed him before. Not that she was watching for him, of course. She sighed.

It was only minutes later that Carmen blinked in surprise. *Sí*, there he was, as though she had conjured him up, riding towards Comandante Diego. Her heart beat faster. She stood on her tiptoes and leaned forward, the better to see.

A loud bawling of cattle sounded from behind. Carmen, distracted by the tall figure of the scout, watched the approach of his horse. Puma—she remembered his name—looked as fine in the leather clothes of a seasoned scout as he had in the armor of a *soldado*.

Though Puma was some distance from her, she knew it was he. She recognized his shoulder-length black hair, now braided, with a red cloth around his head. She recognized the way he rode the horse, as though he and his steed were one. *Sí*, it was he.

The bawling sound came again, louder this time. One of the two oxen pulling Carmen's cart answered with a bellow of his own. Carmen, startled, almost lost her grip on the side of the cart. She swung around to locate the source of the noise.

To her surprise, several cows were running on either side of the line of ox-carts. The long sharp horns of the cattle jostled and further provoked one another. So far, none of the carts looked damaged, for the cows were steering clear of them, but the situation did not look safe to Carmen. Carmen watched with wide eyes as the bellowing lead cows ran past her cart. Behind her, she heard the cry, "Stampede!"

She gasped. Doña Matilda, awake, pulled herself to her feet to see what the noise was all about. "Stampede," repeated Carmen as she met the older woman's questioning look. Her companion crossed herself with one hand and held on for dear life with the other. Carmen gripped the sides of the cart until her fists were white.

The cart began to roll faster, jerking about in the ruts. Now both the oxen were bellowing. Cattle surrounded the cart, their heaving brown backs a moving sea. Then, to Carmen's further dismay, she saw the lead cows leave *El Camino Real* and start running off to the right, toward the creek bed, possibly drawn by the smell of water.

"Oh, no," moaned Carmen. Her own oxen followed blindly. It was a full-blown stampede! Around them, the excited *soldados* were racing horses and trying to stop a cow here, a calf there, but actually doing very little to halt the chaos.

Carmen's heart thundered in time with the pounding hoofs around her. Doña Matilda's mouth opened and closed several times, as though she were screaming silently, then Carmen saw no more as her attention was jerked to what lay ahead of the cart. There, no more than two hundred feet ahead, lay a drop-off marking an old flood height of the river.

Several of the cattle were already stumbling over it and disappearing. To Carmen, standing in a cart hauled by frantic, panicked beasts, the thin dark line loomed like a steep cliff.

Carmen's cart was now a little to the north of the furiously racing herd of cattle. No longer quite surrounded, the cart and oxen still hurtled at a headlong pace. Carmen watched, face bloodless, as the thin line came closer and closer. Doña Matilda gasped as she realized the danger. No matter how short a drop that cliff was—and there was nothing to indicate it was short—the cart would never make it. It would skid and fall, and the two occupants would be thrown onto the hard rocks of the river bed and killed.

Suddenly the cart lurched and Doña Matilda teetered, poised on the edge of the cart. In horror, Carmen watched her dueña fall off the cart, bounce and collapse in a heap on the hard ground. "Dueña!" cried Carmen. The cart sped onwards. Gaping, shaky, Carmen swung to face the oncoming cliff.

"No!" she screamed at the sudden realization that she was about to die. Every fiber of her being came alive. Never was her life so dear as in this leaving of it.

Carmen's wide eyes were fastened on her quickly narrowing horizon. A brown blur galloping in from the north did nothing to break her concentration on the impending horror. Suddenly she noticed a man racing alongside the cart. His horse was blowing flecks of foam that landed on her.

Then a strong brown arm shot out and yanked Carmen off her feet. He plucked her out of the cart and, in one motion, plunked her down behind him. Carmen clung desperately to the rider's waist. The horse kept to its frantic pace.

Quickly, the rider swung the horse away, a single pace from the very lip of the drop-off, and they rode furiously to safety, leaving the oxen to their fate.

Carmen and the rider stopped at some distance. Horse, man, and woman all panted heavily. The rider carefully dropped her to the ground, then dismounted.

Carmen's shaking legs would not support her, and she sank to the sand. She watched in grim silence as several head of cattle disappeared over the side of the drop-off. Red dust obscured their view, but loud bellows and cries told the painful story.

At last, still trembling, Carmen got to her feet and turned to face the man who had so bravely rescued her. She gaped as she found herself staring up into blue, blue eyes. Her whole body, already shaking from fright at her ordeal, now trembled anew at seeing who her rescuer was. It was the *indio*, the scout, the very man that Comandante Diego had insisted she keep away from! Carmen's bloodless face suddenly flushed crimson. This man had just saved her life! Social prejudices mattered naught in the face of that powerful fact.

"I—I—" She tried to choke out the words that would tell him she was grateful, that she owed him her life, but she could not; she was still too shaken from her wild ride. Instead, arms out, she tottered the few steps to him and collapsed against him.

His arms went around her to steady her. Carmen felt the embrace and suddenly found herself hugging him, clutching him in gratitude and weak-kneed relief, never wanting to let him go. Warmth shot through her as she realized that at last she was safe. Death did not wait for her. She was not going to be dashed to the ground and killed.

She clutched him tighter, her face buried against his broad, hard chest. She was safe!

Puma looked down at the top of the blond head pressed against his chest. He murmured soothing Apache words to her, and she gripped him all the tighter. His mind raced in the aftermath of his rescue. Had he been even a single heartbeat later, the woman pressed against him now would be lying dead in the gully alongside several score of cattle.

When she looked up at him at last, Puma was still not prepared for the onslaught to his soul. It was like the first time he had looked into those turquoise eyes, those eyes that gave so much, that said everything. He felt a violent wrenching of his heart. He could not name the strange feeling that came over him, but he pulled her even closer to him, knowing that it was right, that she belonged in his arms. They stood, hugging each other, bodies trembling. He looked down at her upturned face, her lips trembling. Slowly, gently, he lowered his lips to within a breath of hers. . . .

"Hey!" Pounding hoofbeats caused them both to turn. Comandante Diego rode up, a ferocious glower on his face. "What the hell are you doing, Apache?"

Puma stiffened, then slowly, regretfully, released the woman.

Carmen reluctantly let him go. He had almost kissed her! She touched her lips, then glared at Comandante Diego. Nothing, not even Comandante Diego's glowering presence, would make her take a step away.

"Just because you saved her life doesn't mean you can hold her! Or kiss her!" cried the Spaniard. "Get away from her!"

All three heard the jealousy in his voice. Carmen stood, stunned. The comandante, jealous? Whatever for?

Carmen faced the angry comandante. "This man just saved my life! I will not have you insult him!"

"*He* insults *you*!" screamed Diego. "He dares to hold you!"

"He was comforting me."

"He was seducing you!"

Carmen and Puma looked at Diego as though he had lost his mind. Which mayhap he had.

Puma took a step away and reached for the bridle of the sorrel. He climbed onto the horse's back, nodded briefly to Carmen and, rode away.

She swung upon the comandante. "How dare you! That man saved me—"

Comandante Diego nudged his horse closer and leaned down, his piercing black eyes fixed on Carmen's white face. "He is nothing, I tell you. Garbage." The sneer on Diego's face made him look ugly. Carmen took a step back. "Sí, you would be wise to be afraid," added Diego. "Do you know where I got that piece of human filth from? Do you? Well, I will tell you." He leaned closer. "I got him from the Mexico City prison, that's where. He's a murderer and a thief, just like all my *soldados*!"

Doña Matilda, her face roughly scratched from her fall, staggered up in time to hear his words. She and Carmen gasped.

Comandante Diego looked satisfied. "I thought you would be interested to know that he's even worse than the rest of the diseased lice—uh, others. He's an Apache. He killed one of my best men. He was sentenced to hang the very day we rode out of Mexico City!"

Carmen's eyes were wide with shock. "So the good Churchman did not tell you these little facts, eh?" Diego spat. "I thought not. Now you know. Stay away from the *indio*!"

With this last word, Comandante Diego straightened, jerked his horse's head in the direction of the red dust cloud, and rode off, leaving Carmen and Doña Matilda staring after him in disbelief and horror.

Chapter 9

The next morning, Carmen and Doña Matilda were once more riding in the now battered ox-cart. Miraculously, the two oxen had not been killed, only scraped. They did move more slowly today, though, thought Carmen.

Later, she glanced up from *How To Be A Perfect Wife* and watched as Comandante Diego rode by. His armored helmet gleamed dully. He sat his white stallion very straight and carried his spear upright as he rode. He was a fine figure of a man, she thought. He was a leader, the man whom the caravan members depended upon to make wise decisions.

Yet try as she might, Carmen did not feel anything for him except wariness. Sometimes when he rode past the ox-cart, he would stop and speak politely to her or even ride alongside and cheerfully discuss the countryside. At such times Carmen had to force herself to answer the man. And now, since he had revealed that his *soldados* were all thieves and criminals, Carmen had shrunk into herself, all confidence in her safe passage to Santa Fe gone. And she did not even want to think about the *indio* scout—that he was worse than the others, that he had killed a man, that he had been sentenced to hang . . .She moaned. How could she have found the man attractive? And yet he had saved her life—twice. Did that not count for something? Carmen moaned again.

"You cannot hide behind that book all morning," said Doña Matilda, looking over sharply at the sound. "I think you had better come out and tell me why you are groaning. Are you sick?"

Carmen slowly lowered the book and stared across at her dueña. They hit a particularly nasty bump in the road and she was saved from answering for a moment, but when Doña Matilda continued to watch her, Carmen sighed and glanced out the slats of the ox-cart. "No, I am not sick."

"Speak up, child! I cannot hear you over all the racket this cart is making." Another jostling bump caused the older woman to grasp the side of the cart.

"I will be glad," said Carmen, "when we reach Santa Fe. I have had enough of this caravan."

Doña Matilda muttered an acknowledgement.

Carmen raised the book to her face once more.

A few minutes later, Doña Matilda pointed out helpfully, "Your book is upside down."

Carmen turned the thick volume right-side-up. "Thank you." She turned two crinkled pages.

They rode in silence for some time, jolted now and then when the ox-cart hit a particularly deep rut.

At last the caravan halted for the noon meal. The horses and animals were given a chance to rest at that time. Carmen's meal consisted of dried meat and leftover corn cakes from breakfast. She swallowed the food as she stared across the vast plain at the mountains. "Drink more water," encouraged Doña Matilda. "You need it in this heat." She handed the skin flask of water to Carmen, who dutifully took a sip.

Carmen sighed. She wanted to do something, anything, to relieve her feelings of being lost, of having her world suddenly become no longer safe, but what could she do?

Doña Matilda climbed back into the cart. She offered a hand to help Carmen up, but Carmen shook her head. "I will walk."

Doña Matilda nodded and went to lie down for a nap upon a pile of blankets. The caravan started moving again.

Though the dust threatened to choke Carmen, she kept walking. The movement of her body, the stretching of her muscles, felt good and it helped her organize her thoughts. Very well, the *soldados* on the caravan were not the fine men she had thought them to be. Nevertheless they had got her this far on her journey. Safely.

That the *indio* was something other than what she had hoped—well, that too, mattered little. She realized now that she was attracted to him and had built him up in her mind. Since he had saved her that night in El Paso del Norte, she had looked at him with awe. She had expected something of him, but what? Nobility? A heroic, honorable character? She snorted and kicked lightly at a loose rock as she walked along.

That he had further saved her life last night during the stampede complicated things. His heroism was real. That was not something she had made up. Comandante Diego could not take that away from him with cruel words. But Carmen decided she would be wise to take the comandante's words to heart: the *indio* scout was capable of heroic acts, but was he a man she should admire or look up to or trust? Her head told her 'no'. Her heart told her '*sí.*'

Carmen straightened her shoulders. She would continue on her journey regardless of the character of those around her. She would let no one, not Comandante Diego, not the *indio* scout, dissuade her from her purpose.

Carmen Yolanda Diaz y Silvera had a destination, a goal in life, and that was to marry Juan Enrique Delgado in Santa Fe. Very well, she would concentrate on that. She firmly fixed her fanciful image of Juan Enrique Delgado in her mind's eye and plodded on.

One of the oxen pulling Carmen's cart began to slow down. Then he stopped walking altogether and stood bawling. The ox-cart behind Carmen's almost ran into hers. Carmen hastened to the front of the cart to see what ailed the beast. He was favoring his right foreleg. He had gone lame. She bent closer. His injuries from the stampede yesterday were worse than she'd thought. Now what?

"Get outta the way!" yelled a man impatiently in the ox-cart behind. With frantic tugs, Carmen led her beasts to the side of the trail and stood watching helplessly as the eight other carts drove slowly by, some of the cooks waving.

Carmen stood at the side of the trail, wondering what she should do. "Help," she called tentatively. None of the cooks turned around. *'Rule Number 227: The perfect wife never yells or raises her voice'.* Now where had that thought come from? She needed to raise her voice to get help. Torquemada obviously had not written his guide for women stranded in ox-carts on the side of the road, she thought in frustration as she brushed a heavy lock of hair out of her eyes. Doña Matilda slept on. Where were those men? Carmen asked herself irritably. "Help!" she yelled.

"Heeeeellllllllpp!" she tried again.

Finally, one of the *soldados* riding herd on the cattle saw her standing there and rode over.

When she told him that the beast was lame and that she needed Comandante Diego's help, he just grunted and rode off, leaving Carmen standing in the sun. She took heart that he had disappeared into the red dust billowing up from the front of the caravan, where she knew Comandante Diego was riding.

Carmen peeked into the cart. Her dueña snored gently. Above Carmen a hawk circled lazily. Her eyes watered from squinting up into the blue sky watching him. Next, she watched the receding dust cloud from the cattle herd. She coughed. How long was she supposed to wait for Comandante Diego?

Now the horse herd came alongside. She put her arms over her face to protect her nose and mouth from the ever-present red dust kicked up by their hooves. Coughing and waving her arms, she stood there, miserable and hot. How could anything be worse?

The horses finished passing her by. Carmen caught the occasional whoop from a *soldado* who noticed her standing there at the side of the trail, but none of them approached. She fumed some more. Why didn't anyone come to her aid? Still she waited.

At last, out of the red dust galloped Comandante Diego on his white horse. Relieved, Carmen straightened her drooping shoulders. Doña Matilda awoke from her nap just as Diego rode up.

He frowned. "Injured animal."

Carmen nodded, feeling grateful for his presence on the caravan for the first time.

Comandante Diego pushed back his helmet while he thought. "Need another ox. Don't have any oxen. Just cows and a few bulls." He jerked a thumb in the direction the herd had taken.

"Well, what am I to do?" Carmen felt like screaming at the man, she felt so hot and tense and frustrated. If she didn't scream, she would break down and sob.

Doña Matilda stepped out of the cart. "Well, get us a cow or a bull then, young man."

Comandante Diego looked at her, and for a moment Carmen had the ludicrous thought that he wanted to gnash his teeth at the old woman. She perked up.

"If I put a bull in with your ox, you'll have trouble. They won't like each other. Won't pull together." The look on Diego's face indicated that he was tempted.

"Then get us a cow!" Doña Matilda stood, arms akimbo, eyes bright and challenging.

Comandante Diego shrugged and rode off. He returned some time later with a large, dirt-colored cow. Carmen thought the animal's big brown eyes looked gentle. Comandante Diego was followed by another ox-cart. Standing in it was the cook who had served Carmen her dinner many times. He was grinning.

"Here is a cow," said Diego, dismounting and reaching for one of the beast's horns. "I don't know how well she'll do at pulling the cart, but Lopez assures me she is docile."

Lopez hopped out of his cart and pulled the injured ox off the traces. Then Diego placed the cow in them. She looked huge, but she seemed to accept the pushing and pulling the men were doing to get her in the traces. At last all was arranged to their satisfaction.

"Get going," said Diego, giving the cow's rump a swat. The cow jerked forward and the cart started rolling. Carmen looked at Doña Matilda, and the two women started walking after the cart. Behind them Carmen heard a sudden shot ring out. She turned to see that Lopez, the cook, had shot the lame ox and was now loading it onto his cart. She knew fresh beef would show up on the menu for dinner.

Carmen slowed her steps, still watching the cook tussle with the big carcass. Life was hard in this land. She felt sadness that the ox had died. Though she had not given him a name, he had pulled the cart faithfully since they had left El Paso del Norte. She had relied on his great strength to pull her possessions, and his efforts had been a part of her journey. Now he was gone. A tear welled up. She trudged along, the sand beneath her feet blurring from the tears.

After a while she joined Doña Matilda in the cart.

Resolutely, Carmen turned to face the front. It had been a trying day. She picked up the thin volume of poetry and turned a page. Gritting her teeth, she vowed that she would get to Santa Fe. Nothing would stop her!

Chapter 10

The members of the caravan were fortunate this eve, Carmen observed. They were going to stay at a mission. She would attend vespers in the mission church.

Carmen leaned forward in the cart, the better to admire the high white adobe walls that enclosed the town. Towering above the town, she could see the thick white column that housed the church bell.

Carmen watched as Fray Cristobal approached the padre of the mission. The padre also had a spare look about him, but instead of being pink, like Fray Cristobal, his skin was a leathered dark brown from the sun.

Two *indio* children, a boy and a girl, played in the dirt outside the gates. A thin *indio* woman hurried through the gates and ran over to them.

111

She bent low, her head swinging back and forth as she watched the oncoming caravan and spoke to her children. At her words, two pairs of small dark eyes focused on the *soldados* with Fray Cristobal, then both children jumped up and ran to seek shelter behind the broad gates of the town. The woman followed at a regal pace. Carmen watched as the woman gave one last look over her shoulder before disappearing.

It was a scene that Carmen had witnessed before, at other missions where the caravan had stopped. Women and children never stayed for long in the vicinity of the Spanish *soldados*. It was a pity, Carmen thought. The children were always so beautiful and she would have liked to speak with the women, but alas, she never had the opportunity. They always fled.

A few brave men and women of the town did join the *soldados* as they filed into the mission church, a traditional Spanish sanctuary, to attend vespers. When the evening service was over, they all filed out again, in silence. The *indios* did not look at the Spanish.

Carmen and Doña Matilda, the last to leave, halted in the doorway. Carmen watched the mission padre and Fray Cristobal conferring. Curious to know what they were saying, she approached them and hovered in the background, content for the nonce to eavesdrop.

The two Churchmen were soon joined by Comandante Diego. Though Carmen inched closer, she could not hear what the mission padre was saying, but from his widespread hands, his rounded shoulders, and his earnest gestures, she knew he was asking for something. And Comandante Diego was shaking his head. This, too, was similar to scenes that Carmen had previously witnessed at other stops. She took a few steps closer, followed closely by Doña Matilda.

"But *señor*," the padre was saying, "there has been a drought. No rain for a long time. My people, they are hungry—"

"No," Comandante Diego answered. "I will not give you a single goat, do you hear? And we have no corn to spare! The colonists of Santa Fe need the food we are bringing. Good Spanish folk need the goats. Let the *indios* get their own damn food!"

The padre replied in tones too low for Carmen to hear. She leaned forward, hoping to catch a few words. Doña Matilda frowned at her, but said nothing. Carmen inched closer.

" . . . poor harvest . . . not enough food . . ." The padre's lined face took on more lines in his desperation.

Carmen turned away, twisting her hands together impotently. At every mission they had stopped, it had been the same story—priests pleading for food for the mission *indios*. How were any of the Spanish colonies managing to survive in this vast land? From what Carmen could tell, the lack of food was a widespread problem. And the colonists of Santa Fe no doubt did need the food. But so did the padres and the Christianized Indians along the route to Santa Fe.

The padre was still pleading, " . . . and Apaches attacked our town just last week. They took the seed corn, and the little we had left from last winter's harvest . . . carried off one of the women . . ."

"Apaches!" Comandante Diego whirled upon Fray Cristobal. "Did you hear that? Apaches! I told you they were no good. And yet you insisted upon bringing—"

"He has been a good *soldado*," proclaimed Fray Cristobal stoutly. "And he makes a fine scout. Why, you yourself rely on him for information."

"I do not trust that son-of-a-bitch as far as I can spit, do you hear? More so now that the first I hear of Apaches in this area is *not* from my Apache scout! He has seen them, no doubt, and not said a single word to me."

The padre watched the two men. "It was seven days ago, *señor*. The Apaches are far away by now." He paused, then added, "Please, gentlemen, can you not spare a small bit of meat, a handful of corn? These are good people here in this town. They do not deserve to starve. They have been good Christians. They built this church." He pointed to the white adobe structure, then turned back to his guests.

The hopeful look on his face pained Carmen. She marched up to the men. "There are several cow carcasses in the wagons. One of them is my own ox." She swung to face Comandante

Diego. "If you will not give these people food, then I will!"

Comandante Diego flinched. "Doña Carmen!" He said in a mollifying tone, "There is no need for you to involve yourself in this, Doña Carmen. We men will decide what shall be done." He turned to the padre and said smoothly, "And I can see no reason why women and children in this town must go hungry when we have meat to spare. I was just about to make that suggestion myself. Of course, we have plenty of meat to give—all those cows from the unfortunate stampede." Though he was speaking to the padre, Diego's eyes slid to Carmen. His chest puffed up a little as he saw her glance at him. Carmen could not believe the man's audacity. She watched as he strutted over to where some of the *soldados* were gathered.

"Lopez," bellowed Diego suddenly, causing Carmen to jump. "Get the salted meat."

Soon a wagon piled with stacks of meat rolled up to the church. Lopez jumped off the cart.

Word swiftly spread through the town that food was available. *Indios* swarmed around the ox-cart, and Lopez began handing out pieces of dried and salted meat. All Carmen could see of Lopez was his head and arms as the press of people cut him off from view. Within minutes the ox-cart was empty and Lopez was alone once more.

Comandante Diego strolled over and smiled at Carmen, bowing. "You see, Doña Carmen. We Spanish can be most generous, when we need to be." He waved a hand in the direction of the departing *indios*. "Of course they will all be hungry next week. And there will be no food for them then. It is too bad." He shook his head.

In confusion, Carmen watched him walk away. He knows, she thought, he knows that I do not like him. Is he sincere in wanting to help these people? Or is he trying to impress me? Her lips tightened. It mattered little, she told herself. Soon she would be in Santa Fe, with Juan Enrique Delgado, and Comandante Diego's motives would count for naught.

The bonfire cast a flickering orange light on the pale buildings of the town. Everywhere were people—talking, laughing, dancing, singing in celebration of the meat the Spanish had brought. A mouth-watering aroma of roasting beef filled the air. The scent of baking corn drifted through the town. Fray Cristobal had generously ordered that three bushels of corn be distributed.

Carmen stood with Doña Matilda at a little distance from the heat of the flames and watched several young men dance. One man's head was thrown back as he did a shuffling dance. A pretty *indio* woman ran up and threw a flower at him, then retreated, laughing.

'*Rule Number 161: The perfect wife does not dance. Certainly not the brazen dances that some women do these days,*' wrote Thomas of Torquemada two hundred years previously. Carmen smiled. Obviously the pretty *indio* woman had not heard of Torquemada's advice.

It was a welcome moment of levity in her long journey. To see people laughing and singing did her heart good, she realized. She wished the evening would never end.

Fray Cristobal approached the two women. "It is a lovely evening, *sí*?" His usually pink face looked orange in the reflected glare of the fire.

Carmen and Doña Matilda agreed enthusiastically that it was. Comandante Diego strutted over. Carmen could feel her muscles tense at his approach. Diego was chewing lustily on a meaty rib of beef. He waved it at the dancers. "These *indios* could teach us Spanish how to dance, no?"

The ladies politely agreed that the dancing was very picturesque.

Diego eyed Fray Cristobal. "*Sí*, they dance very well, indeed," said Diego in a louder voice. "These *indios* certainly know how to live!"

Fray Cristobal stiffened but said nothing. It was obvious to Carmen that Comandante Diego was up to something.

"One thing I admire about the *indios*," continued Diego, "is their religious dances. Look at that boy over there." He pointed to the male dancer that Carmen had been admiring earlier. "Look at him dance! Now that's fine dancing, a dance to his barbaric gods." Diego glanced at Fray Cristobal.

The Churchman's face was painfully red.

"And the singing," continued Diego blithely, waving the rib. "None of that monotonous chanting that we Catholics do. Why, I think all the *indios* should be encouraged in their religious dancing and singing. Rather quaint, aren't they?"

His face a blistering red in outrage, Fray Cristobal turned to the comandante. The good brother's mouth opened and closed like that of a beached fish. "What," he managed to grind out, "do you think we Spanish have risked life and limb to do for these people?" Not waiting for Diego's answer, Fray Cristobal rushed on, "The Church has a mandate here! We are to save souls! To encourage these people in their heathen dances is to condemn their souls to hell! Is that what you want?"

Carmen thought she detected a tiny smile on Diego's mouth, but it was difficult to tell as he chose that moment to gnaw on the rib.

"When our explorers and conquistadors first came to this New World," went on Fray Cristobal, his voice shaking, "they found a pile of human skulls, sir. A pile of one hundred thousand human skulls! Is that what you want? For the *indios* to go back to killing each other for their heathen gods?"

"I suppose you counted," answered Diego in a bored tone.

"Father Olmeda did," snapped Fray Cristobal.

Commander Diego looked a little taken aback. Father Olmeda was the priest who had accompanied the first, legendary conquistadors to the New World.

"We are in a battle, sir," said the thin churchman, drawing himself up with dignity. "A battle for men's souls. We are here to cast light on the darkness of ignorance and save a whole population who have never known the true love of God! You do not help matters when you say that the *indios* should be entitled to their heathen practices!"

Diego tossed the rib in the direction of the bonfire. A brown dog intercepted the bone and was jumped on by a larger black dog. Snarling and snapping, the two fought over the bone in a frenzied fight. When the loser slinked away, Diego turned to Fray Cristobal. "I still say—"

"May I have a word with you, Comandante Diego?" Out of the shadows suddenly appeared the *indio* scout. Carmen's hand went to her throat as she gasped. Her heart beat faster.

Comandante Diego looked at the dancers, looked at Carmen, then lastly turned to the scout. He sighed. "What do you want?"

"Privately, Comandante."

"Very well." The two strode some distance away to stand beside the church. Carmen could see them talking and Comandante Diego gesticulating, but she could not hear their words. When Commander Diego returned, he was alone and his face was grim. "Apaches have been seen."

"We know that," said the padre patiently. "I told you earlier that last week they stole our food and one of our women—"

"Tonight," interrupted Diego tersely. "My scout tells me that he spotted several of them in a ravine north of here. He thinks they may

119

be planning a raid on the caravan." All trace was gone of the needling, provoking man he had been when he had taunted Fray Cristobal. Comandante Diego was once more very much the commander of the caravan.

"Doña Carmen, Doña Matilda, if you will excuse me. I must see to our preparations." He bowed politely to the women. "Sleep well, ladies."

Chapter 11

"Carmen."

She was having a lovely dream. She stirred, her legs entangled in the thick blanket that covered her.

"Carmen."

A handful of feathers, bird down, drifted across her face.

"Carmen."

She woke then and sat up. "Who—what?"

"Shhh."

Carmen blinked, struggling to understand. She grasped the blanket. "It is the middle of the night," she hissed. "What do you want? Who are you?" This last with a quiver. Doña Matilda moved fretfully on the other side of their dead campfire, then slept on.

Carmen's hands moved to clutch the throat of

her nightgown, eyes wide, as she waited for the man to identify himself. Her heart pounded. He came closer. Now he was a shadow. Closer.

"You!" she cried.

He clapped a hand over her mouth and she drew back, frightened. "Shhhh. I will not hurt you." When she remained still, frozen from fear, he took his hand away. She could see him now. It was Puma, the Apache scout.

"What do you want?" she rasped. Her fingers that clutched the neck of her nightgown were white at the knuckles.

"I have come to warn you."

She leaned forward. "Warn me? Whatever are you talking—"

"Shhhh. I have no time for games."

"I am not playing games," she said indignantly.

"The Spanish play games. Strange games. And, if you do not be quiet, I will not tell you the warning."

Carmen clamped her lips together, effectively silenced. When he said no more, merely continued to look at her, she prodded, "Well?"

"So impatient," he murmured, and reached out to stroke her hair. "Are the Spanish always so impatient?"

"*Sí.*"

He chuckled. Puma wondered briefly why he was here, warning this woman. By rights, he should have said nothing to Comandante Diego, and certainly nothing to this woman. But something had impelled him, and it was too late now for reflection.

Carmen could see the strong line of his jaw. Her eyes had adjusted to the light shed by the waxing crescent moon. Her nostrils dilated. She could smell him, a leather smell and horse and smoke. His deep voice soothed her, though his presence invoked fear.

"I saw you tonight," his deep voice invaded her thoughts. "By the fire."

Her eyes widened. "You were spying on me!"

He chuckled again. "No. I was watching the dancing, from near the wall."

Carmen glared at him. He was amused; they were talking as though he had wakened her for a pleasant conversation. "I think," she said severely, adopting her dueña's strictest manner, "that you had better warn me and leave."

He dropped the lock of her hair and sighed, and she felt a pang of sadness suddenly. His voice was serious when he spoke. "There are Apaches—"

"I know," she said. "Comandante Diego told me."

He shook his head slowly. "Impatient woman, wait until I have spoken." Imperiousness laced his voice.

She thought he was displeased with her, and her face fell. Then she gathered herself. What was it to her if an *indio* scout did not like her? But she remained silent, waiting.

Puma gathered his thoughts. How much to

tell the woman? He looked at her, knowing that he could see her much better than she could see him. The moon was behind him, and the light fell on her face. Her eyes were wide, looking black in the night, and he wondered briefly if he would have found her as attractive if her eyes had been brown and her hair black. *Sí*, he decided. It was *her*, something undefinable about *her*. "My people," he began, "live near here."

Carmen's fingers on the throat of her nightgown loosened imperceptibly. She nodded.

"There is a man of my tribe who"—Puma sought the Spanish words—"who broke away from my people. He is an outlaw."

"What has this to do with me?" asked Carmen cautiously. While she did not want to offend the scout, at the same time, she found his presence unsettling. He was big, he was strong, he had saved her life twice, she felt a sense of indebtedness to him that she did not want to acknowledge, and she knew he was dangerous. She just wanted him to leave. And the longer the story, the longer he would stay.

He sniffed, and she knew she had offended him again. "Impatient," she muttered at the same time he did, and they both chuckled.

Then Puma went still. He did not want to laugh with this woman, to find her amusing, to feel comfortable with her, and that was what he was doing and feeling as he spoke with her like this while the others were asleep. She was Spanish. How could he forget it? That was the reason he was here, talking to her, warning her.

Carmen felt more relaxed with him now, and her hand dropped from her throat. She leaned toward him to say something, but he drew back. She froze.

"Do not leave the caravan at any time," said Puma. He saw her flinch at the coldness in his voice, but he could not help himself. He just wanted to warn her and get it over with. "Have someone with you at all times. Dress in dull-colored clothing, none of the bright dresses you like to wear."

Carmen thought she detected a note of regret in his voice.

"Nothing to attract attention. Keep your hair covered. Blonde is too—" Puma hesitated. *Beautiful, striking, lovely*, his mind supplied. "Unusual." He stared at her. "Apaches are stalking the caravan. They mean to raid it."

He stood. Carmen stared up at him. He was going to leave. "I—"

He waited.

"I thank you." Carmen got the words out. "I know you take a risk to tell me this."

"No risk," he said, his voice harsh. "I do not want your blood on my conscience."

Her hand went to her throat.

"Angry Man is not a kind man," he said enigmatically. "I do not want him to capture you." *I want you for myself.*

Carmen gave a little moan.

Puma strode away, leaving her sitting there,

eyes wide, fingers trembling. He shrugged his broad shoulders, angry, disconcerted at his foolish thought. Want her? That . . . Spaniard? *Dios*, if the Spanish woman was foolish enough to get captured now, after his warning, well, that was not his responsibility.

Chapter 12

Screened by the branches of a scrawny tree growing atop a hill overlooking *El Camino Real*, Puma waited. Two leagues behind him rolled the caravan. Sitting astride his Spanish-bred sorrel, Puma studied the trail. He leaned over and whispered in the sorrel's ear as he gently patted the stallion's neck. The horse shifted his footing, then was still. Puma noted that he did not try to bite.

Puma wiped a palm across his forehead and shook his braids. He had taken the direct route ahead of the caravan. The other scout, a Comanche, had taken the west. Puma did not trust the Comanche.

Puma sighed. He had already waited for two long days. He had first seen Angry Man and his renegades two evenings before. It had been a

127

brief, tense interview. Angry Man had thrown a few taunts, shaken a Spanish-made sword at Puma, then retreated into the hills. But he had not gone far. Puma could tell that from the tracks he kept seeing. Angry Man was still watching the caravan and the thought made Puma uneasy.

He wondered if he dared spare any more time on what could possibly be a fruitless watch. While he was here at the front of the caravan, Angry Man could be attacking the rear. It was even possible that Angry Man would not raid the caravan because there were so many Spanish *soldados* protecting it. But Angry Man had never been accused of being a cautious warrior, and Puma was not going to make the assumption that he had changed his ways. Puma's guess was that the renegades would raid.

Puma had told Comandante Diego of the meeting with Angry Man because he felt he owed it to his Apache People not to let Spanish wealth or weapons fall into renegade hands. Spanish arquebuses would greatly increase Angry Man's killing power. Who was to say he would not use them on his old tribe?

Also, if Angry Man were successful on his raid, then the Spanish would surely seek revenge indiscriminately on the nearest Indians they could find—likely Puma's tribe.

Puma shook his head. No, either way it was best to do all he could to prevent Angry Man's raid.

* * *

The sorrel lowered his head and chewed at a clump of tough grass. With a sigh, Puma dismounted. He had seen no sign of the renegades this day. The stallion nosed another clump of grass. Behind Puma loomed boulders. Cactus dotted the landscape.

The stallion snorted and his ears twitched. Puma stiffened and glanced in the direction the skittish horse was looking.

Suddenly a hand reached around and covered Puma's mouth. Puma reached back and grabbed the arms of his assailant and tossed him forward onto the ground. He dived on top of the man and struggled for a hold on his attacker's throat. When he saw who he was choking, he loosened his hold. Slightly.

"It is you," he said to the sputtering youth.

Takes Two Horses sat up and rubbed his throat tenderly. "You are getting old, letting someone sneak up on you like that," he croaked. "Why, I could have killed you."

Puma's blue eyes flashed. "When? After I had choked the life from you?" He did not like the fact that Takes Two Horses was correct. Puma leaned over to glare at the erstwhile friend in front of him. "I heard you."

Takes Two Horses got slowly to his feet. Puma straightened.

The two men stood regarding each other warily. "What brings you so close to our caravan?" asked Puma at last. "I told you not to come near the Spanish."

Takes Two Horses glanced nervously about. Then, apparently satisfied that they were unobserved, he said, "I have come to tell you that Angry Man does not like it that you told him to stay away from the caravan. He says that it is *his* place to make decisions for his men, not yours. He is also angry that you are still alive. He had hoped the Comanches would kill you—or break your spirit." Takes Two Horses' chin jutted out as though he, too, were offended. "He spits every time he hears your name."

Puma shrugged. "*Shi Tsoyee*, my grandfather, chose to keep me alive." He glared at Takes Two Horses. "I did not expect *you* to sell me to the Comanches." Puma's face was as set as stone. "We were once friends, you and I."

"Pah, not since boyhood." Takes Two Horses shrugged carelessly, and Puma felt a wave of rage rush through him at how little their friendship had meant to the younger warrior. "I am a man now," continued Takes Two Horses. "I have thrown in my lot with my leader."

"He will lead you to your death."

An enigmatic smile. "Possibly." The two adversaries stared at each other. At last, Takes Two Horses broke the silence. "I am not your friend. You are part Spanish. You are part of the Spanish dog tribe."

Under Puma's rage he felt a dawning sadness that his old boyhood companion had so turned against him. "It made no difference when we were younger," he pressed.

"It does now." Takes Two Horses' eyes were flat and black.

"Why did you sell me?" Puma demanded.

Takes Two Horses' chin jutted out again. Puma guessed suddenly that his former friend had not been in on the initial plot to capture and sell him. "It was something my leader wanted done," Takes Two Horses said stonily.

Puma shook his head in disgust. "That kind of loyalty will lead you to an early death."

Takes Two Horses clenched his fists and took a step towards Puma. "What do you know, Spanish one?"

Puma sighed. He was getting nowhere trading insults with this man. "Is Angry Man going to raid the caravan?" Puma half-expected no answer but the rapid departure of Takes Two Horses.

To his surprise, his opponent stayed. "Yes," acknowledged Takes Two Horses. "He wants the weapons. He would sell any prisoners he takes, too." Takes Two Horses sounded defiant. "He would sell you."

Puma laughed. "He will not get the chance."

"He did, once."

Puma's eyes narrowed. "He will not get a second chance. Of that, I am certain."

Takes Two Horses eyed him keenly. "You do not seem afraid."

"I am not."

"Perhaps you will be afraid," suggested Takes Two Horses softly, "when I tell you that Angry Man wants the woman."

131

Puma's heart thundered in his chest as he fought to keep his face impassive. "What woman?"

"The one you watch. The one with hair the color of ripened corn silk."

Puma felt himself go cold. The Apache renegades had been closer to the caravan than he had thought. For Takes Two Horses to know this much, they must have observed the Spanish—and Carmen—at very close range. Puma wanted to lunge at Takes Two Horses and choke the very life from him for threatening the woman. Instead, he glanced away so that his opponent would not read the rage in his eyes.

When he had his rage and fear under control, he turned back to the younger man. "And you?" he asked. "Are you going to do this thing?"

Takes Two Horses shrugged. "It will prove exciting. We are young men. We have hot blood."

Puma snorted. "Take care that your hot blood does not spill all over the sand."

The other stuck out his jaw. "I will be safe." He sobered. "I thought you would want to know this plan because it is against the Spanish, and you ride for the Spanish. You are no longer Apache!" There was a taunting note in his voice. The younger man reared back, and Puma clenched his fists, prepared for an attack.

The sorrel stopped munching and lifted his head to watch the men.

"Why do you tell me of your plans?" demanded Puma. "You warn me. And you warn the Spanish."

Takes Two Horses observed slyly, "I wanted to see the fear in your eyes."

Puma glared at him. "And do you see it?"

"Perhaps," answered Takes Two Horses mockingly as his flat black eyes watched Puma.

Puma refused to look away until Takes Two Horses shifted his gaze. Puma motioned to the stallion, who bumped him and sniffed his hand, looking for a treat.

"I wanted to see the Spanish tremble in fear. I wanted to see *you* tremble in fear."

"Do you hate me so much?"

Takes Two Horses' glare answered Puma's question.

Puma shrugged. The sorrel nudged him, his nose in Puma's other hand. Puma leaned back and patted the horse's nose. He was surprised at the sorrel's seeking him out.

Takes Two Horses yawned. "I would leave now."

"Wait." Puma needed more information. "Why does Angry Man wish to challenge the Spanish? They are a large tribe and growing larger all the time. It is not good to anger them."

"Pah," Takes Two Horses jeered. "One little raid on a caravan will not be noticed by the Spanish dogs. And we will get weapons, as I told you."

"You are low on weapons and running out of food and trade items, then. Nothing else would make Angry Man attack the Spanish."

Takes Two Horses shrugged disdainfully. "And there *is* the woman. The Comanches would give many horses for her."

Puma's big fists clenched. Imagining Carmen as a prisoner of the Comanches made his stomach churn.

Takes Two Horses turned on his heel and gave a single shrill whistle. A large black mare trotted out from behind a boulder.

The stallion's nostrils flared and he took a step toward her. Puma grabbed the reins and gave a tug. The sorrel halted and swung around, ready to bite. Puma took a step back.

Takes Two Horses threw his leg up and jumped onto the mare's broad back. Without a glance back, he kicked the mare and galloped along the sloping trail that descended the hill. He was gone.

The sorrel snorted once and went back to munching grass.

Puma turned back to the horse. He shook his head. "I do not like it," he muttered. "It is not like Angry Man to warn me." For Puma was certain that was what Takes Two Horses' visit was—a warning. The younger warrior would not have spoken to Puma without first receiving Angry Man's permission. Puma knew that now. He had seen how fully his old boyhood friend was influenced by the renegade.

"Angry Man must be very certain of his success. And that, my friend," he added, gently patting the listening horse, "means danger. We must be constantly on guard."

Puma swung up on the horse's back and noted with satisfaction that this time the sorrel did not try to bite his leg. "Come, Horse. We will warn Diego. Again. If it's not too late."

On another hill, one and a half leagues to the south, another Indian waited, his hard black eyes squinting against the sun. He watched the long pink cloud of dust. Soon he could see the horses and cattle and ox-carts that looked tiny from his vantage point.

The renegade warrior lifted his hand as a signal to his young riders. They waited, poised and tense on the hillside. Then a wave of his hand brought them to life. They dashed forward, riding silently—for they were Jicarilla Apaches. No war cries warned the caravan as the renegades stormed down the sandy slope, small pebbles rolling in their wake.

135

Chapter 13

Carmen stood up in the ox-cart and stretched. At that moment the cart hit a rut and she had to grab for the sides. She coughed from the red dust and wiped her forehead in the heat. Behind her sat Doña Matilda reading the book of poetry, her legs hanging over the back of the cart.

Suddenly, a line of men on horseback caught Carmen's eye. She watched with interest as the line fanned out and proceeded at a steady pace toward the vanguard of the cavalcade. "Look," said Carmen. "Visitors."

Doña Matilda scrambled to her feet, her curiosity evident.

Eight *indios* galloped steadily towards the caravan leaders. Comandante Diego held up his hand to indicate a halt. He and his men stared at the oncoming men.

The *indios* rode their horses hard. Suddenly, terrible howls issued from the riders' throats, and Carmen felt her hair stand on end. They must be demons, she thought desperately. Sister Francisca had been correct after all. There were such things! She closed her eyes and crossed herself hastily. When she opened her eyes again, the *indios* were still there. Beside her, Doña Matilda's lips moved feverishly in anxious prayer.

All of a sudden the *indios* reined in their ponies, ceased their bloodthirsty screams, and milled around in apparent confusion—unfortunately just out of range of the arquebuses. Then they shook their weapons at the *soldados* and yelled insults. The terrible screaming began once more and then, as if only now realizing their danger from their foe's greater numbers, the *indios* whirled and raced back the way they had come.

Comandante Diego squared his shoulders. He glanced over his shoulder, grim-faced, and yelled an order. Then he swung round to the front and spurred his charger. The white horse leapt forward, giving chase.

Behind Diego streamed the eight *soldados* of the vanguard, waving swords and firing arquebuses.

Many blurred shapes joined him, racing past Carmen to the front. They were the *soldados* who had been guarding the cattle and horse herds. Drawn by the action, they yanked swords from their scabbards and arquebuses from their waistbands as they flew by. Carmen counted forty of them.

Her heart beat frantically. It was all so exciting! "Those *indios* cannot hurt us," she cried to Doña Matilda. "See how Comandante Diego chases them! All the *soldados* are chasing them!" Her cheeks were flushed and her eyes sparkled. What need had she to fear? "Oh, Comandante Diego is so brave!" Carmen missed the sardonic look that her dueña shot at her.

The *soldados* quickly disappeared into a great cloud of dust, and there were many shots fired and much yelling. The sounds grew fainter as the brave *soldados* pursued the fleeing *indios* farther into the desert.

Carmen waited, her hand to her throat, as the screams and yells grew still fainter.

A little time passed, and Carmen thought she could still hear an occasional yell, but she could see naught. A sharp exclamation caught her attention. She whirled in time to see Doña Matilda point to the rear of the caravan. Her face was pale. Her mouth opened and closed but no sounds issued forth.

"*Madre de Dios!*" Carmen's eyes grew wide as she spotted trotting towards them ten more *indios* on horseback. These were in no particular hurry as they called back and forth to each other as they drove a small herd of horses ahead of them—horses of the caravan!

Carmen watched in disbelief as two of the *indios* cut out several fat cows and moved them in with the small herd of horses. Her jaw dropped. The *indios* were calmly plundering the Spanish herds while the *soldados* were off pursuing those other Indians. "It's a trick!" cried Carmen as she suddenly realized what had happened.

She ducked down into the cart, her mind whirling. "A weapon!" she whispered hoarsely to Doña Matilda. "We must have a weapon!" Grimly, the older woman nodded. On hands and knees, the two women scrambled on the floor of the cart for a stick, a knife—anything they could use for a weapon. Carmen's fingers felt the slim volume of poetry, and she cried out in disgust. "Poetry!" She picked up the book to fling it out into the desert, but Doña Matilda lunged and seized it from her.

"No," she cried. "Not this book!"

"*Madre de Dios*," muttered Carmen. "We are about to fight for our lives and you worry about a book of poetry!" She glared at her dueña, who glared back. "We're wasting time," snapped Carmen. "We need a weapon!" The two went back to their furious search of the cart.

There was nothing she could defend herself with! Carmen halted her frantic scramblings when her fingertips touched the small sack of jewelry. Beads of perspiration stood out on her forehead, and she bit her lip to keep from crying out her frustration at such a paltry weapon. She wanted to hurl it across the ox-cart in her fear and anger, but she restrained herself—barely. The ox-cart lurched. She dared another peek through the open slats.

Closer, they were closer! Merciful God, do not let them catch us!

The Indians kept coming. What should she do? She and Doña Matilda would be killed—slaughtered like deer and their possessions stolen. The red sands would turn brown with her blood, and Juan Enrique Delgado would never know what had happened to her. Tears formed in her eyes at the thought, and she dashed them away. "No," she muttered desperately. "No! I don't want to die. Life is too sweet!"

Doña Matilda, too, had given up the search and sat across from Carmen, a stricken look upon her narrow face.

Two *indios* were trotting alongside the ox-cart now. Carmen could have reached her hand out and touched the sweating, mahogany-colored neck of one horse. Instead, she shrank back into the cart, her big turquoise eyes wide with alarm. The drumming of the hooves and snorts of the beasts sent fear spiraling through her. One of the *indios*, a man with a large head and hard black eyes, slowed his bay to an easy walk alongside the cart. "You come with me," said the *indio* in broken Spanish.

Holy Mary, Mother of God, pray for us sinners now and at the hour of our death. . . .

Carmen got shakily to her feet. "Never!" she croaked. She watched as the *indio* on the roan sauntered up to the yoked oxen. The roan bumped into the side of the ox, and the rider added a kick of his own. The big beast lurched to the right to get away from the rider.

After several sudden lurches and a loud thump, the ox-cart began to leave the rutted track. They were being forced off the trail! The *indios* were driving them as easily as they drove the herd of horses!

"What now?" cried Doña Matilda. "Will they kill us?"

Carmen could only stare back at her, lips frozen, eyes wide in fear. There was no way to tell which of the women was more terrified.

With kicks and yells, the *indios* goaded the yoked ox and cow to move faster. Soon the cart was bumping across the desert, leaving the caravan behind.

"Should we jump?" asked Carmen, the dry wind tearing her words away.

Her companion shook her head, hanging onto the sides of the cart for dear life.

They rolled at a goodly speed for some time across the desert. Then they crossed over some hard shale rock. The cart jerked and bumped. After that, they followed the horse herd into a canyon that Carmen had not even noticed until they were almost upon it. Once in the steep-sided canyon, the ox-cart gradually slowed its pace until it rolled to a halt. There was silence as Carmen looked around. Ahead at a little distance, the stolen horses and cattle milled around a small pool fed by a narrow stream.

Carmen and Doña Matilda gazed helplessly at each other, their stark terror mirrored in each other's eyes.

The *indios* trotted up to the ox-cart and the man with the big head and hard eyes, the one who had ordered them to come with him, dismounted. He walked over to the cart and climbed aboard.

Doña Matilda shrank back. Carmen steeled herself to show no fear.

Two more *indios* leaped aboard the cart; it was now very crowded, and Carmen could smell the wood smoke scent from their bodies. Carmen's clothing trunks, which had been stored in one corner, caught their eyes, and they dragged them to the edge of the cart and threw them down onto the sand.

Carmen gasped in fright as she saw the three turn to stare at her as they spoke amongst themselves. Her stomach churned as she thought of what these men would soon do to her and her poor dueña.

For the nonce, however, their attention was focused on the chests. The trunks were broken open, and all of her clothing spilled forth. Grunting, the men ploughed their brown arms through the frothy stuff. Costly garments of brilliant yellow, red, plum, peacock blue, green, and turquoise velvet spewed forth in a jumble over the ground. Pale creams, lavenders, and ice blues joined them. The men chortled away in their guttural tongue.

Carmen groaned. Some part of her registered the violation of the ruthless hands running through her undergarments and dresses, dresses that the best dressmakers of Seville had slaved over for weeks. But another part of her mind, in shaking fear, could only stare at the *indios*, horror and fear and hopelessness vying in her heart.

The *indios* tired of their play with the clothes, and except for a few bright dresses that seemed to catch their fancy, they left them on the ground. They held a hasty conference, then six of the *Indios* mounted their horses. With shouts and kicks, they moved the horse herd farther on into the canyon. They rounded a corner and vanished from sight.

Carmen stared after them with hopeless eyes. Now what? she wondered.

"Will they kill us now?" murmured Doña Matilda, voicing Carmen's own fears.

The four remaining *indios* marched over to the women. Two of them seized Carmen. Their hard hands on her arms made Carmen wince. Her nostrils flared as she smelled the wood smoke, sweat, and pungent horse smell of the two *indios* holding her. Her heart pumped thunderously in her chest. She summoned every ounce of courage she had. She must get through this ordeal!

The other two *indios* seized Doña Matilda and dragged her from the cart.

Carmen closed her eyes, wishing desperately that this was merely a terrible dream. She opened them again as she, too, was dragged across the rough wooden boards of the cart and then thrown to the sand. She scrambled hastily to her feet, determined to give them no advantage.

Doña Matilda glared up from where she had been roughly deposited on the ground. She looked pale and shaky and defiant. Carmen took new heart from the old woman's courage.

The brutes laughed.

The leader—for Carmen had determined that the one who had spoken to her in broken Spanish was the leader—walked up to Carmen and suddenly grabbed her hair and yanked, hard.

She cried out and pushed at him, trying to get him to release her hair. With a grunt, he let go and stepped back.

Carmen glared at him, daring him to try to touch her hair again. One of the *indios* said something to the leader, and the other three laughed. The leader glowered. Evidently goaded, he approached Carmen once more and reached for her hair. Carmen, teeth bared, sharp-nailed fingers curled into claws, took a swipe at him. "Leave me alone!"

He jerked back from her, and his small eyes watched her warily then. He barked something incomprehensible. The men with him chuckled.

Carmen steadied herself, refraining from rushing at him, though she badly wanted to. She sensed that to antagonize this cruel man would be to court instant death. But if he attacked her, she vowed she would go to her death fighting!

The leader backed away from her a little, and Carmen glanced swiftly from him to the others. They were all young, bare-chested, brown-skinned men, dressed in leather trousers with leather moccasins up to the knee. One of the men wore a red bandanna headband in the Western Apache style to keep his shoulder-length black hair out of his face. The three others wore braids. Knives slung on belts rode low on flat hips.

They stood in a silent half-circle around her and studied her. Doña Matilda, they ignored. After a while, one of the *indios* yanked his dagger from his waistband. He gestured with it at Carmen, threatening loudly. After his threats, he waved the dagger several times in front of her face, then placed it between his strong jaws, his lips pulled back in a ferocious grimace to reveal strong white teeth. Carmen shuddered.

The men continued to stare at Carmen, talking amongst themselves. They pointed at her hair, then to the leader, and laughed, evidently enjoying a good joke.

Carmen, shaking in terror, wondered when they were going to kill her and get it over with. Her nerves were taut with fear and she wondered how long she could last without falling to the desert sand and sobbing.

At last the nerve-tautening silence was broken when, surprisingly, the leader grunted and turned away.

With disbelieving eyes, Carmen watched him walk over to the ox-cart. He began rummaging through it, and his actions soon drew the curiosity of the others. They, too, drifted away, leaving Carmen and Doña Matilda alone.

Thoughts of running blindly into the canyon raced through Carmen's mind, but she shrugged them away. The *indios* would easily catch her and might use her attempt to escape as an excuse to kill her. Now that the immediate threat of death had passed, she wanted to cling to life in any way that she could.

She sent a prayer of thanks skyward, then, glancing at the *indios* in the ox-cart, sent another prayer swiftly on its heels. She prayed that they would not find her precious sack of jewels. For a few moments, it looked as if her prayer would be answered. Then she heard a guttural cry of triumph and watched the leader jump down from the ox-cart, triumphantly waving aloft Carmen's dowry—her leather sack of jewels.

Carmen's shoulders slumped, and she hid her face in her hands and sobbed quietly. When she looked up, she realized, too late, by the *indio's* grinning face that he had read her reaction correctly—he had found something very valuable. Her hopes plummeted. Now these demons would profit from their savagery! Not only would they kill her and Doña Matilda, they would have Carmen's jewelry, too!

Feelings of helplessness and rage swept over her. She clenched her fists in impotent fury as she watched the leader walk over to his horse, where he had stored some of Carmen's more colorful dresses.

He tied the leather sack to the rest of his loot.

The three other *indios* in the cart must have realized the importance of their find, for they were grinning and speaking excitedly. *Making plans about how to spend my dowry after I am dead*, Carmen thought bitterly.

Just then, a violent push on her back caught her unaware. She heard the leader's guttural voice say something unintelligible to her as she stumbled, lost her footing, and fell to the ground. Someone laughed—cruelly, she thought. *This is it*, she told herself. *This is how my life ends. Here, in the desert with these demons killing me.*

Doña Matilda sobbed loudly and one of the *indios*—dagger still in his teeth—leapt from the cart and hit her across the face. She spun backwards and crammed her fist into her mouth, trying to stifle her new sobs.

The man's casual brutality to the older woman suddenly enraged Carmen. She rose and flew at him with her nails out, intent on gouging his smooth, cruel face. Surprised, he held her off, both her wrists trapped in one hand. He growled—he could not do much else with the knife in his teeth. Then, casually, he tossed her away from him and she fell once more upon the hard ground.

Angrily brushing wisps of blond hair from her face, Carmen got to her feet and screamed, "You horrible man! Leave her alone! She has done nothing to you!" Carmen screamed at him, at them all, in Spanish. She used every insulting, horrible word she could think of. Unfortunately, there were not many, her convent training having not prepared her for such a moment. But she knew with some satisfaction that Sister Francisca would have been properly mortified at the words that she *did* yell at them. And mayhap Sister Francisca would have been proud of her defiance of these demons. She yelled louder.

The *indios* appeared stunned at all the yelling and gesticulating she was doing, for they only stared open-mouthed at Carmen. Clearly, they had never been screamed at by a beautiful, enraged Spanish noblewoman!

As her voice was reduced to a hoarse croak, she noticed several more riders appearing over a hill. They were galloping fast, on a course towards the captured ox-cart.

Carmen moaned and wanted to throw up her hands in defeat. Merciful heaven, not more *indios*!

She suddenly realized that these must be the *indios* she had first seen, the ones who had led the *soldados* on a decoy chase away from the caravan.

The *indio* who had so casually back-handed Doña Matilda was distracted by the newcomers. The others, too, watched the new arrivals come closer.

Carmen stayed silent, unwilling to focus the men's attention on herself again. She edged over to her sobbing dueña and put her arms around the wretched woman. They stood together and watched the approaching riders.

There were about the same number of riders as there were of her captors. These men, too, were bare-chested and wore leather leggings, bandannas, and moccasins.

Their horses were lathered in sweat. They had traveled a long distance at a fast pace, Carmen surmised. She hoped the Spanish *soldados* were not far behind.

Carmen watched the new arrivals closely. They did not appear concerned about being followed, however. They happily joined their fellows. One broad-chested *indio* scooped up a dress of Carmen's, the golden yellow velvet dress she had worn in her last interview with her Tío Felipe before she left for the New World. The *indio* held up the dress admiringly. Then he tried putting it on, getting all tangled in the process. The watching *indios* chortled at his clowning. Someone draped a black mantilla over the yellow velvet. Disgust, like bile, rose in her throat.

A festive atmosphere prevailed as the new-comers continued to play with Carmen's precious things. Her cherished copy of *How To Be A Perfect Wife* was ruthlessly handled as the *indios* passed it around. Suddenly, a mock struggle broke out between two of the *indios* and the precious volume was torn in two. The freed pages blew away on the wind.

Theresa Scott

Carmen gave a little cry, then turned away, sick with despair. No, the *soldados* would not be coming. She knew that now. She and Doña Matilda were alone. Alone with the feared *indios*.

Chapter 14

Puma pressed the sorrel as fast as he could. The stallion's sides were lathered and heaving by the time Puma pulled atop a hill that overlooked *El Camino Real*.

He was too late.

Spanish *soldados* straggled back to the caravan across the plain. To Puma's practiced eye, the horse herd looked smaller. The ever-present dust cloud obscured his view of the rest of the cavalcade.

Nudging the sorrel forward, Puma leaned back as the horse slid and skittered to the bottom of the hill, then he urged the stallion forward. The sorrel tossed his head once, as though in protest, and leapt ahead. They traveled at a punishing pace to the caravan.

When he saw Puma ride up, Comandante Diego swung to face him. "Where were you?" he snarled viciously.

The Comanche scout smiled smugly at Puma, the only sign that he enjoyed seeing the Apache, traditional enemy of his people, so humiliated.

"Pedro here," Diego said, indicating the Comanche, "returned an hour ago." Another smug smile appeared on the scout's face. Puma ignored it. He said nothing, but looked beyond Diego, striving for a glimpse of the ox-carts. Was Carmen safe?

"I said," sneered Diego, "where the hell were you?"

Puma swung back to him at last. "Scouting."

"*Sí*," sneered the commander. "And a lousy job you did of it, too." He waved a hand carelessly at the caravan. "*Indios* have stolen our horses, stolen our cows." A look of worry replaced the anger on his face. "Stolen two women."

Puma's heart thundered. His mouth went dry. "Doña Carmen?"

"What right have you to call her by her name?" roared Diego, as if proprieties mattered at such a moment. He visibly calmed himself. "The two women taken were Doña Carmen Diaz y Silvera and her dueña, *sí*." He leaned forward, blustering, "And it is all your fault! You gave us no warning!"

The Comanche smirked.

Puma eyed Diego uneasily. Something in the comandante's tone did not ring true. "I told you last night to watch for Apaches," said Puma.

"It was your job to watch for them!" roared Diego. "I have the whole caravan to take care of!"

"What exactly happened?"

Diego looked distinctly uncomfortable. "You are dismissed from being a scout," he said. "Ride with the caravan to Santa Fe, but I will not have you as a scout. You are worthless!"

Puma could feel his cheeks grow warm in humiliation. He struggled to keep his face impassive. Somehow he knew that if he were to show any emotion in front of this man, he would be even further humiliated.

The Comanche was grinning delightedly.

Puma nodded stiffly in the general direction of Diego, but he refused to look at the Comanche. Comanches fought like women, anyway.

Before he left, Puma wanted the answer to one question. "Did you send *soldados* after them? Did you track the women?"

Diego snorted. "*Sí*, we sent *soldados* after them. What do you think I am? I know my duty."

"And?"

"And we did not find them." Commander Diego looked distinctly uncomfortable. He shifted in his big saddle. The white stallion pranced under him. The big horse's white sides were lathered yellow. Yes, they had been on a chase, Puma observed. He nodded shortly to Diego and turned the sorrel away, intending to find Miguel

Baca. The little thief might have some honest answers.

Miguel Baca looked grim when Puma questioned him. "We went on a chase, *sí*," he acknowledged. "Did old Guts n' Thunder tell you that we went on a big chase, all forty-eight of us?"

Puma shook his head.

"Well, we did. Guts n' Thunder led us on a great chase and at the end we caught"—he held out his hands, empty—"air." To Puma's uncomprehending look, he said, "Nothing. No one."

Puma frowned.

Baca smiled. "This is how it was, *amigo*. I am happily riding along, when I have to stop for a piss. All of a sudden about ten *indios* come riding toward Diego. They stop, yell, and run back the way they came. Ol' Guts n' Thunder cannot help himself. He wants to chase them. So I get back on my horse—fastest piss I ever had in my life—and we ride after them. All of us ride after them." He shrugged as he saw Puma's frown deepen. "I know, I know. We left no one to guard the caravan."

"And when you came back, the horses and women were gone." Puma could not keep the disgust out of his voice. "Comandante Diego knows nothing." Puma spat. "*Nothing!*"

"*Sí*," agreed Baca amiably. Then his amiability vanished. "It is most unfortunate about the women. The young one—"

"*Sí*," agreed Puma. As casually as he could, he asked, "Who did Diego send after them, to track them?"

Baca named two soldiers. "And the Comanche scout, of course."

"None of those would know what to do." Puma spat in disgust. "And a Comanche cannot track Apaches."

Baca shrugged. Suddenly a braying note was heard, and Puma turned to see Fray Cristobal. "My son," intoned the good brother, "have you heard the sad news?"

Puma nodded.

Fray Cristobal shook his head. "Dead, they are. Gone. It is as if they are dead." He crossed himself. "We must pray."

Puma turned away. While he liked Fray Cristobal, Puma had no use for the Spanish god. Now, *Shi Tsoyee* was different. Raised in the ways of the Apache gods, Puma had full confidence that *Shi Tsoyee* would help a man on his life's journey. From what he could tell, the Spanish god was too violent, too destructive— or at least, his followers were.

Grim-faced, Puma got together a small cache of meat and supplies. When he had packed his belongings in his blanket and rolled it up neatly, he took the reins of the sorrel and walked over to where Baca was still talking with Fray Cristobal.

"Good-bye, Miguel Baca, *mi amigo*."

Baca looked at him in surprise. "You leave?" He glanced around. "Does old Guts n' Thunder know about this?"

Puma shook his head. "And you are not to tell him. At least, not until I am gone." Puma needed the sorrel and knew that Diego would not give permission for him to take the horse. Puma shrugged. He needed the horse—he'd take him.

Fray Cristobal made the sign of the cross over Puma's head, and Puma wished he had not done so. He did not want any misfortune attaching itself to him. He wondered briefly if Fray Cristobal was a witch. To the Apache, witches were very dangerous.

"*Vaya con Dios*, my son."

Puma nodded, deciding he would just have to ask his god to keep the churchman's witchcraft and spells away.

Puma mounted the sorrel. The stallion did not try to bite, and Puma leaned forward and whispered praise in his ear.

Miguel Baca gave a sad little wave. "Goodbye, *mi amigo*." There was a wistful look on the scrawny soldado's face.

Puma felt a sadness sweep over him. Miguel Baca had been the kindest to him of all the Spanish he had met in his long journey to Mexico City and back. And now Puma was leaving him behind. Yet, it had to be. "Mayhap we will meet again," observed Puma.

Baca shook his head. "I think not, *amigo*." He gave another little wave and swallowed.

Puma turned his horse. He kicked the sorrel, and they trotted away from the caravan, Puma's thoughts already on the trail ahead and the mission he had set himself—to find Carmen Silvera.

Chapter 15

It took Puma until the next morning to find the old woman. She lay several steps from the stream, in the shadow of one of the canyon walls. Puma surveyed her dispassionately, wondering if she were still alive.

The canyon was well-hidden. He himself had been unaware of it, and this was close to the territory he had roamed as a young man. Angry Man had done a good job of fooling the Spanish, Puma thought in disgust. And he had been correct about one thing. The Comanche scout would never have found this canyon. The Comanche probably got lost when the renegades ran the stolen horse herd and cows and ox-cart over that slick shale deposit. No tracks. Only an Apache could track another Apache, Puma thought grimly.

He went up to the old woman and knelt beside her. To his surprise, he saw her eyelashes flicker and her chest move slowly up and down. She was alive.

Still with the same dispassion, Puma took out his knife and sliced off a piece of material near the hem of the old woman's dress. He rose and went to the stream and laid the material in it, wringing it out. He walked back and placed the square of cloth over the old woman's face. After a few trips to the stream and back, he heard her moan. He lifted the dark material off her and saw that she was staring. She tried to sit up.

"Easy," he cautioned. "Move slowly."

The Spanish words reassured Doña Matilda, and she relaxed as she took a deep breath. Then, when she saw who was helping her, she gasped. "You!"

Puma sat back on his heels, waiting. When she saw that he was not going to hurt her, Matilda tried once again to sit up, and this time she succeeded. Puma noticed a large purple-and-yellow bruise across her cheek. Angry Man's mark, he thought in sudden fury.

Gently he helped the woman to her feet and led her to the stream. He retrieved his Spanish-issued tin cup from the back of the sorrel and filled it with cool water. The old woman drank, then wanted more. He shook his head. "Later," he cautioned. "You may have more water soon. Too much will make you sick." The Spanish did not know about running for miles with a mouthful of water for sustenance, thought Puma. After the first thirty miles, *then* you could drink the mouthful.

The old woman stared at him, her pointed nose and dark eyes suspicious. He smiled.

"Thank you," said Doña Matilda with dignity.

"*De nada.*"

"But it is not nothing, young man. You saved my life."

Puma shrugged. The old woman glanced around. "Where is Doña Carmen—" She stopped. "Carmen—oh *Dios*, my Carmen!" Evidently, whatever she had remembered had not been welcome. "My poor, poor Carmen."

Puma's gut tightened at the old woman's tone. "What did you see?" he asked, dreading the answer.

She turned back to him, her gaze bright with unshed tears. "The *indios*. The one with the big head and the little eyes." Puma recognized a fair description of Angry Man. "He put her on a horse and led her away! When I ran after her, he—he kicked me away, like a dog!"

Angry Man, certainly.

"How many were with him?" Puma hoped his calm tone would reassure the flustered woman.

"Sixteen, seventeen, I—I am not sure." She stared at him, her eyes beseeching. "Oh, please, please, señor, please go after her. Please help her!"

He regarded her thoughtfully. "What about you?" He glanced around the canyon. "You are here alone. Have you no thought for yourself?"

160

The old woman flushed. "Of course I do, young man. But now Doña Carmen is in more danger than I am!"

He smiled grimly at that, liking the old woman's spirit. Yet he could not, in good conscience, leave her alone and stranded in an unknown canyon. Even were he to make a shelter for her and leave her some food, intending to return after he had found Carmen—if something happened to him, if he were injured or killed, no one would ever find the old woman. And yet, if he were to return her promptly to the caravan, he would lose valuable time in tracking Carmen. What should he do? He sat back on his heels, thoughtful, and closed his eyes. When he opened them, he saw that she was watching him steadily.

"Come," he said, rising. He helped her over to the sorrel. As he was lifting her onto the big horse's back, Puma felt a breath on his back and heard a snort. He whirled quickly and tapped the sorrel on the nose, not hard, but enough to let the stallion know he would suffer no biting. The horse jerked his head, one eye watching Puma knowingly. When Doña Matilda was settled on the sorrel, Puma climbed on and they set off.

"Where are we going?" his passenger asked.

"I'm taking you back to the caravan." Puma squinted at the sun. There was still plenty of daylight left to get the old woman to the caravan and then return to the canyon and pick up the renegades' trail.

He urged the sorrel into a faster trot, knowing that the delay might cost Carmen her life. He only hoped that she could survive whatever Angry Man had decided to do to her. The sorrel increased his pace effortlessly, and Puma whispered a prayer. "*Shi Tsoyee*, For this powerful, swift horse I thank you, *ihéedn*. And let me get to Carmen in time. *Ihéedn*."

Chapter 16

Carmen was in shock. Captured by *indios*, torn from Doña Matilda, dragged away and thrown upon a horse and led on a bone-jolting ride through countless hills and canyons until she was hopelessly lost, Carmen had withdrawn into herself. She did not notice the reds and golds and pinks of the spectacular sunset as she rode along the crest of yet another hill. She did not hear the occasional murmurings of men's voices that went on around her. She was completely inward-looking, trying desperately to make sense of what had just happened to her. But her thoughts would not sort themselves into any coherent order.

She felt numb. All she could do was hang on to the black mane of the horse beneath her. Her body jerked rhythmically with each step of the horse, but her feelings would not come back to life. How could this have happened? Slowly, gently, she began to tiptoe out of the fog that was in her mind. *How could this have happened to me?*

At last they halted in yet another canyon. The *indios* urged the horse herd over to a rough corral made of wooden poles set across the narrowest end of the canyon. Carmen's glazed eyes looked dully around. She felt little surprise at seeing ten or more cone-shaped hide dwellings grouped near a stream.

She was in some kind of a tiny village. Three *indio* women emerged from three dwellings and ran up to greet their men. Carmen stared at them, not really understanding much of what she was seeing. When one of the women came over and stared up at her with narrowed black eyes, Carmen met her gaze wearily. The woman said something to the others and stalked away. Indifferent, Carmen watched her go.

Carmen waited, as though glued to the horse's back, but no one came up to her after that or said anything. It was all very strange, Carmen thought, but no stranger than what had already happened to her. She was still numb and thought mayhap that she had passed some critical stage of fear that came from being so afraid for so long and had moved into a stage of merely breathing and moving her limbs and not actually thinking or feeling.

Slowly, when she realized that no one was going to bother her or even speak to her, Carmen stiffly dismounted, sliding the last few feet before collapsing on the ground. Even her legs could not hold her up anymore, they shook so badly.

After a while she got to her feet and glanced around. The *indios* were occupied with the horses, the cattle, and building fires near the *tipis*. No one was paying any attention to her.

An *indio* youth came over and reached for her horse's lead rope. From somewhere deep inside herself, Carmen found the strength to glare at him. He grunted and blinked at her, then led the mare away, leaving Carmen standing there. *Now what?* she thought, sinking down in the sand and leaning her back against a rock. Behind the boulder, the *indios* laughed and chatted and went about their business.

Carmen peeked behind the boulder. She watched as two *indios* singled out a cow and swiftly killed the beast. She turned her head away as they began butchering it, the sight of the bloody entrails making what little there was in her stomach rise to her throat.

After that, there was much activity in the camp; men and women roasted great chunks of meat, people visited, men refought battles. An air of merriment and celebration permeated the place, but Carmen was not a part of it. She slumped back down.

Dark descended. Listlessly, more to stretch her fatigued muscles than out of any curiosity, Carmen lifted herself slightly and once more peered over the top of the boulder. Two *indios* were trying on her lovely dresses. She sank back down to the sand. She barely cared, she realized. Let them have her dresses. They already had her jewelry.

All she wanted was to get away from here and back to the caravan. Thoughts of the Apache scout rose in her mind. Where was he? Did he know she'd been captured? Did he care? Oh, what was the use! She had to get to Santa Fe and Juan Enrique Delgado. Juan Enrique Delgado. Thoughts of her *novio* did not move her. She had no feeling left. But she must be firm. Marriage to him would give her a civilized life. It was what her uncle had planned for her. It was why she'd traveled so far. Was that way now to be closed to her forever? Frustration and despair suddenly flared in her. Face crumpling, she put her head on her knees and sobbed, uncaring of the movements of the *indios* behind the rock. Wherever her hot tears fell, they scorched her skin.

As her tears flowed, she shook like a leaf in the wind. She was fortunate to be alive, she knew, but she was terrified about what was to come. Would the *indios* hurt her? Kill her? What were they waiting for?

She wrung her hands, sobbing in the darkness. She was so alone! The terrible loss of Juan Enrique Delgado blended into the terrible loss of Doña Matilda. Her dear Dueña, who had been a faithful companion to Carmen through her long journey. A deep wave of sadness engulfed Carmen. Her dueña had kept Carmen company, had read to her, given her advice—wanted and unwanted—and now she was gone. Carmen had never had a mother. Tía Edelmire, the closest female relative she had, had always been kind, as had Sister Francisca at the convent. Yet Carmen thought that Doña Matilda had been as much a mother to her as any older woman had ever been. And now she was gone. Fresh tears dripped down Carmen's cheeks.

Her body shook with the sobs, and she did not try to stifle them. More ripping sobs burst forth as she realized fully how alone she was, how she had no one to rely on but herself. All that was familiar to her was now lost. Juan Enrique Delgado gone. Doña Matilda gone. Hope . . . gone. Helplessness added to her pain.

After some time, she found that the tears had actually released some of her pain. She drew a shaky breath and wiped at her eyes. Her face felt swollen from crying, but she did not feel the overwhelming despair, the numbness she had felt before she had started to cry.

Marveling a little at the peace she now felt, she sat up. At that moment, a drum began beating somewhere behind her. She looked around. She peered into the darkness away from the camp and could see no one. She peeked back over the boulder. The *indios* were laughing and chanting in time to the drumming. A shiver went through her at the thundering sound.

When they merely continued to drum and chant, she began to relax once more. The rock against her back was still sun-warmed, and the gentle, radiating heat made Carmen feel sleepy.

Her eyelids, swollen from crying, drooped heavily. She leaned back and closed her eyes—tired, so tired. Gently, gently, she fell into sleep.

When she awoke in the morning, her blinking gaze fastened on hard brown eyes staring at her.

Chapter 17

"Get up," said the renegade leader, for it was he. Carmen looked at him, still dazed from sleep. She closed her eyes, willing the cold face in front of her to be but part of a bad dream.

He gripped her wrist, hard, and yanked her to her feet.

This was no dream. Carmen swayed to her feet, her turquoise eyes wide. Warily, she watched the short man standing in front of her. His eyes were as cold as his face. She wanted to shrink from him, but a little voice warned her that he would pounce upon her as a coyote does a rabbit if she were to show him any fear or weakness. She swallowed, straightened, and pulled her wrist out of his grasp. "Keep your hands off me."

The Spanish words meant nothing to him, or if they did, he showed no sign of understanding them. He sneered at her and said something in his own language. The two glared at each other, then he grabbed her by the shoulders and swung her around towards the charred embers of last night's fire. He gave her a rough push between the shoulder blades.

Carmen staggered a few steps in that direction, and he said something again in a low guttural voice. She whirled, her breasts heaving, her breath coming short. "Stay away from me!" She scowled fiercely.

He walked up to her and pushed her again, in the direction of the fire. He wanted her at the fire pit for some reason, but Carmen did not know why. She turned, lips pressed tightly to keep them from trembling, and walked with as straight a back as she could manage toward the fire, expecting another blow between the shoulders at any moment.

They reached the fire and he pointed at the few embers still smoking. He grunted and said something, then pointed at the blackened remains of the cow carcass from the night before. Carmen began to understand. He wanted her to make him breakfast. She crossed her arms and stared at him, her jaw hard.

His jaw was set just as firmly, his black eyes flat. They would have fought a longer battle of wills, but Carmen decided to do as he demanded. She remembered all too well the careless blow the younger *indio* had given Doña Matilda. She

would not antagonize this man if she did not
have to. He was dangerous, and she sensed
from the lines on his face that he was cruel.
She would go along with what he wanted—
for now.

He grunted when he saw that she was heading
for the carcass, and he followed her. As they
approached, a huge cloud of blowflies rose
from the carcass, turning it from black to red
and white. Carmen put a hand to her mouth to
stem the sick feeling that rose in her.

The *indio*, oblivious, knelt and whipped out
a lethal-looking knife. Carmen jumped back,
and he grunted. Then he began slicing several ribs off the dead cow. These he flung
at her.

Carmen caught them in her skirt. The red
meat left blood streaks on her dress, and a
dollop of fat left a large splattery mark, but
she pressed her lips together. She would pick
her battles carefully, she decided. A dirty dress
was not worth dying for.

Carmen set about the task of gathering some
nearby wood, and the *indio* leader turned away,
apparently satisfied for the present that she was
doing as he ordered.

Later, when the ribs had been roasted, Carmen stood up and glanced around for the
indio leader, but he was not in sight. With
a shrug, she squatted near the flames again
and started to nibble on a chunky rib. She
tried not to think about the flies that had
already tasted the stringy meat, but she was

hungry, having had no food since early the day before.

'Rule Number 150: The perfect wife allows the servants to serve her choice morsels. The choicest ones go to her husband.' Carmen recalled irreverently. She almost giggled. Thomas of Torquemada had never eaten roasted cow in the New World wilderness, that was evident.

Then the *indio* leader was standing beside her, his face furious, his voice low and cruel. He shook her arm, dragged her to her feet, and pointed to the ribs. His exclamations were loud and vehement. Evidently, Carmen decided, he did not want her eating, or mayhap he wanted the choicest morsels for himself.

She flung the rib aside and stepped back. He glared at her, then reached for the roasted ribs and took them, all of them, and walked away towards one of the tipis.

Carmen stared after him, hands on hips, fuming. Just what was she supposed to eat? Not getting an answer from the receding back of the *indio*, she sauntered over to the cow carcass once more.

She waited for someone to stop her. No one did. Picking carefully, Carmen was able to glean a few pieces of meat from the white bones. Then she caught herself. What was a Spanish noblewoman from one of the noblest families of Seville doing picking through this dead cow carcass, looking for leftover meat?

For a moment she wanted to throw the hard-gained handful of meat away. Then she ground her teeth together. Seville was far away, half a world away. Torquemada and his world of the perfect wife was half a world away. If Carmen did not eat, she would die. It was that simple.

She glanced around, the hills in the distance catching her eye. Above her, the blue sky was huge. *Sí*, she was far from Spain, far from the noble families, from Tía Edelmire, Sister Francisca, her cold uncle. And no, the noblest families of Spain would not approve of her digging through a fly-covered cow carcass. Mayhap they would even think it better that Carmen held on to her pride and ate nothing.

But then she would starve to death.

Carmen frowned. She hesitated. She glanced around once more. Here there were no Spanish noblemen. Here there was only the sky, the hills, the canyons, these *indios*, and herself. Her world had changed suddenly, immutably, and what was she to do? She knew herself to be a Spanish noblewoman, deep in her heart, and that could never be taken from her. But what of her outward circumstances? Those had changed drastically. Must she change with them? What choice did she have?

From somewhere deep inside Carmen, there surged a sudden, explosive desire to live. She would survive this ordeal and get to Santa Fe. Somehow. And to do so, she would eat. For strength, for survival.

She bent her head and looked inside the carcass. Tentatively, she pulled at a rib. It came loose in her hand, and she smiled in satisfaction. She gathered several more, then trotted away from the carcass toward the fire, intent on cooking her meal. She would survive.

Chapter 18

"You have come far enough, son of the hated Spanish!" Angry Man's voice snarled at Puma. "This is our encampment. What are you doing here? You leave!"

Puma halted a little distance away, the sorrel stallion moving restlessly beneath him. Puma had tracked the Apache renegades through some very rough country. Even now he was amazed that he had found them. Their hide-out was well hidden, even by Jicarilla standards. He dismounted and walked toward the renegade leader. The air between the two crackled with hostility.

Puma's narrowed icy-blue eyes scanned the scene, taking in the tipis, the colorful garments spilled near the creek, the remains of the fire, and the cow carcass. To one side, he caught a glimpse of blond hair. *Do not think about her*, he warned himself. *Think about Angry Man, your enemy.*

Puma's jaw clenched. Angry Man had easily taken the woman. And the herd of horses.

Puma's gaze searched Angry Man's. The renegade leader looked furious. Out of the corner of his eye, Puma saw the blond woman move towards him. He wanted to tell her to move away. He finally glanced at her; he could not help himself. She looked pale and defiant. She watched him steadfastly, with something like hope in her turquoise eyes. He turned away.

"Leave us, I say!"

Puma swung back to Angry Man, his thoughts racing. He had had no plan. He had merely rounded the bend of the canyon and there they were. It was unfortunate that he had stumbled upon them in daylight. He sighed. His tracking instincts were better than he had thought; the interlude in the Mexican prison had not dulled them. But his timing—ah, his Apache timing—that had to improve!

Several men gathered around Angry Man. Takes Two Horses met Puma's gaze defiantly and smirked. From the corner of his eye, Puma saw a woman duck into a tipi. Puma thought he recognized her from his tribe. She looked like Morning Dew, Takes Two Horses' sister. If it was she, then Morning Dew had chosen a violent life, on the run with the renegades. She would have done better to stay in the village of Man Who Listens.

Puma's eyes and thoughts returned to Angry Man. The volatile renegade leader would probably fight with little provocation. But Puma did not want to fight, not unless he saw no other choice. What he did want was the blond woman. And perhaps some Spanish weapons—then Angry Man could not attack an Apache village, should he get the notion.

Puma frowned. He did not want to risk his life if there was a better way than fighting to get what he wanted. And, he mused, there just might be. . . .

"I want to travel with you for a while," he said softly. "I wish to join you."

Angry Man stared at Puma, clearly disbelieving what he had heard. He growled, "I do not believe you. What do you want? Why are you here? I do not want you with me. My men do not want you with us. Look at them." It was true. None of the faces watching Puma were friendly. Most of Angry Man's band were men he had grown up with, though some were strangers. One had the markings of a Comanche. Puma gritted his jaw.

He watched his opponent with an impassive face. Puma would not lie, yet he could not tell the truth, either. It was a difficult path he had chosen. Puma shrugged casually. "I bring knowledge of the Spanish, a good horse, and weapons. Surely you can use such."

Angry Man stuck out a belligerent jaw. He eyed Puma carefully. "I do not believe you," he said at last. Then he sneered, "What is the matter? Did your Spanish dog people kick you out?" Puma heard the contempt in Angry Man's voice.

Puma's eyes flashed, but his voice and stance were calm as he said, "I do not like the Spanish. They put me in prison. As you well know."

Angry Man sneered, but his eyes shifted from Puma's briefly.

What was this? Guilt? wondered Puma briefly. "Why did you sell me to the Comanches?" he demanded aloud. "Why did you try to kill me? Why do you hate me so?" He was suddenly weary from the weight of Angry Man's hate and wanted to know the truth.

Angry Man's flat black eyes watched him. "I, too, dislike the Spanish. Even more than you. They take over my country. But you, you make my stomach hot. You are Spanish." A bitter look crossed Angry Man's face. "Yet my father allowed you to live with us in our village. He favored you to be the next *cacique*, over the other young men. More worthy men." Angry Man's voice was a low growl.

Puma kept his face impassive, but he was startled. The headman preferring him? Where had this come from? Was jealousy behind Angry Man's hate and contempt?

"The headman, my own father, threw *me* out of the village, but kept you. That alone should tell you why I hate you." Angry Man's fists clenched at his sides.

It was true then, marveled Puma. Angry Man hated him because his own father had thought that Puma should be the next headman. Even

178

a stronger man than Angry Man would have felt the rejection, the blow to his manly pride. So Angry Man had merely done what he had always done, even as a boy—lashed out.

"Why should you throw your lot in with me?" Angry Man was demanding. "You know I wanted to kill you. I still do."

Puma shrugged again. He allowed one corner of his mouth to pull down in a twist of a grin. "I can protect myself." His answer made Angry Man stand a little straighter. The surrounding men grunted and shifted their feet.

Clearly, Puma's confidence had surprised the renegades. "And," continued Puma, "I do not fear you. Why should I not join you if it is to our mutual benefit for a time?"

Angry Man said nothing. He glanced at Puma, then to his men, then back at Puma. He was weighing his decision. His next statement surprised Puma. "I will not stand and bandy words with you all day," he said at last. "If you want to join my band, then you take orders from me. Understand that!"

Puma nodded, relief surging through him. Angry Man had believed him. He wanted to glance at the blond woman, but he steeled himself not to.

"Pick up those clothes from the desert. Let us see you do that!" The cruel hate in Angry Man's eyes was a palpable thing and Puma knew the man would do his best to attempt to kill him again. Puma must be very, very careful.

Puma began gathering the colorful dresses.

Angry Man started to mock him. His men gave a hoot or two, then quieted, perhaps remembering Puma's earlier confidence. They, too, had grown up with him and knew the measure of the man. Takes Two Horses was the first to turn away. Puma steadfastly kept heaping garment after garment into a pile, his gritted jaw the only sign that Angry Man's words humiliated him.

Angry Man sauntered over to where Puma knelt, gathering the clothes, and sneered. "And do not expect any share of the horses!" Angry Man sneered.

Puma kept piling clothes. He did not trust himself to speak.

Finally Angry Man walked away.

Puma let out his breath. He tightened his fist on the voluminous turquoise dress he was holding and glanced across at the woman. She was watching him, had been for some time.

He saw that the her gaze was riveted upon him. He stared back into beautiful turquoise eyes that matched the dress he was holding. Dark, thick lashes framed her eyes, and she did not try to hide her vulnerability. His fingers tightened on the garment he was holding, and he half rose to his feet to go to her.

Then he caught himself. Angry Man was nearby, might be watching even now. He must not guess Puma's motives. Puma's world started moving once more, but his rapidly beating heart told him that the woman had deeply touched something in him. And he had answered.

He glanced away from her to see Angry Man

suspiciously watching them both. Puma bent back to his task, his mind suddenly grateful for this humble work.

Out of the corner of his eye, Puma watched the woman. She was still staring at him. Her cheeks were no longer pale, but flushed a lovely pink. Her eyes were bright, bright with hope.

Puma's heart sang. He had done right to follow Carmen Silvera here. Puma's lips twisted in a grim smile. At first, he had feared greatly when Angry Man had guessed his ruse so easily. But now he knew he would find some way to save her. He was strong, and he was smart. And he wanted the her. He would outwit Angry Man and his band of renegades to have her.

Puma picked up another dress, a gold velvet one this time, and held it to his nose. It smelled of her. Yes, he would have her, the woman with the beautiful turquoise eyes, and he would do anything, brave anything to have her.

Chapter 19

Carmen caught herself glancing hopefully once more in the direction of the *indio* scout from the caravan. How had he arrived here? She had watched, hand to her throat, as the scout and the *indio* leader, her captor, had talked. Though she had stood at a distance, Carmen had easily detected the hostility between the two.

If only he would look at her. She could not make eye contact with him, however, for his full attention was on picking up her dresses.

Carmen shook her head impatiently.

Finally the *indio* leader walked away, and Carmen at last caught the scout's eye. The two stared at each other. The scout lowered the gold velvet dress he held in his hands. Carmen wanted desperately to let him know of her trouble. Or mayhap he knew? Ah, but did he care? She watched him, her soul in her eyes as she wordlessly pleaded with him for help.

He stared at her, saying nothing.

At last Carmen could stand it no longer. "Please," she begged, taking several steps towards the blue-eyed *indio*. "Please! Do not leave. *Please* help me." It struck her then that a good Spanish noblewoman would never beg, but then no Spanish noblewoman that she knew of had ever been captured by *indios*, either. Carmen squashed the little insulting voice that castigated her for throwing her pride away. Hers was a changed world, she must remember that. Here, she needed all the help she could get.

And, by heaven, begging was nothing compared to being left in this encampment with people who either hated her or were indifferent to her.

"Please!" Carmen reached out red, scraped hands imploringly.

Puma looked at the beautiful, teary face turned up to his and swallowed. He could do nothing. Nothing. To help her now would give away the game too soon. He glanced away from those hope-filled pools of turquoise, and his heart smote him. How galling it was to feel so powerless with Angry Man's captive! It was yet one more cruelty to hold the chief's son accountable for.

Puma felt the renegade leader's eyes upon him once again, and he shrugged. Swinging away from the woman, he kicked at the pile of clothing. When he looked up, he saw Angry

Man smiling, his hard eyes narrowed. The blond woman had turned away, shoulders slumped.

Puma somehow reached his horse's bridle and tugged. The sorrel stallion started to follow him toward the corral. Puma knew he could not stay and meet Carmen's entreating turquoise eyes a moment longer. He would be unmanned if he did.

It was sunset, and the Indians were preparing the evening meal. Puma listened to the beautiful Spanish captive's rapid-fire words. He almost pitied Angry Man. Almost, but not quite. The Spanish woman had been railing at the renegade leader for some time. Puma marveled that Angry Man tolerated it.

Carmen was expressing her fury that Angry Man had ordered the old dueña abandoned in the nameless canyon where Puma had found her. Puma wondered what desperation drove Carmen to taunt the man who was her captor in such a reckless fashion.

Yet Puma admired her daring in telling Angry Man what she thought of him. And he admired the sense of loyalty that drove her.

He grinned to himself. Not that Angry Man understood much of what she said. But Puma did. He understood most of the words, though one thing puzzled him. He could not fathom why, in her anger, she did not use the nasty words that he knew, the ones he had learned in the Mexican prison. He shrugged to himself; it was not the words she said that were so powerful, it was the fire in her voice.

He paused in his gathering of wood for the fire—the most humiliating task that Angry Man could find for him, for only Apache women fetched wood and water—to admire her once more.

Carmen was furious. "I do not care who you are," she cried at the renegade leader. To herself, she had nicknamed him El Cabezón, because of his large head. "I tell you that *no* old woman deserves to be left in this desert. In this heat! She will die! She may already be dead. And it is all your fault!"

Carmen realized that she was not getting through to El Cabezón; she could see that, but then she had given up on doing that some time ago. She did not speak whatever language he did, and he did not speak much Spanish. She glanced over at the tall *indio* with the blue eyes—the one she had earlier pleaded with for help. Some help! All he did was gather wood and let the others laugh at him. She curled her lip at him, disgust plain on her lovely face. Then she went back to chastising El Cabezón.

Puma caught the sneer and turned away, his face stony. So she thought him worthless, did she? After what had passed between them, that look when she had allowed him into her soul, her contempt was all the more bitter to him. How easily she gave up on him. How quickly she expected betrayal. But then, what could one expect of a Spanish woman?

Then he thought of the old woman whom he had found in the canyon. The scorching heat would have been a death decree to her, and Puma felt glad that the beautiful woman was railing at Angry Man. She was justified in her contempt of him. But she was wrong about Puma. Puma had found the old woman and taken her back to the caravan. But he could not tell Doña Carmen this, not yet.

Puma ground his teeth. Carmen's disdainful sneers hurt. Grim-faced, unable to bear her open contempt any longer, he went to gather wood at a distance and check the horses once more before darkness fell.

Later, Puma sat beside a glowing fire with Angry Man and his men. Throughout the day, Puma had known Angry Man was watching him. As was Takes Two Horses. And the others. It was not a good situation to be in, thought Puma. He must get out of it soon. And he would—as soon as he figured out how he was going to take Doña Carmen away with him.

By now, Puma had also learned of the valuable jewelry that lay in the leather sack dangling at Angry Man's waist. Angry Man had boasted that he would trade the pretty colored baubles for many weapons, even arquebuses and armor, from the Spanish. Puma shuddered at the thought of Angry Man's renegade band being armed with arquebuses and protected by Spanish armor. Not only would the renegades terrorize the Spanish and other Indian people, Angry Man might think he could raid his own people, too. It was not a welcome thought.

It was beginning to appear to Puma that he would have to steal Carmen *and* the leather sack. And a few deep-chested horses as well, to flee upon. Glumly, Puma stared at the flames, wondering how he was going to accomplish all that needed to be done.

A fluid cascade of angry Spanish caught Puma's attention. He looked up to see Carmen leaning away from Angry Man. The renegade had come up close to her and now grasped the woman about the waist, pulling her toward him. Angry Man was in an amorous mood, and it was not a sight that Puma liked to see. He wondered if the woman would be able to fend off the tough, determined Apache. So far, Angry Man was contenting himself with sighs and gestures, but Puma knew the renegade's patience would wane swiftly. The woman could obviously sense it too, for her voice was rising.

Not once, Puma noted grimly, did she look to him for help. Irritated, he threw a stick into the fire. She thought so little of him now, he mused, that she would fight the determined Apache leader off by herself. In disgust, Puma rose from the fireside. As one, five other renegades rose with him. Angry Man's watchdogs. He should have known. As he gazed at the narrowed eyes and clenched fists of Takes Two Horses, Puma wondered how he was going to rescue the woman if he was watched this closely. He shrugged noncommittally and sat back down.

Puma turned back to watch the woman. She was throwing off Angry Man's arm, and he did not look pleased at her rebuff. Puma kept his face impassive, but it did amuse him to see the man frustrated. Still, the situation did not sit well with Puma. He did not like it that the woman was alone in defending herself. He wanted to be there to help her. But he had to wait.

Later, while the other men lay stretched out by the fire or asleep in the tipis, Puma lay tense. Carmen seemed safe for the night because Angry Man had decided to leave her alone. But Puma felt suspicious. It was not often that Angry Man gave up so easily on something he wanted.

Carmen wrapped her turquoise dress closer around her legs and shivered. She lay with her front to the fire and her back to the cold night air. She could feel that her cheeks and breasts were flushed and too hot, but her backside was freezing as a night chill descended on the hills.

Carmen wondered at her own bravery in staving off that horrible man, El Cabezón. She wondered to herself how she had ever found the courage to fend him off, never mind scold him for abandoning Doña Matilda.

She closed her eyes and shivered despite the fire's heat. And that other man, Puma, the scout with the icy blue eyes . . . She sniffed. Why, he had turned out to be no help at all. He had just stared at her with those blue eyes and left her to yell at horrible old El Cabezón.

Carmen moaned and let her head drop onto her crossed arms. How alone she felt. So alone. And afraid. She sighed and rubbed her head, trying to relax and get some sleep. Somehow she thought she would need it.

But her thoughts went on. She was surprised that she was still alive. She had been close to death several times that day. She rolled over and gazed up at the huge yellow moon and the silent stars, small dots of white light, and wondered if she would still be alive tomorrow.

She must have dozed off, because when she awoke it was to feel the prick of a knife at her throat. Terrified, she lay there unmoving. A rough hand at her shoulder urged her to stand up, and then she moved, her whole body quivering.

She turned to face her opponent and saw by the light of the moon that it was El Cabezón. He was grinning evilly as he motioned her away from the encampment toward the entrance of the canyon.

She did not know what he wanted, or what he had wanted all evening when he had been touching her, but she knew it was something that *she* did not want. She wished for once that the nuns had been more forthcoming with information about what went on between a man and a woman, but Sister Francisca had seemed to know little or nothing, and there had been no one else Carmen could ask. Once she had tried to ask Tía Edelemire, but her aunt had merely tightened her lips and looked away.

Now, with this evil man beckoning her with his knife toward the trees, Carmen knew it was too late. She would find out what he wanted in a terrible way. She walked slowly along, stumbling frequently, the harsh oak brush and sage scrubbing at her legs. She knew she irritated the man with her slowness, but she could not help it. Twice he prodded her in the back with his knife, and she felt a tiny sting through her dress each time.

They reached a spot in the canyon where the canyon's walls were only as tall as a man was high. The *indio* urged her up the steep slope to the top. Now they were on a hillside. Nearby Carmen spotted a thicket of brush. This was her last chance. She must break and run into the brush if she was going to save her life. Just then, El Cabezón stumbled. At the same time a cry rang out. A thundering sound came from below, and Carmen watched in astonishment as the horse herd that the *indios* had captured galloped madly down through the narrow channel of the canyon and hurtled toward them.

With a loud cry, El Cabezón spun around and jumped down the slope, racing after the horses. By the light of the moon, Carmen could see several of his men running behind him, trying to stave off the stampede.

Carmen scrambled off to one side and raced away from the thicket, heading for a group of large boulders. Mayhap she could hide there.

She ignored the sharp branches that slapped at her tender skin. *Must get away, must get away*, pounded her brain as her feet pounded the dirt. She did not stop. She wanted to get away from that horrible man and whatever it was he planned to do to her.

She heard no sounds of pursuit. The *indios* must have been concentrating solely on the horses. The only sound now was of her own frantic breathing. Upon reaching a tree near the boulders, she ducked around it and peered desperately back into the darkness the way she had come. She could see very little. She waited, holding her breath so she would not give away her hiding place. Her lungs burned. She heard nothing but silence.

Chapter 20

The she heard it. A branch crackled. Fear struck Carmen and would not let go. El Cabezón was back!

But where was the man? Why was he stealthily stalking her out here through the brush? Why did he not just march up and catch her? New fear paralyzed Carmen, this time a roiling, heart-pounding, helpless fear. Her fingers gripped the rough bark of the pinyon tree and it pressed painfully into her skin as she clung for dear life. The tree was protection, the tree was friend, the tree . . . She shook her head, trying to stave off the panic. But still she held on.

She heard a low animal growl. She lifted her head, alert. *Madre de Dios*, what was this? Carmen would have flown from the tree to the boulders but for her fingers which would not give up their death grip on the bark. Her wide eyes stared into the darkness as her brain tried to make sense of the sound she had heard.

An animal! That was it. It was not El Cabezón, but a wild animal that was stalking her!

New fear, even greater than before, gripped Carmen. She clutched the tree even tighter, the bark biting painfully into her skin. She welcomed the pain. At least it meant she was still alive.

Wait! The sound was getting louder. Carmen heard the crackling sound of underbrush, heard some grunts and groans. Then came an earsplitting scream. Lastly, she heard a long sigh. Then more silence.

She waited in utter fear. She could feel the fine hairs on the back of her neck standing straight up. Was she next? Merciful Father, merciful Maria, please. . . .

Someone was coming towards her, someone who did not try to silence his steps.

She stayed there, plastered against the tree, waiting for Death to find her. *Madre de Dios*, merciful Father. . . . How long could she survive this fear?

Then, out of the darkness, strode the *indio* scout, leading two horses. The scout's face was closed and shadowed in the moonlight. She could see, however, that his eyes were narrowed as he silently appraised her.

Carmen's eyes flickered over him, then widened. She saw that he wore her leather jewel sack at his waist.

Her eyes went back to his stony face. She waited, as the longest moments of her life crawled by.

With one more step he stood beside her.

She kept her eyes on his. Awe, relief, fear coursed through her body in waves. Merciful Father, how much terror could one woman take?

Puma reached out and tried to pry her arms slowly away from the trunk of the tree.

She smelled the scent of him, smoke mixed with some indefinable masculine smell.

"Come with me," he said in Spanish. His voice was deep, comforting.

And Carmen slowly let her fingers uncurl from the tree. The palms of her hands were bleeding, but she did not see them. She let her arms drop. She took a step toward him and collapsed to the ground.

Face impassive, the Indian reached down and picked Carmen up. He lifted her and placed her on the bare back of a gray mare. "Margarita," whispered Carmen in surprise.

The scout stared at her.

"This horse," stammered Carmen. "She looks just like my Margarita . . . my Andalusian mare. . . ." Bewilderment was in Carmen's face and voice.

"We must hurry," said the scout. "Angry Man will soon come looking for you."

"*Sí*, of course," Carmen's strived valiantly to retain some kind of sanity. She would think about the mare later. For now, she would clutch the black mane and not let go. She buried her face momentarily in the horse's mane and inhaled. She was safe.

Puma thought the woman was going to drop off the horse, and he reached forward to push her upright on the mare's back once more. "Hang on," he said.

He grabbed the lead rope of the mare and mounted the sorrel. He had to ask himself why he had chosen the biting sorrel stallion again when he could have had the pick of Angry Man's horse herd just before he stampeded them out of the corral. Then he shrugged and looked over the canyon. He liked the sorrel, plain and simple. And the stallion was biting less. He was a good horse. Puma smiled grimly. Angry Man and his renegades would be occupied for some time with running down their scattered horses.

He glanced back at the woman. She met his gaze.

Carmen stared back at him—no fighting, no protesting. Her terror had sapped the fight out of her. She clutched the mare's mane for dear life.

Puma led them back toward the edge of the canyon. The sorrel snorted. The gray was pulling on the lead rope, tossing her head. "Easy," soothed Puma.

"What is it?" came the woman's voice. Puma thought he detected a quiver in her voice.

He pushed the sorrel forward, then the stallion stopped, refusing to take another step. The scout pointed with his chin to the ground. "Cougar."

Carmen gasped as she stared at the huge cat lying dead on the ground. A thick stream of blood trickled black into the light fur of its neck where a knife had pierced the beast's jugular vein. Flies were already gathering for the feast.

Puma added, "He was stalking you."

Carmen shuddered.

"Let's go."

"Wait!" Carmen's voice shook in earnest now. "You—? He—?" She could not get the words out.

"*Sí*, I killed him," acknowledged Puma. He pulled on the sorrel's head, urging the stallion away from the dead cat. "We go now."

Carmen shuddered once more, then kicked her heels against the mare's gray sides. As the horses put distance between the dead cat and themselves, Carmen breathed easier.

And she found herself staring at the broad back of the scout as the horses' ground-eating strides carried her far away from the renegades' encampment. Where was the *indio* scout taking her? she wondered. Then she decided she did not care. She was free of El Cabezón. She was safe from the cougar. She was alive. That was really all that mattered.

Chapter 21

On top of a hill overlooking a pine forest, Puma led the Andalusian gray mare to a stop. The two horses snorted and nosed clumps of dry grass as the riders dismounted.

They were in mountainous country now, Carmen saw. The sun was coming up. As she stretched her aching muscles, she stared to the east. The colors were lovely, and the air smelled fresh.

"It is a good day to be alive," observed Puma, watching her.

Carmen smiled and nodded. They stood, watching the sun, listening to the little sounds of life as the animals of the desert began to wake up.

At last Carmen turned to him. "Thank you," she said earnestly. "You have rescued me. Again."

Puma shrugged, his face impassive.

Carmen faltered a little, then continued. "I am concerned about Doña Matilda. She is somewhere in the desert. . . ."

Puma shook his head. "She is with the caravan."

"How do you know?" Carmen's eyes were wide.

"I found her. Took her to her people."

Carmen gave a little cry of joy. "Dueña is safe! Oh, thank you!" Relief flooded over her. The old woman was safe! This *indio* scout, Carmen was beginning to find, was a man of few words. Yet what he did not say, other men would have boasted about for a long time. She thought of the dead cougar.

Carmen watched him thoughtfully as he stared out at the rising sun. His nose had a hawklike thrust to it in profile. His face looked stern. Yet she was not afraid of him, she found to her surprise. He had rescued her several times, beginning with the first time she had met him. On the journey from the renegade's encampment, he had pushed both her and the horses, but he had found time to stop for a rest once. He had even found water for them where Carmen thought there was no water to be found. He knew the secrets of the desert well, she thought. She could not have asked for a better guide.

She tried to remember what she knew about him. She knew his name—Puma. She knew he was one of the fearsome Apaches. She knew he had spent time in a Mexican prison, killed a man, and had been sentenced to hang. She knew he had a friend on the caravan, the skinny *soldado*, and that the others treated him respectfully, warily almost. She knew he was brave.

Carmen thought some more. Try as she might, she could come up with nothing else. Curiosity welled in her. At last she asked, "Do you have any family?"

Puma continued to stare over the vast landscape. He nodded.

"Where is your family?"

He pointed to the ponderosa pine forest. Carmen thought somehow she must have mistaken him. "No," she said gently, speaking Spanish a little slower so he could understand her fully. "I mean, where is your father, your mother? Mayhap some sisters and brothers?" She paused. "A—a wife?"

Puma turned to her, his face unreadable. He shook his head. "No wife." He pointed to the pine forest once more.

Carmen stared in that direction, her heart beating a little faster at his answer. He had no wife. "All I see are trees."

"Look."

She continued to stare. At last she was rewarded. She saw a blue curl of smoke. Then she saw a low mist of blue smoke. "There are people down there!" she exclaimed.

Puma grunted.

Carmen stood excitedly. "Let us go to them," she said. "Mayhap they can help us."

Puma eyed her, then shrugged good-naturedly and got to his feet.

"We can talk to them. Find out where *El*

Camino Real is." Carmen was full of plans. "Mayhap they will help me get to Santa Fe."

Puma looked at her. "Why do you want to go to Santa Fe?"

Carmen met his eyes warily. Why did she feel a strange hollowness in the region of her heart? "Why, to marry my *novio*, of course."

Puma stared at her. The turquoise eyes looking into his were veiled. He grunted. "A *novio*." He shook his head. He did not like the thought of this woman planning to marry. A *novio* might come after her.

Carmen smiled tightly. Of course she must get to Santa Fe. She felt exasperated with Puma suddenly but willing to tolerate his wordless ways now that she knew people were close by. "*Sí*," she exclaimed gaily. "When I get to Santa Fe, I will marry Juan Enrique Delgado. He is the reason I traveled to New Spain in the first place." Wasn't he?

Puma regarded the woman thoughtfully. "New Spain?" he said at last as his mind grappled with what she had told him.

She waved her hand at the landscape. "This."

Puma shook his head. "Apacheria," he grunted.

She smiled at him, not willing to get into an argument when help was so close by. "Come," she said. "Let us go down to the mission and meet the priest."

"Mission? Priest?" He wondered if all Spanish women hopped from topic to topic like jackrabbits.

Carmen pointed impatiently to the blue smoke. "People," she enunciated carefully.

Puma grinned. She thought the smoke was from her people. What a surprise she was going to get when she realized that the smoke was from *his* people, the Jicarilla Apache. Only Jicarilla Apaches would be in this area. He would ask this group of The People if they knew where Man Who Listens' tribe was camped. "Come," he grunted.

When she went to get on the mare, he waved her away. "On my horse."

He mounted the sorrel, then extended a hand to help her up.

Carmen looked at him. Why did he want to ride double on his horse? The Andalusian mare was strong. Shrugging, she decided to humor him. After all, he had saved her life. She reached for his hand and climbed aboard the stallion.

Puma grinned to himself. When he rode into his people's camp with the woman on the back of his horse, it would be an announcement to all of them that she was his woman. He urged the stallion forward.

Chapter 22

It was past dawn when Puma let Carmen slide slowly off the sorrel stallion in the middle of the village. He dismounted after her, and they stood in the midst of cone-shaped homes strewn widely among ponderosa pine trees. A swift-moving creek lay a short distance away.

An old man stepped out of a tipi near the center of the village. Startled, Puma recognized Man Who Listens. Puma's heart beat faster. God had smiled upon him. Puma had found his people. He looked about for his mother's lodge.

When he swung back to Carmen, he noticed that her eyelids drooped, her whole body slumped, and she lacked the energy to push away the voluminous amount of hair that had fallen over half her face. She was tired, his little Spanish captive—tired and still beautiful.

He spotted his mother's dwelling, recognizable by the painting of a horse and rider on her deerskin door. Puma pointed casually toward the lodge. The Jicarilla Apache tipi was ideally adapted to their nomadic wandering. It was easy to build, did not require a great deal of upkeep, and provided protection against the hot sun, the mist, and the occasional violent rain showers that descended on the mountains.

Puma's mother, Sky Flyer, drawn by the excited voices of her neighbors, appeared in the doorway. She stared at the newcomers, then hurried forward.

Puma saw that she had aged in the time he had been gone. The hair that framed her face was now streaked with gray.

"My son, my son," she cried when she reached Puma. Tears rolled down her cheeks as she stared at him. "I thought never to see you again. . . ."

He hugged her tightly for a long while. With eyes closed, he thought how good it was that he was with his people once more. Sky Flyer was the first to recover. She stepped back, brushed the tears from her eyes, and glanced behind Puma. Then she met his eyes once again.

In the Jicarilla language, he answered her silent question. "My Spanish captive." His blood pounded in excitement at his own words. The Spanish woman was his, truly his. And she was in his power. His blue eyes brightened as he glanced at her, possessiveness sweeping over him.

Sky Flyer gazed intently at her son, then dropped her eyes and nodded. Puma turned back in time to see his mother drop her gaze. He frowned. Then he shrugged. It was his business what he did with his captive.

Soon other people of the village—men, women and children—began crowding around him, asking questions, welcoming him back. Several of them repeated his mother's words. They thought he had been killed. Evidently no one in the village knew that Angry Man had sold him to the Comanches. Well, Puma would inform them when the time came. But not now.

Puma noticed one young woman hanging back, watching him. He was surprised to see that it was young Bird Who Plays in the Pinyon Trees. She had grown up in the time he was away. When Bird Who Plays saw him return her glance, she smiled shyly. Puma turned back to a man who was asking him something. When he felt he had answered their questions as best he could, he looked to his mother. She nodded. Together they moved towards her tipi, and the others stepped respectfully aside.

Carmen followed Puma. People murmured as she went by. Carmen smiled weakly. No one returned her smile.

"Welcome to my mother's home, Doña Carmen," Puma said now and waved his hand at the structure.

Carmen started. He knew her name. Then she gaped at the hut he had indicated. She swallowed the quick retort that rose to her lips. She was not in Spain any longer, nor with her countrymen. She had seen huts like these before, at the renegades' encampment. She smiled with trembling lips, but words failed her.

"You may stay with my mother until you can build your own tipi," he said stiffly, annoyed at her reaction.

Carmen turned to him. "Build my own tipi?" Her voice was faint.

Puma nodded. "Women's work."

Now Carmen was the one who was frowning.

"I will show you how." And have every man in the village laughing at him, he thought grimly. Then he smiled at her reassuringly. He would make it easy for his captive. And the sooner she built a tipi, the sooner he could bed her. He felt his groin tighten at the thought.

Sky Flyer said something in the Jicarilla language and pointed up the hill to tipi poles set off at a little distance. Puma answered her, his grin widening.

"My mother says that you have a fine opportunity to build your first tipi. There is the start of one." He pointed to the poles his mother had indicated. "An aunt's family was called away quickly. It is yours now."

Carmen stared open-mouthed at the tall, naked poles tied in a cone shape.

The sun's early rays reached across and touched the gold highlights of Carmen's thick hair, and Puma stared at her, fascinated. He noticed that she had quickly revived from her bone-jarring ride across the desert. That was good. Only strong women survived the Apache life.

Puma's eyes burned a darker blue as he studied Carmen possessively. He felt strong and alive around this woman. She touched a chord of desire in him that was so intense that he had to have her, had to sate his desire. Since he had first seen her, he had wanted her. That wanting had grown until it was a pulsing, live thing.

She was extremely beautiful, this Spanish woman, and she was at his mercy. She was his captive, and he could do with her what he willed. What he willed was to keep her in his lodge until he had seduced her and then, once she was his, she would be willing to please him and stay with him as his captive. It would be a good life. He was an excellent hunter and could provide enough meat and skins for his own tipi and more. The Spanish woman would never go hungry. She could do much worse, and would have, had he not rescued her from Angry Man. Puma smiled grimly as his hungry eyes swept Carmen's frame.

He did feel a twinge of conscience. He was not going to help her get to Santa Fe and her *novio*. He was going to keep her. In a way, he was deceiving her. He sighed. He supposed he would have to tell her eventually that he had no intention of letting her go.

But if she knew he planned to keep her and enjoy her bountiful favors—his eyes dropped to her breasts—she would no doubt fight him with every ounce of her strength. And her strength might be considerable, given the stamina she had shown on the desert journey.

Puma's blue eyes looked so earnest, Carmen thought as her gaze met his. Carmen's stance softened somewhat. At least he was trying to help her. Mayhap he would take her to a nearby Spanish settlement. He knew she wanted to get to Santa Fe. And he had rescued her. Carmen tried a smile.

Puma's eyes glittered as he watched Carmen's tentative smile. He realized from the struggle on her face that she was naive and innocent of what he planned for her. His lips twisted in a half-smile as he saw her relax.

His teeth shone white against the dark tan of his face. Anyone who looked that handsome could not be dangerous, thought Carmen. And he *had* shown her nothing but kindness since he had rescued her from El Cabezón.

She shivered and looked around, spying several of the cone-shaped structures. More people. More *indios*. It would be essential to have a champion in this strange village. But to live in one of these hide dwellings—it was so very different from what she was used to! She stared. Still, it would not do to turn away from the only man who had helped her thus far.

'*Rule Number 327: The perfect wife is always gracious to her husband, and kind in word and deed.*' Husband? How foolish to think of Rule Number 327. She wasn't his wife! Carmen turned back to him, her turquoise eyes bright. "Very well," she said as graciously as she could manage. "I—I accept your kind hospitality. Tell your mother I thank her very much for the . . .

tipi." He was still watching her; Carmen smiled uncertainly. She suddenly wondered where Puma would stay. No doubt he would stay at another abode. And if his mother was in residence nearby, surely nothing untoward would happen, would it?

Puma's smile was a half-twist of his sculpted lips. He swung away and walked up the hillside toward the vacant tipi. Carmen stumbled after him.

He stopped in front of the framework, frowning. He had to get a buffalo hide covering for it and a deerskin flap for the doorway. "Stay here while I see to the horses. I will return."

Carmen watched him stride away, his broad back straight, his strong legs moving effortlessly. Then, feeling the effects of the long night, she took a deep breath and sank down under a ponderosa pine to wait for him. *'Rule Number 350: The perfect wife works with diligence at her husband's side, never ceasing in her labors to make his life easier.'* "I need to rest," groaned Carmen aloud. "And he's not my husband!"

When Puma returned, he was lugging several articles. He disappeared inside the hut. Carmen heard grunts and groans. Dust and dirt came flying out of the doorway. Whatever was he doing in there? she wondered. She watched Puma make several trips down to his mother's home and return with still more articles.

At last, dusting off his hands, he stepped outside the tipi and signalled Carmen over. A deerskin flap now hung at the door.

Carmen peeked inside. It was surprisingly neat, she thought, as she surveyed the inside of the dwelling. A ring of stones outlined a fire pit in the center. Off to one side stood a large clay pot and two beautifully woven baskets. Spoons, bowls, and several square packets of something, food perhaps, were stored nearby. Carmen wanted to tiptoe over and look inside them, but she withheld her curiosity, conscious that she was a guest. The light was dim, but she could make out a bed of fur robes and three blue and cream and black patterned blankets on the other side of the fire pit. Weapons of war hung from a pole—bow, shield, spear, quiver with arrows. She recognized a Spanish arquebus. The Spanish saddle that had been on the sorrel stallion was set alongside the pole. Everything looked well cared for.

Carmen turned when she heard a sound behind her. Puma had entered the dwelling. "Sit down," he insisted, as he placed an armload of sticks to one side of the fire pit. With efficient movements he laid the fire and soon had it burning cheerily. "Hungry?" he asked.

Carmen looked at him warily, wondering what Apaches ate. But her stomach felt empty, and she knew she needed sustenance. "*Sí*," she answered hesitantly.

Puma smiled and left the tipi, returning with two steaming bowls of stew. He gave her a satisfied glance. In the space of a short time, he had managed to shelter her and was now feeding her. The Spanish woman would know that he could provide well for her.

Puma handed a spoon and bowl to her and sat down cross-legged across from her to eat his stew. Carmen gazed into her bowl. Big chunks of meat and some unknown vegetables floated in a savory-scented gravy flavored with herbs. She took a small bite of the meat and chewed it consideringly. Very tasty. She took another bite. And another. They ate in companionable silence. When she was done, Puma politely asked, "More?"

"*Sí, por favor,*" answered Carmen without hesitation. "That was delicious. What was it?"

"Dog meat."

Puma did not see Carmen's eyes widen as he left the dwelling to fill up her bowl, but he did hear a choking sound. And when he returned, he noticed that she no longer seemed hungry. Shrugging, he finished off the extra bowl of stew himself.

Setting the bowls aside, Puma stood up. "We rode all night and need rest. You retire there," he pointed to a fur robe across the tipi.

Carmen's hand went to her throat. "Where—" she began nervously, "where are you going to sleep?"

Puma picked up two of the patterned blankets and laid them on the other side of the tipi from the robes. "Here," he said, sitting down on the comfortable bed he had made for himself.

"Th—there?" she asked. She tried to keep the trembling out of her voice. "I—I thought you would sleep somewhere else." She hurried on. "With your mother."

Puma raised one black eyebrow. His blue eyes laughed at her. "Apache men do not sleep with their mothers," he said at last. "Do Spanish men?"

Carmen thought she saw the hint of a curled lip with this question. She straightened. "Not at all! That is, I mean to say, I thought—" She tried again. "I thought you would retire somewhere else," she cried in desperation. "Not here. Not near me. It is not proper!"

"It is very proper," pronounced Puma. "This is my home. This is where I sleep." He looked at her, his blue eyes still laughing.

Carmen ground her teeth. He was being purposely obtuse. "You cannot sleep here," she said succinctly and clearly. "*I* am sleeping here."

Puma sat down on a fur robe, leaned back, and smiled.

"I do not have to stay here, you know," Carmen said nervously. She rose to her feet and took an uncertain step towards the deer flap door. "I can leave."

Puma said nothing, only watched her.

Those intense blue eyes were unnerving Carmen. "Very well," she said, flouncing to the door. "I shall leave. *I* shall sleep with your mother."

Puma shook his head in amusement. "No," he said.

"No?" cried Carmen. "You dare to tell me no!"

Puma stood up then and walked to the door. Gently, he removed Carmen's hand from the deer flap. He took her hand and pulled her toward the bed. "No!" cried Carmen. "You must not!" She struggled to free her hand from his grip. When he would not release her hand, she used the other to push at his arm, trying in vain to free herself. "Let me go. You cannot—must not—"

"Must not what?" Puma was grinning down at her. The little Spanish captive was certainly struggling to free herself. He loosened her hand suddenly, and she fell back on the robes.

He dropped down beside her and reached across her.

When Carmen lifted herself to her elbows, it was only to find herself in Puma's arms. She saw that their struggles had placed them squarely on her bed.

She lay there looking into his blue, blue eyes, his firm mouth mere inches from hers. Why, he even had a cleft in his chin. She groaned. The man was maddeningly attractive. She could feel the strength of his powerful arm muscles as he held her. "Let me go," she whispered.

Puma bent his head toward her, his breath soft on her lips. She looked so delectable, felt so soft. He ran his hands soothingly along her back.

Carmen watched him, her lustrous eyes locked on his. "No," she whispered again. His touch was gentle, relaxing, and she wanted to let him continue, but she knew she must not.

"*Sí*," he whispered back. "I have been wanting to kiss you ever since I first saw you." His head came down then and gently, ever so softly, he touched his lips to hers. It was a sweet kiss, the sweetest he had ever tasted. And he wanted more.

When his lips met Carmen's, her eyes widened in alarm. He smelled of smoke, of man. As his lips nibbled delicately at hers, he slowly pushed his tongue into her mouth. Tentatively, she touched it with her own. They played like that for the rest of the kiss, then he slowly, reluctantly, broke the kiss. Carmen stared at him, her eyes huge. She slowly brushed her lips with her fingers. "You—you kissed me." There was wonder in her voice. "That was my first kiss."

Puma dragged her back and molded her to him. "I can do more than that," he assured her. And he bent his lips to hers once more. He groaned then at the sweetness of her and clasped her closer to his hard frame. He threw every bit of himself into the kiss. It was hot, it was reckless, it was powerful, it was sweet—so sweet. . . .

Carmen was breathing heavily. She felt caught up in a maelstrom of sensation she had never experienced before. Her body felt hot, her face felt flushed, and her thoughts were whirling. This man, this strong, powerful man, was holding her and doing things to her that felt wonderful. . . .

Puma was running his hands up and down the contours of her back. The cold, smooth material of the dress she wore frustrated him. He wanted to feel her flesh, warm and supple. He cupped her firm buttocks in his hands and pressed her against him and moved his hips.

Carmen moaned. What was he doing to her? She had never felt so light, so floating. She pressed her hips into his. "Please . . ." she moaned.

In answer, Puma ran his tongue along her lips, then plunged inside again, opening her mouth to his. He groaned as he flicked his tongue over the soft places in her mouth.

"Oh, *sí*," she moaned. Carmen's arms went around his neck, and she shivered as he caressed her. His hands were running the length and breadth of her, seeking, demanding, and she wanted more of his touch.

Her fingers took on a will of their own, and she tugged at the long hair at the back of his neck to pull him closer to her. "Mmmmmm . . ." she moaned. He tasted so wonderful. He tasted of smoke and sweat and . . . man. She pushed into him, instinctively trying to become as one with him.

Their lips were in a frenzy now, each trying to devour the other.

Puma clasped her, his arms like steel bands that held her as he strained against her. She felt so good, so sweet. He closed his eyes, striving for breath. He must have her. He could not live another heartbeat without having her, feeling her soft body welcome him. . . .

His lips fused to hers, Puma plunged his tongue into her mouth again and again. Shifting his weight, he moved on top of her. His knee sought the V of her thighs and he pressed against her.

He lifted the hem of her dress and ran his warm hand along the length of her leg. Closer and closer his hand moved to that which he craved. With a groan, he reached her and pushed aside the flimsy undergarment she wore in one fluid motion.

The mounting pressure against the center of her being brought Carmen to her senses. She pushed ineffectually at the hand holding her so securely. "Stop! Stop!" she cried. She stared at him, her eyes wild. "What are you doing?"

He smiled and kissed the tip of her nose. "I am making love to you."

"But you cannot," she wailed. "I do not know you! I am not married to you. I cannot! Sister Francisca said—"

Puma waited for her to continue, but she did not. He eased himself off her and watched her. His body throbbed from arousal, and he gritted his teeth in frustration.

Carmen bolted up and stared at him, her mouth swollen from his kisses, her hair in disarray, her body heaving with each breath. "Oh, no," she moaned. "What have I done?"

She looked so upset that Puma, despite his own discomfort, sought for words to reassure her. "Nothing," he said at last. "You have done nothing."

"Oh, no," wailed Carmen. "You cannot deceive me. This is how babies are made, is it not?"

Puma looked at her curiously. "Of course," he said.

Carmen threw one arm over her eyes so she did not have to look at him. "I am going to have a baby," she moaned.

Puma stared at her. "You are pregnant?" He could have sworn she was inexperienced. Still, the ardor with which she had returned his kisses should have warned him. Drawing back, he too, sat up. Stiffly, he asked, "Who is the father?"

It was Carmen's turn to stare at him. Her face crumpled as she cried out, "You are."

"Me?" Puma was stunned. "How can I be the father? We did nothing—"

"We did *everything*," sobbed Carmen. "Oh, no, how can I ever return to my people? My *novio* will have nothing to do with me. I am ruined. Ruined!" And she fell to sobbing helplessly.

Puma felt baffled. What was the matter with the Spanish woman? Thoroughly confused, he reached over and patted her arm.

She sobbed louder.

Puma sat quietly beside Carmen as she cried. He picked up a lock of her soft blond hair and stroked it thoughtfully, putting it to his lips and kissing it. Then he began to stroke her head gently.

Carmen allowed him to do that, and gradually her sobs died away.

"Do you think you shall have my child because of what we did?" Puma struggled to understand this woman's thinking.

Carmen sobbed once more and nodded her head into the furs, reluctant to face him.

"Did your mother not tell you about babies?" asked Puma.

"My mother died when I was born." More sobs.

Puma accepted that answer patiently. "An aunt, perhaps?" he suggested.

She shook her head. "There was nobody. Sister Francisca was going to tell me, someday."

"Ah," said Puma. "Your sister did not tell you."

Carmen looked at him then. Her eyes were red from weeping, but she still looked beautiful to him. "She was not my sister. She was a nun."

He looked at her blankly.

"A nun at the convent where I was raised."

When Puma continued to gaze at her unwaveringly, Carmen grew exasperated. "She was not my sister, she was a nun—a woman of God."

"Ah," Puma nodded. "I understand."

"How is it that you speak Spanish and do not know about nuns and convents?"

Puma smiled. "Perhaps because the prisoners who taught me Spanish did not know much about them."

"Oh." Carmen could not think of anything to say to that. She pushed herself up onto her knees. Struggling to regain her composure, she said, "You will have to leave now."

Puma stared at her. This woman blew in more directions than the wind.

"I am going to go to sleep," Carmen said impatiently. "So you must leave."

"After what we shared?" Puma was incredulous. He thought for certain that now she would accept him in her bed.

"*Sí*," she said firmly, the streaks from her tears still wet on her face. "*Especially* after what we shared." She gulped. "And what we are going to share."

Puma looked and felt puzzled. "What is it we are about to share?" he asked.

"Why, our child."

"Oh, *sí*. That. I had forgotten." And in truth, he had forgotten what had first set his little Spanish captive to groaning and weeping.

He took her hand gently.

She drew it back. "Oh, no, you must not," she said. "That is how this all started."

Puma looked down at the fur robes for a moment, struggling to keep from laughing. At last he said, "I will explain to you where babies come from."

And he did. When he was finished, Carmen was watching him with wide eyes. "You wanted to do that to me?" she cried. She sputtered as words failed her. "Never!"

Puma smiled. His Spanish captive was certainly entertaining. "Women do it," he said simply.

Carmen leaned closer and looked him straight in the eye. "Well, I will not."

Puma raised an eyebrow. "What about your *novio*?" he shot back.

"That is different. I am going to marry him."

"And you will not marry me?" Puma's voice was dangerously quiet.

"Never!" cried Carmen. She crossed her arms over her breasts and sat there defiantly.

Puma stared at her, feeling the blood rush to his head. This woman, this Spanish spawn of a Spanish dog, refused to marry him! He was a respected warrior, a hunter of renown. Apache women, yes and even some Spanish women, sought his favor with beguiling glances and sweet smiles, happy if he deigned to look their way. And this captive—this, this slave—refused to marry him! The insult of it all hit him full in the face.

He rose at once. "You have had an eventful day," he said angrily. "I will leave you to your rest."

Carmen watched dumbfounded as Puma walked to the door. What had happened? Somehow she had insulted him terribly. "Wait!" she cried.

He placed a hand on the deerskin flap, ready to push it aside. Then he turned. "*Sí*?" Stiff pride was in his voice.

"I—I am sure it was a very great honor for you to offer marriage. It is just that I already have a *novio*. . . ."

Her voice died away. It had not exactly been an offer, now that she thought of it. More of a roared insult. She rubbed her brow. Oh, she did not know what to think. But she must not let him go off like this—angry and sullen at her. The kisses they had shared had been so wonderful. . . . "How is it that you know my name?"

"The caravan," he snapped. At her blank look, he added, "Lopez, the cook, told me."

"Oh." What now? He made another motion to leave. "I know your name is Puma," she said hesitantly. "Do you have another name?"

He frowned thoughtfully at her. "Apaches do not use their names. Not their real names." He stared at her for a long moment. No, he would not tell her that his true name was Snarling Mountain Lion. She would have to make do with his nickname.

Carmen wanted to wilt under his stare, it was so harsh.

"Puma," she said softly, "thank you, again. For rescuing me today," she said at his puzzled look.

He nodded once. "*De nada.*" He turned to go but stopped. "What is your full Spanish name?"

"It is Doña Carmen Yolanda Diaz y Silvera."

He heard the pride in her voice as the long name rolled off her lips. He found himself thinking of how sweet those lips were, how soft. . . .

"I come from an old family, a very old, noble family. In Seville, Spain," Carmen finished brightly.

Puma nodded shortly. "I see," he answered at last. And indeed he did. The prisoners from whom he had learned the Spanish language occasionally had spoken of Spain, of the wonders there, of the wealth. Seville was a city they had spoken of. It was the major trading city for the New World.

So, Puma's captive was from a rich family, was she? No doubt a family with status such as Puma would never have or hope to have. She was beyond him. He could see that now. How foolish he had been even to think of marrying her. She would never consent to marry a wandering Apache, someone who did not even own the land on which he built his hide house.

Puma glanced around at the home he had fixed up so hopefully. Suddenly, it did not look so fine to his eyes. He glared at the woman sitting on his bed. His nostrils flared. She was there on *his* bed—the bed of a half-blood Jicarilla Apache. Not on the bed of some Spanish nobleman. His lip curled and he almost snarled aloud. If that was the way it was to be, so be it. He would keep her. He would not offer her marriage again, for she would only spit on his offer as she had already done. But he would keep her. Keep her and her 'very old, noble' blood. He smiled then, and it was a cruel smile.

Carmen, sitting on the fur robes, shivered when she saw him smile at her. She drew a fur around her shoulders, suddenly conscious of the coolness in the air.

Puma's eyes were hooded as he gazed at the beautiful woman on his bed. He no longer felt guilty that he had compromised her in front of the whole village by riding in with her behind him. No, not after the way she had refused his offer to marry him.

Let her sit there thinking she was safe from him. She was in greater danger now than when she had first entered his dwelling, and he relaxed at the knowledge. He would enjoy taming this Spanish captive.

"Sleep," he said gruffly.

"*Sí*," said Carmen obediently, lying back down. She felt relieved that he was leaving. The tension between them had suddenly become thick. "I—I will."

He glared at her a moment longer, then strode out the door.

Behind him, Carmen wondered at the change that had come over the man she had first kissed so ardently. Her fingers went to her lips. Her first kiss . . . and her second and her third . . . She blushed.

Carmen crawled into the fur robes and lay back, her thick hair fanning out around her head. She closed weary eyes. The man who had rescued her had left the dwelling but not her mind. She wondered about him, about the blue-eyed *indio* who spoke Spanish. She lay there, conjuring up his tight embraces, his warm lips, and his questing hands.

She flushed anew at the memories, at the way she had pressed herself upon him. She must remember that she was going to marry another man. Juan Enrique Delgado seemed so far away. Santa Fe seemed so far away. She must get there, she supposed. She *was* to be married, after all.

She wondered then if Juan Enrique Delgado kissed as well as Puma. Curling her toes at the memory of the passionate kisses she had shared with Puma, she felt doubts creep into her mind, doubts that Juan Enrique Delgado could ever kiss that well. She sighed. Nobody could ever kiss that well.

She must get back to her people, back to the Spanish. She must not linger in this village; she might fall under the spell of Puma. He was far too enticing. No, she should not stay here at all. . . .

Chapter 23

Carmen slept through that day and into the next night. She awoke sometime past dawn to a faint noise. Someone was coming up the hill to her tipi. Then she heard the faint murmur of voices. Carmen could not resist peeking through the door opening.

There stood Puma, near a small fire, speaking with his mother. It was she who had come up the hill. Carmen's eyes hungrily roved over Puma. His broad back was to her as he spoke with his mother. He stood straight and tall in the clear morning light.

Then Carmen spotted his bedroll still lying on the ground. Her heart pounded thickly. Puma had been sleeping just outside the tipi for the entire time Carmen had been asleep. She knew it. Mayhap his proximity was why she had slept so long and so soundly.

Carmen let the doorflap fall. She must not come to depend on the handsome *indio* too much, she thought. She must tell him once again that she was determined to reach Santa Fe and her *novio*. She tried to conjure up her favorite image of Juan Delgado, sitting at her feet, gazing up at her adoringly, but this morning the image would not come. Carmen sighed and gave up. She would get to Santa Fe. It would be enough. She would see what Juan Enrique Delgado looked like then.

With renewed determination, Carmen got to her feet. She found a wooden comb placed alongside her bed and she wondered at Puma's thoughtfulness. Had the comb been there when she had first entered the dwelling, or had he entered while she was asleep and placed it there? The thought of him watching her as she slept gave her a tingle of excitement. She quickly squashed it. Juan Enrique Delgado, that was the man she must think of.

Carmen stepped out of the tipi and walked sedately over to the two Apaches. Before she got close, they ceased speaking and Puma turned to greet her, his face impassive. Sky Flyer, his mother, looked a little more friendly. Carmen had the distinctly uneasy feeling that they had been speaking of her.

"*Buenos días*," she said with a tentative smile.

The two nodded. Puma stared at Carmen. She looked fresh and beautiful this morning, and he wished for a moment that she looked old and tired. Then perhaps his heart would not beat faster, his breath would not quicken so, and his stomach would not clench as though struck when she turned those wide turquoise eyes on him.

Sky Flyer stepped forward and murmured in Apache. Carmen looked questioningly at Puma.

"My mother says she will take you to gather food on the hillside. Sky Flyer says she will teach you the ways of the Apache women."

Carmen looked from Sky Flyer to Puma and back again. She smiled weakly and said, "That is very kind of your mother. But it is hardly necessary. I must travel to Santa Fe, not stay here."

Carmen wondered at the cloud that passed over Puma's stern face. His jaw was set mulishly. She shrugged. That was his problem. Turning to Sky Flyer, Carmen murmured some very polite, flowery words in Spanish, thanking the woman for her offer of assistance and assuring Sky Flyer that Carmen's family would ever be indebted to Sky Flyer for her kindness and deeply regretting that Carmen was unable to stay long enough to learn the ways of the Apache women.

Sky Flyer appeared to understand her. She giggled and then glanced at Puma, her face in a half-smile. Carmen had seen the same twist of the lips on her son's face. Sky Flyer started back down the hill, her broad back descending with dignity. Carmen smiled as she watched the older woman leave. What a gracious woman she was.

When Carmen turned back to Puma, she saw that he was glaring at her.

The time had come, thought Puma, to tell his captive exactly where she stood.

"Doña Carmen," he said coolly, "I will not take you to Santa Fe." He waited, arms crossed, for her answer.

Carmen blinked. Frowning, she said, "But you know I must get to Santa Fe. . . . my *novio* . . ." How would she ever get there without Puma's help? What did he expect of her? Anger began to grow in her. "You know that is where I must go. I have traveled half-way across the world to get to Santa Fe. Juan Enrique Delgado is waiting for me."

Face impassive, Puma stood there. Then he shrugged, as if he cared little about the waiting *novio*, which was true.

Carmen's anger grew. "What do you mean you will not take me to Santa Fe?" When he continued to stare at her out of a stony face, she glared back at him. Hands on hips, she marched up to him. Her head came level with his broad chest. "I demand," she said succinctly, speaking in slow Spanish so that he would not misinterpret a single word, "that you take me to Santa Fe." Furious turquoise eyes stared into icy blue ones.

"No."

She wanted to kick him. "That," she explained as calmly as she could, "is where I am going. I have a *novio*"—Puma looked singularly unimpressed—"who is waiting to marry me." She leaned closer, feeling the risk was justified. "If you do not take me to Santa Fe," she declared proudly, her voice was still even, "then I will walk!"

"No."

"Oh?" she inquired archly. "And what do you propose to do with me?" A small frisson of fear tingled down her spine as she began to get the first inkling that mayhap this handsome, stern man was not as kind as she had thought. "Have me stay here and learn the Apache woman's ways?" That should jolt him, she thought; such a thing was clearly impossible.

"*Sí.*"

She stared at him, then clamped her mouth shut. Her brows lowered ferociously. "I will not," she snapped.

For the first time, Puma smiled. He had won. There had never been any question of his not winning, actually. She was in his power, and in his possession. The thought made him magnaminous in victory. "You may live here," he indicated the tipi with his chin. "You will gather food for me. I will hunt for you, protect you. You will give me children."

She gasped, her memory suddenly refreshed as to how such children would be made. Her turquoise eyes wide, Carmen stammered, "But—but you cannot—" She swallowed. "I am Spanish," she said desperately. "My people will not let you do this. They will follow me here."

She struggled to hold onto her sanity. This could not be happening to her. Again.

Puma looked her directly in the eye. "Your people will not find you here. They do not know where to look." As he stared at her, some part of him wondered why he so strongly wanted to unite with this woman. She was Spanish, as she had so desperately reminded him, and he did not like the Spanish. His face took on the stony, impassive look again. He had decided to keep her, and keep her he would. She could learn Apache ways. He knew enough of Spanish ways to know that he did not want to live with them.

"Am I to have no say?" Carmen was still struggling with what he had said. She was to live here, with the *indios*, gather his food, bear his children. . . . She closed her eyes. This could not be happening to her. When she had ventured forth from Seville, she had known there would be danger on her journey, but never, in her most desperate dreams, had she ever imagined anything like this happening to her.

"No." Suddenly it was too much for Carmen. She broke and ran, running she knew not where, anywhere to get away from him and what he was telling her.

Her feet pounded the uneven ground. Rocks that would normally have caused her to wince, she ignored. She must get away.

Puma was after her in a heartbeat. Though she was as fleet as an antelope, he easily ran her down. He leaped at her, threw his arms around her waist, and brought her tumbling to the ground. They finally rolled to a halt, he on top of her. He held her wrists above her head and pinned them to the ground. Both were panting heavily, she from fear, he from exhilaration.

"You will stay with me," he snarled through gritted teeth. "You will not leave."

She glared up at him. "I will! You cannot keep me!"

"I can." He loosened her wrists and she quickly tried to buck him off. "There is nowhere for you to run," he said thickly, her actions causing him to notice his own personal reaction. "If you go out into the hills, or the desert, it is certain death. There are wild animals. Renegades."

She remembered the cougar and El Cabezón. She went still.

"You do not know how to find food, where to find water. You would die."

She looked at him, unseeing for a moment. A vision of herself lying helplessly in the desert, lips dried and cracked, left alone, like Doña Matilda, came to her.

Puma saw that she had grown quieter and was listening to him, understanding him. Now he would win her over. "I will take care of you," he said thickly. "I will feed you, clothe you, shelter you. I will not let wild animals hurt you. Or Angry Man, either. Do you understand?"

Staring at him dazedly, she nodded.

"You will be safe with me. I will not hurt you," he emphasized.

She nodded again and shuddered. He was correct, the thought came crashing through her brain. There was nowhere to run to. She was dependent for her very life upon him. She gazed up at the stern face and blinked.

"My people will help you. You will live with us. After a time, you will come to like your life with us. With me." He hoped that part was true for her. He had seen it happen that way before. Children were readily adopted into the tribe and took well to the Apache life. And women, after their first child, seemed to be more accepting of living with the Jicarilla.

Carmen was calmer now, thinking of what he had told her. A quiet had descended upon her, and she felt almost listless in her despair. Mother of God, had her soul gone away?

She tried to get up, and he moved off her. She sat up and looked around. The mountains still looked the same. The ponderosa pine trees were in the same place. The cone-shaped dwellings had not changed. Only *she* had changed. Her life was here now, with the *indios*. He had told her that. She looked at him, a part of her wondering why she believed him so easily. Then she knew. It was because she felt powerless, felt that she had no say in what happened to her—that was why she was feeling this uncaring dead feeling.

"No!" she cried and scrambled to her feet. He stared at her, disbelief in those icy blue eyes. "You cannot keep me like some kind of a . . . some kind of a wild horse!" she cried. "I am human, like you! I have a soul! I have done nothing that God should let this happen to me! No!" Every ounce of her being was in the cry. She turned and fled to the tipi, throwing herself down on the furs. Sobbing, she cried and kicked and cried some more until at last she had no more tears left to cry.

She might be his captive, his prisoner, but she was not dead. She would fight to stay alive, to keep feeling alive within her breast.

Puma stood in the doorway, watching her thoughtfully. Perhaps it was good that the woman did not take easily to captivity. She would make a strong, powerful mother for his sons. And daughters.

He, of all people, should know that to accept captivity willingly was a form of death. He himself had not been calm and accepting of his fate in the Mexican prison. He had railed against it, sought his freedom, vowed he would survive. And he had.

And now his little Spanish captive was doing the same thing. He smiled. It was good, he thought. He had chosen wisely. Even if she was Spanish.

Chapter 24

Reluctantly, Carmen realized that she was accepting her new life with the Apaches. She followed Sky Flyer over the rough ground as they were heading for the stream. They would have a soothing, cool drink and mayhap even a bath. Life's pleasures were simpler for her now.

She lugged a heavy basket full of edible roots in her arms. She would be thankful for the chance to rest. Jicarilla Apache women worked hard, she had learned over the past few weeks. They gathered berries, roots and nuts, whatever the mountains had to offer that was edible. Most of the food that she and Puma ate seemed to be what Carmen had gathered. No, to be honest, he had provided some very welcome meat. Antelope was becoming a great favorite of hers. She liked the taste. But she refused, absolutely refused, to eat dog again. She always gave her portion away to Sky Flyer when their family group sat down to eat together.

Family, she thought uneasily. She supposed she was being accepted as family by Puma's people— his mother, his mother's husband, Puma's aunts, and assorted cousins. Or were they brothers and sisters? She found it hard to tell because the words they used to call each other were the ones for brother and sister. Yet she thought that Puma was actually Sky Flyer's only offspring.

Sky Flyer and her husband, One Who Hunts, were kind to Carmen, she had to acknowledge. Some of the other members of the tribe were not. Most kept their distance. One young woman, Bird Who Plays in the Pinyon Trees, often glared at Carmen. Carmen had no idea what she had done to offend the young woman, but Bird Who Plays made rude comments to her and laughed and giggled about her to her friends. Bird Who Plays' friends did not seem particularly friendly to Carmen either. Carmen tried to ignore the nasty words and whispers, but at times she felt sad because of it. She did not ask Sky Flyer any more about what they were saying. She knew they were insults because when Carmen had first repeated to Sky Flyer what Bird Who Plays had said, Sky Flyer had tightened her lips, shaken her head, and refused to answer. Later, Carmen had seen Sky Flyer speaking to Bird Who Plays, and then the young woman had glared sullenly at Carmen. No, it would do no good to speak of it again.

The Apache men ignored her completely. That was fine with Carmen. She wished that Puma would ignore her, too. No, she did not, she corrected herself hastily, since she was being completely honest today. Actually, she liked it that he talked with her. Her heart beat faster every time he came near her. To her surprise, he had not come to her at night, to make babies. She wondered why. She thought that was why he had wanted her. He had certainly spoken of it that first day in camp. She sighed. Would she ever learn the workings of the Apache mind?

The few weeks she had been with The People had passed in a blur. She was learning the Jicarilla language and the ways of the women. Sky Flyer spoke some Spanish, though not as much as Puma, who seemed very much at home with the language. She realized now that he had merely toyed with her when he had let her think that he did not understand Spanish well.

He seemed pleased with how much she had learned. He encouraged her language lessons and complimented her about what wonderful plants and roots she found. But Carmen was not fooled. She knew he wanted her to fit in with his people; he had not given up on making her an Apache.

And he watched her closely. Several times she had caught his alert blue eyes upon her when she wandered from the village to answer nature's call. If she did not return swiftly, he came after her, causing her more than one embarrassing moment. He seemed to think she would bolt again. And she would, if she got the opportunity, Carmen acknowledged. But she was confounded as to where she would run to. The mountains were not territory that she knew, and she had not seen a single Spaniard since she came to live with the Apache. She did not know in which direction to bolt.

She thought of Puma. He had treated her well, she had to admit. He brought her delicious meat, gave her favored portions of antelope. He made certain when the thunderstorms came that their shelter did not leak. If it did, he helped her to repair it.

On the second day she was with the Apaches, Puma had returned with the skin of the cougar he had killed to save her. Puma informed her that Angry Man and his renegades had moved on. Holding out the hide to her, he told her that the cougar meat was too rotten by the time he had arrived at the carcass, but he had managed to save the skin. Carmen had merely nodded, not being too anxious to sample cougar meat. With Sky Flyer's help, Carmen had tanned the hide, and now it lay as a covering on her bed. She felt very proud every time she looked at the fur.

She noticed that Puma kept the jewelry sack with her dowry on his person at all times. She wondered if he knew what it was. He seemed to understand it was valuable. Carmen tried not to look at it too often; she did not want to rouse his suspicions, but she was very aware that if she were to escape, she would need the jewels to help her resume her life with the Spanish.

Days went by before she would think about Juan Enrique Delgado. Each time she remembered him, she would feel guilty. Puma was so much

more present to her. She saw him every day, ate
his food, prepared his clothes. She even breathed
in his scent when he stood close to her.

But Juan Enrique Delgado . . . Carmen wondered if he ever thought about her. She wondered
if Doña Matilda had reached Santa Fe and told
him what had happened to her. She wondered
if he cried in the night for her. That thought
pleased her, and she moved her image of him
in her mind from sitting at her feet, gazing up at
her adoringly, to lying sleepless in the cold hours
of dawn, crying out her name. *Sí*, she liked that
scene. She was happily contemplating Juan's
tear-streaked face lifting from the pillow as he
reached for her absent body, when a loud crack
of thunder broke into her thoughts.

The thunderstorms in Apacheria were savage and violent. Just ahead of her, Sky Flyer
had halted, searching the landscape. Pointing
in another direction from the stream, she
started to run. Carmen ran after her, the heavy
basket she was lugging slowing her steps.

They reached the shelter, a cave, just before
the torrential rains started. Heavy lightning
bolts lit the late afternoon sky. Huddled in
the cave, they waited out the rain. They spoke
now and then, Sky Flyer telling her a story of
the Apache, but mostly they waited for the rain
to stop. When it did, night had fallen and the
sky was black. It was a long, wet, and cold walk
back to the village. They did not arrive until
quite late.

Puma walked up to greet them, his usually

stony face openly showing his relief. "I thought you were lost," he said. "I was about to start looking for you." Several of the men stood nearby, and Carmen guessed that they had been willing to help him search. A small, warm feeling started in her heart that the Apache people would care about what had happened to her. Then she stopped herself. Of course, they would be worried about Sky Flyer, not Carmen. Sadly, she turned away, not seeing the joy and light in Puma's blue eyes as he watched her.

He walked her to the tipi and entered behind her. She did not ask him to leave. After the loud thunderclaps and waiting out the storm, she wanted—no, needed—his company.

He sat down beside her, and she saw that he had prepared the evening meal. "Do Apache men usually do this?" she asked, pointing to the waiting food. She sniffed. Not dog meat, she noted in relief. It smelled like antelope. She smiled.

Puma regarded her thoughtfully. It had scared him, badly, when he realized she was missing. He had feared for his mother, too, but his strongest concern had been for Carmen. If anything had happened to either of them . . . With an effort, he drew his mind away from what could have happened. She was safe.

He shrugged. "Sometimes." He smiled back at her. "I am glad you are back here safely, *Chihonii*, my friend."

She looked up at the odd note in his deep

voice. She wondered if he had worried about her after all.

They ate in silence, and when they were done, she expected him to get up, stretch, and leave as he had done so many nights before.

But he did not. He watched her move over to sit on her cougar skin, the usual sign that it was time for him to leave. Instead, he stayed where he was, looking at her. She noticed the blankets of his bedroll and gave a start.

It had been difficult, Puma mused, staying away from her these past few weeks, letting her get used to the Apache ways, not forcing himself upon her. He felt he had done enough to force captivity upon her, but now he wanted more. He wanted her body, soft and willing. The storm had showed him how much she meant to him, and it had reminded him that life in the mountains could be short. He would take her now.

Carmen's heart began to beat faster when she saw him leaning on his elbow, his body easily at rest, those blue eyes warm for once in the flickering firelight. "Tonight, I stay," he said, and she could not tell if it was a warning, a plea, or a challenge.

She stared at him for a long time. Then, slowly, she nodded. He got up and walked over to her. She looked up at him, still not saying anything. Indeed, she could not. Her heart was pounding in her throat as she stared at him. Then, impulsively, she scrambled to her feet and ran out the door.

With a yelp, he was after her. He seized her before she had gone more than a few steps. "Come back, my little Spaniard," he panted in her ear. Fighting him, she knocked at the strong arms holding her, but it did no good. The rain had started once more, and they were both wet when he dragged her back into the tipi.

He sank to the floor with her and began tearing off her clothes.

"Stop, stop!" she cried. "Do not do this!"

He looked at her then. She was pale and shaking. Her lips trembled, and his own words came back to him. *I will not hurt you.* Whether he repeated them aloud or merely to himself, he did not know. With a grimace of self-reproach, he let go of her dress and rolled away. He lay very still for some moments, teeth gritted, willing his pounding pulse to slow down, his aching groin to quiet. At last he got up and walked over to the bed he had made for himself earlier. "Very well," he said quietly. "I will sleep here." He would give her time to get used to him, he decided, to get used to his presence at night. But, in the end, he would have her.

Carmen stared at him, her heart beating frantically from what had just happened. The drumming rain on the hide sides of the tipi kept time with her heart. In her relief, her shoulders slumped. Then her head came up. Would he try such a thing again?

Puma was watching her, his fingers laced behind his head. "You are safe," he said softly in answer to her unspoken question.

Giving a little moan, Carmen dived under the fur blankets and pulled them over her head. She lay there in the darkness, listening to the pounding of her heart. What had almost happened? She felt as though she had had a reprieve, but she was not certain from what. When Puma had announced that he was staying inside the tipi this night, she had nodded her agreement. She understood that he did not want to sleep out in the wet, nor did she. The tipi was the logical choice. But by the look in his eye, it had come to her that she was agreeing to much more than he had spoken of. To run had been instinctive on her part. When he dragged her back, he had turned into someone strange, someone frightening, someone she did not know. On the heels of these troubled thoughts, she became drowsy and then sleep claimed her.

On the pallet on the other side of the tipi, Puma lay tossing and thrashing through the long night. The hours before dawn found him tired and awake. Had he actually chosen to torture himself thusly? To live with a woman, to see her, to want her, and then to deny himself? What was the matter with him? And yet, if he were to force himself upon her, he would be destroying the trust that had been building gradually between them. And he would be going back upon his own word that he would keep her safe.

What was he to do? Was he to suffer night after night with the physical wanting of her? Or was he to suffer the torments of his conscience as he made her into a beaten, cowed, destroyed woman? God must be laughing at him, he decided, to give him such a choice.

He glanced over at the woman, her blond hair above the covers now, her face quiet in repose. She did not suffer, he thought viciously. She was not dying with the wanting of him.

And then it came to him. He did not have to choose either one of the ugly choices. Instead, he could make her want him, make her desire him and then—then he would have her *and* her body. She would give herself freely. He could keep his word that way, and she too would have a choice.

Puma glanced over at her; a slight smile played on his weary face as he watched her breathe. There had been a lesson in this night for him. Feeling freer now than he had in weeks, Puma fell asleep just before dawn.

When he awoke, she was gone.

Chapter 25

Santa Fe

"Stupid *indio*! How many times have I told you to knock?" Juan Enrique Delgado lolled between the white sheets, his arm around the dozing, burgundy-haired woman at his side.

A peon stood bowing in the bedroom doorway, sweat running profusely down his face. "Very sorry, señor. I had no choice. *Soldados* ask for you. An old woman with them, too. They will not go away."

Juan Enrique Delgado sighed heavily and reached under the sheets to regretfully squeeze the pale plump breast of his companion. The eyes of the trembling Pueblo Indian caught the movement, and he hastily turned away, bowing his way out of the room.

Once the servant was gone, Delgado turned to the woman, whose sandy-brown eyelashes fluttered. She opened them, revealing green eyes. *"Cara mia,"* whispered Juan Enrique Delgado. "I must get up. Do not leave our little love nest. I will fly back to your arms."

The woman yawned and snuggled down further under the sheets. She idly ran her hand along his pale arm. "Do hurry back," she replied languidly. "I await your return with the greatest anticipation." Then she rolled her eyes and fell asleep.

He patted her shoulder delicately. "I, too, Maria Antonia," he assured her. "I, too. Sleep, my little *rubí*, sleep," he murmured. She truly was his little ruby, he thought. Her deep red hair was the very color of the valuable gem, and Juan Enrique Delgado could think of nothing he treasured more than an ice cold, hard, red jewel.

Maria slept, needing no further encouragement.

Delgado hastily threw off the bedclothes and jumped out of bed. *"Soldados,"* he muttered, throwing on a white shirt. He reached for his dark trousers and paused. "What can they want? I do not like it."

Minutes later, panting, he stepped into the cool courtyard of his home. The evening breezes refreshed his pasty skin and dried the sweat on his frowning brow. The tell-tale spiky leaves of the century plants and prickly pear cactus decorated the miniature desert scene of his yard.

In the center was a tiny pool with a gurgling fountain.

Delgado proudly surveyed his lovely home, built at some distance outside the gates of Santa Fe by the sweat of local *indios*. He could have chosen to live within Santa Fe, in the neighborhood of the rich *peninsulares*. He certainly coveted a position among the judges, bishops, generals, and governors sent from Spain to fill the top positions. And someday he, too, would be one of them. But for now, Delgado was content to live away from them, out in the desert. Of course, it was more dangerous to live outside the city, which was why he kept the two bodyguards, Alvarez and Medina. They were hulking men he had hired away from the previous governor whose bodyguards they had been. But now Delgado grumbled under his breath that he should not have given Alvarez and Medina the day off.

He paced swiftly through his fine home. The silver mine almost paid for the heavy mortgage on it.

Three Spanish soldiers in their round helmets waited for him near the tinkling pool. A woman in black, dusty clothing stood behind them. Behind her was an equally dusty trunk.

Delgado mentally dismissed the woman as he marched up to the *soldado* who appeared to be in charge, the one with the long mustache and the pot belly. Bowing slightly, Delgado said in crisp, commanding tones, "What brings you here?" He paused to wipe his brow while he waited for his answer. The military made him distinctly uneasy.

The *soldado* bowed in return. "Señor Delgado, we bring this woman from the city of Santa Fe. She claims to be a relative of yours."

Delgado gave the woman a haughty once-over. "Never saw her before," he said shortly. "Now, please leave. I have important business—"

"You have not changed a bit," interrupted a prim voice, and Delgado turned to look at the woman again. Her voice sounded vaguely familiar. He frowned.

"You are still the same liar you always were."

Delgado reared back. "How dare you, señora," he huffed. "I do not know you—"

The woman drew herself up as tall as she could. "I did not survive *indios* and wild animals of the desert and the terrible heat to come here and be turned away from your door," she exclaimed. "I am Matilda Josefa Delgado, late of Seville, Spain," she announced proudly.

"Matilda Josefa?" he gasped in disbelief. "Tía Matilda?"

"The same," she answered.

"But—but," he sputtered, "where is my *novia*? Where are her things.? Her dowry? Why are you here with the *soldados*?"

"We were attacked in the desert," said the his aunt coolly. "*Indios* stole your *novia*. She is gone."

"But—but," Delgado struggled, his face showing complete bafflement.

"That trunk," said Doña Matilda, pointing to the dusty object, "is all that is left of Carmen's possessions."

"Carmen?"

"Your *novia*," she snapped.

"Oh, *sí*, of course." Delgado wiped his brow with a heavy white handkerchief while he tried to think. "Of course. I—I—you will excuse me," he murmured to the *soldados*. "This is all too much of a shock." And indeed it was. He had not been expecting his *novia* for at least three more months, three months in which he had expected to further enjoy the delights of the ravishing Maria Antonia de Mendoza, his little *rubí*. He wiped his face once more. "Blast the heat," he said to no one and everyone. And blast that *novia*, he thought. Why did she have to go and get herself captured by *indios*? Now what was he going to do? He could not marry her, that was clear. He would not want a woman who had been despoiled. . . . "What kind of Indios?" he asked the fat *soldado*.

"We do not know, señor," came the answer. "Could be Teyas, could be Apaches, could be a band of renegades." He shrugged his ample shoulders. "This woman just arrived by caravan and came to tell us what had happened."

Juan Enrique Delgado eyed the *soldado* with open dislike. He had little respect for *soldados*. All they did was drink and carouse and chase women. Unlike himself, a fine, upstanding member of the community. Why, he owned a silver mine, two salt mines, a beautiful house . . . with a heavy mortgage. Which was why his *novia's* arrival was so important. She carried her dowry.

With a small cry, Delgado ran to the dusty trunk. The lock was broken, and he sank to his knees, throwing open the top and staring at the contents. Then, like a man gone mad, he started rifling through the dresses, all black, plucking each one from the trunk and throwing it onto the courtyard floor. He worked through the trunk that way, and with each dress he seemed to become more frenzied.

The *soldados* watched him in bewilderment, the old dueña with narrowed eyes. "You will not find it," she said at last, when they could all hear the scrabbling of his fingers on the bottom of the trunk. "Those are *my* things in Carmen's trunk. What you are looking for is not there. It is gone—with the *indios*."

Delgado rose slowly and turned to face his relative. "Do I detect a note of satisfaction?" he cried in frustration, prowling towards her. He leaned into her face and said, "Are you glad that it is gone and that I am—" He was about to say penniless, but thought better of it. It would not do to let the *soldados* know too much; they would blab it all over Santa Fe. Instead, he gripped the woman's shoulders and pulled her towards him. "Answer me, you—"

"Please, señor," interrupted the fat *soldado*, laying a restraining hand on Delgado's arm. "This is most irregular. . . ." He had grown to admire the prim woman whom he and his men had escorted out to the hacienda. She had courage to face this fool.

Whereas this rich man—this lazy *peninsular*, sneered Sergeant Carlos Garcia to himself— why, he had yet to see what his bravery was like. So far he had not been impressed watching Delgado scrambling on his knees through women's clothing. No, this was not a man. This was the type of person who thought he was better than those born here. He thought he could come from Spain and take any position he wanted. The sergeant nodded to himself, satisfied with his deduction. Carlos Garcia was well acquainted with the type.

Sergeant Garcia squeezed Delgado's arm. No muscle, he thought, feeling the soft flesh give way beneath the thin shirt. He is a weakling.

The sergeant turned to Matilda Josefa Delgado and bowed. "You do not need to stay here," he offered. "You may come with us back to Santa Fe, and we will find you accommodation. Decent accommodation."

Matilda Josefa thoughtfully regarded the portly *soldado* before her. She was sorely tempted by his offer. Life with the Juan Enrique Delgado that she remembered would be no holiday. Still, he was her nephew . . . very distant, but family nonetheless. "Thank you," she said at last to the *soldado*. "But I will stay with my nephew."

Sergeant Garcia bowed. "Very well," he answered. He shot a glance at Juan Enrique Delgado. "But should you reconsider, please do not hesitate to ask for Sergeant Carlos Garcia. I am well known in Santa Fe."

Matilda Josefa nodded. *"Gracias,"* she said again. She felt shy, almost girlish, in the presence of this confident man. She would like to see him again. Then she caught herself. She was an old woman. She should not be having dreams . . .

"Sí, sí, go, go," Delgado was saying irritably and urging the *soldados* towards the door. "Thank you very much. Good-bye." He closed the door just as Garcia was opening his mouth to say something else, but Delgado did not want to hear another word. He had heard enough.

Delgado hurried back to the doorway leading upstairs to his room and the delectable Maria.

Doña Matilda watched him go. In disbelief, she watched him put a foot on the first stair before she called out, "Nephew, where am I to stay?"

Juan Enrique Delgado turned back and stared blankly across the courtyard at her. "Oh, *sí*, forgive me," he said. "The shock . . ."

"Sí," she answered dryly. She could just imagine the shock to Delgado. But the shock probably stemmed from the loss of the dowry and not the *novia*, Matilda Josefa thought. No, Juan Enrique Delgado had not changed.

Chapter 26

Apacheria

She was gone.

Puma yanked on his leather trousers, not even bothering to lace the fly, and grabbed a spear. He should have known that she would leave after last night. He had scared her away. And it seemed, he thought grimly, that she would rather face the mountains and wild animals than him.

He raced out of the tipi and skidded to a halt. There was Carmen, bending over the small outdoor fire they used on hot days or when they did not want to smoke up the interior of the tipi.

Carmen glanced up at him, surprised, her eyes going to the spear in his hand. Sheepishly, Puma lowered the spear, his blue eyes narrowed.

He looked good this morning, Carmen thought. Her eyes ran over his broad chest with its arrow of black hair that dipped down to the leather trousers. Her eyes widened as she realized where she was staring, and she jerked her gaze back up to his face. Her own face flushed hot.

Puma grunted, turned his back on her, and re-entered the tipi. What kind of a fool was he to rush out after her? She was only preparing the morning meal.

He rummaged in the tipi and when he came out, he was fully dressed, fly laced and leather shirt on. He had braided his hair neatly. The Jicarilla, his people, favored braids instead of the red headbands worn by other Apache groups. He sauntered to the fire and greeted Carmen pleasantly, as if he had not just started the day off with a race out the door.

Carmen smiled to herself and handed him a bowl of stew. They ate together, wordlessly. Carmen wanted to ask him what he was going to do today, whether he planned to hunt, or if he could accompany her and Sky Flyer on their sortie to gather roots, but he looked so distant that she decided to let him speak first.

Puma watched Carmen when he knew she was not looking. He sighed, setting the empty bowl aside. It had seemed so simple the night before when he had decided to make her want him, to make her strong with desire for him, but now, in the morning light, he wondered where he should start.

Carmen took the bowl and started to gather up the cooking utensils. Puma pulled his knife out of the small scabbard at his waist and started sharpening the already sharp blade. Wooing a Spanish woman would probably be different than wooing an Apache woman, he thought. A Spanish woman, especially a rich Spanish woman—here he shot an unreadable glance at Carmen's neat backside as she bent over, fiddling with dishes— would probably expect singing and poetry. So did an Apache woman, but while he knew many Apache songs and could play the flute, he knew only two Spanish songs. Both were drinking songs with nasty words that he had learned from the *soldados*. He did not think Carmen would like to hear those songs.

He sighed. What would impress her? It would have to be something very marvellous, to make her want him. He looked at her again, wondering if she felt the same passion when he kissed her that he did. He shook his head and went on sharpening his knife, pondering how he would get the woman into his bed. Capturing her had been easy. Capturing her heart appeared to be much more difficult.

Carmen watched Puma as he sharpened his knife. His hands were large and well-formed. She thought of those hands as they had been on her body and had to turn away to hide the flush that rose to her cheeks. One dark braid lay across his chest, and she stared at it. What was he thinking? she wondered. Was he remembering the kisses they had shared the first night she had come to the tipi? *She* was remembering them, had thought of them often. He had been so distant since then. He had seemed, to wear a cloak of aloofness when he was near her—until yesterday, when she had returned late and had seen that cloak of aloofness tear.

She studied him with sidelong glances when he was not watching. She had come to depend on him, she realized. One could not help it, given the way of life of the Apaches. Living as close to the natural world as they did, she was finding herself aware of how much he did to make her life easier—bringing meat, teaching her the language, protecting her from wild animals. He even interceded with his people for her if he thought someone was being unkind to her. But she had not told him about how rude Bird Who Plays in the Pinyon Trees was. Carmen feared he would just shrug off the pretty young woman's insults to her.

And he had saved Carmen's life. Several times. That she found the most amazing part of her time with him. She would be dead if it were not for him.

He was strong, he was wily, he had different qualities from those she had observed in Spanish men. She tried to imagine Comandante Diego fighting off a cougar to protect her—and failed.

Next she tried to imagine Fray Cristobal living in a tipi, hunting antelope and talking easily with the Apache people of the village. She failed in that too.

The Alcalde of El Paso del Norte was next. He, she knew, could never have tracked her down through leagues of desert and winding canyons to rescue her from a renegade's hideout. Nor would the Alcalde have rescued Doña Matilda, she thought. The Alcalde remained stubbornly behind his desk, try as Carmen might to pry him away from it.

She gave up the comparisons in disgust. Puma was just different, she had to acknowledge. It was not fair to the Spanish males she knew to compare them to him.

And what of Juan Enrique Delgado? asked the insinuating little voice that came to her on occasion. Was he braver, stronger, better at surviving than Puma? Carmen was shocked at the very question. She wanted to dismiss the question in scorn, but found she did not know the answer. Mayhap she never would.

Puma, she realized now, would make a very desirable mate for some fortunate young Apache woman. That thought gave her pause. Was that why Bird Who Plays was so insulting? Did she have tender feelings for Puma? She frowned. Jealousy would certainly explain the Apache woman's taunting behavior.

Carmen glanced quickly at Puma. Was he attracted to Bird Who Plays? She thought back over when she had last seen him with the young woman. No, he seemed to act no differently with Bird Who Plays than he did with anyone else. If Bird Who Plays was in love with Puma, it was completely one-sided. With a slight twinge of conscience, she resolved to watch the two more closely.

"Carmen."

She looked up guiltily. "*Sí?*" She frowned at him, noting he had dropped Doña, the polite form of address. Had his feelings for her changed too? Was he less respectful? His advances toward her last night made her think so. Yet, he had stopped when she had told him to. She cleared her forehead of the frown.

"I will come with you today," Puma said. "I will do some hunting near you." He did not tell her that she and his mother would probably scare away any kind of game. He was actually accompanying them so he could be with Carmen.

Carmen nodded, not hiding her delight. "It will be good to have your company," she said.

He looked at her, then grunted. Her words seemed sincere.

They got ready and joined several other women heading out to the berry fields. Puma was the only male in the group. He carried a bow, arrows, and spear. Carmen saw that Bird Who Plays was one of the women, and she grimaced. She hoped the young Apache woman would not make trouble on this day.

Bird Who Plays made some comment to her two friends and they all giggled as they stared at Puma. He manfully ignored them.

Once at the berry grounds, the women gradually separated, each drawn by a particular patch of the luscious red berries. Puma stayed near

Carmen for some time. Once in a while, he added berries to her basket. She smiled, but she wondered how he was going to get any hunting done if he stayed near the women. At last, she noticed him move off to a screen of trees and brush.

Puma lay down in the cool shade and placed his spear at his side. Flies and bees buzzed nearby. He could hear the murmur of the women's voices. It was hot. He would just take a little nap.

Carmen was satisfied to know that Puma had gone off to hunt. She hoped he brought down an antelope. A deer would be tasty also. Her basket was getting quite full. No doubt the baskets of the other women were as full.

She swatted at a fly as she looked around for the other women. She could see the tan-clothed forms of Sky Flyer and some of the other women. She did not see Bird Who Plays.

Carmen wiped her brow and spotted a patch of berries near the screen of trees where she had last seen Puma. She worked her way over to the patch.

To her surprise, she heard the murmur of voices. One voice was deep, the other one higher. It sounded suspiciously like Puma and Bird Who Plays!

Unable to help herself, Carmen dropped her basket and crept closer to hear what they were saying. A tiny voice in her mind questioned whether Spanish noblewomen made a habit of eavesdropping on other people, but Carmen quickly squashed the voice. As she crept closer, she wished briefly that her command of the Apache language was better so that she could fully understand what they were saying.

When she peeked into the screen of bushes, she gasped. She did not need to understand the Apache language to understand what those two were up to!

Bird Who Plays sat beside Puma, staring into his face, speaking earnestly. Once she reached out and stroked his face. They looked very cosy together, thought Carmen spitefully. Quietly, she lay down on her stomach, the better to watch.

Puma had awakened suddenly to find Bird Who Plays sitting beside him, a lovely smile on her pretty face.

"Greetings, Puma."

He blinked rapidly, trying to orient himself, and sat up.

"I wanted to speak with you. Privately. This is the first opportunity I have had."

"Bird Who Plays," he reproached her. "A proper Apache maiden does not meet with a man in the bush."

"Puma," she said earnestly. "It is important. I must speak with you."

He nodded stiffly. "Very well."

"I know what happened to you. I know that Angry Man and Takes Two Horses and the others captured you and sold you to the Comanches."

He looked at her sternly. "How do you know this thing? Have you spoken of it to others?"

Her lips tightened for a moment, then she said quietly, "I learned of this terrible thing from Takes Two Horses. When he was courting me, he thought to impress me."

"And were you impressed?"

"Not at all! Oh, Puma, I was very distressed. I told my father that I did not want to hear Takes Two Horses' suit for my hand any longer. I told my father I would never consider marrying Takes Two Horses."

Puma nodded slowly. It was beginning to become a little clearer why Takes Two Horses bore him such enmity. The warrior had been boasting to his maiden and she, instead of being attracted to him, had rejected him to take Puma's side.

"I did not tell anyone," continued Bird Who Plays. "I knew it would do no good because he told me a long time after they had sold you. And I did not want to shame you."

Puma nodded again. He still intended to tell the cacique, Angry Man's father, but had not yet found the best time. He knew the old man would be sorely troubled by this additional betrayal of his son.

"Thank you, Bird Who Plays," Puma said at last.

She smiled at him then, a sad, lovely smile. She touched his face. Her touch was as soft as gossamer. "I—I want you to know that I am very glad that you are back with the Jicarilla people."

Puma looked into her dark eyes, eyes that said so much more. "You once loved Takes Two Horses, did you not?"

She frowned and her eyes flashed. "I did—as a child." She tossed her head. "Now I am no longer a child. I do not love him. It was wrong of him to sell you. Apaches do not do that to other Apaches."

She was correct about that, thought Puma. Takes Two Horses had lost the love of an honorable woman.

Bird Who Plays was looking at him again in that soft manner. "Do you care for the Spanish woman?" she asked.

Puma kept his face impassive to hide his surprise. "Why do you want to know?"

She shrugged. "I but wondered if she had a place in your heart."

A small rustle came to Puma's ears. He concentrated on the beautiful brown eyes fastened so trustingly upon him. Carefully, he said, "I care for the Spanish woman, yes."

Bird Who Plays' face crumpled, and for a moment it looked as if she was going to cry. When she had herself under control, she got up and moved away. Puma watched her leave, sorry to have hurt her. But he knew he could not give her false hope that he would become the suitor to replace Takes Two Horses. Bird Who Plays was young and beautiful. There would be other young men, and one day the young man that she would marry. But it would not be Puma.

He heard another little rustle and smiled to himself. He wondered if Carmen had overheard anything of interest to her.

Chapter 27

He was ready to woo her again. Puma watched Carmen as she sat quietly on the cougar skin, sewing red and yellow-dyed quill beads on a leather shirt.

Carmen determinedly poked the bone awl through the softened deer leather. Sky Flyer had helped her tan the skin, her first deerskin, and Carmen was very pleased with how soft and beautiful the leather was. She had decided that she wanted to make a shirt, the kind the women wore, with decorations. If she ever left the Apaches, the shirt would be a reminder of her time with them.

She was coming to find that she liked this part of her adventure—she was back to thinking of her life as an adventure. She liked Sky Flyer's gentle voice and manner as she instructed Carmen on how to melt the deer fat and brains to rub on a prepared hide. She liked the clear mountain air and the slower way of life of the Apaches. She liked riding the horses, Puma had let her ride the gray Andalusian again. She had even liked berry-picking today. Carmen decided that she would pound some of the berries and then mix them in with fat and dried deermeat to make a delicious pemmican in the way that Sky Flyer had taught her.

She was certainly learning much from the Apaches. She thought of the families that she watched, day after day. They treated each other with kindness for the most part. It did seem a little odd to Carmen that a man never spoke to his wife's mother. Grown sisters and brothers spoke little, either, from what she could observe.

The training the Apaches gave their children amazed Carmen. A common game was for a boy to sneak up and steal grilling meat right from his mother's fire. Then the boy dashed off with the meat, leaving behind a laughing mother.

And the running! A half-grown boy would be told to run to a mountain and back. And when he returned he had to spit out the mouthful of water that he had started out with, to show that he had breathed through his nose properly. Even little toddlers were encouraged to run distances that Carmen thought were impossible for them. Once she overheard an old man telling a group of boys that when they wanted to sleep, they should not sleep in the deep shade under a tree. That was the first place a Spaniard or an enemy or a cougar would look. Instead, they were to choose a place in the grass or in the bush, so that they could sleep safely.

"My mother says that you are learning well." Puma's comment broke into Carmen's thoughts.

"*Sí.*" Carmen was proud of how much she had learned and how fine her quill-work looked.

Puma swallowed. What else could he say? "Your cooking is improving, too," he noted encouragingly.

"Thank you," she said dryly. She still refused to eat dog meat or cook it. Puma had never questioned her on her choice.

Carmen looked at him. Puma was looking distinctly uncomfortable, now that she thought on it. She stared at him. His breath was coming faster, and he was gazing at her very seriously. Was he planning to kiss her again? Something of her thoughts must have shown on her face, for he looked away.

Carmen let out a breath. She suddenly remembered the words she had overheard earlier that day when she had been eavesdropping on Puma and Bird Who Plays. "I care for the Spanish woman, yes," Puma had said.

Carmen had run the words through her mind several times since, wondering if she could have misunderstood. Her grip on the Apache language was still tenuous. Yet the words had been spoken slowly enough that she was certain that that was what he had said. *He cared for her.* Smiling a little to herself, Carmen went back to poking the deerskin with the awl, humming softly under her breath.

And when the women were returning from berry-picking, Carmen remembered that Bird Who Plays had given her a dark glance, a sullen look upon her face, but she had said none of the cruel, taunting words that Carmen had come to expect from the pretty Apache woman.

Carmen glanced swiftly at Puma, still smiling to herself.

He should be glad that she was a cheerful worker, Puma told himself. And that she was beautiful. And that she was kind to his mother and the others. And he was glad about all of that.

It was, he thought irritably, casting about for some reason why he felt so confused, only that she was Spanish. He did not know what to do about her. He did not know how to woo her. And if he did woo her, and she gave herself to him, what would he do then? He would have a Spanish woman living with his people. There would be much anger directed at her. He was surprised that no one had said anything cruel to her yet. He had certainly heard enough comments directed at himself about his own Spanish ancestry, though since Angry Man was gone, there really was no one to taunt him. And no one had said anything since he had returned. Soon he must tell Man Who Listens about the time he had spent in the Mexican prison. Puma realized he was putting it off because he felt shamed—shamed that he had been sold by his

266

own people and shamed that he had spent time as a prisoner of the hated Spanish. He felt somehow tainted and unworthy. He wondered if he had felt these feelings before his captivity. If he had, it had taken harsh events to bring the feelings out.

He glanced at Carmen. She would be a constant reminder of the Spanish, he thought, were he to take her into his lodge and his life. She would be here every day, with her blond hair, her Spanish language, her turquoise jewel eyes—eyes that were staring at him this very moment.

Puma's indecision galled him. Was it because she was Spanish that he hesitated like this? With any other woman—a Ute, even a Comanche—he would not have this hesitation. What was it that the Spanish did to their women to make them so strong? What was it that the Spanish had done to *him*?

With a sigh, Puma got up and left the tipi.

Startled, Carmen watched him go. Something was bothering him this night. She wondered if it had to do with her.

Puma walked the river path, his moccasins making little sound as he walked. The moon was out, and the silver light cast shadows along the path. His senses were alert, but he felt at ease back in his own country.

He was thoughtful as he sauntered along. The question he had set himself was to decide what to do about the Spanish woman. Should he woo her?

He knew he wanted her. Her beauty lured him. But she was more than just a physical presence. She was Spanish and all that that stood for. She was one of the tribe of conquerors who had taken over the land and many of his people. Did he want such a one in his village? He stopped. What was he thinking? He himself had Spanish blood. He himself was one of them, the conquerors. He shook his head. No, he had been raised Apache. His mother was Apache. There was no Spanish in him; it had been eradicated.

Yet, Puma had fit in with the Spanish. He had learned their language, probably with more ease than most young Apache men. And he had learned some of their customs. They were fierce fighters. They were dedicated to their religion. And not all of them were evil. Fray Cristobal, for instance, who had defended Puma to Comandante Diego, was not an evil man. Miguel Baca had tried to be a friend. And even Diego—he, too, had his strengths. He had used all his cunning and arrogance to get his people through the long journey from Mexico City. No, not everything Spanish was bad. Why then, did Puma feel so torn? Why did he feel that the Spanish part of him was some awful mistake, something that should not have happened?

Puma pondered as he walked along. Was it because his Spanish father had deserted him? It hurt to ask that question, Puma realized. For years he had avoided thinking of the man who had sired him. He had rarely questioned Sky Flyer about him. Her gentle answers were not what he wanted to hear. Something fierce inside him rejected his father, just as his father had rejected him.

He had some early memories of his father. Later, Sky Flyer had told Puma that his father had been an explorer. He had ridden into the Sangre de Cristo Mountains one day and joined Sky Flyer's tribe. Teodoro Manuel de Sierra wrote down black marks on white paper about everything he saw. He had drawn pictures of plants, some of them so accurate that Sky Flyer easily recognized them. He had asked many questions about Apache ways. To do so, Puma realized now, his father must have learned the Apache language. But the thought did little to comfort Puma. His father might have been interested in the plants, in the Apache people, but he was not interested in staying with his wife, Sky Flyer, and his son, Puma. When Puma was five years old, his father left, telling his wife that he wished to return to his people. He headed west, out of the mountains, and never came back. The young widow had mourned her husband for a year and then, to protect her son and to survive the Apache life, she had accepted the marriage proposal of One Who Hunts. Together they had raised Puma. Puma loved his stepfather, but the rejection by his birth father was a deep wound from which Puma had not recovered.

Puma sighed. How had capturing one lovely Spanish woman caused all this grief to rise in his heart? Puma halted suddenly, seeing someone sitting on a rock that overlooked the river. Drawing closer, he saw that it was Man Who Listens.

The old man beckoned him to approach. Puma did so and the two sat for some time listening to the water. At last the old man said, "You have not told me what happened."

"No." And Puma did not want to tell the old man now, either. He wanted to be alone with his thoughts. He sighed. But perhaps it was just as well they spoke of it now, in this place. Then it would be done with.

"I was sold to the Comanches."

Man Who Listens nodded, and Puma wondered if the cacique already knew what had happened. After all, Bird Who Plays knew.

"The Comanches sold me to the Mexicans. I spent a year in their prison." Puma got the words out hastily, wanting to pass quickly over the topic. But his face flushed, and his hands tightened into fists. He hated letting the cacique know what had happened to him.

"My son did it." The cacique's voice was forlorn.

Puma's felt relieved. "Yes."

The old man continued to stare at the river. After a while he said, "I have no son."

Puma fidgeted, uncomfortable. He knew it was difficult for the old man to accept how Angry Man had behaved. "You banished him for four years, not a lifetime."

The old man turned to look at Puma. "Yes, that is correct. But the man who left here, full of hate and anger and jealousy, wanting to kill you, that was not my son. The man who sold you to the Comanches, that was not my son." Man Who Listens shook his head. "He is no longer the young man I raised in my tipi. Something happened to him. Something turned him to hate."

Puma pondered. "He wanted to be cacique." Everyone in the Apache tribe knew this.

"He did," agreed Man Who Listens. "But where would he lead our people? I could not agree to let him be cacique. I felt I must pick the wisest man, not give in to my love for my son." Puma saw the old man shake his head. "My son would have made a poor leader for our people."

It was true then. His own father had chosen another to be cacique instead of Angry Man. For a moment, Puma could understand Angry Man's bitterness. He, too, had bitterness toward a father. Then he remembered his own time of slavery, brought on by Angry Man's betrayal, and Puma's empathy vanished.

"You would make a better leader for our people." So, Angry Man had been telling the truth when he said that his father preferred Puma for leader rather than himself. Despite a feeling of sadness for Angry Man, Puma felt jubilant that, despite his Spanish blood, his own people wanted him for cacique. It was a heady honor, one that carried much responsibility and demanded much wisdom.

"You are still young," Man Who Listens was saying. "I do not say that you are ready yet. But you will be."

Puma shook his head. "I cannot even manage my own lodge," he said sadly.

"The Spanish woman?"

"Yes."

Man Who Listens observed, "It is difficult when

a man is at war in himself."

Puma started. Was his dilemma so obvious? Or was Man Who Listens only a keen observer? Puma hoped it was the latter.

"When the war is won, then you will make a fine leader."

"What if the Spanish side of me wins?" asked Puma softly. "The Spanish woman is very strong. I can hear her calling to me, pulling me into her life."

Man Who Listens shook his head. "What you hear is your own voice, your own strength. From within you." He turned to look at Puma out of deepest black eyes. "The woman has no strength if you do not give it to her."

"I need my strength."

"Yes."

"How?" asked Puma. "How do I keep my strength?" He would put her from him if it came to that.

"You give it away."

Man Who Listens was not making sense. "If I give my strength to the Spanish woman, I will become a puppet, a toy."

"Perhaps." Man Who Listens paused. "Then I have chosen unwisely. And lost my son."

Puma felt bewildered. There was much to ponder on. Why did he feel that the fate of his people rested on his decision of what to do with the Spanish woman?

Man Who Listens seemed to sense his confusion. "You have been condemned before for your Spanish blood."

Puma nodded. He could understand the old man again.

"And you have condemned yourself."

Puma nodded reluctantly.

"Perhaps you would do better to thank *Shi Tsoyee* for it."

Puma wanted to explode in anger. With difficulty, he kept his voice under control. "That is part of the problem," he stated evenly. "Why would *Shi Tsoyee* do this to me? I feel torn in half. I did not ask to be born Apache and Spanish!" The anger in his voice was clear, even to himself.

Man Who Listens shrugged. "I do not understand, either," he said.

Puma's anger lessened a little.

"I have lived a long life," continued Man Who Listens. "This will be the first time I know of that *Shi Tsoyee* has made a mistake."

Puma stared at the old man. Was the cacique laughing at him? Puma thought he saw a twinkle in the old man's eye, but it could have been the reflection of the moon.

"This is serious," Puma said with dignity.

"Very," agreed the cacique.

"You have lost a son."

The old man nodded and sighed. "Very serious," he repeated.

"I have lost a father," mused Puma, referring to his Spanish father. He thought for awhile. "How do you know that I will make the right choice?"

The old man shrugged. "The choice will be right. It always is."

"And your son, does he make right choices?"

273

Man Who Listens shook his head. "Not when his head is clouded by jealousy and hate, no."

"Will he ever make right choices?"

Man Who Listens shrugged. "My son also is at war inside himself. There may come a time when he chooses what is right. There may not."

"Like me?"

"Something like you."

Puma did not know if he liked being compared to Angry Man. They were so different. "What makes us different?"

Man Who Listens shrugged. "Some would say the soul. Some would say that you follow the honorable life-way. I do not know."

Puma was disappointed. He wanted all his questions answered. As he stared at the old man, Puma thought he saw the cacique grow smaller. Soon he was staring at an old man, hunched on a rock.

"Good night," said Puma.

Man Who Listens gave a little wave, and Puma turned and strode into the night.

Chapter 28

When he re-entered the tipi, Carmen was still sewing. She glanced up and saw, by the firelight, a disgruntled look on Puma's handsome face. She raised an eyebrow. "What is wrong?" she asked.

He ignored her for a few moments, then with a sigh, he lowered himself down on the blankets. On *his* bed, she noticed. She tried again. "What is the matter?"

Puma stared at her, his fingers draped across his leather-clad knee and flicking restlessly.

Obviously something was bothering him this night, she thought. She wondered if he would tell her, and she marveled even more that she cared.

Silence filled the little dwelling. The soft hoot of an owl came from a distance.

"Damnation!" Puma jumped to his feet.

Carmen stared at him. "Will you sit down?" *What was the matter with him*? she mumbled under her breath.

"Do you know what that means?" He whirled upon her. She jumped at the sudden movement.

"What?" she asked nervously.

"There, that!"

"The owl hooting?" she asked.

He snorted. "That's no owl. That's a ghost. Don't you Spanish know anything?" he sneered.

Carmen's eyes widened. "We, uh, think that when an owl hoots, that is all it is. An owl hoot."

"Well, you are wrong. It is the restless spirit of a dead person, wandering near the tipis. My people know this."

Carmen's lips tightened. "My people know things, too."

Puma snorted. "Like what?" He could not stop himself from stepping closer to the edge of this particular precipice. Damnation, he wanted an argument!

Carmen took a breath. "They know that ghosts don't take the form of an owl. They remain in the form of a person. And Spanish ghosts like to stay around graveyards, not tipis."

"*We* don't have graveyards," said Puma in a superior tone of voice. "We bury our people in a shallow grave on a mountainside, or in a cave."

"Well, I am sure that is all very well for you," remarked Carmen. "But we did not do that in

276

Seville. Why, if we did, the whole mountainside would be covered, there are so many people. Seville is a big city." It was her turn to sound superior.

Puma was silent. He had seen Mexico City. He knew what a city was. He gnashed his teeth. This argument was not going well at all. "I do not like cities," he observed. "I like to live where there is open space and desert and cactus and rocks and mountains and freedom."

Carmen eyed him consideringly. "It is lovely here," she conceded.

Puma was not expecting that. He wanted an argument. An argument would make him feel better. He could release his anger, his pent-up frustration at what to do with the Spanish woman, his recent shame at telling Man Who Listens about his imprisonment. Yes, he needed an argument.

But he was not getting one.

" . . . fresh and clean. Not like our cities. There is nothing but garbage and human waste and dead animals in the streets of Seville. Here it is clean."

Puma grimaced and searched his mind for another way to achieve his argument. But before he could say anything, Carmen was adding, "The mountains are beautiful, *sí*, but you have not seen real beauty until you have been on the ocean!"

Her lips widened in a lovely smile, and for a moment Puma was enchanted. Then he quickly

277

caught himself. In irritation, he snarled, "I do not care about the ocean."

"You would," said Carmen, "were you to see a sunset at sea." Impulsively, she added, "It is so beautiful, Puma. The blue sky, the aquamarine sea, the white sails of a ship . . ." But she was speaking another language to a man who had never seen an ocean or a ship. "And the fish," she exclaimed. "You would like the fish, too! They taste delicious."

"Apaches don't like fish," he grunted.

"Oh." Carmen paused.

Puma stared at her. He wasn't going to get his argument, he could tell. He leaned forward. "I was in Mexico City, the great city of the Spanish."

Carmen nodded.

"And parts of it were very beautiful." Damnation! Now where had that come from? He had wanted to rail against her and her people, not compliment them! "Of course, since I was encaged in their prison, I mostly saw the poverty and squalor and dirt that the Spanish bring with them. That was very ugly, I can tell you." There, that was better. Keep his anger up. "I saw people come and go, Spanish people—*soldados*, farmers, children, women . . ."

Carmen sighed. "It must have been very difficult for you in prison. Your freedom gone. No one to speak your language, no one to—"

"I am not asking for your sympathy," Puma snapped, slanting her a glance.

"I wasn't giving any," she snapped back, eyes furious.

Silence. Carmen concentrated on her sewing, poking viciously at the skin with the sharp awl. Puma drummed his fingers on his knee and listened for another owl hoot. None came.

"About this *novio* of yours," Puma said after a while, unable to tolerate the uncomfortable silence. "What is his name again?" Puma remembered the man's name very clearly. Juan Enrique Delgado. He just wanted to start an uncomfortable conversation.

Carmen's turquoise eyes flashed, and she tossed her head. Puma could tell she did not wish to answer him. Smiling slyly, he leaned forward and put his hand under her chin. "I'd wager your *novio* would certainly like to know where you are right now."

Carmen jerked her chin out of his grasp. "Be careful," she warned. "If I cannot go to him, he may come to me." She could not resist adding, "He will kill you."

In satisfaction, she saw his icy blue eyes flash.

Puma snorted. "Hunh! Some skinny, useless Spaniard will not kill me! I will kill *him*."

"Juan Enrique Delgado is not a skinny, useless Spaniard! He is a tall, noble, graceful man!"

"When did you meet him?" Puma asked with interest.

Carmen faltered. "I—I, well I, that is—"

Puma started to laugh. He could not help it. He lay on his bedroll and snorted and chuckled. Carmen watched him in mingled exasperation and disgust. "What is so funny?" she demanded.

"You," he choked. "You were going to marry a man you had not met." He went on laughing.

"That is the way things are done in Spain," she observed loftily. "I was betrothed to him. Our families agreed—"

"*Sí, sí*," sputtered Puma. "We do that too. The families agree. But always, always there is a chance to see the one you are to marry." He chuckled. "Why, Delgado could be a little round cactus of a man for all you know." And Puma started laughing again.

Carmen observed him indignantly. "He is not," she announced. "He is tall and handsome and "—she paused, thinking of Puma's ice blue eyes—" he has lovely dark eyes, and—and a mustache." She was guessing, making things up about Juan Enrique as she went along, but she would not let this man laugh at her. "And he has a silver mine and plenty of servants, and he is very rich and extremely charming and writes beautiful letters and—"

Puma stopped rolling on the blankets and sat up, the laughter gone from his eyes. "What letters? Give them to me!"

"I don't have any," she wailed. "The letter was left behind in my trunks in the oxcart when El Cabezón stole me!" If only she had the letter. She would read it to this big oaf and prove to him that somebody loved her and cared about her!

She was in anguish that she could not produce the letter. "But I have memorized it," she rushed on. "It starts off beautifully, like this—'My dear little Spanish flower,'" she quoted. "'How I long for the day when I will hold you in my arms, when you will truly be my wedded wife at last—'"

"Enough!" barked Puma. "It turns my stomach to hear such words."

"He *is* poetic," admitted Carmen happily with a toss of her head. "He is *very* poetic." She almost added, *something you will never be*, but she thought better of it when she saw the anger spark in Puma's ice-blue eyes.

Damnation! Puma was getting his argument, but not quite the way he had envisioned.

"There is more," Carmen crowed happily. "'The city of Seville, one of the greatest in Spain, will be so much the poorer when I make you my wife. The sun itself will hide its face in jealousy when I make you mine. The exquisite beauty of your face, your lovely red cheeks, your serene blue eyes, make my heart thump in my chest in anticipation of seeing you—'"

"What red cheeks? What blue eyes?"

"My uncle sent him a portrait of me. Just a tiny one," she added as she saw Puma glower. "I—I had face paint on."

Puma bent her face back and stared at her, his eyes roving over her. "I like the way your cheeks are now," he pronounced. "Pink. And your eyes are turquoise, not blue." He stared at her, then released her. "And they are not serene."

281

Carmen sat back, her hand going to her throat. "*Sí*, well, I—"

"The man's a fool," snapped Puma in irritation. He was done with seeking an argument.

"He is not! He is a very fine, upstanding, noble—"

"Cactus," interjected Puma. "He is a fine cactus of a man." He turned over, his back to her.

Carmen's mouth snapped closed. Now what? She eyed Puma's broad back. Her eyes drifted down to his lean buttocks, where the leather material stretched tightly. She marveled at his strong thighs. She smiled to herself, a small feeling of satisfaction growing in her heart at having bested Puma. She smiled broadly at his back. She could afford to be magnaminous in victory.

"Puma." She said it in a breathy, sing-song voice.

He stirred and grunted.

"Oh, Pumaaaaa . . ."

"What?"

"Are you sulking?"

It took a moment for him to understand the word. When he did, he whirled to face her. "No, I am not sulking!" he roared. "Apaches do not sulk."

"Oh." She chortled to herself because he *had* been sulking. And he thought he was so smart.

Puma did not like the smug look on her face. He stalked over to her. She dropped the awl, her eyes widening uncertainly.

282

Carefully, he removed the skin and needle from her grasp and set them aside. "Do the Spanish sulk?" he asked smoothly.

"S—sulk?" Carmen could not think clearly with him leaning over her like this. She closed her eyes, trying desperately to focus her thoughts. When she opened her eyes, his face was closer, if such a thing were possible.

"I distinctly remember a time or two—" she began. But her words were silenced by the gentle pressure of his lips on hers. He held the kiss and slowly leaned into her. She fell back, and he caught her head.

The kiss caught her off guard. A warm sensation came over her as his lips moved on hers. She moaned and reached up. Lethargically, she put her arms around his neck, the better to get comfortable. When Puma broke off the kiss, she remained there, looking up at him as the firelight flickered on his face. She could hear his breathing quicken and thought, *I did that. He is excited because of me. Because of my kisses.* It was a powerful, exciting thought. Carmen's own breath started to quicken.

She reached for him lazily and pulled his face back down to hers. Their lips met, and this time Puma pushed with his tongue at her mouth. Carmen, curious, let her lips open, and he surged in. She gasped at the warm feeling pooling in her womb. His tongue searched through her mouth, now darting, now mating with her tongue. Carmen moaned.

Then she felt something else. His hand—warm, firm, grasping her hair tightly—holding her head. She could feel the strength of his arm beneath her head and her heart beat faster. He was strong, this man.

He lay upon her, but his weight did not bother her. She could feel that their lower torsos were entwined somehow, and she arched up, the better to press against him. She wanted—no, she needed—to press against him. By now, his breath was coming in quick gasps, and Carmen felt excitement radiating through all of her body.

Puma pulled back a little and covered her face with moist, hot kisses. Then, slowly, stealthily, he reached for the deerskin dress she wore. He gave a little tug, and Carmen moaned, placing a hand on his. She would not let him take it off. *Very well*, he thought. *I have other ways.*

He began stroking her legs. She liked that and let him. He could feel the strong muscles of her legs, and the thought of those legs wrapped around him spurred him on to other, more sensuous movements.

Carmen could feel his hands stroking the skin of her thighs, then gasped as he gripped her buttocks. He squeezed them and she found herself pressing rhythmically against him. Her head was floating. Her body was floating. She felt wonderful!

One hand was approaching the front of her now, his fingers moving gently in and out of the crisp curls of her womanhood and for a moment she stiffened at this new feeling. Then she relaxed. It felt good, it felt warm, and she let him touch her.

Puma was ready. He was more than ready. He was fit to burst. It was all he could do to move slowly and easily so as not to scare her. When he saw that she accepted his gentle stroking, he positioned himself, moving on top of her. Then, propping himself on arms that trembled with excitement, and keeping his movements as gentle as he could, he lowered himself until his manhood touched the very entrance of her.

He pushed. Carmen's eyes flew open. "What?"

"Easy," he moaned. "Let me . . . ." And he was inside her, using all of his strength to pause for a moment to let her sheathing muscles accept him. He could not, would not, take his satisfaction until he knew it was good for her, too. He heard her moan, and then she clutched at him, her legs open and urging him on. Thankfully, eyes closed tightly, Puma pushed once more. Then he was surging into her, then out, then in, his body unable to stop in his excitement. They moved as one in the age-old rhythmic dance.

Carmen was caught up in a maelstrom of emotions and physical sensations. She could hear his heavy panting, her own echoing his. She could feel his strength as he surged into her, and she marveled at her own as she met him, arching. She wondered at her body withstanding the powerful force of his and she exalted in the new knowledge of their bodies coming together. She wrapped her legs around him, holding him to her tightly in ever-increasing need as his whole body went stiff. Then she, too, stiffened and joined him as a welling, beautiful sweetness rippled in arcs outward from her womanhood. *"Dios!"* she cried.

Puma hugged her tightly until her gentle spasms stopped. For a short while, the only sound in their tipi was their own heavy breathing. Carmen could see a sheen of sweat on both their bodies. She attempted to lift a lock of his hair, and then she let it fall, too exhausted to do anything more.

Puma was the first to recover. He gave her a long, slow kiss on her lips, then covered her face with kisses.

Carmen smiled and accepted his worshipping attentions as her just due. She lay looking up at him, replete with lazy satisfaction. "That was wonderful."

Puma grinned back. "There are some things we Apache and you Spanish know how to do very well together."

She laughed and raised herself until she was sitting up. She tugged at her dress. She finally got the garment off and tossed it across the tipi. Then, leaning back on her elbows, she smiled. "Very well, indeed," she agreed. She reached out and pulled him to her. "Come here," she purred. Puma went willingly.

Chapter 29

Puma staggered out of the tipi. *Dios*, that woman had stamina! She could give an Apache a challenge in endurance any day, he thought. And here he had been worried that she would not take to the Apache life, that she might prove too weak. Had he been wrong! If anyone was proving too weak, it was he.

He stirred at the dry ashes of the outside fire, wondering what he was going to make for breakfast. Carmen's lovemaking tended to make him forget about going hunting. Now that he thought of it, she had not been out gathering any roots or berries lately either. That was what happened when one spent as much time in bed as they had done recently.

Puma chuckled to himself as he recalled his stepfather, One Who Hunts, taking him cautiously aside one morning last week. Puma had just dragged himself out of the dwelling. The older Apache had mentioned sternly that too much lovemaking was not healthy, that once or twice a week was sufficient. Puma almost laughed aloud, but he caught himself in time. One Who Hunts would have been astounded to know that once or twice a day was little enough for him and Carmen. Once or twice sufficed for a morning! Puma groaned. Would he ever get enough of this woman?

In the tipi, Carmen was smiling serenely at the tanned hide wall above her head. Puma had shown her a whole new world. He had shown her the world of sensuality. A month had gone by since they had first made love, and in that month Carmen had explored new sensations that she had never known existed. Puma was an extremely virile man. And to think that married people did this all the time! 'Twas a well-kept secret that no one talked about—the fun of lovemaking.

She sat up slowly, easing her lithe body from under the cougar skin cover. Stretching, she yawned and thought of the day ahead. They really must get some food.

Chapter 30

Santa Fe

Her lips pursed, Doña Matilda Josefa Delgado regarded her nephew stolidly across the breakfast table. Even the crisp tortilla and the spicy meat placed in front of her by the obsequious peon did not cause her to blink an eye. No, her gaze was upon Juan Enrique Delgado. Her toe started tapping on the hard brick floor. When he still did not look up from his reading, she lost patience and said, "Are you going to speak with me, or are you going to keep reading those useless reports?" She delivered this in her best maiden-aunt voice.

It got indifferent results. Delgado looked up, and she noted how shiny the top of his balding head looked. He had had a full head of black hair before leaving Spain, she remembered. Now just the sides of his scalp sported hair. A fly buzzed about the kitchen and finally landed on his shiny dome. He swatted it away, no doubt wishing he could do the same to his aunt.

"Well?" he sighed wearily.

"What," she demanded, "are you going to do about Doña Carmen?"

"Doña Carmen?"

"Your *novia*."

Juan Enrique Delgado sighed again, even more wearily. "What is there to do?" Then he shrugged and went back to reading his silver mine reports. "She is with the *indios*," he mumbled. "Let them keep her."

Matilda Josefa Delgado drummed her fingers vigorously on the table. Delgado looked up at the noise and frowned.

"A month has gone by," Matilda Josefa said as slowly and as clearly as she could. "And in that time, you have done nothing—*nothing*—to get help for that poor girl!"

"The *soldados* are looking for her," answered Delgado sullenly. He looked toward the doorway, and suddenly his whole demeanor changed. He beamed, his black hairy eyebrows rising to meet his forehead. "Ah, Maria, my little *rubí*. What a pleasant surprise!" He leaped up, letting the reports on his lap slide unheeded to the floor. He stepped on them as he pulled out a chair for the approaching redhead.

Matilda Josefa took one look at Delgado's mistress and sniffed disapprovingly. She turned to gaze out the window. Ever since she arrived, she had known what was going on here—oh *sí*, indeed she did. It was shameful the way Juan Enrique was carrying on with this loose hussy when all the time La Carmencita was somewhere out in the forsaken desert! The very thought gave Matilda Josefa a pain in the stomach. Her thin lips turned down in distaste. If only there was some way she could make her nephew realize his responsibility to Doña Carmen.

Then Matilda Josefa went suddenly still, staring thoughtfully. Slowly she turned back to her nephew and his loose hussy. Mayhap there *was* a way. . . .

She watched with veiled eyes as Maria Antonia de Mendoza languidly sat down, accepting Delgado's fluster as her due. The woman's pale skin stood out starkly against the deep red of her hair, and she was wearing a green robe that matched her eyes. She towered over Juan Enrique. Matilda Josefa watched her nephew return to his place, clattering awkwardly into his chair.

"I will have one of those and two of those," said the pleasantly rounded Maria, pointing to the plate of sliced meat and the plate of warm tortillas. Maria glanced at Matilda Josefa out of her long green eyes and yawned as Juan Enrique jumped up to fill her plate. Maria knew that the old Aunt heartily disapproved of her. She gave her a slow perusal. "When are you leaving?" she asked bluntly.

291

Theresa Scott

For a moment, Doña Matilda was taken aback. She liked Delgado's mistress about as much as she liked rattlesnakes, and she had found the woman to be as friendly as one. She had never actually carried on a conversation with the hussy, preferring to let the occasional contemptuous sniff speak for her instead. And now the hussy was actually asking her a question?

She pursed her lips and decided to ignore the impertinent redhead. Matilda Josefa was out for bigger game. "Your *novia*," she reminded Juan Enrique Delgado smoothly, sliding a glance at Maria. "We were speaking of your *novia*."

Maria Antonia wilted a little, and Matilda Josefa smiled to herself. "When did you say you were sending out a search party for your *novia*?"

"I am not sending out a search party for my *novia*," snapped Delgado. "She is of no use to me. She is with the *indios*, used by every man in the tribe by now! Her dowry is lost. Of what good is she to me?"

Maria Antonia murmured approvingly as she nibbled at a tortilla.

Matilda Josefa leaned forward. "Doña Carmen is pretty," she offered enticingly. "Actually, she is *very* pretty."

Maria Antonia slanted a glance at the older woman and stuck out her tongue when Delgado was not looking.

His mouth full, Delgado pushed another tortilla consolingly in the direction of his mistress.

"Of what use is pretty when she has no money?" he sneered.

"Aaah, so that is it."

"Of course. That has always been it. That was why I wanted to marry the woman. She was supposed to bring me a large dowry—one that would pay for more miners to work my silver mine, for the expensive upkeep on my house . . ."

"How you do go on, Juan," giggled Maria Antonia.

Delgado patted her knee. When he saw that his aunt was staring thoughtfully out the window, he let his hand slide a little higher. His breathing quickened. "My little *rubi*," he murmured.

Matilda Josefa frowned thoughtfully. It was obvious that her nephew had not changed—had, if anything, grown more calloused over the years. Yet his infatuation for Maria Antonia surprised her. It did not fit with the Juan Enrique she remembered. She sighed. She supposed she would find the answer to that riddle some day, but it would probably mean speaking with Maria Antonia, not something that Matilda Josefa particularly relished.

"Tell us again how Juan's poor, poor *novia* was stolen," said Maria Antonia, her green eyes sparkling with mischief—or was it malice? "I believe you said an ugly *indio* put her on his horse . . . ?" Maria pretended to shiver deliciously; her action was noticed by Delgado, and he frowned.

Matilda Josefa sniffed. She would not speak to that woman if she could help it. Then she paused. If she could tantalize Maria Antonia's curiosity or lust, or even Juan Enrique's greed, then mayhap one of them could be convinced to search for La Carmencita. Slowly she turned to face the irritating redhead. "He was not ugly," she corrected. "He was handsome." *Dear Lord, forgive me for lying,* she prayed and barely refrained from crossing herself.

Maria Antonia's eyes opened a little wider and she sat up. "Handsome?" she murmured. "Oh my, how—how terrible!" With her green eyes wide, Maria looked to be more titillated than scandalized.

And Matilda Josefa was not loathe to supply the details. "Quite, quite handsome," she added helpfully. "In fact, every single one of them was handsome." In truth, she could not remember what the *indio* men looked like, she had been so terrified.

Juan Enrique Delgado looked up from reading his mine reports. "Women," he snorted and possessively squeezed Maria Antonia's leg, lest she forget who was keeping her. Maria gently removed his hand and looked questioningly at the other woman. "Do tell us more," she whispered.

Matilda Josefa smiled to herself. Deceit must be bred into the blood of the Delgado family, she decided, and plunged on. "I believe he was the one who stole the dowry. I distinctly remember seeing him hold the sack of jewels. The dowry," she explained kindly, "was all in jewels." She tapped her lips thoughtfully. "*Sí*, now that I think of it, I am certain that it was him."

"Sack of jewels?" piped up Delgado. "You did not tell me that you saw someone with the sack of jewels. You only told me that the dowry was gone!"

"I forgot."

Juan Enrique Delgado glowered at her. Maria Antonia frowned.

Matilda Josefa cleared her throat. "The—the terror of it all, you know," she said. "I have only just been able to think of it . . ." She touched her forehead, trying to think. There was more to this deceit than met the eye. How did Juan Enrique Delgado do it? "Often La Carmencita would open up the sack and show me her jewelry. Diamonds, pearls, rubies, and emeralds made into necklaces, bracelets, rings, that sort of thing." Matilda Josefa smiled with what she hoped passed for blissful reminiscence. "We spent many fond hours playing with the baubles." *Dear Father, forgive me. It was only a tiny lie. La Carmencita played with her jewelry and I dozed.*

Delgado carefully folded the report he was reading and placed it on the table. "Would you," he began, watching her like a coyote does a rabbit, "recognize those pieces of jewelry if you ever saw them again?"

"Of course," assured Matilda Josefa brightly. "I saw them so many times. . . ." She waved a hand airily.

"I see," said Juan Enrique thoughtfully. There was silence in the kitchen. Maria Antonia nibbled on a tortilla, then brazenly nibbled on Juan Enrique's puffy little ear. He pushed her away absently. "So, it is likely that the *indios* will not know the value of those jewels or what to do with them. . . ."

"Oh no," laughed Matilda Josefa, cringing inside at how easily the Delgado deceit had come to her once she had started. "Why, Carmen herself practically told them! She cried and screamed and held onto the sack. They finally threatened to cut off her hands to get her to release it." *More lies*, she thought. *Saints preserve me. . . .*

"How exciting!" cried Maria Antonia.

"*Sí*, my little *rubí*," said Delgado with a grim smile. "But not for the reasons you think." Turning once more to his aunt, who looked a trifle pale this morning, he asked, "I wonder, if we were to search the area . . . asking for the jewelry, we might have better luck. . . ."

"What about La Carmencita?" shot back Doña Matilda.

"Oh, *sí*, *sí*, her too." Juan Enrique looked irritated. "We could ask about her. Why, who knows? Once we find the jewelry, it might be very easy to find the woman." Privately, he thought that if he found the jewels, he would not waste time looking for one lone white woman lost in the Land of the Apaches. But he would say nothing of this to his aunt. After all, she seemed rather fond of the lost Doña Carmen.

296

"Here," he said to his aunt, shoving a piece of paper under her nose. "Draw a picture of each necklace, each ring, every brooch, every single piece of jewelry that you can remember."

"Ah, well, you see, I must . . ." Doña Matilda swallowed as she stared at the blank piece of paper. "I must have a little time. To remember, you see." That was true, by the saints. Mayhap she could remember if given some quiet. "Let me retire to my room. . . ." She rose.

Juan Enrique rose with her, bowing slightly. "*Sí, Tía* Matilda." He rubbed his hands together. "Take all the time you need," he added graciously. He sat back down on his chair, a smirk on his face as his aunt hurried from the room. "It has already been a month," he observed to Maria. "What is another few days? And if we can find the jewels . . ."

Maria giggled. "Do you think we shall find your *novia*?" she asked idly, as she ran her fingers through the thin fringe of Delgado's hair.

"Doña Carmen?" he answered in surprise. "I am not going to hunt for Doña Carmen. I am going to hunt for the jewels. If we circulate drawings of the jewelry pieces to traders in the area where she was stolen, talk to peons, talk to any *indio* we can find, we might yet track the jewels down. Especially if we offer horses or arquebuses for information. *Indios* love horses, and weapons too," he sneered. "But we had better not let the *soldados* know we are offering guns to the Indians. They do not like that. They fear the guns will be used against *them*!"

Under Maria's wide-eyed green gaze, Delgado snorted at the cowardice and poor reasoning of the *soldados*. "If the jewels are still around," he continued, "I will find them! I am not going to lose a fortune if I can help it!" He frowned. "I just wish I had thought of it sooner," he muttered.

"Oh, Juan Enrique," Maria breathed. "You are smart. . . ." And she gave him a peck on the cheek.

Juan Enrique Delgado blushed and took her plump white hand. "My little *rubí*, I have an idea," he said eagerly. "After we find the jewels, let us—let us get married!"

Maria's other pale hand went to her full breast in a gesture of surprise. "Us, my dear Juan Enrique? Why, this—this is so sudden! Why, it is—" Her long green eyes narrowed even more as she visibly searched for words. It would be the hope of a lifetime to marry a rich man like Juan Enrique Delgado. And she had thought that to be his mistress would be satisfaction enough! The cast-off wife of a deserting *soldado* left to fend for herself in Santa Fe would finally be worth something in this forsaken frontier!

Maria smiled secretly to herself. She was so glad that she had decided to fake the loss of her virginity that first night that Delgado had claimed her. Why, everything he had done since then showed how much he was besotted with her. And now, to propose marriage . . .! It was better than she could have hoped for! A shine came into her green eyes as she leaned closer to him and whispered, "Why, *sí*, dear Juan Enrique. Let us do that."

Chapter 31

Apacheria

Sky Flyer came to call upon Carmen. A group of about six women were going out to collect the last mescal of the season. Soon the plants would flower and be unfit for use. When Sky Flyer inquired whether Carmen cared to join them, Carmen quickly agreed. While it was important to the Apaches to gather and roast and store plenty of mescal for the winter, it was more important to Carmen to have some time away from Puma—to think.

The women walked until they came to a large flat field some distance from the village. Many mescal plants grew there.

Because the lower part of the plant, the crown, was as heavy as it was delectable, the women decided to build the roasting pit in the field, rather than carry the heavy crowns back to their tipis. The whole gathering and cooking process would take two or three days, depending on how big the mescal heads were.

Carmen had just pushed her sharp-pointed digging stick into the head of a particularly stubborn plant when she noticed Bird Who Plays in the Pinyon Trees approaching. Dragging a basket behind Bird Who Plays was a pretty little girl, about seven years old. Carmen had noticed her frequently accompanying Bird Who Plays and thought mayhap she was a younger sister or cousin.

Today Bird Who Plays' face looked sullen, and Carmen felt her stomach tighten. It was the first day of her monthly flow, and she did not need or want a confrontation with Bird Who Plays. But the girl showed no sign of being distracted from her course towards Carmen. She came steadily onward, her eyes focused directly on Carmen. She looked to be spoiling for a fight. Mayhap it was the first day of *her* flow, too, thought Carmen irritably.

Carmen kept working at the stubborn crown of the plant. She saw Bird Who Plays' feet stop directly in front of her, yet Carmen kept working. She finally stopped when she realized that the woman was still staring at Carmen's efforts to get the mescal crown to roll out. And laughing.

Wearily, Carmen straightened and wiped a dirt-encrusted hand across her sweating brow, leaving a streak of brown earth on her pale forehead.

Bird Who Plays saw it and smiled. The white woman looked particularly foolish with the streak of dirt on her face.

"What do you want?" asked Carmen.

"I came to tell you that you are a no-good woman."

"What do you mean?" Carmen did not like the sound of this.

"You are not married to Puma. You are a no-good woman."

Carmen stuck her chin out. She saw the little seven-year-old watching her, her bright eyes curious. Carmen lowered her voice. "It is none of your business."

"Hah," snorted Bird Who Plays. "No Jicarilla man wants a woman who is not a virgin. Apache woman must stay pure until marriage. Spanish woman does what she likes, eh?" Bird Who Plays spat insolently on the ground. "No Jicarilla man wants such a woman for his wife."

Carmen's lips tightened. "I fail to see how it is any of your business what I do."

Bird Who Plays smiled. "Puma will throw you away. Then he will marry me."

"A good Apache woman," observed Carmen sarcastically.

"Just so."

"Fine," snarled Carmen. She was feeling degraded and hot and tired and humiliated. It was not the Spanish way to have relations with a man before marriage either. But she would not tell Bird Who Plays that. "I want to return to my people, anyway." In truth, she had not thought of her people, or Juan Enrique Delgado—here she winced slightly—in over a month. She had thought only of being with Puma, of loving him.

Carmen sighed in irritation. Why had Bird Who Plays chosen today of all days to badger her, when her her emotions were pulled in every direction? Mayhap the Apache woman spoke the truth. Mayhap Puma would tire of her and her non-Apache ways and cast her aside. What would happen to her then? Would she be digging mescal for the rest of her life for some other Apache man? The very thought sent a shudder through her. And now that she thought on it, Puma had not asked her to marry him, not since that one time when he first brought her to his village. She wondered suddenly if mayhap he did not really want to marry her. Their lovemaking was wonderful, but mayhap that was all he wanted.

She realized now that she had been building little plans in her mind, just beneath the surface, and one of those little plans suddenly jumped out at her. It was that Puma would love her and want to marry her—this fantasy certainly legitimized for Carmen what they were doing in bed night after night. And now, here was this Apache woman telling her that Puma would never marry her! It was too much.

"Go away," Carmen muttered, taking the easiest way out. She did not want to talk about this.

Bird Who Plays smiled. "You will see. Puma will get tired of you. Throw you away. Marry me." With a confident smile, Bird Who Plays turned and walked off. The little girl dragged the burden basket after her.

Carmen sighed and swiped at her hot and sweating forehead once more, leaving another dirt streak. In sudden anger, she tore into the plant, poking viciously with her stick. Then she picked up a rock as Sky Flyer had shown her and pounded at the plant. The crown rolled out. It was a big one. Swiftly Carmen turned the plant over and cut off the outside leaves to expose the white underpart. In satisfaction, she dropped the heavy crown into her basket and grimaced. Would that she had dealt as well with Bird Who Plays in the Pinyon Trees!

The roasting pit fire was lit. The flames leaped and flickered in the large pit, as broad across as a man is tall. The deep pit had first been lined with rocks, then layers of wood had been placed in its depths. Next, a layer of rocks covered the burning wood. After the fire had reduced the wood to ashes, the mescal heads would be placed on top to cook. Wet grass would cover the mescal with a layer of dirt over that so that the vegetables would roast and not steam. Carmen had seen this done several times already during her stay with the Apaches. She had helped Sky Flyer lay out their mescal heads in preparation for placing them on the fire later.

The sun had just retreated behind the mountains and Carmen lay back, resting and listening to the night sounds here and there in the distance. Suddenly one of the women ran to the center of the mescal camp, next to the pit. She dropped the load of wood she had been gathering and screamed, "Where is Snowberry? Where is Snowberry?"

Carmen sat up when she recognized the frantic woman as Bird Who Plays. Snowberry must be the pretty little seven-year-old, Carmen guessed.

Sky Flyer got to her feet from where she had been sitting and ran up to Bird Who Plays. "What happened? What happened?"

There was a babble of voices. Several women were speaking at once, in panic. Eventually Carmen understood that Bird Who Plays and Snowberry had gone to gather wood for the fire pit one last time before nightfall. Snowberry had wandered off a little distance from Bird Who Plays, though not far enough to alarm the woman. But when Bird Who Plays had finished gathering her bundle of sticks, Snowberry was nowhere in sight. Bird Who Plays had called and called, and now she was deathly afraid that something had happened to the girl. Tearfully, she begged the other women to come to her aid to help find the child. It did not help that Bird Who Plays had heard an owl hoot just as she became aware that Snowberry was gone.

Despite Bird Who Plays' unkindness to her in the past, Carmen could not turn her back on the other's frantic pleas and the obvious fear evident in that usually sullen face. Carmen found herself volunteering, along with Sky Flyer, to go with Bird Who Plays into the dark to look for Snowberry. No other women volunteered because of fear of the ghosts that lurked when the owl hooted.

What am I doing here? Carmen asked herself as she trudged along in the dark. There was a sliver of moon out this night. *I don't like the dark*, thought Carmen. *I feel afraid, too. But I am an adult. Adults are not supposed to fear the dark*.

She could barely see Sky Flyer.

Carmen heard an owl hoot again. She watched Sky Flyer pause, heard her clear her throat, then continue on, calling anxiously for Snowberry. Carmen's estimation of Puma's mother increased. She knew the older woman was fearful of the hovering Apache ghosts, yet she was forcing herself to continue searching for Snowberry. Carmen took heart from Sky Flyer's bravery and called out the child's name—her real name. No answer. Bird Who Plays, too, kept on searching.

Carmen walked along for some time, keeping Sky Flyer in sight as much as possible. Though Carmen called Snowberry's name over and over, she received no answer. Neither Sky Flyer nor Bird Who Plays seemed to hear anything either. Then came two more owl hoots. Still the three women kept searching. At last, Carmen was dragging her feet. Her legs ached. How long they had been calling and searching, she did not know. She halted, listening to the sound of her own heavy breathing.

"Let us go back," Carmen heard Sky Flyer call. "It is very dark. We will search again in the morning."

Bird Who Plays in the Pinyon Trees soon joined Puma's mother, and Carmen watched as they both turned back to the warm glow of the distant fire pit.

Carmen had briefly explored a shallow ravine, and she stood there now, willing herself to give one last try. "Snowberry! Snowberry, please answer!"

But there was only silence. The other two women were now walking together, back to the firepit. Carmen could see them move through the brush. She had better hurry if she expected to catch up with them; otherwise she would be out alone in the desert. Like Snowberry.

Carmen said a brief prayer that the child would be found safe, then looked around once more. There were lumps and bumps on the ravine floor. She knew they were rocks, having stubbed her toes several times.

She walked along the little ravine, heading back to the firepit. She was careful to keep Sky Flyer and Bird Who Plays in sight. The ravine widened, and Carmen had just started to scramble up the side of the slope when she tripped and fell, putting out her hands to catch herself. Her hand touched something soft and warm. She drew back in alarm, then whispered, "Snowberry?"

The slope of the ravine was in darkness and she could see nothing; the moonlight bounced off the other side of the ravine. "Snowberry?" Gingerly, Carmen reached out to touch the softness and warmth. It was a little arm. She followed the arm to the trunk of the body as though she were a blind woman. "Snowberry?" Her hands patted the little face; she could feel warmth. Quickly she sought the up and down movement of the child's chest. She was alive!

"Snowberry!" Carmen's shout had alerted Sky Flyer and her companion.

"Over here!" Carmen yelled. The two women ran to join Carmen. Sky Flyer must have been able to see something for she said, "There is blood."

Carmen gasped.

"On her head," explained Sky Flyer. "Heads bleed much. Help me lift her." The three women struggled to lift the nearly lifeless child and somehow managed to get her dead weight aloft. They headed back to the firepit, staggering and stopping for occasional rests.

All three were breathing heavily with their precious burden when they finally staggered into camp—Carmen carrying Snowberry at the shoulders, Sky Flyer at her feet, and Bird Who Plays wringing her hands and groaning over every twitch of the child's arm or leg.

The women carefully placed Snowberry on a blanket, and Bird Who Plays dropped to her knees muttering endearments the whole time. She murmured and ran her hands swiftly over the little girl. Carmen thought she was pleading with the child to wake up.

Sky Flyer gently pried Bird Who Plays away from Snowberry, assuring the older girl that Snowberry needed rest. Sky Flyer explained in a soothing voice that in the morning they would take Snowberry back to the village and the shaman would help her.

Bird Who Plays allowed herself to be led over to her sleeping place, but she would not sit down. Instead, she snatched up her blanket and marched back to Snowberry. Bird Who Plays spread the blanket out next to the unconscious child and lay down, her arms creeping around the frail girl. Carmen saw her give the child a tender kiss on the forehead.

Carmen turned away, tears in her eyes. *Holy Mother, if there is anything good in this world, any justice, any love, then let that little girl live*, she found herself pleading desperately. *Let her live and be healthy*.

Chapter 32

The women brought the injured child back to the village early the next morning. Carmen stood with several women and watched as Snowberry was carefully laid on a blanket in front of the shaman's tipi. Dried blood still covered one side of her head, and there was a large purple lump on her forehead. She looked very pale, and her breathing was shallow. Carmen guessed the child had tripped in the night and fallen, bumping her head. It bothered Carmen that the child had not yet awakened. She certainly was sleeping a long time.

The shaman, an old, wrinkled man, knelt down, eyes closed, beside the child. After some minutes, he called out for water. His assistant, a much younger man, brought a bowl of water and wiped the blood from the child's hair and head. She still looked pale and sickly.

"The owl wanted this child," announced the old shaman. "That is why she had this accident. She is in great danger from the darkness sickness. The owl wants to snatch her spirit."

Gasps were heard here and there. A murmur ran among the women, and Carmen leaned closer to listen to two women whispering. They both agreed that the hooting owl they had heard the night before had been the spirit of an old man who had died earlier. It must be he who was after the child. Yes, the shaman knew this. He was very wise.

Carmen frowned. Privately, she had her doubts. She still thought that the child had bumped her head.

The old shaman started to sing. People began drifting away, disturbed by the words of his song. It was very frightening when a shaman must challenge a ghost. Carmen stayed to watch him moving colored sands into a design—a sand painting. Sky Flyer came up and ushered her away before she could see very much.

Carmen carried her basket of roasted mescal heads to her tipi. Puma was not there. Mayhap he was hunting, she thought. She began pounding the roasted heads of mescal to make them into flat cakes. Then she laid them out to dry in the sun. They would be stored for winter after they were dried. As she worked, she could hear the shaman singing and she thought of Snowberry. She hoped the shaman had the power to stop the little child's death. His voice would rise and fall, stop then start up once more. Evening was falling, and he was still singing.

Puma had not returned. Carmen began to grow lonely for him. Sky Flyer stopped by and invited Carmen to partake of the evening meal with her. Carmen quietly refused the invitation, though she liked the older woman. She wanted to be at the dwelling when Puma returned.

Carmen ate her simple dinner of roasted mescal and dried meat. She was becoming used to *indio* foods now and liked them. But what she would not give for a hot cup of chocolate! She sat there reminiscing about how she drank hot chocolate at every meal back home in Spain. She wondered if hot chocolate could be found in Santa Fe. She doubted it; Fray Cristobal had not mentioned it as one of the items he was bringing to the colonists. She sighed and set aside her cup of plain water. Where was Puma?

Carmen walked to the door of the tipi and stared outside. Night had fallen, and the village had grown quiet. The old shaman was still singing, and his voice taking on a peculiar intensity, to her mind. Men who did battle with ghosts, she thought, must be very brave.

The little fire she had lit inside the tipi had almost died down. Carmen glanced at it, wondering if she would sleep well with no fire and no Puma. Probably not. She was just reaching for an armful of the wood stacked near the door when an owl hooted. The shaman heard it too, she guessed, for he suddenly stopped singing. Then he began chanting again, loudly, and this time his assistant accompanied him. If one must do battle with ghosts, it helped to have a companion, Carmen thought approvingly.

She retreated into the tipi, putting sticks on the fire. She snuggled under the covers of her bed and listened to the chanting. She fell asleep listening to the chanting.

She awoke to here a twig snap outside the door. All her senses were alert, and her heart was pounding. Then she heard a muffled curse and a thud. Puma! She would recognize his voice anywhere.

Puma lurched into the tipi. "What was in that basket?" he demanded.

Carmen smiled. He looked so good, his big body outlined in the tipi's small space. How she had missed him! "Mescal heads," she answered calmly. "Roasted, pounded, dried mescal heads."

He grunted. "They are scattered everywhere now," he growled. "I did not see them." In truth, he had been so intent on finding Carmen that he had not paid any attention to the several baskets scattered near the entrance to the tipi. His Apache night vision definitely needed improving!

"Come here," Carmen invited, holding out her arms.

Puma stripped off his clothes and dived into bed beside her.

"How I have missed you," she murmured, hugging him.

"Me, too."

They snuggled together until their passion overwhelmed them. When their lovemaking was

313

over, Puma grabbed a fistful of her thick hair and held her fast. He gazed possessively into her turquoise eyes. "You are mine," he murmured, as if to himself.

Carmen went still. She regarded him steadily, feeling a little sad all of a sudden. "*Sí*," she said slowly. Bird Who Plays' words came back to her then, and she wondered if he would ever again ask her to marry him. "Puma?"

"Mine," he said. "No one else's."

Her eyes widened in astonishment. "There is no one else, Puma. Only you."

He pulled her face closer to his. He studied her, his eyes roving over her pale, delicate face, her slim shoulders. "I will keep you, Carmen. No matter what."

She was about to ask him what he meant, when several shouts outside the tipi interrupted their intense interlude. Shakily, not knowing why her heart was pounding as it was, Carmen got dressed and followed Puma out of the tipi. The whole village was in an uproar.

"Snowberry is better! The shaman has cured her!" yelled a woman as she ran past the tipi. Carmen and Puma hurried with the others to gather at the shaman's dwelling.

To Carmen's surprise and delight, Snowberry was sitting up, taking a drink of water from the shaman's assistant. Carmen ran up to her. The girl looked much better. Her eyes were alert, though she still seemed very pale, and her body seemed limp. She needs rest, thought Carmen.

Bird Who Plays in the Pinyon Trees was pushing through the crowd of people gathered around the newly recovered child, and Carmen smiled to herself to see the happiness in the young woman's face.

Bird Who Plays hugged Snowberry. Then the woman glanced up and her eyes met Carmen's. Then Bird Who Plays looked away. Carmen could still feel the smile on her face, but she wondered at the strange look that had passed between Bird Who Plays and herself. She was given no more time to think about it before Puma drew Carmen away from the happy little scene.

"What is it?" Carmen asked in bewilderment. "Snowberry is better! Are you not pleased?"

"I am pleased," he said in his deep voice. His hand on Carmen's arm tightened. "Do not leave the tipi tomorrow. Nor for the next several days."

"But Puma, I have work to do. Your mother needs help—"

"Let someone else help my mother. You stay in the tipi."

Carmen frowned. "Why?"

He did not answer.

"Puma, I have a right to know why you are demanding this of me. It is a small place, that tipi. I do not want to stay in it for several days."

"You will do it," he said and the harshness in his voice surprised her.

When he saw her toss her head and set her jaw, he relented a little. "Spanish strangers have

315

been seen. They have been asking about a pouch of colored rocks. And about a blond Spanish woman, taken from a caravan."

Carmen gasped.

Puma's eyes narrowed, and his grip grew even tighter on her arm. "*Sí*," he acknowledged. "Your *novio* is looking for you."

Chapter 33

Somewhere in Apacheria

Juan Enrique Delgado wiped his sweating brow. A piece of white cloth that he had tied over his head for protection from the sun flopped on his head whenever a tiny breath of wind breezed by.

Doña Matilda privately thought he looked ridiculous, but she kept her opinion to herself.

And the little *rubí* who sat atop her donkey looked more like a chunk of rock today than a precious jewel, thought Doña Matilda acidly. On this, the fifth day of the expedition, Maria Antonia was covered from head to toe in a dress of heavy brown velvet shot through with threads of gold. On her head was a thick mantilla of brown and gold lace. And, most ridiculous of all, perched on top of her uptilted nose was a huge pair of spectacles. They made her long green eyes look warped and round.

Matilda Josefa had no one to blame but herself for the spectacles. Maria Antonia had taken to wearing them because once, in a desperate moment, as Doña Matilda had cast about for something spritely to say in a most trying conversation with the redhead, she had suddenly remembered the tidbit of information that spectacles were the most fashionable article of clothing in all of Spain—or at least they had been when she and Carmen had departed that country.

She quickly came to regret having told the plump woman about spectacles, however, because now Maria Antonia owned seven pair and refused to leave the Delgado villa without putting a pair on.

Not that she could see through any of them. And Maria Antonia *would* insist on dragging four pair along upon the expedition. She had even presented a pair to Doña Matilda—the ugliest pair of the lot, black-rimmed with thick, distorted glass that made everything one looked at wave back at one—and Matilda Josefa had utterly no use for them. Though she had stiffly thanked Maria Antonia, she had stowed the useless things in a case on her donkey's back where they bounced up and down with every step the donkey took. Doña Matilda secretly hoped they would break.

It was obvious that Maria Antonia considered her elaborate outfit, especially the spectacles, proper dress on this expedition outfitted to find her rival's jewelry. Doña Matilda noticed irritably that she preened and posed whenever Juan Enrique called a halt to wipe the sweat from his eyes or to water the mounts.

But for now, Juan Enrique Delgado was glaring at the black scout he had hired. Juan Enrique and the women had been wandering around in the desert for two days and had not found a single *indio*. After listening for two days to Maria's whining and his aunt's sharp witticisms, Juan Enrique had hired the black scout at the last mission they had come to. The scout was dressed in the usual manner of *indios*, in leather leggings, high moccasins, and a disgustingly stained deerskin shirt with fringe. The scout said he knew about *indios*, especially Apaches. Juan Enrique, his eyes darting to his little *rubí* with her pinched, tight little mouth, steeled himself for another outburst of whining. Before she could open her mouth, he hired the man on the spot.

Juan Enrique wiped at his forehead once more. He had noticed that the red bandanna wrapped around the scout's forehead kept the sweat out of his eyes. Juan Enrique had borrowed the idea, with modifications. Having no bandanna, he had tied the arms of one of his spare white shirts around his head. The shirt made a most splendid shield from the sun, protecting his eyes and his bald dome.

"Let's get on with it," Juan Enrique ordered now, kicking the large mule he rode. The mule, whom Maria Antonia had named Balky in a fit of whimsy, refused to move. Once more, Juan Enrique gave the beast a kick, then slashed hard with his whip. The mule brayed and took a step. Then another. He began to trot. "Whoa!" yelled Juan Enrique Delgado, yanking on the reins. The beast skidded to a halt.

How Juan Enrique wished that the black scout would stop staring at him out of those cold, flat, black eyes.

"I thought you said we would find them by now," he snarled. The scout looked at him. Just sat like a lump and looked at him. Delgado wanted to snap his whip across the man's face, but he did not quite dare to do that. This scout did not act like the African slaves that Delgado had sold upon his arrival in New Spain. Nor did he act like those who worked for their Spanish owners in Santa Fe. This one acted free, and Delgado sensed that he would not accept any cruel treatment. The black would probably leave them if Delgado expressed his true feelings and lashed out at the man. And then where would Delgado be? Stuck in this merciless heat in the middle of the desert with his precious Maria and the old bitch, that's where.

"I said we'd find them. I did not say when." He had probably made a mistake when he hired on as a guide for this Spanish fool, thought the black scout. Originally born a slave in Spain, Stefano had been sent by his Spanish master to Santa Fe in the New World to set up a silversmith shop. Stefano's originality and business acumen had made such a success of the business that he had been able to buy his freedom within three years. Once he was freed, Stefano had vowed never to be a slave to any man again. And he had kept that vow. He had married into a tribe of Jicarilla Apaches and knew their ways well. When his beloved wife had died in a difficult childbirth, he had stayed on with The People; he preferred their ways to those of the Spanish. But he could not forget Spanish ways altogether. Occasionally he would visit Santa Fe or a mission. That was what he had been doing when Delgado had hired him for a guide. Now Stefano wondered if the five arquebuses and five spears that Delgado had promised were worth putting up with the man himself.

Maria Antonia giggled. "He sounds so funny when he speaks Spanish, don't you think?" She had thought the scout rather attractive. She imagined she saw passion in those cold, hard eyes. She studied the scout intently. He ignored her. "Let's call him Balky Two," she giggled.

The scout, Juan Enrique, and Matilda Josefa all turned as one to stare at her. "Mayhap I will think of another name," observed Maria lamely.

Matilda Josefa snorted.

Suddenly the scout straightened in his saddle. He was looking up at a nearby hillside. "There," he grunted.

"Where?" cried the other three.

"I see nothing," complained Maria.

The scout urged his horse in the direction

321

of the sloping hillside. Juan Enrique Delgado shrugged, whipped Balky, and the mule condescended to trot after the scout. Maria followed on her smaller donkey, Isabel, whom she had grandly named after a Spanish queen of two hundred years ago.

Doña Matilda followed on her nameless donkey—she had refused every one of Maria's suggestions as to what to name her mount. Holding her back stiffly, she jostled after Maria, riding as though she and the beast were clearly two separate entities, which they always would be in Matilda Josefa's eyes.

Her donkey was slower than Maria's and it stopped to nibble at some dried grass on the hillside. By the time she she finally persuaded the animal to begin moving again, the others had gathered at the top of the hill. Matilda Josefa rode up to see that her companions were in deep conversation with a band of formidable-looking *indios*.

Juan Enrique looked pale. Even Maria Antonia looked a little frightened. As she drew closer, Matilda Josefa gasped. The leader of these *indios* was the very same savage who had stolen her and Carmen from the caravan!

She wanted to warn Juan Enrique, but she could not catch his attention. The black scout, normally taciturn, seemed suddenly to have much to say to the band of fierce *indios*. Matilda Josefa did not want to risk drawing the renegade *indios'* attention to herself. What if they recognized her? And what had they done with Doña Carmen?

She fidgeted with her hair, hoping that she did not look the same as when these cruel men had left her to die in the canyon. What had she worn then? She closed her eyes, trying to remember. Her gray hair had been up in a bun, as it was now. Surreptitiously, when she hoped no one was watching, she pulled at her hair until most of it came down loose and hung in wisps around her shoulders. Mayhap they would not recognize her. Oh, but she was still wearing black—the very dress, she now recalled, that she had worn when first captured by them. Mayhap they would remember her!

Then she remembered the odious spectacles. Fumbling in the case tied at the back of the donkey, her fingers finally located the hard spectacles at the very bottom of the case. She muttered a prayer that they were not broken.

Without looking at the *indios*, indeed trying to shrink into the donkey, Matilda Josefa whipped out the spectacles and put them on. She straightened. Her stomach swam. Now the whole desert, *indios*, cacti, Juan Enrique, and Maria Antonia waved in front of her eyes. How could she wear these infernal things? But what else could she do? She had to have a disguise. To be recognized by the *indios* would be dangerous—why she would do better to walk into the offices of the Inquisition and announce that she was a witch!

Suddenly the renegade leader pointed at her

and said something to the black scout. The other renegades laughed. Even the scout smiled a little. Doña Matilda clutched the pommel of her saddle as the desert, rocks, and *indios* swam nauseatingly before her eyes. Had the renegade leader recognized her?

"What did he say?" asked Maria Antonia coyly. She looked expectantly at the scout for an answer, her green eyes round and huge behind her glasses.

The scout grunted and swung to look at the older woman. He stared at her a moment and then translated, "He asks, where did we find this wild woman with the owl eyes?"

Maria Antonia giggled, and even Juan Enrique's thin lips split in the merest glimpse of a smile. Matilda Josefa slumped in the saddle, her fingers on the saddle's pommel slippery with sweat. They did not recognize her!

Now the renegade leader was saying something else. The taciturn scout laughed, actually laughed. He turned to translate and Matilda Josefa's stomach clenched. "He wants to know if we will trade the wild woman to him when he brings us the jewels."

Juan Enrique's face lit up. "Anything," he nodded. "Tell him he can have anything."

Maria pouted.

Matilda Josefa paled and leaned over the side of the donkey, expecting any moment to vomit from fear. Her balance had been very bad ever since she put on the spectacles. And now this! The *indios* wanted her, badly enough to trade for her! How terrible! Her plan, her disguise, all of it had been useless.

The black scout watched her clutching the pommel as she leaned over the side of the donkey. Her knuckles were white. "Just a joke," he explained solemnly.

Matilda Josefa sagged in ill-disguised relief.

Maria Antonia perked up. "They can have me instead," she said coyly.

"No, they cannot," snapped Juan Enrique. "Silence!"

Maria pouted.

"What about the jewels?" Doña Matilda dared to ask weakly. She had to get the topic away from herself.

"*Sí*, the jewels . . ." It worked; Juan Enrique's attention was once again taken up with his pursuit of the dowry. He glared at the scout. "Find out when they will bring us the jewels." What a stroke of luck that they had run across *indios* who had seen the bag of jewels, had even seen a blond Spanish woman in a turquoise dress, and best of all, claimed they knew where to find them! Juan Enrique could feel his heart beat faster as he thought of all the wealth just waiting for him.

The scout turned to the renegade leader and said something. The two spoke for some time, and finally the scout nodded. Then he urged his bay horse to a walk and moved away from the renegades.

"What did he say?" demanded Delgado.

The scout stared at the impatient Spaniard.

"He will bring the jewels. The woman, too." He started to ride.

"When? Where?" cried Delgado. "How much?" He grabbed at the scout's horse. "Answer me!"

The scout glared at him. Now he knew he should not have taken a scouting job with this fool. The weapons the Spaniard had promised did not seem worth it at this moment. And the scout did not like dealing with Angry Man, either. Though his deceased Jicarilla wife was of another tribe, Stefano had heard of Angry Man and his banishment by Man Who Listens. "Angry Man will find you when he is ready."

"What do you mean?" screamed Juan Enrique. "Goddamn it! Talking to you is like talking to a—a—" Words failed him.

"Juan Enrique," his aunt reproved him, "please curb your temper."

Juan Enrique glared at her. "Shut up," he snarled, "or I *will* trade you to the *indios*."

Matilda Josefa clamped her mouth shut and sniffed disdainfully. Inside, she was seething.

Maria Antonia watched the interchange and smiled slyly. "They don't want her. They were only joking. Nobody wants her."

"Silence!" yelled Juan Enrique.

The scout sighed.

Juan Enrique heard and swung to glare at him. "You! It's all your fault! You started all this!"

The scout glared back. "Angry Man wants the weapons you promised."

"He'll get them when I get the jewels!"

"That is what I told him. He did not like it that you had no weapons with you."

"I am no fool."

Privately, the scout disagreed.

"I hid the weapons." Juan Enrique puffed up his chest at his own cleverness.

"Go get them. I told Angry Man that we'll camp by the river and wait for him."

"Is that all we do? Wait?"

The scout shrugged. "Better to do that. He will bring the jewels to us."

Juan Enrique stared at the scout thoughtfully. He wondered if he could get the jewels from the *indios* without trading the weapons he had promised them. After all, that would save him much money. Weapons were very expensive.

The scout watched him. "Angry Man is mean. He does not like Spaniards. He wanted to kill you."

Juan Enrique jerked his head. "He could not kill me," boasted Juan Enrique. Inside, he worried. There had been—how many? Eight or nine *indios*. Juan Enrique only had four in his expedition—the two women were useless, and who knew if the scout would back him in a fight? Not good odds. "I am strong."

The scout thought that was very unlikely. "Get the weapons," he advised. "Angry Man will return soon."

"How many days? When will he give me the jewels?"

The scout shrugged. "He did not say. Just said

'soon'. We get the weapons, then we wait." The scout glared at Juan Enrique before urging his horse forward. He did not trust the Spaniard. If there were no weapons at the meeting place, Angry Man would kill the Spaniards, and probably the scout, too, if he could catch him. This Spaniard had better produce the weapons, because Angry Man would surely produce the jewels.

Juan Enrique gnashed his teeth. He jerked his mule's head around and started down the hillside after the scout. He saw his aunt, the spectacles perched on her nose, hanging onto the donkey. "You!" He glared at her. "There had better be many jewels in the dowry," he snarled. "Many, do you hear! This expedition is costing me a fortune!"

Maria Antonia followed after him, sitting primly on Isabel. She stuck out her tongue at Doña Matilda as she passed by her.

Matilda Josefa tightened her lips and yanked on the donkey's reins, trying to turn him around to follow the others.

Juan Enrique looked over his shoulder and frowned at his aunt. His white headpiece flopped with each step of his mule. "And take off those spectacles! They look damn foolish on you!"

Chapter 34

At the Jicarilla Apache Village

It had been five days since Puma had warned Carmen to stay in the tipi. And she had done so. But oh, how tired she was of the dwelling. It was fortunate that the days had not been as hot as usual. Carmen glanced out of the doorway. Today looked as if it was going to be hot. She sighed in dread. She did not want to stay and sew in the tipi, not another day! She had dried food, sewn clothes, sharpened all her knives—everything she could think of to do within the confines of the tipi had been done.

She sighed. The worst thing about staying in the little dwelling was that Puma was not there. He had gone hunting with a party of men because meat supplies were needed to prepare for winter. How she missed him.

She started to tidy the already neat tipi one more time. This time, Carmen decided, she would tidy *everything*. *'Rule Number 191: The perfect wife directs the servants to keep the home clean of dust and grime.'* Carmen rolled her eyes. "Except I am not his wife at all," she muttered indignantly. "I am his mistress! And," she added ruefully, "where are the servants?"

It was as she was lifting the blankets on Puma's bed that she found the leather pouch containing her dowry. She smiled to herself and peeked in. Every piece was there. She took out a long string of pearls and wrapped them around her neck and peered down at herself. Somehow, the pearls did not fit with her Jicarilla-style deerskin dress. With a sigh, she unwound the pearls and put them back in the pouch. She hung it on a pole next to Puma's weapons. He really must take better care of it, she mused. After all, it was worth a fortune!

Her eyes fell upon the little straw doll she had made while confined. Unfortunately, she had not been able to visit Snowberry, but she hoped the child would like the doll. A tiny Spanish mantilla draped from the head, and a little lace dress decorated the straw body. Carmen had taken the lace for it from her turquoise dress, which she now seldom wore.

Carmen knew that Snowberry was getting better, but she wanted to see for herself how well the child had recovered. Sky Flyer had kept her informed as to the child's progress, but it was not the same as visiting her.

Carmen sighed. Puma should be back soon. Mayhap this very night. Then she would only have to get through the day before she found herself in his arms again. She smiled to herself. He loved her; she sensed it. She certainly loved him. These past days had given her the opportunity to think about him, about her feelings for him. Though she was betrothed to Juan Enrique Delgado, it was Puma she loved.

Knowing that her *novio* searched for her had helped her to clarify her feelings. She would stay with Puma. If, by chance, her *novio* found her, she would tell him that the betrothal was ended. She would wish him well, of course, and then bid him farewell.

An image of the Juan Enrique Delgado that she had always pictured in her mind's eye rose before her. He was crying, on his knees, pleading with her to marry him, but she, alas, though she had compassion and was truly touched by his pitiful plight, could only bravely turn away, mayhap a tear or two running down her own cheek. She reached for Puma and he was there, taking her into his arms. Carmen sighed. Ah, what a satisfying fantasy.

She sat in the tipi, looking around for something else to do. The sun had now risen enough to beat down upon the dwelling, and it was heating up. It was going to be a long, miserably hot day. Her hair lay heavy and thick upon her neck. She tossed her head. A fly buzzed.

Finally, Carmen could stand it no longer. She must get out, go somewhere, talk to someone. Puma would be back soon. There was no danger; three Apache braves guarded the village. Mayhap she would just go and see little Snowberry, see if she was feeling better. It would not take long. *Sí*, that was what she would do.

When Carmen arrived at Snowberry's tipi, she could see that the girl had a tipi full of visitors. Two women even stood outside because there was no room inside. One of the women was Bird Who Plays in the Pinyon Trees.

Carmen's stomach tightened as she looked at the Apache woman. Bird Who Plays met her eyes directly, and before Carmen could take a step further towards Snowberry's family's tipi, Bird Who Plays nudged her. "Come with me," she said.

Curious, for the Apache woman's tone had been unusually polite, Carmen followed her. At a little distance from the village, Bird Who Plays stopped. Her large brown eyes met Carmen's in a direct look. "You were very brave to find Snowberry. When the owl hooted, I was afraid. You must have been too. But you kept looking. Very brave."

Carmen stared at Bird Who Plays. Was this an Apache apology? "You will make a good wife for Puma." Bird Who Plays nodded once, and Carmen still stared at her. *Sí*, this was definitely an apology.

"Thank you," said Carmen uncertainly. "I am glad that I found her."

Bird Who Plays shrugged and headed back to Snowberry's tipi. Carmen watched her walk away, feeling mystified. It was an apology, but hardly an undying vow of friendship. With her own shrug of the shoulders, Carmen sauntered after Bird Who Plays. On her way, she stooped to pick a handful of pretty wildflowers. When she reached Snowberry's tipi, she ducked her head and entered.

The girl looked up at her entrance. The crowd of women had gone, and only the child's mother was in attendance.

Carmen walked over and squatted down beside the child. Snowberry smiled at her. She looked much better. Carmen handed her the wildflowers and then presented the Spanish doll. Snowberry gasped in delight and hugged the doll to her chest. Carmen stayed to watch Snowberry's nimble little fingers weave a basket. Her talent was obvious to Carmen. The Jicarillas were well-known for their basketry art and Snowberry was proving true to her heritage. Ending the visit, Carmen took her leave politely. She was in high spirits at seeing how well the child had recovered. Now, if only Puma would return, everything would indeed be well!

Puma rode along, the sorrel moving swiftly across the hills and easily bearing the twin load of rider and dead antelope. Far behind him was the Apache hunting party. Puma had departed early, while the others still hunted, because he wanted to return to Carmen. He would not have left her if they had not needed the meat.

Puma felt strangely driven to return to Carmen. He did not want to spend another night away from her. Perhaps he should have returned before this, he thought uneasily. He tried to reassure himself that her *novio* would never find her.

As he rode, Puma mused on why he was so drawn to the woman. She was Spanish, after all. He reminded himself that he, too, was part Spanish, then quickly denied the thought. He was Apache, all of him. *She* was the problem, not him.

As a Spaniard, she was the enemy of his people. Though it was true that she did the work of an Apache woman, she still looked Spanish and would always look Spanish. He sighed. Yet she had become a very important part of his life in the time that he had taken her to live with him. Their lovemaking was wonderful. Even now, his manhood stirred as he imagined her, naked and willing and waiting for him. He nudged the sorrel to a faster pace.

It was only her lovely body, he told himself. That was what he wanted. That was why he kept her as his mistress and kept her from her *novio*. So he could enjoy her.

But he wanted more, he told himself. He wanted marriage. Then the humiliating memory intruded of how she had haughtily spurned him when he had offered marriage. His lips tightened, and a cruel look came over his face. Oh, she had tried to couch her rejection in that flowery language of hers, but it was rejection just the same. She could not fool him.

And why should she marry you? taunted a little voice. *She is rich. She is from a noble Spanish family. What would she want with a man who does not even own the ground on which he builds his tipi? What do you have to offer?*

Puma grimaced in humiliation. He had his love to offer.

Love, came the sneering little voice. *Love? You would love a Spanish woman? You hate the Spanish!*

Puma urged the sorrel to go faster, thoughts of his humiliations at the hands of the Spanish goading him on.

It was midnight when he reached the tipi. He jumped off the stallion and raced to the dwelling.

She was in there, sleeping. Her hair spilled over the blankets, and the moonlight shining on it gave it a golden glow. Her face in repose looked serene.

Serene. The very word that Juan Enrique Delgado had used to describe her in his letter. Puma felt sick at the reminder.

Then Puma's icy blue eyes narrowed at the thought of the searching *novio*. Juan Enrique Delgado thought he could take Puma's woman, but he was wrong. No one would take Carmen from him, Puma vowed. Certainly no Spaniard!

He approached the woman, throwing off his clothes as he did so.

He sank down beside her, still panting from his long ride.

Carmen awoke. Her wide turquoise eyes fastened on him, and a sleepy smile crossed her face. She opened her arms and he went to her. He entered her, desperate to join with her, to hold her to him, to never let her go. Then they were both gasping from their combined pleasure. When breathing was restored once more, Puma lifted himself on his elbows and gazed down at Carmen. "He cannot have you," Puma muttered.

Carmen, wide awake now, pushed him off her and sat up, disoriented. She put a hand to her throat. "Puma? How—? What—?"

He glared at her.

"What is the matter?" Carmen's eyes widened in alarm. She had seen that half-twist of a smile on his face before and knew it did not bode well. "Puma?"

He reached for her and grasped her chin. His grip was firm, hard. "Look at me," he said evenly.

She met his icy eyes without flinching. "Do not try to contact him. I will not let you go."

"Who?" Bewilderment was evident in her voice.

"Your *novio*." The words were clipped.

She gazed at him, seeing his agitation. "Puma, I wanted to speak with you about my *novio*."

"No tears, no pleading," he said harshly. "You stay with me!"

I do not want to go to him, Carmen wanted to cry out, but the stormy look on Puma's face stopped her. Mayhap when he cooled down she could speak with him, reason with him. She dropped her gaze for a moment, her mind trying to grasp what to say. When she looked up, he was donning his clothes.

"Where are you going?"

"There is an antelope for you to dress. I am going back to the hunt. I will return."

His words were cold and harsh. She wanted to shrink from him. Instead she managed, "When?"

"I do not answer to any Spanish woman," said Puma in a low, cruel voice. And then he was gone into the night.

Carmen heard the thick, pounding gallop of the sorrel fade into the distance. Then her tears started.

Chapter 35

Carmen lay face down, sobbing into her blankets. She had lain like that for a long time after Puma left. Now she slowly put on her deerskin dress; she suddenly could not stand the vulnerability of her nakedness, not after he had treated her so heartlessly.

Then she heard footsteps outside the tipi. He had returned! Puma had returned!

Carmen sat up, dashing her tears away. With bated breath, she watched the door. Relief swept over her. He must have realized what he had done, that he had treated her unfairly. He was coming to beg her forgiveness! Elation swelled in her.

But the man who strode through the door was not Puma. It was El Cabezón. He was naked to the waist, and his face was painted in fierce black designs. His eyes glittered. In his big hands, he held several lengths of leather rope.

Carmen's elation turned to horror. No! It could not be! But before she could choke out a scream, El Cabezón seized her and clapped his sweaty hand over her mouth to prevent an outcry. Carmen's eyes were huge above his hand, and her heart thudded against her ribs.

With smooth, swift movements, El Cabezón tied Carmen's hands behind her. Next, he efficiently placed a gag over her lips and tied it. Then he looped rope over her feet and tugged until she writhed her whole body in protest at the tightness. With a grunt, still not saying a word, El Cabezón lifted her over his shoulder like a sack of corn. He glanced around the tipi, grabbed the leather dowry pouch off the pole, and strode out the door. It had all happened so fast that Carmen could scarcely believe she was not dreaming. Only the tightness of her bindings convinced her that she was awake.

The Apache renegade threw her over a horse, tied her arms and legs beneath the animal's belly, then mounted his own horse and led hers off. Carmen struggled, wanting to cry out, to alert someone in the village, but all was quiet in the night and she could do no more than make helpless grunts.

This could not be happening to her, Doña Carmen Yolanda Diaz y Silvera! But the smell of the horse was real enough. And so was the broad back of the animal. She could feel the bony backbone digging into her stomach. When

El Cabezón led the horse in a trot, Carmen thought she would die.

Fortunately, they did not ride far like that. Just as dawn cleared the sky, they halted near a pile of boulders and several more Apaches joined El Cabezón.

Wordlessly, one of them undid Carmen's feet and helped her to sit upright. Though he did not untie her hands, he undid her gag. She was grateful and surprised by his gentleness. For a moment their eyes met, and she thought she saw sympathy in those dark depths. She thought of Puma. Mayhap this man knew Puma, was kind to her because of him. . . . Then the renegade returned to his own mount without another glance at her.

El Cabezón walked up to her, the leather dowry pouch dangling in his hand. On his broad face was a grin that looked utterly out of place on him.

Before he could say anything, she snapped, "Why have you stolen me? Let me go!"

The renegade just stared at her, amusement on his face. His grin looked particularly incongruous with the black paint.

"Puma will find me," stated Carmen confidently. "He will track you down and rescue me!" There, that should scare the foul man.

The smile disappeared from El Cabezón's face. "Puma is the one who told us to steal you."

For a moment Carmen had difficulty interpreting the man's rough Spanish. Then, when she realized the import of his words, the blood drained from her face. "What?"

"*Sí*, Puma sold you to us."

"No, no—he couldn't have," wailed Carmen in disbelief. "No! Puma loves me—" She snapped her mouth shut, not willing to divulge any further information about her connection with Puma. True, he had stormed out of the tipi, but he would never have sold her!

"That is why there was no one to stop us," observed El Cabezón. "It was very easy to walk into your home and take you."

Carmen swallowed. She had wondered why no one in the village had awakened or been on guard to stop her from being stolen. No, El Cabezón was lying. He had to be!

"Puma," continued her captor, "hates the Spanish."

Carmen lifted her chin. She knew that statement to be true. *But he liked me, mayhap even loved me,* she thought defiantly.

El Cabezón must have seen the imperious rise of her chin. He grimaced. "He told me to take you away. Said that he did not want to see your hated Spanish face anymore."

Carmen's jaw dropped. Would Puma say such a thing? No, surely he would not, she thought desperately. Then her wits returned and she inquired archly, "I suppose he told you to take that leather pouch?"

"No, he did not." There was no flicker of amusement on that dark face now.

Carmen reluctantly guessed that El Cabezón spoke the truth about that. *If* Puma had sold her, he would not have allowed this man to steal the dowry, too, would he? Puma would keep it, knowing its value.

But he did not sell her, she reminded herself sternly. This man was lying. Yet, if he told the truth about the pouch of jewels, mayhap he was telling the truth about Puma selling her.

No. Carmen could not, would not, believe it. Puma would never sell her. Why, he had asked her to marry him! *Only once, and that was long ago*, said the little voice. *Mayhap he grew tired of you. Mayhap Bird Who Plays in the Pinyon Trees was correct in saying that Puma would not marry you, that he would 'throw you away'. Mayhap this is how the Apache throw someone away . . .*

The bridle of her horse was yanked roughly and her chaotic thoughts interrupted. The renegades started off in a southwesterly direction.

During the long, aching ride Carmen had plenty of time to ponder her fate. And the possible duplicity of the man she loved.

Chapter 36

Carmen's drooping shoulders and spirits lifted when she saw that the renegades were headed toward a river. She wondered if it was the Rio Grande. A thicket of willow trees grew near the water.

Glimpsing a movement, she leaned forward. Was that a man? Wait, no it was two men—and two women. How odd.

Her heart began to beat erratically. For a moment she faltered. One of the men looked Spanish, the other like a very dark Apache, but it was difficult to tell at this distance. Straightening on the back of the horse, she focused her eyes, her attention, her whole being on those four people.

As she got closer, Carmen's jaw dropped in disbelief. Why, one of the women was—no, it could not be! It was her dear duenã—Doña Matilda!

Without further thought, Carmen kneed the horse, urging it forward. She passed the renegade who held the bridle. He watched her in a surly manner, but did nothing to stop her. Indeed, he kicked his horse also to keep pace with her.

"Dueña!" Carmen yelled. She pulled up at one of the willows. She would have jumped off the horse if her hands had not been tied. She glanced impatiently around for El Cabezón. Oh, would he release her?

The Apache renegade had dismounted and was walking over to the Spaniard. Carmen ignored him. Oh, who would undo her hands so she could dismount?

Fortunately, the same renegade who had shown her some kindness earlier appeared at her side. With his knife, he slit the leather bindings on her hands. Carmen winced with pain when the blood surged through her freed hands, then all was forgotten as she jumped off her horse and ran to Doña Matilda.

But how strange she looked, thought Carmen as she ran. The older woman's gray hair hung in long wisps over her shoulders, and she was wearing huge spectacles. If Carmen had not traveled with her from Spain and known her so well, she doubted she would ever have recognized the woman.

She threw herself into her companion's outstretched arms. The two women embraced each other. "You must be very, very careful," whispered Doña Matilda. "These men are dangerous. Say nothing. We will try and get help."

Carmen drew back and searched her dueña's deepset dark brown eyes. She saw sadness there—and worry.

Doña Matilda took the opportunity to hug her again. "That is your *novio*," she whispered, pointing to the Spaniard who was engaged in loud negotiations with El Cabezón.

Carmen whirled to stare at the man. *That* was her *novio*? That stocky man with the white material flapping around his head?

"Surely there must be some mistake," she whispered back. "Juan Enrique Delgado does not look like that—"

The sardonic look on Doña Matilda's face cut her off. Then Carmen realized she had never actually seen Juan Enrique Delgado, only imagined him. Still, he looked so different from what she had imagined. He looked so . . . so insignificant. "Who is that?" Carmen pointed to a red-haired woman.

"That," sighed Doña Matilda, "is Maria Antonia de Mendoza. She is Juan Enrique's— *novia*."

The woman, her dark red hair shining in the bright sun, was staring at Carmen. And not with favor.

"Juan Enrique's *novia*?" squeaked Carmen. "I—I don't understand."

"You will," said Doña Matilda grimly.

The men's negotiations had reached a high pitch, Carmen could tell from their voices. El Cabezón was swinging the dowry pouch and Juan Enrique Delgado was pounding the ground with the butt of an arquebus. The black scout was standing, arms folded, a defiant look on his face. The renegades, who stood looking on, were all frowning.

"What is it?" asked Carmen.

Doña Matilda shrugged her shoulders. "Juan Enrique is trading weapons for you."

"He is?" faltered Carmen. "How . . . very kind of him."

"Hmmm," said Matilda Josefa noncommittally. "Juan Enrique wants the jewels," she stated. From the tone of her voice, Carmen guessed that the other woman was trying to tell her something, but what it was she could not guess, so she too shrugged her shoulders and watched the men.

Finally the black scout stepped in and barked several short, sharp words at both men. El Cabezón and Juan Enrique stared at him, then looked at each other.

"I wonder what they are saying," mused Carmen.

Evidently, the men were now in agreement, because the renegades began loading the weapons onto the horse that Carmen had ridden. When they were done, the Apaches mounted their horses and started off.

Carmen watched them go. As he rode away, the one renegade who had been kinder to her than the others glanced over his shoulder at her, his face unreadable.

Carmen did not have long to wonder at his action. Maria Antonia de Mendoza marched up to her and thrust her face at Carmen.

"So," sneered the redhead, "you are Juan Enrique's precious *novia*." The word was an epithet the way she said it. "Understand," Maria said, staring down at Carmen, who was the shorter. "Juan Enrique is *mine*! We are going to be married. He does what *I* tell him."

She had no chance to say more, for Juan Enrique himself came sauntering up to them. "Doña Carmen," he said ingratiatingly. His smile looked like a grimace to Carmen. "Welcome."

"Thank you," said Carmen, "for rescuing me from those *indios*."

"*De nada*."

Juan Enrique's black eyes were running over Carmen in a manner she did not like. She looked around nervously. "Are we far from Santa Fe?"

"Ah, forgive me. You must be anxious to come to my home after your—uh, ordeal." His dark eyes had settled on her bosom.

Carmen put a hand to her throat nervously. He was still staring. She ran her hand through her tangled hair. "I—I would like to leave now," she said. "If that is not too much trouble."

"No, no. No trouble." He was still looking at her with that oily look.

Doña Matilda was mounting a donkey. Maria, her full lips in a pout, was climbing aboard another donkey. Juan Enrique mounted a mule. The scout helped lift Carmen up on his big bay stallion, then held the bridle. Evidently he intended to walk.

Carmen could not help but contrast the figure that Juan Enrique made mounted on his donkey with what Puma looked like mounted on his sorrel. She turned away. She did not want to think about Puma, about his possible betrayal. . . .

"It was most unfortunate that you were captured by *indios*," said Juan Enrique politely. "We were, all of us, most heartbroken to learn of your capture—myself most of all, of course."

Carmen stared at him, wondering if he spoke the truth. His eyes were veiled and small and she could not tell.

Juan Enrique Delgado's eyes were busy roving over Carmen's exquisite body. Whatever had been done to her had not marred her shape or her skin, he decided. While of course he would not consider marrying a woman after such adventures as Doña Carmen had doubtless had—still, he would consider making her his mistress.

He smiled pleasantly in Carmen's direction at some murmured response she had made. *Sí*, he thought. He could have Maria Antonia as his wife and Carmen Diaz y Silvera as his mistress.

And now that he had the jewels, he could of course afford to be more generous to both women. He eyed Maria uneasily. She might not like it if he took the Silvera bitch as mistress. Then he brightened. What could Maria say? He was the one with the power, the money.

Delgado smiled and leaned over politely to murmur more considerate words to Doña Carmen. She was beautiful, he saw. Mayhap it was fortunate after all that the Apache renegade, Angry Man, had forced him to trade for her. Juan Enrique had not wanted her in the trade, but Angry Man had insisted. Mayhap things would work out well after all. . . .

He flashed a quick smile at his neglected, pouting little *rubí*. *Sí*, things might work out very well indeed.

Chapter 37

The plodding ride back to Santa Fe gave Carmen too much time to think about things she would rather have ignored—about how there was truth to El Cabezón's statement that Puma hated the Spanish, and about how Puma must have hated her. He had said deliberately cruel words to her before El Cabezón had stolen her from the tipi. But to sell her!—*if* he did—was an incredibly vicious thing to do. It did not fit with the Puma she knew. Yet she had seen hardness before in him and knew he had had to be tough to survive his imprisonment in Mexico City. Would his toughness extend to rooting out the growing love he had felt for her? Because Carmen kept telling herself that he did love her. Or at least she thought he had. But where was his love if he had sold her? Her thoughts kept going round and round until she wanted to scream.

Finally, Carmen gave in to the sadness and despair she felt. Puma did not want her. She loved him, but he did not want her. She was alone. Oh, there was Doña Matilda, true, but still Carmen felt alone. And the older woman had said few words to her on the ride to Santa Fe, which was unlike her. Her reticence had added to Carmen's despair.

What would she do? She could not marry Juan Enrique Delgado, not when she loved Puma.

Her shoulders slumped as she rode the bay stallion; her own thoughts claimed her.

They finally reached Santa Fe and rode through the town. The walls of the mission stood white against the brown hills, and for a moment Carmen roused herself to look around. It was a pretty town, and the men and women who crowded the narrow streets were dressed in bright colors of Spanish and Indian origin. Children played in the small yards.

Carmen felt a twinge of disappointment that Juan Enrique Delgado did not stop. He determinedly escorted his small party through the heart of the town. He pointed out a church, San Miguel de Santa Fe, and the Palace of Governors, built in 1610 when the city was founded. They passed through the rear gates of the city and pressed on for some distance down the road until they reached his villa.

Carmen was surprised to see a large, pleasant two-story dwelling done in the Spanish style of white adobe and red tile roof. A large curved doorway led into a small courtyard decorated to look like a miniature desert. Steps led up to the second story, and Carmen glimpsed four doorways indicating rooms that let out onto the second-floor balcony. She strained forward for a better view of the imposing residence.

"I am sure you will enjoy my home, Doña Carmen," said Juan Enrique Delgado, dismounting. He helped Carmen to dismount, then turned to aid Maria down from her donkey. Carmen smiled to herself as she watched the redhead stick out her tongue at Juan Enrique and flounce off through the arched doorway, leaving a servant to unload her belongings from the donkey.

Carmen wondered briefly at the relationship between Maria and Juan Enrique. Doña Matilda had said that Maria was Juan Enrique's *novia*. But Carmen was supposed to be his *novia*. Fortunate man, with two *novias*, Carmen thought wryly.

"Peon," barked Juan Enrique to the servant. "Show Doña Carmen to the bedroom at the end of the balcony."

The old man nodded and tottered off, carrying three large sacks, part of Maria Antonia's luggage. Carmen followed, watching him carefully negotiate the stairs. When he reached the top, he stumbled, and Carmen stretched out her arms to catch him and prop him up.

Once he was steadied again, the old man continued on his way, faltering along the balcony. Carmen followed as calmly as she could, but

352

she wondered how Juan Enrique Delgado could expect such an old man to serve him. Why, this elderly man should be sitting in the courtyard, dozing in the shade, Carmen thought, not struggling with heavy baggage. Halfway along the length of the balcony, the old man stopped to rest. Carmen could hear him panting, and she chose that moment to discreetly observe the courtyard.

A small fountain bubbled into a little pool. Spiky-leaved century plants and small yuccas were scattered here and there on the smoothly raked desert sand. She recognized a mescal plant growing beside a small rock and smiled. She must see if the plant sported a good-sized crown. Mayhap Doña Matilda, Maria, and Juan Enrique would enjoy some pounded, dried mescal. Then her smile faded, and Carmen turned away sadly at the inadvertent reminder of her time with the Apaches. By now, the old servant was shuffling along the balcony again, and Carmen followed patiently.

He stopped at the third door and pushed it open, staggering into the room with his load of luggage. That must be Maria's room, thought Carmen, as she heard shrill words issue through the thick door. The old man, looking chastened, backed out of the room and carefully closed the door behind him. He shuffled along the balcony to the fourth and last door on this side of the house.

By his gestures, Carmen understood that this was to be her room. She stepped across the threshold and into a warm room. A small, curtainless window graced the wall opposite the door. Below it was a low, heavy, wooden bed with a bedspread woven in cool greens and blues. A large Spanish fan of gold and green was spread across another wall and under it was more heavy furniture—a chest, a bureau, and a chair—all carved in the Spanish style. On the fourth wall was a framed painting of a stern-looking Spanish woman. Pushed against the wall were a table and three chairs.

Carmen regarded the painting. The stern-looking woman's thin lips were pursed and waxen, her plump cheeks held two bright spots of red in the Spanish mode of makeup, and her nose was stubby and turned up at the end. But it was her eyes, deepset and small like Juan Enrique Delgado's, that caught and held Carmen's rapt gaze. The eyes in the painting stared out balefully as though telling the viewer that *this* was a woman to be reckoned with. His mother, Carmen thought with a shiver as she turned away from the harsh, feminine reminder of her *novio*. She really must tell Juan Enrique Delgado that she had no intention of marrying him. Had she not met Puma, she would have married Delgado, but being with the Apaches had changed her life forever.

Hearing loud voices, Carmen wandered back along the balcony and down the steps leading to the curved entrance to the courtyard to investigate.

Juan Enrique stood nose-to-nose with the

black scout. The Spaniard was shouting and cursing. The scout was glaring.

"That is all I am giving you," screamed Juan Enrique, the veins on his thick neck standing out in his anger.

"You said five guns." The scout held up one hand with fingers spread. "And five spears." He held up the other hand.

Two arquebuses and two long Spanish spears lay in the dirt at their feet.

"Be satisfied with what I give you," snarled Juan Enrique Delgado.

The scout shook his head. "No. You told me five. Of each."

"Two."

"Five!" The scout looked stern and unmoving.

Juan Enrique gnashed his teeth. To Carmen's surprise, he whirled on his heel and ran up the stairs. She heard a door slam, then the thump, thump, thump, of Juan Enrique Delgado's feet as he ran back down the stairs. He stopped, panting, in front of the black scout. Delgado raised his arm and pointed an arquebus squarely in the irritated scout's face.

Carmen gasped.

"Leave now," snarled Juan Enrique at the guide. "And do not come back. If you do, I will shoot to kill you. Understand?"

The scout did not look cowed to Carmen, but stood glaring at the furious Spaniard. Finally, just as Carmen opened her mouth to add her pleas to Juan Enrique's threats, the scout bent, retrieved the two arquebuses and two spears from the ground, and turned on his heel. He lashed the weapons to his horse, gathered his horse's bridle, and mounted. When he rode away, he did not deign to glance back at Juan Enrique Delgado.

Juan Enrique has made an enemy of that man, thought Carmen, watching him ride away. She hoped that the scout took Delgado's advice and did not return. She was beginning to suspect that Juan Enrique was neither kind nor honorable. He had evidently promised a greater sum to the black guide than he had been willing to pay. Juan Enrique had gone back on his word. He had also pulled a weapon on a man who was not armed. Neither action fitted the Juan Enrique Delgado that Carmen had built up in her mind as she traveled across the world to meet him. She feared suddenly for her own safety.

Juan Enrique Delgado wiped his forehead with a large handkerchief. Carmen heard him mutter into it. Then he glanced up and seemed to see her for the first time. "What do you want?" he snarled.

Carmen took a step back, and her jaw dropped. Heretofore Juan Enrique had been polite to her, ingratiatingly so.

"Don't look so surprised," sneered Delgado. "You've no doubt seen worse." He prowled slowly towards her. "Staying with those *indios*. Sleeping with them."

The blood drained from Carmen's face.

"Oh, you cannot fool me, you little wanton."

Carmen regained some sense of awareness in her outrage at his crude statements. "I have come to tell you that I will not marry you," she said frostily.

"Ha! As if I would marry you!" he snarled. "I have your dowry. That's all I wanted." His cruel eyes appraised her from belly to breast. "That's all I ever wanted. Though I do admit, now that I have seen you—"

Carmen's hand went to her throat in consternation. This snarling beast was not the Juan Enrique she had dreamed of. Who was this man?

"Consider yourself my prisoner," Delgado added, his voice low. "You can expect me in your bed this evening, Doña Carmen." The title, as he said it, was as insulting as his tone. "You will show me all the dirty little tricks you learned while fornicating with the *indios*!"

Carmen opened her mouth to speak, then closed it again, too aghast to speak. She was pale; her world was falling apart around her. She closed her eyes, unable to believe what he was saying to her. Finally, words reached her lips. "You cannot," she gasped. "You cannot do this. . . ."

He laughed, the sound unexpected and coarse to Carmen's ears. "I can do anything I want." He waved a hand at the desert vista before them. "The nearest neighbor is half a league away. Who is going to help you?" He laughed. "No one. You are at my mercy, you *indio* strumpet. For as long as I choose to keep you!"

Chapter 38

Puma returned to the village with the rest of the hunting party. The night he had stalked off, leaving Carmen, he had been angry and determined that no Spanish woman was going to mean anything to him. But once he had cooled down, a sense of desolation set in. Then he had had to face the truth. He loved her; how could he keep denying it to himself? That she was Spanish was an irrevocable part of her, as it was of him. She could not change what she had been born into any more than he could.

After he had rejoined the hunt, he had had plenty of time to think. Lying in wait for antelope and deer had given him time to grapple with his own Spanish heritage. While he was not gleeful that he was Spanish, he was more accepting of it. His blue eyes, his height—both came from the Spanish invaders. They were an indelible part of him. And his treatment by Spaniards in prison had affected his life in ways that other Apaches had never known. Being Spanish was a part of him and would be until he died. He could no longer condemn Carmen for her heritage, either. It just was.

Now he felt guilty. When he glanced at the tipi he shared with Carmen, he grimaced. The hunting trip had been very successful, and he found himself hoping that the big supply of meat he was bringing would make Carmen relent a little toward him, for he knew she would be angry. It had not been fair of him to blame her for being Spanish; he could see that now. She had had as little choice as he. The difference between them was that she had been raised Spanish and felt proud of her heritage, whilst he felt ashamed.

Puma delayed going to the tipi. He fed and watered the sorrel and brushed the stallion's coat. Then he set the horse loose to run with the tribe's small herd. Puma watched the sorrel gallop over to one side of the corral where the Andalusian mare stood. Puma smiled to himself and shook his head. Both he and his horse had fallen under the spell of Spanish females.

The sorrel was a fine, strong horse and did not bite now. The stallion and the mare were gifts from the Spanish, Puma reminded himself humorously. Some of the things that the Spaniards brought to Apacheria were good. Certainly Carmen was.

His pace quickened as he approached the tipi.

"Carmen?" he called softly. There was a rustle inside and out came an Apache woman, her head bowed. Puma stared at the shining black hair where he had expected to see blond. "Bird Who Plays in the Pinyon Trees? What is it?" He could not remember Bird Who Plays ever visiting Carmen before, but perhaps they had become friends in his absence. One never knew about women's friendships. "Where is Carmen?" he asked.

Bird Who Plays looked up at him, and her brown eyes were sad. "She is gone."

"What do you mean?" Dread seized Puma but he struggled to keep his body stiff, his face impassive. "Gone?" His mind reeled. Her *novio* had found her and taken her away! That had to be it. Fear seized Puma's vitals and twisted them. Too soon he had thought the danger of her *novio* was past, that the inhospitable desert would have caused him to give up. Instead, the cursed Spaniard had continued the search. Puma should have stayed and protected Carmen instead of running back to the hunting party!

Castigating himself, Puma brushed past Bird Who Plays and dashed into the tipi. It was empty, and Carmen's favorite deer dress was gone. He yanked up the blankets where he had hidden the little pouch of colored rocks and necklaces that had been so important to Carmen. Gone, too!

He sank back on his heels. In all his anger at her, he had minimized the danger of her *novio*'s search for her. And now she was gone. Despair clawed at Puma.

"Carmen disappeared," came Bird Who Plays' voice from outside the tipi.

Dully, Puma rose to his feet and staggered out the door.

"One evening she was here, the next morning she was gone."

"Were any Spaniards seen?" It had to be her *novio*. Who else would have taken her?

"There were two horse tracks outside the tipi."

Only two? Was her *novio* so fearless that he would ride into an Apache village alone and steal another man's woman?

"Did anyone see her go?"

Bird Who Plays shook her head.

"Anyone at all?" pleaded Puma. "There must be someone who saw her, heard her—"

"She was very quiet when she left. As if it was planned."

Suddenly thoughtful, Puma stared at Bird Who Plays. No, it could not be, his heart cried. Carmen would not willingly leave him—he had to keep telling himself that. "No," he muttered aloud.

Bird Who Plays shrugged.

"Where is my mother?"

"At the river getting water."

"Perhaps she can tell me more. . . ."

"Perhaps," agreed Bird Who Plays. "What are you going to do?" She held Puma's gaze boldly for a moment, an uncharacteristic gesture for an Apache maiden.

Puma knew then that she still cared for him,

still hoped. With as much gentleness as he could summon in this terrible moment, Puma said, "I do not know. I want to go and find her, but I need more information. Perhaps Sky Flyer can tell me." He started to turn away.

"Snarling Mountain Lion." The sound of his real Apache name stopped him. Whatever Bird Who Plays wanted to say would be important. He swung to face her.

Softly she asked, "Is there any hope that you will marry me?"

He stared at her. Bird Who Plays in the Pinyon Trees must feel desperate indeed to be so blunt. His keen eyes saw that her lower lip trembled, that her hands were clasped tightly together to keep from shaking. To ask the question had cost her much.

He took a step toward her. "I care for you. You are like a cousin to me, or a sister. I have seen you grow into a fine woman. And you are part of my tribe. But it is Carmen that I want to marry." He wondered if Bird Who Plays would hate him for wanting to marry a Spanish woman, then pushed the thought away. He loved Carmen; she was precious to him, and her Spanish heritage was no longer a part of the reckoning.

A sad smile flitted across Bird Who Plays' face. "She is a good woman," she said softly. "I hope you will be happy."

"First I have to find her," observed Puma dryly.

Bird Who Plays nodded. Then she glanced

about quickly. No one was paying any attention to the two of them. She took a step toward him. Her eyes darted nervously once more. "I—I have something else to tell you."

"Yes?"

"Takes Two Horses wants you to meet him."

Puma stared. "What are you saying?" He eyed her. "What do you know of Takes Two Horses?"

He thought Bird Who Plays blushed, but he could not be sure.

"Every night when the moon is high, he comes to the big boulder down by the river path. He waits for you."

"For *me*?"

This time she did blush. She went on hurriedly, "He has done this for five nights. He will wait three more nights for you, then he will go back to Angry Man."

"What does he want?"

"I do not know."

Puma's face looked suddenly grim. "I will be there tonight."

"What do you want?" Puma asked guardedly. He stood with his back to the boulder, his eyes narrowed upon Takes Two Horses. Puma did not trust Takes Two Horses, not any more.

Takes Two Horses met his stare, his black piercing eyes giving away nothing. "I have come to warn you."

"Why should you warn me? You do not like me. You have said so clearly."

Takes Two Horses said nothing. After a long

pause, he sighed. "It is not as I thought it would be, riding with Angry Man."

Puma grunted. He wondered if Takes Two Horses was attempting another betrayal of him with this kind of talk. Puma could not forget that it was Takes Two Horses who had delayed him with talk while Angry Man and his renegades had stolen Carmen from the caravan. He would let the other man talk a little longer, Puma decided, but if he felt suspicious, he would leave.

"At first it was merely stealing," continued Takes Two Horses. "I enjoyed the excitement. Then Angry Man began killing. Now *I* am killing. We kill anyone we see." He shook his head in self-disgust. "My stomach churns at the sight of blood now."

Puma waited.

"Have you ever killed a child?" Takes Two Horses stared at Puma. "Have you ever looked into his eyes as you stabbed him in the belly with your spear, all because he was the son of a Spaniard?"

Puma gazed back, his blue eyes icy. He was the son of a Spaniard. Takes Two Horses seemed to have forgotten that in his own anguish.

The Apache renegade looked away. "That is what we do, sometimes," he admitted sullenly. "I hate it."

Puma observed coolly, "You *have* changed."

Takes Two Horses swung back to him, his eyes hostile. "I have! Now I kill women, children—" Suddenly the hostility seemed to drain out of him, leaving him weary in the moonlight.

"It is not what I thought it would be, following Angry Man."

Puma waited in silence. There was nothing he could say to ease the man's anguish.

"There is going to be an uprising of Indians against the Spanish."

Puma jerked in surprise at this news.

"The Indians, all of them who have had their towns and pueblos and hunting lands claimed by the Spanish, are going to rise up and fight. They are going to kill every single Spaniard— man, woman and child."

"Where did you hear this?"

"It is a secret message that is being sent to all Indian males. To the Pueblos, to the Tewas, to the Apaches, to everyone. But no women are to know. A runner from Taos carried the message to Angry Man's encampment fourteen moons ago. He wanted Angry Man to join the rebellion."

Puma was stunned at the enormity of Takes Two Horses' revelation. "All the Indians," he murmured. Man Who Listens' tribe was well hidden in the mountains. That would explain why no Taos runner had found the camp and passed on the news of the rebellion.

"The leader, Popé, is a Pueblo Indian who wants to drive the Spanish away from our lands forever. He hates them." Takes Two Horses looked thoughtful. "Almost as much as Angry Man does."

Both men were silent for a long while, Puma trying to make sense of what the renegade had just told him. "When?" he asked finally. "When is this going to happen?"

Takes Two Horses held up a little knotted cord. "When this last knot is reached." There were six knots on the cord. "Each day I take off one knot. This is how all the Indian tribes will know when to fight. Popé is very clever; he is a Pueblo shaman. The messenger said Popé learned his hatred of the Spanish when he was thrown into prison."

Neither man made the comparison, but it was there, unspoken. Just as Puma had been thrown into prison.

"Are you going to fight?" Puma was curious.

Takes Two Horses shrugged. "Why not? I already kill Spanish women and children. What are a few more?" But under the callous words Puma heard the bitterness.

"Why are you telling me this?" Puma asked.

Takes Two Horses eyed him. "I do not know," he said at last. "I thought I did it to warn you, since you are Spanish, and we will kill every Spaniard." Puma relaxed. Takes Two Horses was telling the truth. "But then when I saw what happened to Carmen . . ."

"What happened to her?" Puma's hands were at Takes Two Horses' throat before either man could blink.

"Easy," muttered Takes Two Horses, choking. He clawed at Puma's fists and Puma slowly released him, but he did not step away. "Where is Carmen? Tell me!"

"Angry Man sold her."

"To whom?"

"To a Spaniard from the town they call Santa Fe. He was a short, round man."

"You were there?"

Takes Two Horses nodded warily. "I was there when Angry Man gave the woman to the Spaniard. Angry Man received many weapons in return. He traded the little sack of colored stones to the Spaniard, too."

"Yes, it was missing from my tipi."

"The Spaniard behaved strangely. At first he did not want the woman, only the colored stones."

Puma frowned. Only the stones. That did not make sense. Perhaps it was not Carmen's *novio*, but some other Spaniard. But who? And why?

"Angry Man forced him to take the woman. For some reason, the chief's son did not want to kill her, though I do not know why." He watched Puma carefully. "I can guess."

"Why?" Puma's voice was rough. He feared greatly for Carmen now.

"For revenge."

At Puma's demanding look, Takes Two Horses explained, "Angry Man holds many things against you. You are half-Spanish, and he hates the Spanish. You stole the woman and the sack of stones away from him once, and that humiliated him."

Puma nodded.

"He hates you because his father banished him and kept you. The old chief even wants you to be the next headman, not Angry Man.

For that, Angry Man cannot forgive you."

"And so he seeks his revenge against me by stealing my woman." Puma's face was hard and grim.

Takes Two Horses sighed. "Angry Man knows you, knows your weaknesses. He used them against you."

"What do you mean?"

"He told your woman that you hate the Spanish, that you hate her."

"Surely she would not believe such a thing!" But inside, Puma's mind was screaming that it would be all too easy for Carmen to believe.

"And," continued Takes Two Horses, "Angry Man told her that you sold her. To him."

Puma groaned, remembering how he had stormed out of the tipi.

"Angry Man was very clever about it," observed Takes Two Horses. "He did it very carefully so that the woman would believe him."

Puma's dread deepened. He knew Angry Man's cunning. When he was done, Carmen would believe the lie.

"Where were they going, after the trade?" Puma demanded tersely.

Takes Two Horses shrugged. "Santa Fe is my guess. That is where the Spaniard was from."

Puma met Takes Two Horses' gaze. "My thanks for this information. I will go after her."

Takes Two Horses shrugged. "And I will go to kill Spaniards."

"Can I not talk you out of it?"

Takes Two Horses shrugged again. "There is nothing left in my life now but killing," he said bitterly. "And I do it well."

"There is Bird Who Plays . . ." muttered Puma.

Takes Two Horses' eyes flickered. "Bird Who Plays?"

"She loved you once."

Takes Two Horses's shoulders slumped. "Once perhaps. But she does not love me now. She would not want me. If she was disgusted with me for selling you, think how she would feel if she was to learn of the many killings I have done." He shook his head.

"She is a good woman," Puma urged. "Change your life's course. Stop killing, come back to your people. We need you."

Takes Two Horses stared at Puma, clearly doubting his words. "I see ghosts at night," he said softly. "Children's ghosts. They hide just beyond the next rise of the desert and beckon me with long, thin arms. Sometimes I hear them call me, hooting like owls on the night wind."

Puma felt his skin crawl.

"No, there is no way back to the tribe for me." Takes Two Horses' words were sad.

"We have a shaman," reminded Puma.

"That old man can do nothing for me," snorted Takes Two Horses.

"He drove away the ghost that was chasing Snowberry. The child is completely recovered."

Takes Two Horses said nothing.

"And Bird Who Plays cares about you." Puma watched his old comrade carefully. "We have a shaman, and we have Bird Who Plays in the Pinyon Trees. That is more than Angry Man can offer you. He can only offer you more death, more ghosts." When Takes Two Horses was still silent, Puma advised, "Think on it."

When Puma turned and walked away, the tortured warrior still stood there, but Puma did not notice. He had to find Carmen—or she would be killed!

Chapter 39

Santa Fe

"Come out, my little *rubí*," cooed Juan Enrique Delgado. "And you, too, my little desert flower."

Neither woman bothered to answer. They glared at each other. The bed was pushed up against the door, as was the heavy wooden chest and every other article of furniture that Carmen could add to the barricade.

"Come out," pleaded the voice on the other side of the thick frame. "Let us talk."

"I thought you said you were not interested in my *novio*," spat Maria Antonia de Mendoza.

"I am not," answered Carmen, her turquoise eyes narrowed to furious slits.

"Then why is he pounding on your door like this so late at night?"

"Mayhap because he did not find *you* in your room," replied Carmen acidly.

"Hah!" snarled Maria. "You cannot tell me he is looking for me—oh no, not when he is talking so sweetly outside *your* door!"

"I had nothing to do with it!" Carmen wanted to scream in frustration. Why would the woman not believe her? "Understand this! I do not want your *novio*. I do not *like* him. I would never let him into my bed."

"Hah! He comes to you in the night! Can you deny that?" demanded Maria in triumph.

"I still say I had nothing to do with it. Quickly, get that chair. I think he's moving the door."

Hurriedly, the two women interrupted their heated exchange to push the heavy article of furniture across the floor. They managed to get the chair up against the washstand. Maria sank down onto the chair for a moment, wiping sweat from her eyes.

Carmen stood, hands on hips, and glared at her. "I do not know why you think I even want Juan Enrique," she snapped. "You can have him. You can marry him."

Maria glanced up suspiciously. "Not until I have his ring on my finger will I believe you."

Carmen snorted. "What makes you think a ring will protect you from his philandering?"

"Juan Enrique does not philander!" shrieked Maria, jumping up from the chair.

Carmen shook her head in disgust. "Whatever you say, Maria."

There was only silence from the other side of the door. Carmen walked over to the window, glad of the reprieve. It seemed that she had been barricaded in this room for hours with this furious woman, when in reality it had probably only been minutes.

"You want to marry Juan Enrique," argued Maria shrilly. "What woman would pass up the opportunity to marry a rich man like Juan Enrique?"

"I would," said Carmen quietly.

"Hmmmmph," snorted Maria Antonia. "Then you have never been poor."

Carmen swung away from the window to face the taller woman. "No, I have not."

Maria Antonia stared at her in contempt. "Well, I have! I know what it is like to be deserted, hungry. As a little child, I went days without food because there was none! And it was no better when I married that son-of-a—!" She gasped, aware suddenly that she had said too much. Her eyes narrowed. "I have been poor, and I won't be poor again, do you hear? I will marry Juan Enrique or anyone else it takes to give me a good life."

"Fine," shrugged Carmen. "Go ahead."

Maria stalked closer. "Don't think I don't see through your little ploy."

"What ploy?" Maria truly mystified Carmen.

"You are trying to convince me that you have no intention of taking Juan Enrique away from me, when in fact, once you have convinced me, you will be free to seduce my own man in my own house!" Maria's voice had risen to a piercing shriek on the last word.

Carmen stared at her. "I must get out of this madhouse."

"Go!" screamed Maria, pointing at the barricaded door. "Go now!"

"And walk into Juan Enrique's waiting arms?" asked Carmen, exasperated.

Maria launched herself at Carmen, grabbing a handful of blond hair and pulling. Carmen screamed in pain.

Then there was pounding on the other side of the door. "Girls, girls! Stop that!" came Doña Matilda's voice. "Cease at once!"

Next, Maria screamed when Carmen yanked on her hair.

"Juan! Juan! They are fighting. You must stop them!" Doña Matilda's voice was frantic.

Running footsteps sounded on the balcony corridor outside the bedroom. More pounding on the door.

By now, Carmen and Maria were wrestling on the floor, both of them panting. They rolled over and over across the hard floor before Maria finally landed on top.

"He is—" Carmen could not stop panting. "He is not worth it," she managed to gasp out.

Maria looked mightily affronted, sitting on Carmen's stomach. "He is so!"

Carmen shook her head and tried to get up. Maria refused to move off her stomach. The woman was heavy. "Get this straight," snarled Maria. "You are going to leave this house, leave

Santa Fe, and not come back. Juan Enrique is mine!"

Carmen glared back at the older woman. Why did Maria not believe that was exactly what Carmen wanted to do? "Get off me!" she yelled.

"No! Not until you say you'll leave!"

Carmen glared at Maria.

Maria glared back.

Dios, the woman was stubborn. At last Carmen nodded her head wearily, as if in defeat, but inside she felt relieved. "I will go," she offered in a downcast voice. "You win. He is yours."

Maria stared back at her. "He always was," she smirked. Warily, she moved off her opponent.

Carmen waited until Maria was completely off her, then she sat up. "I will take Doña Matilda with me," Carmen stated firmly.

Maria must have thought it was a condition for her rival to leave town, for she snapped, "Very well. I have no use for that nosey old woman, anyway."

"And," continued Carmen, "I will have adequate supplies. I will not be driven out of this town with no food or clothing." Her brows were drawn together, her eyes as fierce as she could make them. She intended to find someone, mayhap the black scout, and ask him to lead her back to El Paso del Norte. She would prefer to have him lead her back to Puma's people, but she feared that Puma really had sold her and she did not want to take the risk of falling into his hands again. So, it was best if she returned to El Paso. Mayhap from there she could find her way back to Spain.

"Very well," agreed Maria easily, swatting the dust off her dress from their tussle on the floor. "I will be generous." She smiled. "I can afford to be. Now." Then her eyes hardened. "But if I catch you trying to seduce Juan Enrique, our deal is off. Do you understand?"

"I do not *want* to seduce Juan Enrique," protested Carmen yet again.

"He came to your door!"

They were back to this argument again. "I am not responsible for where Juan Enrique goes in the middle of the night."

"Hah! When he comes to your door, you are!"

Maria was thoroughly unreasonable when it came to that man, thought Carmen in irritation. Well, she could have him. She obviously thought he would make her happy—he and his money.

"Maria!" It was Juan Enrique Delgado, imploring from the other side of the heavy door. "Maria! I know you are in there. Come out!"

Maria glared at Carmen. "I mean it," she warned. "If I catch him sniffing around you, I'll—"

"Maria!" More pounding. "What have you done to my little desert flower? Why is it so quiet in there?"

"I mean it!" hissed Maria.

Carmen did not doubt it for a minute. She began tugging at the furniture in preparation for clearing away the barricade.

"My little desert flower," cooed Juan Enrique. "Are you all right?"

Carmen looked sardonically at Maria, whose eyes flashed. She raised her chin in challenge.

"Go away, Juan Enrique," Carmen called. "Maria and I are"—she hesitated—"visiting."

"Open up," cried Juan Enrique, pounding loudly now that he had been able to raise a response. "What is going on in there?"

"Please open up," pleaded Doña Matilda.

Maria joined Carmen in pushing away the furniture. After the bed was back in its proper spot, the washstand and table up against the wall in their respective places, Carmen glanced about the room. "Ready?" she asked.

Maria nodded.

Carmen opened the door.

"Juan Enrique," cried Maria, opening her arms. Juan Enrique came into them, his head muffled against her full bosom. Maria glared at Carmen across the top of his bald head.

Carmen smiled back sweetly.

"What is the meaning of this?" demanded Maria of Delgado. "Can I not have a little chat with Doña Carmen without you making a fuss?" She pouted her full lips at him.

He glanced up at her adoringly. "Maria," he said softly. "You forgive me?"

"Of course I forgive you, dear man. I can understand a man going to her—once." Her voice was ice as she said it. Evidently Juan Enrique did not mistake her meaning, for he hugged her breasts again. "But now I am going to keep you very busy, and you will have no need to call upon Doña Carmen late at night, will you?"

She lifted her head and glared at Carmen across the top of his head.

Carmen waggled her fingers back at her.

Juan Enrique beamed at his little *rubí*. He was relieved to be back in her arms once more. He must be more careful the next time he visited the Silvera bitch. Apparently his little *rubí* had a jealous streak as wide as the Rio Grande at full flood. *Sí*, he must be careful. He turned a bland smile in Carmen's direction. "You will excuse us, Doña Carmen?"

Carmen watched them leave. The gall of the man! He had acted as though nothing out of the ordinary had happened. Carmen sighed. The sooner she was out of this house the better, she thought.

"Carmen?" It was Doña Matilda. "Did she hurt you?"

Carmen shook her head. "No," she sighed. "Not really."

Doña Matilda's sharp eyes took in her young charge's disheveled appearance. "He meant to bed you, Carmen."

"I know."

"You must watch out for him—"

"Doña Matilda," said Carmen, turning tiredly to the old woman, "I am going to leave here. I will not put up with Juan Enrique and his little games."

Her companion regarded Carmen cautiously.

"It is a lonely land for a woman, even two women alone." Matilda Josefa could not say this was unexpected. The question was, would Juan Enrique let La Carmencita go? She thought not.

"Will you come with me?" Carmen asked, meeting her dueña's eyes directly.

"*Sí.*"

"You do not know where I would go."

Doña Matilda shrugged. "I do not want to live out the rest of my life with Juan Enrique and Maria," she observed dryly.

Carmen giggled at the thought. Then she sobered. "I am thinking that we could return to El Paso del Norte."

Doña Matilda stared at her, then nodded slowly. "Mayhap we can even return to Spain someday."

"*Sí.* I do not know how we will get there, but we will try."

"Having the dowry would help," Doña Matilda pointed out. She regarded her charge closely. "But what about that Apache man, Puma? If we return to El Paso del Norte, you will not see him again." Carmen had been very quiet on the topic of the man who had rescued her, and Matilda found her silence intriguing.

Carmen's shoulders slumped. "He—he does not want me."

The other woman stared in disbelief. "Does not want—! Is the man blind? Insane?"

Carmen smiled tiredly at her dueña's loyalty. She was a kind woman, the best. "No," Carmen replied quietly. "He found it too difficult to live

379

with someone who constantly reminded him of the Spanish. He hates the Spanish."

"As do many," observed Doña Matilda with a shiver. "I tell you, this place—" She stopped. No need to scare the child. No need to let La Carmencita know that on her last shopping visit to Santa Fe, she had seen Carlos Garcia, the portly sergeant who had first escorted her to Juan Enrique's villa. Kindly Sergeant Garcia had warned Doña Matilda to stay close to the Delgado villa because the *indios* were very restive. She had taken his cautionary words to heart. No, she would not tell Carmen of this tonight. The young woman had had enough excitement. "Best you get some sleep," she urged instead.

Carmen smiled wanly. She *was* tired. Softly, she closed the door and retired to her bed. But she tossed and turned until dawn, the icy blue eyes of Puma invading her dreams.

The next morning, when she dragged herself to breakfast, it was to find that Doña Matilda and Maria were still abed.

Juan Enrique was not, however. He was sitting at the table, reading mine reports. He smiled graciously upon seeing Carmen and pushed a plateful of warmed corn cakes at her. "We must be more discreet, my desert flower," he warned conspiratorially.

Carmen blinked. "Whatever do you mean?" Dread clenched her stomach in a knot. She pushed the plate back at him, having suddenly lost her appetite.

Delgado smiled meaningfully at her from across the table. "The next time I come to your room, Maria will not know. She need never know." He leered at her.

Carmen shivered in revulsion. She stood up from the table, turned around, and walked from the room.

"I will not be denied!" he cried out behind her. "I *will* have you!"

Chapter 40

Saturday, August 10, 1680

Puma's rough homespun trousers and tunic and hat were enough to make him look like a Spaniard, he thought judiciously. He tied a red Apache handkerchief around his neck. Spaniards liked color.

He glanced across at Takes Two Horses and grinned approvingly. The Apache warrior looked like a real Spaniard. His long hair was tied back, and his large hat and dusty homespun pants and shirt gave him the look of a farmer as he slouched on his horse.

But One Who Hunts still looked Apache to Puma's narrowed eyes. Nothing, certainly not the clothes they had stolen, could make One Who Hunts look like a Spaniard. Even driving the wagon failed to make Puma's stepfather look any more Spanish. Puma tried a different hat on the older man. He squinted critically. Something more was needed. Puma tossed One Who Hunts a folded Spanish blanket. The purple and black stripes draped across his shoulder made him look a little more Spanish. Puma sighed. It would have to do.

The clothes and wagon were a cunning touch, thought Puma in satisfaction. They had been fortunate to come upon a Spanish family traveling *El Camino Real* several leagues outside of Santa Fe. The small party had camped for the night beside a river. While the family slept, Puma and Takes Two Horses had helped themselves to the Spaniards' clothes, the wagon, and the plodding mare who pulled it.

Puma had not left the family completely destitute, however. He had seen two sleeping children among them and he had decided to leave one of the horses. The Spanish family would eventually arrive in Santa Fe, but not as soon as they had anticipated.

For now, Puma, his stepfather, and Takes Two Horses had the sorrel stallion, Takes Two Horses' mare, and the wagon and horse. They pushed the animals hard to reach Santa Fe. According to Takes Two Horses' reckoning, Popé's rebellion was due to take place in three days.

Puma squinted at the horizon. They should reach Santa Fe in another hour, he thought. They had enough time to find Carmen and take her back with them before the rebellion began.

He knew it was going to happen. As they rode, he had seen bands of men straggling toward Santa Fe. Even now, he could see distant human shapes creeping across the desert. But neither he nor his companions gave any sign that they saw the intruders. Keeping to his role, Puma hoped to appear a harmless Spanish farmer traveling to market in the city.

Suddenly, Takes Two Horses pointed to a small dust cloud behind them. Puma swung around to look. More traveling *indios*, he thought, coming to Santa Fe for the uprising. Puma nodded at Takes Two Horses and kicked the sorrel's sides. They had better go faster.

They rode at a swift pace; the mare pulling the wagon was strong, but her sides were covered with sweat. Puma ordered one stop to rest the mare, then urged them onwards. They could rest again when they reached Santa Fe.

It had surprised Puma when Takes Two Horses had first come to him and said that he wished to join Puma and One Who Hunts on their mission to find Carmen in Santa Fe. Puma had not known what to think. It was unusual that the Apache warrior would leave Angry Man, and Puma suspected a trick. But he had agreed to let Takes Two Horses come along, Puma's curiosity overcoming his caution. And he had been well rewarded. Takes Two Horses had proved to be a valuable ally on the journey. It had been he who had suggested stealing the Spaniards' clothes so that they would be able to enter Santa Fe in disguise.

Puma knew that the Apache warrior was still torn about what he should do. The past two nights on the journey, Puma had heard Takes Two Horses moaning in his dreams. Mornings, the young man looked haggard. Puma wondered what life path Takes Two Horses was going to choose. Was he going to return to the tribe and Bird Who Plays and seek help from the shaman, or was he going to continue along the bloody trail of murder that Angry Man had started him on? Puma shrugged. He was glad it was not his decision to make. Perhaps Takes Two Horses needed this time to decide what direction his life would take.

As for Puma, he had troubles enough of his own. He was riding to rescue Carmen, but he did not know if she would willingly come with him. Perhaps her *novio* had won her over. Perhaps she believed whatever lies Angry Man had told her and never wanted to see Puma again.

Puma's lips tightened and his eyes grew cold. Whether she wanted to come with him or no, he would throw her over his horse and carry her out of Santa Fe. That was one decision he *could* make.

As they approached the gates of Santa Fe, Puma felt his heartbeat quicken. A *soldado* on guard duty called out to them to halt. One Who Hunts sat slouched on the wagon seat, fiddling with the reins. Takes Two Horses slouched on his mare and yawned. Puma listened with a respectful, humble air that he found irksome to don as the guard first berated him and then, thinking him sufficiently cowed, asked him questions. No, *capitán*, they had seen no *indios* on their ride. *Sí*, they were farmers. No, they had no food to deliver. They were coming to take away a dead body, one of their family, you know how it is, *capitán*. . . . Puma shrugged.

The *soldado*, after another intense look at Puma, had nodded briefly and let them go through the gates of the presidio. Puma sighed inwardly. The Spanish must know something of the planned rebellion. They were very wary. This was too bad, for it would make the rescue more difficult. Still, he had three days. . . .

The Jicarillas pulled up the wagon in the center of the town plaza. Puma stared around at the government buildings and a large church. He felt hemmed in and wanted to run, but he squashed the impulse. This town was smaller than Mexico City, and he had survived that place.

Puma spotted a man in Apache garb, watering his horse, a big bay stallion, at the fountain. Puma walked the sorrel over to him and dismounted. The black man met Puma's gaze warily, then looked away.

"I am looking for a man," said Puma conversationally in Spanish. He would not speak the Apache language to this rugged-looking man unless he was convinced the other would help him. After all, finding a black man wearing Apache clothing in Santa Fe was suspicious.

Puma uneasily thought of how he himself had acquired his Spanish clothes. Perhaps the man in front of him had acquired his in like manner. Perhaps he simply preferred the more comfortable style of dress. Or perhaps he was a traitor to the Apache people and was here to warn the Spaniards of the rebellion. Puma decided he would be very, very careful with this man.

The black man stared down at Puma's feet and grunted. "You had better get rid of those Apache moccasins if you want to pass as a Spaniard," he suggested in the Apache language.

It was a surprised Puma who met the man's glance warily. The man's eyes were alert, and there was a firmness of manner about him. His flawless pronunciation of the difficult Apache words reassured Puma. Puma took a breath. "I want to find a Spaniard named Juan Enrique Delgado. Do you know him?"

The black glared at Puma. He spat. "Yes, I know him."

Puma's hopes rose. "Can you tell me where to find him?"

The black's eyes raked Puma, the sorrel stallion, then Takes Two Horses and One Who Hunts. All three stared back at him in the hot sunshine.

"Are you a friend of his?" demanded the scout.

Puma stared at the man, not wanting to answer until he knew more about him.

The scout met his eyes and he seemed to make a decision. "I will take you to him."

This was fortunate—perhaps too fortunate, thought Puma, to find a man who, in all the town of Santa Fe, could lead Puma to his enemy. He glanced at a heavy silver and turquoise necklace the scout wore around his neck. The craftsmanship on the squash blossom design was superb. Puma's eyes went back to the scout's and he nodded warily. "What people are you from?"

The scout told him the tribe he had married into. In return, Puma gave the name of Man Who Listens' tribe.

"One of my deceased wife's sisters lives with your people," answered the scout. "She married into your tribe."

Puma grunted. This was good. The man was less likely to betray him if they were kin. He asked more questions and determined that Bird Who Plays in the Pinyon Trees was the daughter of the scout's wife's sister.

"See that man?" Puma indicated Takes Two Horses. "That man wants to marry your niece."

The black scout stared thoughtfully at Takes Two Horses. At last he nodded and said, "My name is Stefano. Come, I will take you to Delgado."

Stefano mounted the bay stallion, and Puma signaled the others to follow. As they rode through the town, Stefano told Puma how he had come to know Juan Enrique Delgado. He verified that a woman of Carmen's description had been traded to the Spaniard. The scout dwelled particularly on how Juan Enrique Delgado had cheated him of weapons. The more Puma heard, the more alarmed he grew that Carmen was with such a man.

At last Stefano halted in front of the large rear gate of the city. He spoke briefly to the *soldado* guarding it. The *soldado* staggered over to the gate, pushed at it until it finally opened, then stepped back and took off his helmet and made a sweeping bow as if ushering them into a king's presence. With a foolish grin, he plopped his helmet back on his head and ambled back to his wineskin.

Puma sighed in relief as the small party passed through the gate. They followed a winding road for a short time, gazing at an occasional adobe hut along the way, or sometimes a larger villa. At last, Stefano drew up his bay in front of a large, spacious villa.

For a moment, Puma's heart sank. Carmen's *novio* lived here, in this luxurious home? She would not thank him for stealing her away from this, his heart told him.

But he was determined. He loved her and cared about her. This house and the Spaniard in it would be no protection whatsoever to Carmen when the *indios* rebelled. The vastness of the house would merely seal her death warrant as one of the hated Spanish who lived in luxury while others starved.

Stefano urged the bay on past the house, as though they had business farther along the road.

"Who lives in the house besides Delgado?" Puma asked the scout.

"An old Indian servant. Two women come in once in a while to do the cleaning and such. The three Spanish women I already spoke of. Oh, yes, and sometimes Delgado keeps a couple of bullies around, two brutes named Alvarez and Medina."

The servants would be small challenge to Puma's plans. The bullies would be another matter if they were in the villa. He would do well to wait for cover of night before stealing Carmen away.

"You after the woman?" asked Stefano casually.

Puma regarded the other solemnly. What would stop this man from reporting everything Puma said to Delgado? The scout had already worked for Delgado and might still feel a personal loyalty to him, though he did sound bitter about being cheated of the weapons. And there was the kinship tie with Puma's tribe. Puma shrugged noncommittally.

The scout halted his bay and met Puma's eyes. "I do not like Delgado," he spat. "I am offering my help."

"I could use some help," Puma admitted. "We do not have much time."

"The rebellion." The scout nodded.

Dios, did *everyone* know of the planned rebellion?

"I hear," remarked the scout, "that the day has been changed."

"What?" Puma stiffened.

"Yes, today is the day of the rebellion."

The news hit Puma like a blow to the stomach. "No!" he muttered. If this were true, he could not wait for the cover of night to rescue Carmen. He must find her immediately.

He swung the sorrel stallion around, all effort to cover their intent gone. "We must get her now," he said to One Who Hunts and Takes Two Horses. "Stefano," he nodded at the listening scout, "tells me the uprising is to happen today, not in three days. We cannot afford to wait another moment. We must get Carmen out of there!"

Chapter 41

"Did anyone order more sacks of corn?" The old *indio* servant's voice could barely be heard in the dining room.

A substantial lunch was just ending as Carmen, Maria, and Doña Matilda lingered over their hot chocolate. Juan Enrique was savoring his fifth glass of expensive, imported red wine.

The old servant repeated himself, his voice rising a trifle in an effort to be heard. He was drowned out by a burp from Juan Enrique. Carmen glared at Juan Enrique, Maria Antonia pouted at him, and Doña Matilda pointedly ignored him.

Carmen had noticed that Juan Enrique had a definite tendency to wax voluble on the topic of his beloved silver mine at mealtimes. Nothing and no one, not even Maria, could hold his attention as well as his silver mine. Yet Carmen had never seen him actually leave the villa to go to the mine. The mining reports just appeared, usually carried in by Alvarez or Medina, two glowering men that Carmen avoided whenever possible. Delgado seemed to spend most of his time lazing around the villa.

It was true that Juan Enrique said he was planning a journey to the silver mine in the forthcoming month, but Carmen had begun to think that his mine was as fanciful as her daydreams of Juan Enrique had turned out to be. Since meeting him, those daydreams had turned to dust. Juan Enrique Delgado was obnoxious—there was no other word for it.

How could her uncle ever have betrothed her to such a man? And to think that she had spent week—no, months—memorizing every single one of Thomas of Torquemada's four hundred and seventy-three maxims on How To Be A Perfect Wife for this man! What Carmen should have done, she thought viciously, was to drop the heavy tome over the side of the ship the moment they left Cadiz harbor.

"What corn?" asked Juan Enrique lazily, settling himself in his chair once more. Not waiting for an answer, he ordered, "Tell them to drop it off in the kitchen. Why are you bothering us with such trifles?"

"Hey!" The old servant was roughly shoved aside as four strangers pushed their way into the dining room. All three women stared, aghast, at the intruders.

Juan Enrique, whose back was to the doorway, slowly turned around. "What—?"

Carmen gasped. She recognized the black scout, the one whom Juan Enrique had sent away so ignominiously. The scout was holding an arquebus pointed directly at Juan Enrique.

There was also something vaguely familiar about the others, now that she looked closely. One was a black-eyed Spaniard with his hair tied back, and another was a shorter Spaniard with a purple and black blanket draped over his shoulder. Both carried swords, the naked blades sharp. But when her wide eyes met the cold, icy blue eyes of the large man who was the leader, Carmen knew him at once. She wanted to cry out in joy. She wanted to crumple to the floor in fright.

Puma! What was he doing here? She half-rose in her chair, one hand at her throat, trying desperately to scream, when he reached across the table and dragged her out of her chair. Dishes and food flew in every direction.

"You cannot do that!" protested Juan Enrique.

Puma clapped a hand over Carmen's mouth to prevent her scream and held both her arms behind her back. His furious blue eyes glared at the pudgy Spaniard. "Do not stop me, little toad," he said in Spanish.

Juan Enrique gasped. Maria leaped to her feet and threw herself protectively in front of him. "How dare you!" she cried. "You cannot come into this house and—and—"

"Where are the jewels?" demanded Puma of Juan Enrique.

Carmen tried to struggle. What did Puma want of her? Why was he here? Her heart pounded in excitement.

Puma tightened his grip on her arms and she subsided.

"The jewels!" he demanded again. Puma was not going to wait for the Spaniard to come up with a lie about the jewels. "Takes Two Horses, go with him!"

Takes Two Horses pushed the trembling Juan Enrique Delgado towards the stairs.

"I will not tell you," cried Juan Enrique in a terrified voice.

"Then we kill the woman," said Stefano in a lazy voice. His arquebus was now pointing at Maria Antonia de Mendoza's heaving bosom. Despite his relaxed stance, Carmen, Juan Enrique, and Maria believed that he meant what he said.

Delgado stared. He wet his lips.

"Well?" prodded Stefano.

Delgado cleared his throat and cast a glance at Maria. Her life now hung by a thread, and that thread was in Juan Enrique's pale, puffy hands.

Carmen stared in fascination at the battle that waged on Juan Enrique's face. She could almost follow his thoughts as he tried to decide whether to keep the jewels or to save Maria. Carmen shuddered.

Maria herself looked pale. Her eyes pleaded

with the Spaniard, and seeing him hesitate, she murmured, *"Por favor."*

Juan Enrique Delgado did not move.

"Por Dios!" she cried.

An eternity later, Juan Enrique muttered, "Very well, my little *rubí.*" Then he turned towards the stairs. Takes Two Horses followed him menacingly.

Maria sank into a chair, put her head down on the table, and sobbed in relief. Even the scout looked relieved. It had been only a threat, Carmen suddenly realized. While they waited for Delgado and the Apache warrior to return, Maria's sobs echoed through the room. Doña Matilda remained standing stiffly by her chair.

Juan Enrique was soon shoved into the room by Takes Two Horses. Carmen spied her leather dowry sack in the Apache warrior's hand. So. Juan Enrique had not played his little *rubí* false.

Takes Two Horses tossed the leather pouch to Puma. Puma opened it and glanced inside. With a satisfied nod, he tucked it away inside his tunic. "Come." He propelled Carmen towards the kitchen door. They were through the kitchen and outside into the yard in several swift strides.

Puma took his hand away from her mouth. "Where," she gasped, "are you taking me?"

"Get in," he said roughly. "No time to talk." He pushed her into the bed of the wagon and snatched up a coil of rope.

"You can't do this to me!"

Within seconds she was neatly trussed, hand and foot.

"Let me go!" This was not the man she loved! He yanked off the red handkerchief from around his neck and tied it around her mouth.

Carmen glowered at him, her turquoise eyes outraged. Around her were littered several sacks, some of them filled with sand. The "corn," she realized—the effective ruse the Apaches had used to gain entrance to the villa.

Puma swiftly covered her with the homespun sacks. With a bitter sigh, Carmen closed her eyes against the rough material. Tears forced their way through her clenched eyes. She was in a turmoil. He had come to rescue her, screamed one part of her brain. Hard on that thought came: *He doesn't love me, doesn't want me. Oh, why can I not accept that?*

Yet the traitorous thoughts and feeling still arose. For a moment, she'd been overjoyed to see his beloved face. For a moment, she'd forgotten his betrayal. Love, pure and simple, had leaped in her heart. Now bitterness reigned. Why had he come? What did he want of her? To inflict more pain? Seeing him did just that— inflicted terrible pain in her heart. How could he have thrown her away? Sold her to Angry Man? Didn't he realize she loved him?

The wagon began to move.

"Stop!" cried Puma. "Where's Stefano?"

Just then the black scout marched out the front door of the villa, his arms full of arque-buses. A wide grin was on his face as he crossed the yard to his horse. "Delgado should have paid me what he said he would," Stefano announced jovially. "He would have saved himself a fortune in weapons." Whistling happily, Stefano tucked the guns into his blanket roll and mounted the bay.

The wagon started forward.

Despite her tears, Carmen suddenly noticed that Juan Enrique did not run protesting after her. He could have, she thought. He could have run out and tried to prevent Puma from taking her away. But he did not. Juan Enrique was still inside the house, where it was safe, probably being consoled against the big breasts of Maria Antonia de Mendoza at this very moment.

"Wait!" came a loud cry. The wagon ground to a halt once more.

Puma swung around, the sorrel prancing beneath him.

"Take me with you!" demanded Doña Matilda. She stood glaring at Puma from the steps of the villa, one arm on her hip, a small case in her other hand, her gray hair flying loose around her head.

Puma stared at her. "This is an abduction," he explained. "I cannot take you with me."

"*Sí*, you can," she said keeping her eyes steadily upon his as she marched down the two steps and crossed the yard to him. "Doña Carmen is in my charge. Where she goes, I go."

Puma looked helplessly at Takes Two Horses and One Who Hunts. Stefano chuckled audibly.

Puma frowned. He saw he could expect no help from them.

"Señora," he said carefully. "You do not want to come with us. It is a very rough life. We *indios* move around often." Suddenly inspired, he added, "And we eat dog meat."

Doña Matilda made a face. "I am *Señorita* Delgado," she corrected. "I am used to moving around. I have never eaten dog meat in my life, and I am too old to start now." She stood planted firmly in front of the sorrel.

Puma glanced at the villa, expecting Juan Enrique Delgado to come running out after them at any moment. "Please step aside," he said. He had no wish to harm the stubborn old one. "We must leave."

Seeing the direction of his glance, Doña Matilda hastened to assure him, "You need not expect pursuit. At this very moment Juan Enrique is being nestled against the generous bosom of Maria Antonia. And she is busy telling him how brave he is." Her voice rang with contempt.

I knew it, raged Carmen silently. *The little toad*!

Doña Matilda ran to the wagon, flung her small case aboard, and hopped on after it. She glared mutinously at Puma. "I am coming with you. I will not stay another day with that idiot of a nephew," she pronounced.

Puma shrugged. They had wasted enough time. "Let's get out of here," he said, and the small procession moved forward.

Carmen clenched her teeth. She could expect

no less than indifference from Delgado. In truth, she felt relieved to be leaving him behind. Oh, but Puma, she moaned, how could *you* have betrayed me? How could you have turned your back on my love?

Anguish tore at her heart. He was taking her with him, but why? Clearly, he did not love her. Pain gripped her throat, where more tears awaited. Oh, she should never have journeyed to the New World. She should have stayed in Spain—in the convent. Never ventured forth, never learned about love, about men, about Puma. Never learned the agony of a broken heart. . . .

Chapter 42

Puma dug his heels into the sorrel's sides. They had to move swiftly to get away from Santa Fe before the rebellion broke out.

He glanced over his shoulder. Stefano, Takes Two Horses, and One Who Hunts followed, faces grim. One Who Hunts, driving the wagon, was barely able to keep the mare in check. She wanted to run. She must have sensed their fear, thought Puma.

He wondered how Carmen was feeling, under the sacks. He hoped she understood that he was not going to hurt her. Her dueña he ignored.

The rocking motion of the wagon frightened Carmen. She feared that at any moment she was going to be bounced off the flat bed of the wagon. She spent much of her time praying.

Why had he stolen her? She continued to ponder grimly. Had he received so much wealth from her trade to El Cabezón the first time that Puma had decided to repeat the sale? That must be it. What other reason could he have for marching into Santa Fe in daylight and stealing her right from her previous *novio*'s home? Carmen shivered. Puma's icy blue eyes had not looked kind. She wondered if he hated her as much as El Cabezón had reported that he did.

Then Carmen felt Doña Matilda move closer to her. She was suddenly glad of the brave old woman's presence. Amidst all the betrayal of *novio* and of lover, only the old woman had remained firm. The thought brought more tears to Carmen's eyes. How *could* Puma have betrayed her so?

Puma slowed the stallion when he spotted a rag-tag band of men coming down the road. He held up a hand to warn One Who Hunts to slow down the wagon.

Puma's heartbeat quickened as he halted the sorrel. The band was a motley collection of Indians of all different tribes, on foot. Puma could see that the men wore various pieces of Spanish clothing—here a torn blue velvet vest, there a dented pike helmet, over there, stiff armored leggings. And the mob fairly bristled with swords and pikes and spears. One man brandished a bloody sword. Several had arquebuses. Puma hoped they did not know how to fire them.

The mob appeared to be in a high state of excitement. Puma swung back to Takes Two

Horses. The two planted themselves on either side of the wagon. Stefano took up the defense of the rear, behind the wagon.

"Spaniards! Spaniards!" yelled the Indians in the forefront of the crowd as they spied Puma and his companions. The mob began to run toward them.

Puma walked the sorrel ahead, keeping a tight grip on the prancing stallion. The sorrel could sense the excitement and danger. So could Puma.

Puma called out in the Jicarilla language, stating who he was and his companions' names. No recognition from the crowd. Not surprising, thought Puma. He doubted there was a single Jicarilla, or even an Apache speaker, in the bunch. He tried Spanish.

This brought bared teeth and cries of "Kill them! Kill them! Kill the Spanish!"

Puma and Takes Two Horses ripped off their shirts and shook their hair loose. Now they looked Apache, Puma hoped. One or two men in the crowd seemed to realize that they were showing that they were not Spanish. "Not Spanish!" yelled Puma.

The mob took up the cry and began screaming, "Not Spanish!" back at him.

Puma watched them warily. They were behaving in a way he had not seen rational men behave before.

One tall man with piercing eyes was dressed in a deliberately torn and ragged brown padre's robe. It contrasted strangely with the Spanish helmet on his head. He seemed to have some control over his comrades, however, and urged them to be quiet. When he could finally be heard, he demanded, "Where are you from?"

Puma told him, and the man frowned. Puma added, "We want no trouble with you. We want only to leave Santa Fe."

"If you are not with us, you are against us," cried a voice in the mob.

Puma shook his head, his long, straight hair fluttering. "It is your fight," he said. "This is your country. We Apaches are from the mountains. We do not live in Santa Fe. We want only to return to our people."

There were loud murmurings from the crowd. Clearly many of the rebels wanted to kill Puma and his companions. "No!" protested Puma firmly. "We are Indian, just as you are. We do not want to fight you!"

The mob was turning ugly now. Men were pressing forward, pushing against the sorrel. The tall leader seemed to have lost control of the band.

Puma glanced back at his comrades. He waved them forward. Kneeing the sorrel, Puma fought his way through the mob. One man landed a blow on the sorrel's hindquarters. The stallion reared, but Puma managed to retain his seat. Eyes rolling, the sorrel lashed out with several powerful kicks. Men cried out in pain.

"Get back," yelled Puma. "Let us through!" He whirled a sword around his head and out to the sides, hacking in warning.

Men moved away. No one wanted to feel the thrust of the sword or one of the sorrel's powerful kicks. One Who Hunts drove the wagon into the path that Puma and the sorrel created, and he and the scout fought their way through the angry throng. Two men managed to deliver half-hearted blows at the scout, who brought up the rear. He turned and fired the arquebus over their heads.

Someone in the mob fired back. Takes Two Horses slumped forward on his horse. "I'm hit!" he cried. "I'm hit!" He clutched at his stomach; blood seeped between his fingers.

Stefano reloaded his arquebus and fired once more. This time the crowd surged away from them. Stefano fired a third time, and the dirt kicked up by the bullet sprayed a man. He clutched at his face as he yelled, then turned and ran. The crowd ran after him.

Finally clear of the mob, Puma stopped to let the animals calm down. He scarcely noticed that the motley mob ran down the road in the direction of Juan Enrique Delgado's villa. Puma had little time to wonder how the Spaniard and his woman would fare, because he was too busy trying to stanch the deadly flow of blood from Takes Two Horses' side.

Chapter 43

"Oho, what have we here?" leered a tall *indio* in torn monk's robes as he pushed his way into the kitchen. He wore a Spanish *soldado's* helmet on his head.

He and two other men had burst into the villa only moments before. Juan Enrique Delgado lifted his head from Maria's breasts and ordered, "Get out of my house, you filthy vermin!"

"How dare you enter this house!" It was Maria Antonia in her most imperious manner. "Juan Enrique, do something," she added.

Juan Enrique Delgado rose from his chair, a ferocious frown on his face. He hoped to scare these *indios* away. It was most unfortunate that he had given Alvarez and Medina the day off. They were never around when he needed them. First, those accursed desperados and the black scout had stolen his sack of jewels—a loss that still rankled—and now this! Just thinking about the injustice of it all made Juan Enrique furious.

"I said get out!" He took a pace towards the tall *indio*. Juan Enrique glanced at the other two with him. Then, to his surprise, seven more *indios* pushed into the room. They were dressed in a wretched assortment of Spanish clothing. And they all carried weapons, some with blood glistening on them. A terrible silence filled the dining room and Juan Enrique's heart as he realized that these were not the quiet, docile *indios* he was accustomed to seeing in Santa Fe.

"Get out," he tried again, but his voice shook.

The tall *indio* laughed. He was the leader of this band of rebels. He knew Popé personally, had come from the same village as Popé, and all his followers recognized his authority. He prowled towards Juan Enrique, looking like nothing so much as a great brown wolf. "No," he said, openly enjoying Juan Enrique's obvious terror. "You get out. It is our turn. We"— he thumped his chest—"*we* take over the land now. We take over the houses. We kill all the Spanish. We will live like the Spanish. It is you who will get out." He laughed again, showing big white teeth.

Juan Enrique stared in disbelief at the man, unable to believe what he was hearing.

Maria Antonia's slanted green eyes went from one man to another. "Juan Enrique," she squeaked. "Do something."

"Maria," Delgado cautioned. "Be quiet. I need to think."

"Please do," chortled the tall *indio*. "But it will not help you. I, Pepito, claim this house and lands for my people and our great leader, Popé!"

"Juan," whimpered Maria and she pushed closer to him, no longer the imperious lady of the villa. Delgado pushed her away. The wine he had drunk with his luncheon had clouded his mind at first, but no more.

"Well, Pepito," he snarled, rocking back and forth on his heels. "Get the hell out of my house. Go claim someone else's villa!"

"We killed the Spanish," sneered Pepito. "We have killed many Spanish this day!"

"Juan?" Maria, pale, grabbed at his arm. She *would* be comforted. "What he's saying? It cannot be true—"

"Let go, Maria." Delgado shrugged her off. Then he swung quickly and landed a smashing blow in Pepito's unsuspecting face. "Get the hell out!"

Pepito fell back against the wall from the force of the blow. A shot rang out, and Juan Enrique dropped to his knees, a bullet hole through his forehead. He fell to the floor, dead.

"Juan Enrique!" screamed Maria, sinking to her knees beside him. "Oh, Juan Enrique," she moaned, all her plans for being a rich man's wife lying dead before her eyes. "Juan Enrique . . ."

Pepito, his black eyes filled with fury at the punch that the deceased had landed, grabbed her arm and dragged her to her feet. "He is dead," he snarled. "He cannot help you now."

"Let us kill her, too," someone suggested.

Pepito paused, eyeing the woman. "Someone must pay for this." He rubbed his cheek where Juan Enrique had hit him. His black eyes were fastened on the trembling Maria like a stalking wolf watches a doe.

"I say kill her," spoke up one of the men. He was shorter than Pepito, but of heavier build. He tucked the smoking arquebus into his waistband and crossed his arms belligerently across his broad chest. This man had constantly challenged Pepito throughout the morning, ever since Popé had given the order to attack the Spaniards. Pepito knew the man wanted to supplant him as leader of the band of rebels.

"Popé said to kill every Spaniard," pronounced the challenger. "Man, child, or *woman*. I say we kill her." He plucked Maria's arm from Pepito's grasp. With his other hand, he pulled a long knife from his waistband. The razor-sharp blade was stained red. Several murmurings came from the others; the men wanted her death.

Pepito refused to take a step back or to show that he was in any way intimidated. He glanced at Maria. The Spanish woman was beautiful. Her red hair glistened in the sunlight that slanted through the room, her green eyes turned up at the corners, her full breasts . . . Pepito drew a shaky breath.

He felt a hunger come over him to have all that had belonged to the Spaniard. His house, his woman . . . Then, and only then, would Pepito truly be a *man* in his own land once again. Pepito had suffered under the Spanish, God knew. They had killed his brother, forcing him to labor to build their church when he was too sick and weak. The Spanish had killed him as surely as if they'd cut him down with a sword. Yes, it was time that Pepito got something back from the Spanish.

Maria, her desperate instinct to stay alive suddenly on full alert, saw clearly that only this one man, this Pepito with the flashing eyes, stood between her and a death such as Juan Enrique's. The shorter, heavier man was glaring at her with eyes full of hate. It was he who had shot Juan Enrique, she realized. What should she do? She had to save herself. Life was too sweet to let go. Though she had lost her chance for riches, she would not lose her chance for life.

What to do? She could feel the men watching her; her skin crawled from their hate. Slowly she sank to her knees in front of Pepito. She bowed her fiery head briefly, then tossed her hair and gazed up at him, her white throat exposed.

I could kill her, Pepito thought. I have power over her, a Spaniard, a woman of the invaders. I have the power of life and death.

A feeling of omnipotence such as he had never known surged through him. She was on her knees to him, vulnerable, begging for her life. *A*

Spaniard was begging him for her life! Pepito's chest swelled with excitement. He felt his groin stir.

The gathered men watched Maria with a newly awakened interest. Imperceptibly, the tension in the room shifted from one of hate to one of lust.

Maria was unaware of it. "Please," she murmured. She swallowed, forcing the word past her dry lips. Her heart pounded. She could not look at Juan Enrique's dead body. She could not look at any of the men and see the awful hate for her in their eyes, see the blood-lusting demands for her death. Only one man could she look at. She gazed up at Pepito, tears filling her eyes and blurring his image for a moment. "Please," she whispered. "Do not kill me. . . ." She faltered when she saw those flashing eyes harden. "*Por favor . . .*"

Pepito drew his sword and held it above her.

Maria closed her eyes and bowed her head, thinking desperately of some way to stave off his deadly intent. Her hand faltered as she tentatively touched his foot. He jerked it away. She snatched her hand back, her cheeks burning.

"She is mine," she heard Pepito growl. Maria stifled a gasp, then a tiny smile crossed her lips. Hope filled her heart. She lifted her head and her green eyes impaled Pepito's.

Surprise and fascination flared in his eyes before he swung away to glare at his opponent, the man calling for her death.

After what seemed a lifetime to Maria, Pepito's challenger shrugged and took a step back. He tucked his knife into his waistband.

Pepito stretched out a hand towards Maria.

With fingers that shook, she reached out and put her hand in his. His grasp was firm, warm. He lifted her to her feet and she rose gracefully, her life restored to her, a heady triumph singing in her blood. She was alive! She would rule this man and survive! No one would have cause to kill her. She would rule all of them!

With narrowed eyes, Pepito's opponent watched them leave the room. Perhaps he would have a try at the lovely woman himself. Later.

Chapter 44

It was dusk. Puma decided it was fortunate that
Juan Enrique Delgado had chosen to live outside
the presidio walls of Santa Fe. Puma's little party
had a measure of safety as they skirted the city,
keeping well away from the high walls. Nothing
but death and destruction now engulfed the city.
A hellish light lit the sky, and Puma knew that
many of the buildings must be on fire. The rebellion had truly begun.

Puma stopped at some distance to the side of
the city. It was time to bid Stefano farewell. He
wanted to journey north to search out his people
and tell them the news of what had happened
in Santa Fe. Puma thanked him for his help in
rescuing Carmen. To Puma's surprise, the scout
pulled off the heavy silver and turquoise necklace
he wore around his neck. Handing it to Puma,

Stefano said, "Take this gift, with my thanks."

"For what?" Puma was astounded at the stunning beauty of the magnificent necklace. The silver was heavy and exquisitely crafted, the turquoise stone was flawless.

"For allowing me the opportunity to recoup my loss on Delgado." Stefano patted his blanket roll where the arquebuses were hidden. "I have you to thank for these guns. They will bring freedom to my people, freedom from the Spanish."

Puma shrugged. The arquebuses might just bring more death to The People. "You will need powder and shot."

Stefano grinned. "I will get them."

Puma had no doubt he would. They parted with a friendly good-bye, then Puma and One Who Hunts and the women hurried on. Puma felt desperate to get away from the killing.

Puma glanced anxiously at Takes Two Horses. They had placed him in the wagon after he had fallen unconscious and slipped from his mare. Puma had no recourse but to untie Carmen and use her ropes to lash his wounded friend securely onto the back of the rickety vehicle. Doña Matilda bounced along in the wagon beside the wounded man, doing her best to make him comfortable.

What disturbed Puma most was the bloody gash in Takes Two Horses' side and the great amount of blood he was losing. The warrior's breathing was shallow and tortured. Puma feared for his friend's life.

Carmen rode Takes Two Horses' mare. Puma

held the lead rope. Evidently, he did not want to risk his valuable captive suddenly bolting into the desert, she thought grimly.

Carmen felt dusty, disheveled, and disheartened as she sat astride the Apache mare. She recognized the wounded man in the back of the wagon as the renegade who had untied her before she had been traded to Juan Enrique. Carmen hoped the young warrior did not die, but he sounded bad and he looked worse.

She saw Puma glance at the wounded man several times. Puma looked worried. Good, she thought resentfully. At least he cared about someone, even if it was not her.

Then she felt guilty for thinking such a cruel thought. She sighed and wondered for the thousandth time what Puma was going to do with her. Would he sell her? Would he, mayhap, even let her go? But where would she go? The land was in an uproar.

She had been frightened at the sounds she had heard when the mob of unruly *indios* had attacked them outside the villa, but she had not actually seen anything—the sacks had covered her. But when they had passed the rear gates of Santa Fe, she had been riding the mare and had seen for herself the great danger the people of the city were in. Men were killing each other, and even from that distance, she could hear piercing screams of pain.

Puma's small party was now passing the front gates of Santa Fe, but still keeping a goodly distance between themselves and the city. Carmen

415

could see Spanish *soldados* locked in ferocious combat with a large number of near-naked *indios*.

Puma turned to glimpse Santa Fe, or what was left of it, one last time.

Suddenly, out of the gates raced a Spanish woman, her long red velvet skirts tripping her up. She clutched a small bundle tightly to her breast. Puma watched in consternation as she glanced over her shoulder at three Indians pursuing her. One of them stopped, raised his bow and let fly an arrow. The arrow struck the woman's back and she fell, brought low as swiftly and cleanly as a doe. The bundle she had held bounced and rolled several steps from her. In agony, and still alive, the woman clawed the ground, striving desperately to reach the bundle. Her baby, Puma suddenly realized. He saw the mother crawl a short distance, then collapse to move no more. She died facing her baby.

A quick movement to his left caught Puma's eye, and his hand reached out, lightning-swift, to grasp Carmen's lunging mare. She wanted to rescue the baby, Puma realized. Before he could do anything more to stop her, she gave a cry and her face paled as she stared, aghast, at the baby.

Puma swung round in time to see one of the Indians snatch up the baby and race back through the gates of the city.

Grim-visaged, Puma turned away from the scene. He felt suddenly sickened at the slaughter. Why, that dead mother could have been Car-

men, had he not rescued her. And the baby . . .
He shuddered.

"Get moving," Puma urged harshly. He
slapped the mare's flank.

The startled horse leaped ahead, nearly
bouncing Carmen off. She flinched and hung
onto the mare, staring straight ahead. Her
stomach roiled at what she'd just witnessed.
That poor mother! That tiny baby! She dreaded
what would happen to the little one now that
its mother was dead. How terrible this destruction was.

And though Puma and Carmen quickly left
the carnage behind them, over another rise of a
hill, the memory of the dying mother and stolen
baby stayed with each of them for a long time.

They traveled for three days into the Sangre de
Cristo Mountains. In that time, Puma was convinced more than once that Takes Two Horses
was going to die. Twice, the barely healing wound
broke open and blood gushed forth. Doña Matilda tore a strip from the hem of her dress and
used some of their precious water to dab at the
blood and clean the wound. As Puma watched
her efforts, he felt surprisingly grateful for the
old woman's presence.

Once, Puma stopped to scoop up a handful of
cobwebs and stuff them in the wound. He thought
that Takes Two Horses breathed a little better
after that.

Puma found himself praying frantically to God
to let the Jicarilla warrior stay on his earthly jour-

ney. *Shi Tsoyee, let him live until we can get to the shaman*, Puma prayed over and over. *Then he can get help. Ihéedn.* There had been so much killing and death that terrible day in Santa Fe that it seemed vital to Puma that he do all he could to prevent one more death.

At last, late the third day, they reached Man Who Listens' village, and Puma let out a breath of relief. He lifted Carmen from the mare, his eyes meeting hers in mute apology that he had not been able to stop and explain his actions to her before. He hoped she knew he loved her and wanted her. Otherwise, why would he have rescued her?

He set her on her feet, then swung round to call for the shaman. The old man came walking briskly toward him. His assistant shaman came at a run. Carefully, Puma and the two shamans lifted Takes Two Horses off the wagon. Murmurs ran through the crowd of women and children gathered around to watch. Several of the women cried out at seeing the terrible gash in the young warrior's side.

But it was Bird Who Plays in the Pinyon Trees who was most visibly affected. Pale and shaken, she walked along beside the wounded man. She sat down beside the old shaman and watched with huge brown eyes everything he did, from cleaning the wound to packing it with cobwebs. When the shaman called for a hearty meat broth to feed the wounded man, it was Bird Who Plays who appeared with steaming bowl in hand. When he called for more cobwebs, it was Bird Who Plays who gathered and brought them. It was Bird Who Plays who picked the leaves for the tea that would restore Takes Two Horses' blood.

Puma let the sorrel stallion loose in the corral, then looked around to see where Carmen was. He spotted her watching him but warily keeping her distance. Very well, he would deal with her later. She would not try running off deeper into the mountains. He could risk a visit to the old shaman to see if Takes Two Horses would live.

The shaman readily conferred with Puma. "He has stopped bleeding," the old man observed. "He has two holes in his side."

Seeing Puma's surprise, the old man nodded. "One hole is at the front where the bullet entered, and one is at the back, where it came out."

"Is he going to recover?"

The old man shrugged. "He has lived this long with the wound. Three days, is it not?" At Puma's nod, he added, "Since he did not die on the way here, it is very likely that he will get better."

They both watched Bird Who Plays carry another steaming bowl of broth over to where the wounded man lay. She knelt down and began spooning the nourishing liquid between Takes Two Horses' lips. Takes Two Horses' eyes opened and he jerked, coughing, knocking her hand. Broth streamed down his neck.

Puma's lips twitched. "Takes Two Horses has good care," he observed.

"Very good care," nodded the old shaman, a twinkle in his black eyes.

Puma started to walk away, then, remembering something, he walked back to the shaman. "Has he—?" Puma hesitated; it was really not his business. But he was concerned about Takes Two Horses. "Has he mentioned any dreams?"

The old man shook his head. "No." He watched Puma keenly. "Ghosts?" he asked, seeing the younger man's discomfiture.

Puma nodded, relieved. "Many ghosts. Spanish ghosts."

The shaman frowned. "This is serious, then."

"Yes." Puma glanced at Takes Two Horses, who was now sipping at the broth that Bird Who Plays was spooning. "If he is to recover completely . . ."

The old man nodded. " . . . then the ghosts must be driven away."

Puma felt grateful for the old one's understanding. "I will bring you an antelope," he said.

The old man grunted and turned away. He called out to his assistant. "Come, we have work to do."

Puma left them, heads together as they talked. He felt new hope for Takes Two Horses. Now, if he could only solve his own problems. . . .

Chapter 45

Open-mouthed, Carmen watched Puma walk the sorrel stallion in the opposite direction, toward the corral. *Dios*! Why did he go to so much trouble to steal her from Santa Fe if he was going to leave her alone in the village? And why would he not stay and face her? A spasm of fear shook her. He must have planned something awful for her.

She donned her anger as a protective cloak and marched to the tipi. Doña Matilda followed.

"What are you going to do?" asked her dueña, sitting down on Puma's bed. She looked as much at home as if she had been born in a tipi, thought Carmen in surprise.

"Do?" repeated Carmen. "Why, I—I—" She glanced around at the neat dwelling and put her face in her hands. She did not have to pretend, not with her old friend. Anger gave way to pain and fear. "I don't know," she wailed.

"Come, come," chided Doña Matilda. "Now is not the time for tears."

"It is," assured Carmen, wiping her eyes. "If ever I needed to cry, it is now."

Doña Matilda nodded, and sat patiently waiting for Carmen's sobs to stop.

"Do you want to tell me why he did it?" Doña Matilda asked at last.

"You mean why he stole me from Santa Fe?"

The other woman nodded.

Carmen shook her head. "No, I don't." It was too painful, too humiliating to say what she'd been thinking—that he did not love her, but wanted to profit from the sale of her. She sobbed harder.

Doña Matilda watched her shrewdly. "Do you even know why he stole you back?"

Again Carmen shook her head. Then she remembered. This was her dueña, her faithful companion. If she could not tell her, who could she tell? At last Carmen was able to gasp out, "I—I think he wants to sell me again."

She bowed her head and cried. The loss of Puma was too great to bear. Why, *how* could she have loved him? And yet, she knew that even now she loved him; even knowing what he planned, she could not stop her feelings for him. "Oh," she moaned, "was ever a woman more miserable?"

"Sell you?" Doña Matilda flinched. Of all the answers she had been expecting, it certainly was not that one. "He came after you in Santa Fe to take you back to *sell* you?" she asked incredulously.

Carmen nodded morosely.

Doña Matilda looked baffled. "I could have sworn—" she muttered. She straightened. "Carmen, listen to me."

Carmen slowly raised her head at the urgency in her chaperone's voice.

"I was in the canyon. Lost. He found me. He took me back to the caravan. I would have died without his help."

Carmen nodded. "He told me you were safe."

"What I mean to say," said Doña Matilda desperately, "is that I thought he was a good man. Why, he saved my life, saved yours! That does not square with a man taking a woman he has lov"—she cleared her throat—"uh, taking a woman and selling her."

"Mayhap Apaches are different," sobbed Carmen.

Doña Matilda was silent, thoughtful. Then she snorted. "They may be, but *that* Apache man loves you. I can see it in his eyes, whenever he looks at you." She shook her head. "No, I think he has brought you back for another reason."

"What reason?" asked Carmen, eyes red from crying.

Doña Matilda paused, listening. "I believe we will soon find out."

Puma was outside the tipi. He took a breath and pushed at the deerskin flap.

Carmen looked up when he entered. "You!" she cried.

Puma was taken aback. "Of course it's me."

"That is not what I meant!" She watched as he prowled closer to her. She straightened the blankets she was kneeling on so she could gather her thoughts. He was here at last—to sell her. Carmen swallowed. Whatever she had to face, she would do it bravely. He would not have the satisfaction of seeing her cry and plead!

She could feel the heat of his body as he came closer.

He halted. "Señorita Delgado," he said. "Please leave."

Doña Matilda looked mightily affronted. She seared Puma with her gaze. Then a sly look came over her face. "Very well," she agreed meekly and got to her feet. "I will leave."

"Don't you dare leave!" cried Carmen.

"She must," said Puma softly.

Regretfully, Doña Matilda nodded her head. "I must," she agreed. "You have much to talk about." Her glance at Puma was piercing, even threatening.

He wondered if she would stomp on his instep.

"I will go visiting the neighbors." Doña Matilda added, "But I will not be far away." With a last warning glance at Puma, she turned and left the tipi.

Was the old woman trying to scare him? wondered Puma. Then he shrugged dismissively. He would not harm Carmen, ever. He turned his attention back to her, Carmen, the woman he loved. "*Chihonii*," he murmured.

"I am *not* your friend," she snapped. So he was going to pretend friendship, was he?

"Ah, but you are."

"Friends do not sell friends," she sneered. Let him know he was not talking to a fool. She would have the truth between them.

Puma frowned at her, wondering what she was talking about.

"What is the matter?" she continued in contempt. "I know of your plans for me!"

How he hated her contempt. It was so—so Spanish! He watched her carefully. If she knew his plans for her, that he wanted her—why then, was she acting so angry and insulting?

"Didn't you get as much wealth as you expected when you sold me to your *indio* friend?" taunted Carmen.

Puma's frown turned thoughtful. "Angry Man," he said, understanding at last. "Angry Man told you that I sold you to him?"

"*Sí!*" she snapped. She waited for several heartbeats. "Didn't you?" She held her breath.

"And you believed him?" Puma's voice was low and tortured now.

Carmen frowned and took a breath. "Of course. He spoke the truth." But Carmen felt a little unsure. She watched his glowering countenance. Why was *he* so angry? *She* was the one who was hurt! "I know it is true now!" Inside her heart, however, doubt was creeping in.

Puma stared at her. He could scarcely abide looking at her, so great was his fury at her. "It is a lie! It is Angry Man's lie. He told you that to tear us apart. He sought to revenge himself on me by stealing and humiliating you!"

Carmen's heart quickened at his words. She had not believed Angry Man at first—but as the days went by, and she had had more and more time to think, she had finally come to believe that Puma had indeed sold her. The people in her life had had a way of getting rid of her, of pushing her aside—it was certainly true of her father and her uncle—and so Angry Man's words had taken fertile root in her own feelings of rejection. She had finally come to believe that Puma hated her and wanted her sold.

"What else did Angry Man tell you?" Puma demanded. The skin was stretched tight across his high cheekbones. "What else?"

"That you hated me, hated all Spanish—"

"And?"

"And nothing more. He did not have to tell me more. I knew for myself that you hated the Spanish. Have always hated them—hated me!" Her voice was bitter at her loss of him. If it had not been for his hate of the Spanish, mayhap they would have had a chance to stay together. But his hate was too strong; he had transferred that intensity of passion onto her, and it had been the death of their love.

What love? demanded a little voice in her mind. *He never said he loved you.* Of *her* love, then.

His tortured voice cut into her thoughts. "*Sí,* I hated the Spanish," he said. "I hated them for taking my lands, for throwing me into prison, for their brutality to me. . . ." His voice was low, passion-filled. "And I hated my Spanish father for abandoning me!"

Carmen's face paled when she heard that. Now she realized the depth of his hate and exactly what stood between them. His Spanish father had abandoned him. No wonder he hated the Spanish. And there was no way she could ever cross that chasm, she realized now. Her own hopes of love, her despair at Angry Man's words, all of it welled up in her and she knew she could never overcome the intensity of his hate against the Spanish. Her shoulders slumped. If only his father had loved him, stayed with him . . . but he hadn't. He had left Puma and in doing so, created one more enemy against the Spanish.

"But the Spanish are not the only brutal ones," Puma was saying. "There are *indios* who can match them. There are *indios* who are capable of selling their own brother . . . *mayhap* even *indios* capable of leaving their children, as my father left me." Sadly he shook his head. "Let me just say that the Spanish are not the only ones who do cruel things."

"There is much between us," she whispered. "Many things stand between us—our people, our ways, our beliefs, our parents. . . ." *So much misunderstanding,* she thought sadly, painfully. *My love was not strong enough, dearest one, to overcome all the hate.*

"*Sí,*" he was saying heavily. After a long pause, he added, "And yet there were Spaniards who would be my friend. Miguel Baca for one. Fray Cristobal, for another. He intervened for me, even when it almost cost him his life to do so." Puma was remembering the first day he had met the churchman and Fray Cristobal had thrown himself upon Puma to protect him from Comandante Diego's sword. "No, not all the Spaniards are evil," murmured Puma. "I think it is individuals who can be cruel," he said sadly. "But I do not think it is because they are Spanish or *indio.* I think it is because they choose in their hearts to hurt others."

As Angry Man chose to do, as Takes Two Horses had once chosen.

"Do you think that your father chose to hurt you?" asked Carmen. So many things were becoming clear now—his hate for the Spanish, his treatment of her . . . all of it rooted in his own hurt.

Puma looked at her, wondering that he was revealing his deepest pain to her. "My father, I think, had a different set of choices. While I do not think he intended to hurt either my mother or myself, that was what happened. There could be no other result once he chose to return to his own people." Puma shrugged. "My father could have stayed and denied himself, though he

428

longed to return to his people. Or he could leave, and hurt my mother and me. It was a difficult choice—either way someone would get hurt.

"Sometimes individuals must make difficult choices, when someone gets hurt no matter what they do, like my father."

Carmen watched him, her eyes widening. "What are you saying?"

Puma spoke slowly. Understanding was coming to him as he said each word. "Perhaps my father did not care. But I think it more likely that my father did love me, did love my mother, yet he could not bear to stay away from his own people any longer. He tried, but in the end, he chose to go back to his people." Puma paused. "And while I can understand that he had a difficult decision, I still feel angry that he chose to leave. I still feel the terrible pain of his loss. But now my anger and loss is at my father, not at the Spanish people. That is where I made my mistake before. I blamed every Spaniard for the choice my father made.

"Make no mistake, Carmen," Puma said, shuddering, "the loss of my father"—he took a breath—"is a most grievous loss. For you see, I—I loved him." His blue eyes held a world of sorrow.

Carmen's eyes filled with tears. She did not know what to say. Now, when she really needed something to say, to let him know that she, too, was grieved at his loss, that she too, suffered, now the flowery Spanish phrases failed her. They would be insincere.

429

She reached out and touched his hand, giving a gentle squeeze, hoping he would understand her.

Puma squeezed her hand back. Carmen took courage and said, "Puma, my own father died. I feel the loss of his death, but before that, while he was still alive, I felt the loss of him. Do you understand? He was there, alive, living in his villa, but he—he did not know me, not really know me. He did not know the child I was, the girl, the woman I grew to become. There is a loss there, for me." Would he understand that she, too, was sharing a hurt, a buried part of herself?

Puma kissed her and gently encircled her waist, drawing her closer.

"When I traveled to New Spain," continued Carmen, looking up into his beautiful eyes, "to Juan Enrique Delgado"—her voice broke—"it was the journey of my life. I thought I was traveling, at last, to meet the man who would love me, who would want to know me, to be with me, as my father never had. But—" Her voice faltered, and she glanced away, unable to face those eyes. "But Juan Enrique Delgado was not that man. He could not fill that gap in my soul, either. No one can." She put her head on his shoulder, her voice muffled.

Puma smiled sadly. "No one can," he agreed. "We can only understand that the loss is there, and speak of it." He gently placed a finger under her chin and lifted her head. Seeing the tears in her eyes, he added softly, "Let us weep for our loss. And then, perhaps, in time . . ." He did not continue. He could not promise her that the pain would go away, for how did he know? His pain was still with him.

"Mayhap," she whispered hopefully. She did not know if time would heal her, but she suspected that with Puma, some kind of healing would take place. He was so kind, so good. . . .

Puma withdrew his arms from around her. Carmen flinched at the sudden loss of his warm strength. He fumbled at his leather waist and undid the leather jewelry pouch tied there. He held it up to Carmen. "Doña Carmen," he said solemnly. "We have been speaking of choices. Now I give you your opportunity for choice. You are free to go."

She stared at him, stunned.

"I know that there is killing at Santa Fe," continued Puma, "but I could take you to El Paso del Norte, if that is what you wish. There are Spanish people there, and you would be safe, if—if you wish to return."

His blue eyes devoured her. His lips tightened to bite back the words that would call her back to him. She must never know what it cost him to say those words. She would never know that every part of him cried out for her to stay. He could only let her go. That was the only way he could show his love for her.

Carmen stared at him. Did he want her to go? Was this his way of telling her he did not want her, love her? He had already been sorely wounded by one Spaniard, his

431

father, and just now he had shared himself with her, had willingly been vulnerable, to another Spaniard—herself. Was he ashamed of disclosing his feelings about his father, about the Spanish? *Did he want to be rid of her?*

Her heart reeled in agony. He expected her to make a choice! Her hand closed upon the jewelry pouch, and she felt the power of her choice flow through her. Her jewels had the power to set her free.

No, she corrected herself suddenly, her *heart* had that power. She could choose to stay, or to go. Her turquoise eyes locked on his. She took a shuddering breath. "I—I do not want to leave," she murmured. "I—I love you."

He had to lean forward to hear her.

"I want to stay with you," she said, her voice a little stronger. "I love you, Puma." She swallowed. "Do you think it is possible—could you, mayhap, like me? A little?"

"Carmen," his voice broke, and she realized the effort it cost him to speak. "Oh, God, Carmen, I love you!" He pulled her into his arms. She was shaking. He held her tightly. "I love you so much!"

She could hardly breathe, so close did he hold her, but she moved not an inch.

Then he set her away from him, his jaw firm. "But I will not, cannot force you to stay with me."

She stared at him, her heart, her very soul, in her turquoise eyes.

He closed his eyes against the sight. "Carmen, I do not want you to stay for a little while, and then change your mind." He opened his eyes and groaned. She was so precious to him! "I could not bear the loss if you, too, were to go back to your people. If you stay, I want you to stay with me forever, to be my wife." His blue eyes were solemn upon hers. "If you stay, will you marry me?"

"Oh, *sí*, Puma!" she breathed. "*Sí!*" Joy filled her. He wanted her! He wanted her and loved her! She threw her arms around his neck and kissed him soundly. "*Sí, sí, sí*, Puma!"

His nose touched hers. "My name is Snarling Mountain Lion," he murmured.

She tried the name, conscious that he was telling her who he really was. Her heart pounded. "*Sí*, Snarling Mountain Lion. I will be happy to be your wife."

Then he was kissing her with all the passionate intensity of which he was capable. And she responded.

Their lips clung and she felt the life, the strength in him, as he clasped her to him. He was a good man, she realized anew. And she was so very fortunate to have found him.

When the kiss was finally over, Carmen was lying on her back and Puma was on top of her. She smiled and reached up and stroked a strand of black hair at his forehead. "Snarling Mountain Lion, *Chihonii*," she said softly, liking the sound of the Jicarilla word, "I want you to know that Juan Enrique Delgado never, *ever* had my heart. Certainly not after I met him." She shuddered. Then she saw the flicker of anger in Puma's blue eyes. "He never had my body, either," she hastily assured him. "To think that I traveled all that way from Seville, Spain, to marry him. . . ."

Puma grunted.

"I am so very glad I did."

Puma's face went stony.

" . . . Otherwise, I would never have met you!" Carmen smiled, unable to resist teasing this man.

Puma grinned and kissed the tip of her nose. After a moment, he said, "I have something for you, *Chihonii*."

He reached inside his tunic and brought out the beautiful silver and turquoise necklace that Stefano had given him. Carefully, he placed the lovely ornament over her head. "For you," he said. "I know how you like jewelry." His mouth quirked a little. "And this matches your turquoise jewel eyes."

Carmen laughed, and her eyes glowed. She bent her head and fingered the necklace. It was still warm from his body heat. "This is the most beautiful necklace I have ever seen," she murmured. "Why, the silver design even looks like flower blossoms. . . ."

Puma tilted her chin up and drew her back to him. "Carmen," he whispered when she pressed herself closer to him. "I love you. I have loved you since the first time I saw you. You bring me such happiness." He clutched her closer. "Do you know how much I have wanted you?"

She shook her head playfully.

"I have wanted you, loved you, for a long time . . ."

Their eyes locked. "And I want to be with you, always," she murmured.

He kissed her again.

"Oh, Puma," she murmured after a little. "How could I have ever have doubted you and believed Angry Man?" Even now, guilt ate at her.

"Hush," he murmured. "There are great differences between our peoples, and great differences in the ways we have been taught to act. At times we will make mistakes, but we will learn."

Carmen's eyes glowed and she smiled tremulously. "Our love will see us through those times. It is a strong love, Snarling Mountain Lion. A good love."

"It is, Jewel Eyes," he agreed, his lips meeting hers.

Author's Note

The Pueblo Revolt leaders allowed the Spanish survivors of the attack on Santa Fe to leave the city. They fled in a convoy to El Paso Del Norte, now known as El Paso. The Indians held sway in the region for twelve years before the Spanish reclaimed the land once more.

Reference List

Anderson, Joan, Photos by George Ancona, 1989. *Spanish Pioneers of the Southwest*. Lodestar Press. E. P. Dutton, New York.

Baldwin, Gordon C., 1978. *The Apache Indians: Raiders of the Southwest*. Four Winds Press. New York.

Ball, Eve with Nora Henn and Lynda Sanchez, 1980. *An Apache Odyssey*. Brigham Young University Press. Provo, UT.

Basso, Keith H., 1969. *Western Apache Witchcraft*. Anthropological Papers of The University of Arizona. University of Arizona Press. Tucson, AZ.

Blacker, Irwin, 1959. *"Taos"*. First Printing in 1978. Pocket Books, New York, NY.

Bly, Robert, 1990. *Iron John: A Book About Men*. Addison-Wesley Publishing Company, Inc. NY.

Carpenter, Allan, 1978. New Mexico: *The New Enchantment of America*. Children's Press. Chicago.

Cremony, John C., 1970. *Life Among the Apaches 1850-1868*. Reprint of the 1868 edition. The Rio Grande Press, Inc. Glorieta, New Mexico.

Debo, Angie, 1976. *Geronimo. The Man, His Time, His Place*. University of Oklahoma Press. Norman, OK.

Defourneaux, Marcelin, 1979. *Daily Life in Spain in the Golden Age*. Translated by Newton Branch. Stanford University Press, Stanford, CA.

de Leon, Friar Luis, 1583. *The Perfect Wife*. Translated from the Spanish by Alice Philena Hubbard, Sister Felicia, of the Order of St. Anne. Texas State College Press, Denton, TX. 1943.

Farb, Peter, 1968. *Man's Rise to Civilization as Shown by the Indians of North America from Primeval Times to the Coming of the Industrial State*. E. P. Dutton & Co., Inc. New York, NY.

Ferg, Alan, editor 1987. *Western Apache Material Culture: The Goodwin and Guenther Collections*. University of Arizona Press. Tucson, AZ.

Goodwin, Grenville, 1969. *The Social Organization of the Western Apache*. University of Arizona Press. Tucson, AZ.

Gosnell, Charles F., 1938. *Spanish Personal Names: Principles Governing Their Formation and Use Which May Be Presented as a Help for Catalogers and Bibliographers*. The H. W. Wilson Company. New York.

Haley, James L., 1981. *Apaches: A History and Culture Portrait*. Doubleday & Co., Inc. Garden City, NY.

LaFarge, Oliver, 1956. *A Pictorial History of the American Indian*. Crown Publishers, Inc. New York, NY.

Laxalt, Robert, 1970. *"New Mexico, The Golden Land"*, National Geographic Magazine, Vol 138, No. 3. pp. 299-345.

Lloyd, Alan, 1968. *The Spanish Centuries*. Doubleday & Co., Garden City, NY

Maugham, W. Somerset, 1935. *Don Fernando*. Paragon House Publishers, NY. First paperback edition, 1990.

Melody, Michael E., 1989. *Indians of North America: The Apache*. Chelsea House Publishers. New York, NY.

McDowell, Bart, 1987. "New Mexico: Between Frontier and Future", *National Geographic Magazine*. Vol. 172, No. 5. pp. 602–633.

McEwan, Bonnie G, 1991. *The Archaelogy of Women in the Spanish New World in Historical Archaeology*, Vol. 25, No. 4. pp. 33–41.

Moorhead, Max L., 1968. *The Apache Frontier: Jacobo Ugarte and Spanish-Indian Relations in Northern New Spain, 1769-1791*. University of Oklahoma Press. Norman, OK.

Muench, David, 1974. *New Mexico*. Photography by David Muench. Text by Tony Hillerman. Graphic Arts Center Publishing Co., Portland, OR

Opler, Morris Edward, 1965. *An Apache Life-Way: The Economic, Social, and Religious Institutions of the Chiricahua Indians*. Cooper Square Publishers, Inc. NY.

Pike, Ruth, 1966. *Enterprise and Adventure: The Genoese in Seville and the Opening of the New World*. Cornell University Press. Ithaca, NY.

Prescott, William H., 1843. *The Conquest of Mexico*, Vol I, Vol II, Everyman's Library 1909, Dutton, NY.

Schaefer, Jack, 1967. *New Mexico*. Coward-McCann, Inc. New York, NY.

Simmons, Marc, Photography by Buddy Mays, 1979. *People of the Sun: Some Out-of-Fashion Southwesterners*. University of New Mexico Press. Albuquerque.

Sonnichsen, Charles Leland, 1958. *The Mescalero Apaches*. Second Edition. University of Oklahoma Press. Norman, OK.

Stein, R. Conrad, 1988. *America the Beautiful. New Mexico*. Childrens Press, Chicago.

Terrell, John Upton, 1972. *Apache Chronicle*. World Publishing. New York, NY.

Wood, Nancy, With an Introduction by Vine Deloria, Jr., 1989. *Taos Pueblo*. Alfred A. Knopf, New York.

LOVE SPELL

THE MAGIC OF ROMANCE PAST, PRESENT, AND FUTURE....

Dorchester Publishing Co., Inc., the leader in romantic fiction, is pleased to unveil its newest line— Love Spell. Every month, beginning in August 1993, Love Spell will publish one book in each of four categories:

1) *Timeswept Romance*—Modern-day heroines travel to the past to find the men who fulfill their hearts' desires.

2) *Futuristic Romance*—Love on distant worlds where passion is the lifeblood of every man and woman.

3) *Historical Romance*—Full of desire, adventure and intrigue, these stories will thrill readers everywhere.

4) *Contemporary Romance*—With novels by Lori Copeland, Heather Graham, and Jayne Ann Krentz, Love Spell's line of contemporary romance is first-rate.

Exploding with soaring passion and fiery sensuality, Love Spell romances are destined to take you to dazzling new heights of ecstasy.

COMING IN AUGUST 1993
HISTORICAL ROMANCE
WILD SUMMER ROSE
Amy Elizabeth Saunders

Torn from her carefree rustic life to become a proper city lady, Victoria Larkin bristles at the hypocrisy of the arrogant French aristocrat who wants to seduce her. But Phillipe St. Sebastian is determined to have her at any cost—even the loss of his beloved ancestral home. And as the flames of revolution threaten their very lives, Victoria and Phillipe find strength in the healing power of love.

_0-505-51902-X $4.99 US/$5.99 CAN

CONTEMPORARY ROMANCE
TWO OF A KIND
Lori Copeland
Bestselling Author of *Promise Me Today*

When her lively widowed mother starts chasing around town with seventy-year-old motorcycle enthusiast Clyde Merrill, Courtney Spenser is confronted by Clyde's angry son. Sensual and overbearing, Graham Merrill quickly gets under Courtney's skin—and she's not at all displeased.

_0-505-51903-8 $3.99 US/$4.99 CAN

LEISURE BOOKS
ATTN: Order Department
276 5th Avenue, New York, NY 10001

Please add $1.50 for shipping and handling for the first book and $.35 for each book thereafter. PA., N.Y.S. and N.Y.C. residents, please add appropriate sales tax. No cash, stamps, or C.O.D.s. All orders shipped within 6 weeks via postal service book rate. Canadian orders require $2.00 extra postage and must be paid in U.S. dollars through a U.S. banking facility.

Name_____

Address_____

City _____ State_____Zip_____

I have enclosed $_____in payment for the checked book(s). Payment <u>must</u> accompany all orders.□ Please send a free catalog.

COMING IN SEPTEMBER 1993
HISTORICAL ROMANCE
TEMPTATION
Jane Harrison

He broke her heart once before, but Shadoe Sinclair is a temptation that Lilly McFall cannot deny. And when he saunters back into the frontier town he left years earlier, Lilly will do whatever it takes to make the handsome rogue her own.

_0-505-51906-2   \$4.99 US/\$5.99 CAN

CONTEMPORARY ROMANCE
WHIRLWIND COURTSHIP
Jayne Ann Krentz writing as Jayne Taylor
Bestselling Author of *Family Man*

When Phoebe Hampton arrives by accident on Harlan Garand's doorstep, he's convinced she's another marriage-minded female sent by his matchmaking aunt. But a sudden snowstorm traps them together for a few days and shows Harlan there's a lot more to Phoebe than meets the eye.

_0-505-51907-0 $3.99 US/$4.99 CAN

COMING IN OCTOBER 1993
HISTORICAL ROMANCE
DANGEROUS DESIRES
Louise Clark

Miserable and homesick, Stephanie de la Riviere will sell her family jewels or pose as a highwayman—whatever it takes to see her beloved father again. And her harebrained schemes might succeed if not for her watchful custodian—the only man who can match her fiery spirit with his own burning desire.

_0-505-51910-0 $4.99 US/$5.99 CAN

CONTEMPORARY ROMANCE
ONLY THE BEST
Lori Copeland
Author of More Than 6 Million Books in Print!

Stranded in a tiny Wyoming town after her car fails, Rana Alcott doesn't think her life can get much worse. And though she'd rather die than accept help from arrogant Gunner Montay, she soon realizes she is fighting a losing battle against temptation.

_0-505-51911-9 $3.99 US/$4.99 CAN

LEISURE BOOKS
ATTN: Order Department
276 5th Avenue, New York, NY 10001

Please add $1.50 for shipping and handling for the first book and $.35 for each book thereafter. PA., N.Y.S. and N.Y.C. residents, please add appropriate sales tax. No cash, stamps, or C.O.D.s. All orders shipped within 6 weeks via postal service book rate. Canadian orders require $2.00 extra postage and must be paid in U.S. dollars through a U.S. banking facility.

Name_____

Address_____

City _____ State _____ Zip _____

I have enclosed $_____in payment for the checked book(s). Payment <u>must</u> accompany all orders.☐ Please send a free catalog.